D0546520

HOOKED

Also by A.C. Wise

Wendy, Darling

Wise, A.C.,author.
Hooked

2022
33305255017984
ca   08/19/22

HOOKED

A.C. WISE

TITAN BOOKS

Hooked
Print edition ISBN: 9781789096835
E-book edition ISBN: 9781789096842

Published by Titan Books
A division of Titan Publishing Group Ltd.
144 Southwark Street, London SE1 0UP
www.titanbooks.com

First Titan edition July 2022
10 9 8 7 6 5 4 3 2 1

This is a work of fiction. All of the characters, organizations, and events portrayed
in this novel are either products of the author's imagination or are used fictitiously.
Any resemblance to actual persons, living or dead (except for satirical purposes), is
entirely coincidental.

Copyright © 2022 A.C. Wise. All rights reserved.

A.C. Wise asserts the moral right to be identified as the author of this work.

No part of this publication may be reproduced, stored in a retrieval system, or
transmitted, in any form or by any means without the prior written permission of
the publisher, nor be otherwise circulated in any form of binding or cover other
than that in which it is published and without a similar condition being imposed
on the subsequent purchaser.

A CIP catalogue record for this title is available from the British Library.

Printed and bound in the United States.

A TASTE OF THE POPPY

LONDON – 1939

The wave curls above him, poised, laden with panic.

He remembers drowning.

Limbs weighted and wanting to drag him down, lungs screaming with the thwarted desire to expand, mouth poised to open traitorously and let in water instead of air.

James gropes for the table beside him, for the pipe, but the smoke is already in his lungs. He remembers to breathe out. His lungs stop screaming when he does. The smoke coils in the air above him, hanging there a moment, teasing the outline of a shape, but when he looks again, it dissipates.

Hunger gnaws at him and he pulls in another lungful. As he does, James feels himself doubled, a ghost rising from his skin to move about the flat. Slipped out of time, he feels himself once again taking the actions he took moments ago—his hand shaking with need, guts cramping, sweat slicking his skin. He hears the wooden box rattle, the scant amount of opium inside dwindling every day.

A dizzying sensation as he watches himself, feels himself, rolling tar into a sticky ball, pulling it into long strands, filling his pipe. He feels smoke in his lungs. Only a small slip this time, minutes not hours or years, but still, it is disorienting. And it has been happening more and more frequently, his unmooring from time. His guts cramp again, the urge to vomit, and in the next moment, he slams back into his body where he lies on the chaise, gasping for air.

He remembers drowning.

The *drug* should blunt the effect, stave off the memory of the deaths he suffered again and again at the hands of a mere child, a boy. It used to, but now it only makes the sensation worse, stretching him thin between two worlds, this one and...

James refuses the name. He's not there; he is here, in London. Home.

But what manner of home is it without...

He glances to the wooden box beside him. What will he do when the opium is gone? He's an old man, feeling his age now as he never did before. His fingers, once quick-slipping into pockets to relieve them of their bills, once quick with a blade as well, have slowed. What skill does he left to live by?

He lets himself lie back, a rough chuckle taking him and turning into a cough. If he were any other man, he would fear. It would be a race to see what would take him first—starvation, withdrawal, or madness. But he's always been too stubborn to die, too determined. Weary as he is, above all, he knows he will survive.

James lifts the pipe again, using his flesh and blood hand. The other, wood, gleaming warm in the light and chased in silver, rests in his lap. The delicate, articulated joints that allow him to bend or straighten the fingers when he can be bothered to remember curl slightly now, as if cupping something gently in his palm, but his hand is empty. He draws breath and holds it.

"You promised me you'd be careful. Your dreams are dangerous things, James."

The voice is a knife, and James whips around. Another fit of coughing leaves his eyes streaming. Through the blur he sees Samuel standing in the corner, hands folded neatly in front of him, expression mixing admonishment and sorrow.

James forgets how to breathe entirely. He forgets the ache in his leg and the fact that when he walks now, he needs a cane to steady him. He's halfway to rising, going to Samuel, when a twinge in his thigh brings him crashing to one knee beside the chaise. Pain spikes from the point of impact and catches as a gasp in his throat. And still, he almost crawls to the surgeon on hands and knees, a pitiful thing, ready to bury his face in the hem of Samuel's coat.

But James forces himself to straighten.

"Fuck off." The words come out smoke-roughened, harsh with emotion and the effort to speak with conviction. "You're not real."

It's unkind, but then so is Samuel's ghost.

"I don't want you here." James tries to curl his lips into their old sneer.

He pulls the memory of striding the deck in a swirl of blood-red coat, men trembling before him, around him like armor. He must be that, not this pathetic creature, brought low with need. Samuel isn't in the room with him; Samuel has been dead for fifteen years.

Yet the grief hasn't lessened. Always the wave of it is there, ready to swamp him if James lets his concentration falter for even a moment. If he lets his guard down, time comes unstuck and the pain is just as fresh as it ever was—worse than dying, worse than every time he's drowned.

The specter in the corner refuses to waver. Samuel's eyes were never the blue-gray shade fixing James balefully now. Nor was his skin the color of seawater, and just as translucent. James can see straight through him to the wall.

Samuel isn't real. He isn't here. And knowing as much does nothing to lessen James's wanting, the hurt undoing him, unraveling him and leaving him flayed.

"Leave me alone in my misery why don't you?" He snaps the words, angling his body away so he won't have to see whether Samuel obediently fades.

But he feels it. A *tsk*, a disappointed sound pinging directly against the delicate bones of his ear. A sigh of displaced air, and then Samuel is gone. Just like all the other pirates, leaving James alone, the only one.

The sense of loss is immediate. But instead of scrambling to the corner to plead with empty air, he presses down on the feeling of absence like a bruise and lets it ground him. The ache in his chest eases, if only for a moment.

He braces one arm and levers himself up, muscles trembling with the effort. There's a cold pulse of complaint from his thigh where the shards of something that may or may not be metal buried themselves long ago. But his leg holds when he stands, and James retrieves his cane where it leans against the back of the chaise.

He runs his gaze across the shelves crammed with books—of which he has not read a single one—along the wall, and up to the window that peers like an eye out over London, to the bed, far too large for one man alone, to the stove, the kettle, the wardrobe, his coat hung by the door. Last, as always, his gaze comes to rest on the skull sitting on the bedside table.

James moves slowly, limping to the bed. He ignores the grinding pain from his knee where it struck the floor and the steady ache in his thigh as he sits. His hand—the flesh and blood one—touches down atop the skull. The whorls of his fingertips meet the whorls carved into the bone. The pattern chased in silver is the same design covering his other hand, the wooden one. He'd found a scrimshaw artist to do the work, and though the man had balked when presented with a human skull, James's money was good enough in the end.

As he pulls the skull onto his lap, his heartbeat finally calms, his breathing steadies. He is here and now, in London. His name is James, not Hook. And he is no one's captain.

And yet... It is nothing to summon the feel of the deck rolling beneath his feet, the creak and sigh of the ropes and the snap of sails. Neverland—he admits to the name at last; it is always there, and Hook is always there, just beneath the surface. At times, he never left, never fled and fell through the world.

That's what Samuel never understood, what James could never explain. Samuel had warned him that his dreams were dangerous—that the smoke trance he put himself into in place of actual dreaming would act as a beacon, drawing Neverland's eye. But without the drug, James remembers too much. He drinks, he smokes, to dull that other self, to keep Hook and Neverland from rising again.

He did it, always, to keep them safe.

Empty sockets gaze up from under ridges of bone, as reproachful as Samuel's ghost. James replaces the skull on the table, turns it slightly so it looks away. For years, he resisted the pull to keep them safe, to keep Samuel safe, but who is there left to protect now? What does it matter if he's reckless with his own life?

Neverland creeping steadily closer, pressed against the skin of this world, hungering, wanting what it's been denied all these years—James, Hook—as its last meal.

Why should he deny it?

And another thought rises, a sliver of sick hope he shouldn't dare, and yet cannot help. What if some remnant of Samuel waits for him in that other world? Yes, he swore to Samuel, but what does a promise mean to a dead man?

It's been fifteen years, and the pain hasn't grown less, contrary to popular logic. All the while, James kept holding on, promising himself that time would heal him if he could only be patient. But if anything, the hurt has grown worse. As if all this time, the way between worlds has only grown thinner, his memories sharper than the life he lives now, leaving the loss fresher, the wound opened wider rather than scabbed over or scarred. Neverland has always been a beast snapping at his heels; now he can almost feel it, and he's tired of running.

He'd kept his promise, determined to honor Samuel's memory, and yet Samuel's ghost haunts him, pitiless. If keeping his promise brings no relief, what is the point of it? More and more, he finds himself unanchored in time. Now, or then—what does it matter? He is old, he is tired. Hasn't he at last earned the right to rest, to stop fighting against temptation?

James pushes himself up again and returns to the chaise. He draws in another lungful of smoke, and lets himself drift. Lets himself think deliberately of Neverland. After so long, after years of bearing up under the weight of grief alone. He lets himself go.

And almost immediately, waves rock him. He feels the lift and fall of the deck, the peak and trough. The air is salt-crystal—dense enough to crack between his teeth. He is hale and hearty, in a coat the color of blood, armed with a wicked blade.

The ceiling of his flat blurs into a sky smeary with clouds over a scattering of stars. He closes his eyes as he leans back against the chaise. Or perhaps they remain open. It doesn't matter. Waking or sleeping, eyes open or closed, he would still see Neverland. It's been drawing closer all this time, and he no longer has the will to resist it. Among the stars is a place where the sky grows thinnest, framed in sharp-edged silver light.

A door.

It's a thing he's sensed before and never allowed himself to look at fully, but now he turns his attention to it and lets himself see. James lets himself feel the weight of that other world and everything it contains—his ship and his pirates and Pan—all leaning against the imagined door in the sky. Imagined, but also real. Because of course in a world made for a child all ego and desire, wanting would be a door, a literal door. Why shouldn't James avail himself of it too?

Reckless, yes, and ill-advised, but he doesn't care. As he once threw himself wildly into the teeth of a storm, James draws one more breath of smoke and throws all his will and wanting against that door, reaching back for a world he swore he'd never reach for again.

There's a sensation like lightning striking, electricity jumping the gap and snapping through his bones. A rush of displaced air, and on the other side of nowhere, something grabs ahold of his reaching hand.

Breath leaves him in a startled gasp. When the coil of smoke hangs in the air this time it doesn't just tease a shape, it twists slowly, gathering mass, solidity.

Scales and wide-open jaws. The beast rolls in the air above him, lazy and mocking. His chest compresses beneath fathoms of seawater gone the color of blood-dark wine. Fear all at once rushing back when he'd thought himself immune.

Pan's hunting beast. In Neverland, he'd felt it always, moving beneath the world's skin. He'd been aware of it wherever on the island it was, just as it was always aware of him. But he'd come to London, he'd escaped.

Yet now all the beast has to do is turn its eyes like rotten coins upon him and it will know him.

Your dreams are dangerous, James.

Panic freezes James upon the chaise. The old desire to live, almost despite himself, pumps through his veins with an almost painful intensity. He does not want to die, not again. A prelude to a death roll, the beast makes another turn, seeking. Starlight glints from it like light striking a blade. Jaws open, the beast plunges down.

James ducks, throwing an arm up in a vain attempt to ward off the teeth. The motion sends him crashing to the ground, knocking the table over, his pipe and matches and the wooden box scattering. The beast sails overhead, missing him. James presses himself flat, rolling beneath the chaise. The beast whips around, a frustrated motion, its jaws snapping at nothing.

It circles once, and again, searching. James forgets terror for a moment—can't the beast feel him? Can't it see him? But if he closed his eyes, would he know where the beast was in the room? No. It's like a sense has been removed from him, one he'd almost forgotten. He can't feel the creature as he once could, the dreadful awareness of it always clinging to him wherever he was. It seems the beast cannot feel him either. James remains where he is, flat beneath the chaise, waiting, but the pounding of adrenaline in him fades. There must be something else wrong with the creature. It is reduced from its former terror, its former glory, broken. Much like James himself.

The beast turns once more, churning the air, sailing farther away from him and toward the window, blundering like a creature lost. James holds his breath a moment longer; when he dares to poke his head from beneath the chaise, the beast is gone.

His pulse stutters. James blinks at the room, expecting for a moment that it will become the room at the prow of a ship, with a narrow bed hung in rich brocade. But it is only his room, his flat in London. There is no beast.

Perhaps there never was. Perhaps he imagined the whole thing. Another moment slipped out of time. The door, only another illusion, born in smoke and wanting.

Reflex draws his gaze to the corner, hoping for Samuel's ghost, but the space remains stubbornly empty. It hurts more than it should.

James forces himself up one more time, leaving the fallen table and scattered pipe as he makes his way to the eye-shaped window overlooking London. His whole body feels bruised, as much his age as the fall. He lets the cane take his weight. A starless sky stretches over the city. From here, he can see the rooftops of the neighboring buildings. Nothing looks amiss, yet he feels something out of place, something that doesn't belong.

A brass scope sits atop the bookshelf below the window, a gift from Samuel, an old joke, as if this flat perched above the city were a crow's nest. James puts the glass to his eye. He scans the forest of chimneys, the dense world of brick.

For just a moment, he imagines a sinuous shape moving between them, the flick of a tail disappearing from sight. But is that only because he wants to see it? If the beast is real, and remains, perhaps Samuel does too. His breath catches, but when he looks again, there is only the London sky and the city below him.

Perhaps he should be relieved. Samuel is—was—right. Neverland was a terrible place; they escaped it, and it's better left behind for good. He dared too close to the edge tonight, and perhaps his desire did finally crack that door wide. And perhaps something slithered through. A monster. A shadow. A thing of scales and jaws twisting through the night. It snapped once and missed, but will it circle around again as it always has, time and time before? He wishes he could dismiss it as illusion, an effect of the drug, but he fears he has done what Samuel always warned him again and drawn Neverland's attention.

And now the creature is out there. Searching for him. Hunting.

EMPTY

The scent of fresh-baked sweet rolls, glazed in marmalade, wafts from the folded-over paper bag balanced atop the mountain of parcels in Jane's arms. It's maddening, taunting her as she winds through the slushy London streets, cold nipping at her cheeks, wind tugging her coat hem. It took all her willpower not to tear into the bag the moment she made her purchase, but she promised herself she'd save them to share them with Peg.

The sweet rolls, a mutual favorite, are just one part of the celebration they have planned tonight for surviving their first term at the Royal College. Tomorrow they'll both go their separate ways, home for the holidays, and Jane already feels a pang at the thought. She's never met someone she liked as instantly, or got along with as well as Peg. Even though it's only a short break before classes start again, Jane will miss her.

She and Peg met on their very first day at the college, and although Peg ultimately switched out of the medical program into the pharmaceutical program, they've still been together every single day since that first, deciding to become flatmates only a week after they'd met. They'd bonded almost instantly over being the only two female students in the room in their first anatomy class. And they'd quickly discovered that unlike the young men in their classes, they had to work twice as hard to prove they deserved their place there. They'd sworn then and there to always have each other's backs, to support each other, and to not let each other quit, no matter how bad things got.

Jane can't imagine giving up on her dream of becoming a doctor, but there are times when simply getting through a day is exhausting. But knowing Peg is going through the same thing makes it so much easier to bear. Lately there have been rumors that the Royal College is trying to block women from sitting medical exams again. With the war, Jane would think more doctors would be wanted, not fewer, but apparently while dying of sepsis from a treatable wound would be a terrible fate, for some the idea of letting a "lady doctor" do the treating is simply a bridge too far.

As their building comes into sight, Jane pushes the bitter thought down. While she was grateful for her heavy wool coat outside, by the time she climbs the stairs to their door, she's sweating. She manages to get the door unlocked without dropping any packages, and steps inside.

"Is the kettle on?" Jane sets her packages on the table, unwinding her scarf and freeing herself from her coat.

Peg doesn't answer. More likely than not, she's lost in one of her mystery novels. It never ceases to amaze Jane how Peg can read the same book several times over and still get as much enjoyment out of it the third time as the first.

"What's the point after you know who the murderer is?" she'd asked once.

"That's the best part!" Peg had answered her with a grin. "The second time around you get to go back and see all the clever clues the author put in that you missed the first time."

"What about the third time?"

But Peg had only stuck her tongue out. Last Jane checked, Peg was working her way through all of Agatha Christie's Poirot novels again. How she finds time on top of her schoolwork, not to mention spending time with Simon, Jane will never know.

"Peg?" She hangs her coat and scarf from the hook by the door, shaking the last drops of melted snow from her bobbed hair.

Surely Peg must have heard her come in by now. Unless she's with Simon, the two of them holed up in a tea shop somewhere, lost in each other and oblivious to the weather outside. The thought makes Jane smile. She'd met Simon early on too, one of the handful of decent male students who'd never questioned Jane's right to be in the program. She'd been the one to introduce Peg and Simon. Simon had been so painfully shy that Jane never would have imagined a relationship blossoming—not that she'd been trying to set them up—but they'd hit it off, Peg balancing Simon's blushing and tongue-tied speech with openness and enthusiasm.

"Peg?" Jane plucks the pastry bag from the top of her stack of parcels. She sets the kettle on to boil in the flat's tiny kitchen and leaves it heating to knock on Peg's door.

The door swings inward. Jane is about to wave the pastry bag in front of the gap, wafting the scent into Peg's room, but she stops.

Absence breathes out from the open door, making all the hairs on the back of Jane's neck stand on end. There's a kind of missingness that goes far deeper than Peg simply not being there.

Jane pushes the door open all the way.

The pastry bag drops from her hand. Peg lies sprawled across her narrow bed, sheets rumpled beneath her. She is there, Jane can clearly see her, and she is not. Jane's gaze slides away from her flatmate, her friend, and Jane has to force herself to look at Peg, to see her. It's not squeamishness. It's as if Peg no longer belongs in the world and so the world is trying to erase her.

Jane's stomach churns with the utter wrongness. She's watched her professors peel back skin to reveal different muscle groups, crack ribcages to show all the organs lined up inside, saw bones into neat cross-sections to reveal the marrow inside, but this is something else altogether. Jane knows how a human body is meant to work, all the things that make it move and breathe, and what happens when those processes stop. This is not that. Even though she can plainly see Peg, it's as though something fully snipped her from existence, leaving a Peg-shaped hole behind.

Jane forces herself to step farther into the room even though a thickness in the air tries to resist her. She touches the pulse-points at Peg's wrist and below her jaw, even knowing what she will find. She draws her fingers away from the waxen coolness of Peg's skin as quickly as she can. There's an extra pallor to Peg's flesh, as though she's already been drained of every last drop of her blood, but the sheets beneath her remain pristine, the walls unmarred. There's no sign of violence, no marks on her skin, no evidence of a struggle.

A strand of Peg's dark hair lies across her cheek, almost touching the corner of her mouth, which is open as though she died in the act of taking a breath, or was about to say a word. Her eyes stare, and even this Jane must struggle to see because Peg's features want to blur, rearrange themselves, refuse her gaze.

Did someone break in? Jane knows for certain she unlocked the door when she entered, and she certainly would have noticed if it had been forced. She glances around the room; it's a horrible relief in a way she doesn't want to admit, looking away from her friend's lifeless body. The window is open a fraction. Wind slips through, biting cold. But it's not enough of a gap for someone to get inside.

Unless whatever killed Peg isn't human.

The thought drops, unwelcome, like a stone in Jane's mind and sits there. Her thoughts are dull, sluggish, trying to move around it. She stares at the window, the gap, with a sense there's something she's forgotten. She should close the window; Peg will freeze when she returns. Then Jane remembers. She turns back to the thing on the bed, a choked sob rising in her throat.

It's not as though she forgot—how could she forget? Except when she looks away, she does. Peg slides from her mind, because the thing on the bed isn't Peg. It's the absence of Peg. Peg has been utterly undone. Shaking, Jane puts a hand to her mouth. They'd promised to stick together, to have each other's backs. They were supposed to protect each other, and Jane has utterly failed.

She keeps her eyes on Peg even as she bends mechanically to pick up the dropped pastry bag. She steps backward out the door, holding Peg in her sight as long as she can and fixing her in her mind so she doesn't slip away again. In the kitchen, Jane finds the kettle nearly boiled dry and lifts it automatically from the heat, turning off the burner. She should call the police. There's a telephone in the downstairs hall, but at the moment it feels impossibly far away. Jane's body is heavy and all at once, all she wants to do is sleep.

Police. Scotland Yard. She will call. Eventually. She will. But right now, more than anything in the world, the only person she wants to talk to—despite everything between them, the broken promises and the lies, despite the wound that has been eight years healing and only managed to scab—the only person she can fathom talking to at all is her mother.

REUNIONS

Wendy lifts her muffler, covering half her face and leaving only her eyes visible. Beneath her coat, her skin prickles, first hot, then cold, a sense of unease dogging her heels as sure as the December wind. She had no intention of coming into the city today. There's more than enough to do getting the house ready with Jane coming home for the holidays, her brother Michael coming for Christmas, and her other brother John and his wife and daughter coming for New Year's Day. But something is wrong. There is something here that doesn't belong.

Wendy had felt it all at once last night, sitting in the parlor before the fire and putting the finishing touches on a skirt she'd sewed to give Jane for Christmas. It was as though a door had opened somewhere far off, and at the same time very close by, and something cold and dark had come rushing through. She'd stood up so suddenly that the fabric had spilled from her lap, the thread unwinding all the way across the floor so that the spool had nearly ended up in the fire.

Neverland.

The name had risen to her tongue, but she'd clamped it tight behind her teeth, refusing to speak it out loud. Still, she hadn't been able to stop herself from rushing to the window, peering out, looking for a subtle shift in the stars. The night had been brutally cold, brutally clear—no clouds to block the moon or her view of the sky. The only thing she'd seen was the dark, speckled in silver light, nothing amiss, nothing out of place.

No door opening in the sky. No boy who wasn't a boy come to take her hand and ask her to fly away. Her heart had surged, a complicated mix of hope and fear, and then come crashing down again as she'd stood at the glass, her breath fogging against it, looking and hoping and seeing nothing.

Neverland had given her so much as a child. And it had taken more than she'd realized. Eight years ago, it had taken her daughter, and Wendy had stolen her back, bringing Neverland crashing down around them as they'd escaped home again.

So why had it felt as though the way between worlds had opened again, however briefly? She'd tried to convince herself that it must have been her imagination, she couldn't have felt what she'd thought she'd felt. But after reclaiming the fallen skirt and trying to resume her work, she'd found herself unable to sew, her fingers grown clumsy, almost shaking. She'd been unable to concentrate, and later that night, unable to sleep. She'd paced her room half the night, and almost the second it was decently light—despite the storm growing across the sky—she'd taken herself to the station and bought a train ticket into London.

The sense is even stronger now as she dodges last-minute shoppers and puddles of slush. Between the thick-falling snow, the air feels rife with ghosts. Something she can almost see, almost feel, something out of place. If she could only find it.

And then—there. It's as though someone has tugged on a rope tied to her spine. Wendy stops in her tracks like a stone planted in the midst of a river, drawing angry murmurs from the crowd forced to part and flow around her. She ignores them, twisting around to look behind her. But there's only a sea of faces, indistinct in the gray and wrapped against the cold. There's nothing to make her feel once again as though a door opened, as though someone on the far side of it called her name.

Perhaps she's being foolish. Her life has been quiet of late, content and cozy in a way she'd never imagined it could be. At times, though, it feels too quiet, almost stifling. There are times when the urge takes her to simply get on a train without a true destination in mind, or get on a boat and sail as far as she can. As a young girl, she never imagined life as a married woman, as a mother, living in one place and never going off on grand adventures. Last night had she simply let boredom get the better of her, wishing for something, a mystery or an adventure—even a terrible one—to come sweep her away again?

Guilt comes with the thought and Wendy plunges back into the crowd, lowering her head. She's barely taken two steps when the tug comes again, sharper this time. At almost the same moment, a hand touches her shoulder. Wendy lets out a startled yelp, muffled by the wool across her mouth. She spins, instinct raising her hand to strike whoever has ahold of her. The man ducks, raising an arm against her blow and Wendy catches herself. Stunned, she lets her hand drop, staring.

The hand raised to ward off her blow is made of wood, a warm red-brown that strikes to the heart of her, and she knows instinctively that it doesn't belong to this world. Elaborate patterns like curls of smoke flow across its surface—silver gleaming dully despite the gray sky. Where the wooden finger joints bend slightly, delicate rods and pins are just barely visible, so finely crafted that for a moment she almost expects them to move on their own. Tiny pellets of ice land on the man's coat and in his white-gray hair that sticks up from his scalp like shorn wheat stubble.

Despite the weather, he's bare-headed. Actual stubble roughens his chin and cheeks, and his eyes are like no color Wendy has ever seen before. Except they are. Impossibly, she knows them. She recognizes them and recognizes this man. His eyes are slate and storm and looking at them, Wendy feels a deck canting beneath her. Breath catches in her throat and her heart forgets to beat.

There are no oiled curls, no waxed mustache, and the coat the man wears is navy wool, not blood-red velvet. He is shorter than she remembers, but she was only a child when he held her prisoner at the point of a sword, tied her up to the mast of his ship along with her brothers and waited for Peter Pan to come save her. It cannot be, and yet there is not a single shred of doubt in Wendy's mind.

"Hook." She breathes the name, as if it could solidify him in her reality, or banish him. Wendy isn't certain which she means to do.

"James." It comes as an automatic response, a barely conscious correction he's had to make too many times.

He grips a cane, letting it take his weight, and a faint tremor passes through him. Instinct makes Wendy reach to steady him, but she stops just short of touching him. She sees it the moment something shifts in his storm-colored eyes, the recognition that comes into them, and the surprise that isn't as great as it should be.

"And you are… Wendy Darling."

She offers no correction to her own name, merely staring at him. The air around them feels electric and magnetic all at once. Wendy imagines London as a map, folded against itself to bring

24

the two points of their lives together at this precise moment in time. But how can Captain Hook be here? Is that what she felt last night, sitting before the fire, the sense of wrongness, the sense of something slipped into this world that doesn't belong? Or is there something more?

"How…" Too many questions crowd her tongue, leaving her unable to form even one of them.

How did he know her? How is he here and still alive? How did he leave Neverland? How, how, how is he standing before her now in thickening snow?

Hook straightens. Another tremor passes through him, a pained expression following in its wake. Wendy thinks of Michael, her brother, and the way his leg has ached in the cold ever since he returned from the war.

"We…" Her voice falters. What can she say to this man—Peter's immortal enemy, a pirate captain out of a fairy tale? Laughter threatens her, born of a wild jangling of nerves. He cannot be here. The first time she was in Neverland, she watched him die.

"Miss Darling?"

"Yes?" It isn't her name anymore, but it is. Despite her marriage, she has always been, will always be, Wendy Darling.

"I feel as though we were intended to meet." A cough shakes him, and Wendy thinks how frail he looks—gray all the way through, not just his eyes and his hair. "I—"

Before he can say more, it's as though the world drops away from beneath her. Nothing changes, not perceptibly, and yet Wendy feels a terrible shadow hanging over them, worse than the feeling she had by the fire last night. Worse than anything since the night…

Fear goes to the heart of her, piercing like an arrow.

"Jane." Her daughter needs her.

The sense in unshakable, a mother's terrible instinct. Wendy turns, slipping on the icy streets and not caring that she does. Leaving Hook staring behind her, she runs.

THE IMMORTAL CAPTAIN

NEVERLAND – 22 YEARS AGO

His sword—wicked and curved, sharp as a smile—slashes empty air where the boy stood just a moment before. But Pan is already in the air, spinning, a foot, then two, above the tossing deck.

"You missed again!" Pan sticks his tongue out. "Poor old Hook."

The boy lands, dancing a nimble circle as if the boards were not slick underfoot. He waves his sword, not even trying to strike Hook, his movements all flash and show.

A child. Only a child. An infuriating one, but a mere child nonetheless. How is it that he continues to elude every member of Hook's crew, besting them all not once, but dozens of times? Or perhaps it is a hundred by now. Or more.

The fact that he doesn't know unsettles him. Hook swings again to slash away the question of how many times he and Pan have fought. But it continues squatting, a shadow at the corner of his eye, refusing to be vanquished. Much like Pan himself.

There are more gaps in his knowledge than just this one. Parts of his mind are shrouded; there are borders between his own memories beyond which he cannot cross. It is much like the sea bounding this island. He has a ship at his command. It stands to reason that he could simply sail away, as far and as fast as he wishes, and yet always he returns.

Light flashes from Pan's blade, sudden and terribly bright. It strikes Hook's eyes, as sharp as a blow. He staggers back, raising his arm to drag it across his face as Pan's taunting voice sounds again.

"Scaredy pirate! Scaredy Captain Hook."

Anger seethes, sudden and hot, making him careless. Hook drops his arm and slashes, an ugly sweeping motion. Sloppy, when he knows better, coming nowhere near to striking Pan. Not that it matters. Each blow could be expertly timed to slip beneath his enemy's guard, and they still wouldn't land. In all the dozen— hundred?—times they've fought, he's never so much as scratched the boy's skin.

Hook clenches his jaw. Damn elegance and skill. He pushes forward with abandon, hacking wildly at Pan's guard. All he wants is to land just one blow, wear Pan down and draw a spurt of bright blood. To see Pan's eyes widen in fear, hear his mewling cry that Hook isn't playing fair, that he is always supposed to win.

Hook bares his teeth, not giving Pan a moment to recover as he rains blow after blow. Every strike meets Pan's sword, or misses him by inches, but Hook gains ground. Pan's back strikes the rail. Hook's lips stretch in a grin; at last, finally, he has—

A wave swamps the deck, sweeping Hook's feet from beneath him. The ship and the sky change places and he crashes to the boards, blinking saltwater from his eyes. Pan's laughter rings loud and clear as a bell, a sound like a wetted finger dragged across the rim of a glass.

"The old captain's gone all soggy, wet, and moldy! Look at him. He's a drowned rat." Pan's crowing voice reaches every corner of the ship.

Hook sees himself through the boy's eyes—drenched, dark curls plastered to his skin, heavy velvet and ruffled silk—absurd and utterly vain—weighing him down. He looks worse than a drowned rat. He looks an utter fool.

"Captain!" A hand reaches to grasp his arm and pull him up.

Hook pushes the man away. He will not become an object of pity on his own ship. What sort of pirate cannot defeat a simple child?

"Pan!" Hook drags himself upright.

The name hangs in the air, answered by a cock's crow. Then all at once, the boy himself hangs in the air before him. Behind him, the sun blazes so brightly Hook can't look at him directly; Pan is a hole, an absence, a sharp-edged silhouette pinned upon the day.

Where it raged a moment before, the sea falls to calm, the waves going eerily still so that everything seems to hold its breath and wait on what will happen next. Weariness swamps him, as sure as a wave. He's soaked to the bone, his muscles aching from the fight, and Pan remains as fresh as a new-cut daisy.

All Hook wants is dry clothing, and smoke filling his lungs. He wants to drink until he can't remember his own name and sleep for a week. His shoulders slump. The answer to the question he tried to push away crawls from the fog-shrouded corners of his mind to crouch before him, grinning. He has fought Pan thousands of times, countless battles, and he has lost every single one.

The deck rolls. He braces himself as the boy flies a victorious circle, nowhere and everywhere at once.

"You'll never best me, Hook! Perhaps I'll cut off your other hand and feed it to the beast too."

A chill seeps through him, another memory come to join the first. Teeth and scales and terrible jaws. He remembers his death; he remembers drowning.

Blood roars in Hook's ears. He whirls in the direction of the piping voice, bringing his blade around. But Pan's sword is there once again, blocking his and knocking it aside. Hook's sword clatters to the deck. The point of Pan's blade touches one of the buttons gleaming on Hook's velvet coat. With no effort at all, Pan could drive the blade straight through his heart.

"Do it. Do it then." Hook speaks low, barely moving his lips, a desperate, angry wish.

The blade at least would be swift. Pan narrows his eyes.

"That's not how it goes. You must do it right, silly old captain." Despite the gaiety of the words, Pan's tone is blade-bright itself, and just as sharp.

Up in the rigging and hanging from the rails, dressed in skins and smeared with mud, Pan's band of wild boys cheers. They are a nest full of raucous birds, roosting on every part of his ship.

"I know, I shall make you walk your own plank!" Pan's eyes glitter, all malice and glee.

Hook thinks of a geode smashed open, a hollowness studded with jagged crystalline shine. That's what Pan's eyes remind him of; they are nothing human.

Soft waves lap the ship. Why isn't his crew stopping this, coming to his aid? Didn't someone try to help him just now? Hold out a hand? But he slapped them away. He commands a crew of grown men and Pan only commands a ragged band of boys. It should be easy, they should win, but it isn't just Hook himself—they are all wooden puppets dancing at the end of Pan's strings.

Hook clenches his muscles and wills himself to keep still. But Pan's will is stronger. In this place, Pan's will is everything. Hook's arm jerks upward, beyond his control, and he shakes his hook in the air.

"You won't get away with this, Pan! I'll best you next time!"

The boy laughs, delighted at the play unfolding according to his whim.

"I am. Not. Your. Toy." Hook grinds out each word, as painful as spitting up stone, leaving his throat bloody and raw.

If Pan hears the words at all, he ignores them.

"You're a rotten, spoiled child, smashing your dolls together until you break them."

"No more talking now. Talking is boring." Pan's gaze snaps to him, delight melting to reveal something colder, crueler—an ancient being behind the face of the child.

Pan no longer flits back and forth but hangs still in the air, becalmed as the sea. His eyes give Hook the sensation of looking out over dark waters, sensing rather than seeing what lies beneath them. He feels it then, the dull awareness that has been in the back of his mind all along, the thing he's been trying to ignore. But he cannot ignore it any longer. It will rise at any moment, all armor-plated scales and hungering jaws.

Hook remembers drowning. And he has been here a hundred thousand times before.

Fear grabs hold of him, despite his determination not to be unmanned on his own ship, made cowardly before his men. Pan shouldn't have the satisfaction, but his breathing is no longer under control. His pulse gallops, and he's pulled helplessly behind it.

Pan. Panic. A hand slips beneath his skin, takes hold of his heart, and its grip is iron.

His death is an immutable fact. It exists before him and behind him, a thing that has happened before and will happen again—an endless circle. He and Pan and the creature below the waves are three points of a triangle, irrevocably joined. No matter what he does in this moment, nothing will change.

The shadow of a smile, a cold and terrible one, shapes Pan's lips. Then they purse, sounding a whistle that rises and falls, piercing and sharp, skipping across the flatness of the water like a stone loosed from a child's hand.

Hook turns, though he doesn't want to, his legs marching him across the deck when he would dig in his heels. He glances to the side, his crew coming into focus at last as though they'd ceased to exist until this moment when Pan needed them to witness their captain's humiliation.

These men—how many times have they fought together? How many times has he died in front of them? His mind churns and Hook finds he cannot even dredge up a single one of their names. They should be brothers in arms, loyal men willing to die for their captain, and yet he's certain not a one of them knows a single thing about him beyond his shouted orders. Just as he knows nothing about them.

The realization hurts more than it should. The sensation of loss washes through him. There's something missing, someone he's forgotten. He scans his crew with a kind of desperation this time. Rough pirates, dressed in dirt and sweat-stained clothes, grime beneath their torn and ragged nails, hands calloused from the rigging. Except for one. Hook's gaze snags on a man standing apart from the others. The man flinches, as if startled at being seen.

There's a skip in Hook's thoughts, a needle missing its groove. He's never seen this man before, doesn't know his name any more than he knows the others. Except the feeling of loss returns, stronger this time—a phantom limb aching even though he can clearly see it isn't there.

The man meets Hook's gaze, and there's something like distress in his eyes. Hook wishes he could stop walking. If he just had a moment longer. If he could just talk to the man. If only he could remember.

He's almost to the rail now, almost to the plank. He keeps his eyes on the man, trying to hold every detail, memorize him. It feels important. The man is dressed more neatly than the others; he wears no blade. His hair is tied at the nape of his neck, and his hands, Hook startles to notice, appear soft.

They're uncalloused—a gentleman's hands, not a pirate's. It's enough to jolt him from his fear and replace it with confusion. The man's name almost rises to his lips, but just as quickly, the name is gone.

Pan jabs the point of his sword into the small of Hook's back and Hook's crew falls away once again. The entire world narrows, leaving Hook and Pan alone. The sword point stops just short of piercing the heavy fabric of Hook's coat. He lifts one foot, then the other, climbing onto the plank and peering down at the water. The waves churn now, slow and sullen; the thing beneath them continues to rise.

"Now jump!" Pan jabs his sword again, as if Hook had a choice. His knees bend of their own accord and he leaps. He strikes the water hard, his velvet coat blooming around him, petals unfurling and immediately growing heavy, dragging him down.

He remembers drowning.

And he remembers that drowning alone is not enough for Pan.

The beast appears in a rush of silvered bubbles. Jaws close on Hook's leg, bones shatter-snapped as the creature jerks him rapidly through the waves. It's almost fast enough to make him lose consciousness, but not quite. Up and down lose meaning. Water rushes up his nose, burning like fire. A flash of scales winds around him. The creature is vast and he cannot see all of it at once. Couldn't even if his eyes didn't blur with the salt. A clawed foot here, the dead-black center of a golden eye there, a flattened snout opening deadly wide.

It looks like a crocodile, but a crocodile is only an animal. It acts on instinct. It consumes in order to survive. This beast comes to the Pan's call. It is malignant, fired with purpose, capable of hate. And it loathes him.

A small, dispassionate part of Hook's mind tells him crocodiles are primarily freshwater creatures, a useless scrap of knowledge rising from the ether. They prefer rivers and swamps to the ocean. The thought is so out of place, so utterly unhelpful that even as the breath is crushed from his lungs and Hook dies for the hundredth, thousandth, millionth time, he dies laughing.

"Did it get dead again?" Cold fingers poke him.

"Not it, him. This one's the captain."

"Captain. Map-him. Slap-him." The sing-song nonsense words are followed by trilling laughter uncomfortably like the chuckling of sea birds.

"Captain." The third voice is dismissive, dripping scorn. "It still drowned, didn't it? Useless land-thing."

Hook rolls onto his side to vomit up seawater. It burns just as badly coming up as it did going down. His chest aches, his ribs battered. He can scarcely believe that every single one of them isn't broken. Or perhaps they are. His throat, scraped raw, tastes of blood.

"Water." The word rasps from him.

He's lying on something hard. Soaked clothing clings to him. He's too heavy to rise.

"Poor captain." He can't tell if it's the first voice again, or the third, or another one altogether. Either way, the words aren't said kindly, the tone cold, just on the edge of mocking.

He opens his eyes as the rough edge of a seashell pushes against lips. A trickle of water pours into his mouth, and he swallows greedily before remembering the last time the mermaids dragged him from the waves they tried to revive him with salt water. He nearly chokes, but the water is fresh and he swallows again and again until the shell is withdrawn. He struggles to sit.

Dim light comes through the wide mouth of the cave, a silvery-gray that could speak to pre-dawn, pre-twilight, or anywhere in-between. There's no telling how long he was drowned this time, how long it took him to return.

All around him, in shallow pools and deeper ones, mermaids lounge. There's a faint luminosity to the water, algae blooming in the dark. One of the mermaids slaps her tail against the water, a lazy motion. The sound echoes and ripples reflect on the ceiling, creating the unsettling illusion that the cavern is the sea floor and he's still underwater.

It takes a moment to convince himself that oxygen does indeed flow into his lungs. The mermaids watch him, silent, waiting to see what he'll do. They remind him of gulls, placid and stupid, but vicious when there's food at stake.

He's heard the legends of beautiful creatures luring men to their deaths. But whatever loveliness these mermaids have is more akin to the sleek beauty of sharks, or eels. Their faces are human, but subtly wrong. Strange shadows carve their cheeks and jaws, leaving their features a little too sharp, chins a little too pointed. Their flat eyes gleam in the dark.

He tries to forget the way they watch him as he takes stock. His legs are whole, his arms where they should be. Despite the tender ache of his flesh, he doesn't seem more than bruised. The only part he's missing is the only lasting wound the beast has ever dealt him—his hand, replaced by a hook. When he shifts, his bones feel splintered inside his skin, but that's only an illusion—his mind telling him what should be, rather than what is.

The mermaid in the pool nearest him draws closer, curious, and rests her arms on a lip of rock. When he looks at her, she flicks her tail, showering him with water.

"Sad Hook, Mad Hook, Bad Hook. Pretty Peter beat you again." She laughs and the others take it up, the sound echoing through the cavern.

Even this close, he isn't always sure which one of the mermaids is speaking at any given time. As much as they remind him of seabirds, they also remind him of bees—a hivemind, indistinguishable to his eye. He's never been able to tell the mermaids apart, to know whether he's met a particular shoal before. They're changeable, fluid like the element they swim in. Their faces don't stay in his mind. Like those of the boys Pan leads. Like those of his crew.

"Bad, bad Hook. He doesn't know how to beat Pretty Peter, does he?" The voice bounces from the walls, further disorienting him.

The tone is fluting, musical, but also eerie. The mermaids dragged him from the water, but if their mood changes and they grow bored, the lot of them could easily tear him apart.

"It doesn't know anything at all." Another voice, or the same, scoffs. "Stupid pirate. It doesn't know the stories. It doesn't know Pretty Peter's secret."

A flash of teeth and eyes that remind him for a moment of Pan's. Otherworldly. Unreal.

"What secret?" Hook fixes his attention on the mermaid in front of him, the closest, the one he can see most clearly. The others are mere shadows in their pools and on the stone that resembles hardened melted wax. But she isn't the one to answer him, or at least he never sees her lips move.

"Ooh. Buried long ago. Would you listen if we told, scold, bold? No. Mermaids are lowly creatures. Like birds squawking, yes?"

He keeps his gaze fixed on the mermaid in front of him in case she is the one talking. She tilts her head to the side, her gaze canny, unnerving. Can they read each other's minds? Can they read his as well?

"Tell me your story. I'll listen." Something prickles at the back of his skull—a memory from the shrouded corner of his brain?

Has he asked for this story before? More laugher flutters around the cave.

"A secret!" a voice pipes up and others crowd to follow it, spilling one over the other, blurring together.

The mermaids forget their intention to play keep-away with their knowledge, eager to prove what they know and he does not.

"A treasure."

"A knife."

"A door."

The words overlap, and he struggles to pick them apart. The tickling sensation of almost-memory returns. Once again there's something he's forgotten. Something he *wanted* to forget; he feels the shape of it; it feels like hope sliding through his hands, too much to bear.

"A way out."

The words are like fire in his veins. He lunges for the mermaid nearest him, wanting to grab her, shake her, make her speak sense. A flick of her tail carries her beyond his reach, his hand and his hook catching nothing.

"A knife."

"To cut between worlds."

"Old magic."

"Oldest. Coldest. Boldest."

"Mad magic. Bad magic."

"Bad Hook, Sad Hook."

"Mad, madder, maddest."

"Only the maddest can use the knife. Only the baddest."

The words tumble and bounce, striking him like bruising stones. His blood thumps in rhythm with them. Maybe the mermaids are only taunting him. Can their chattering be believed? He might as well listen to the shrieking of the seabirds. Yet hope flutters, a terrible and dangerous thing when he tried to cut itself out of him long ago. When he tried to dull it with drink and smoke. He *has* heard this tale before, and he made himself forget. Because he was afraid.

"More door much gore," one of the mermaids sings.

Door—with the word repeated, he latches onto it. A knife. A door. A blade for cutting between worlds? Could Pan have hidden a secret way to leave Neverland somewhere on the island? Or is the secret older than the boy? Just because the mermaids called it his doesn't mean Pan knows about it at all.

The hope in him flares bright and at the same time leaves him queasy. What is there beyond the world? He's sailed to the horizon before. And always the sea spins him back around and he finds himself once more on Pan's island. There's no other place, has never been. Only this one. Only the endless battle, death after death, drowning after drowning.

The mermaid in the pool closest to him drifts in a lazy circle. "Where is this knife? How do I find it?" He hears and hates the eagerness in his voice, the raw need.

"Knife, knife, knife." She makes the word into a song. "Life wife strife. The drowned captain doesn't know!"

She flips onto her back, her expression dreamy, mouth fixed in a vapid smile. She's growing bored. They all are. If he doesn't get the story now they're likely to forget, if they ever knew.

He imagines a fishhook sunk into the mermaid's cheek, tearing her smile wide. A filleting knife plunged into her gut, opening her from tail to sternum.

If he lets himself get sloppy, lets his anger show, he has no

39

chance against them. He must be the blade forged in the fire, and not the fire itself—honed and useful. He waits for his moment, letting the mermaid pass by him several times without moving, letting her grow complacent.

The next time she strays close, he lashes out with his flesh and blood hand, catching her and hauling her from her pool. Her eyes widen, mouth opening and closing like a landed fish in truth.

"Tell me." He pulls her close; her breath smells of seaweed and oysters slurped raw, rank and cold.

Gasps, splashes, a piping of voices without words. The other mermaids flee, leaving their sister alone. Cowards. He keeps his focus on the one in his grip. A full-grown mermaid could tear him apart, but this one is too stunned. Or too young and stupid to know a powerful motion of her tail could drag him into the water and pulverize him. A snap of her jaws could tear out his throat.

Her eyes shine, the light in them threatening to spill over as tears, but she doesn't fight back. Her passivity makes him loathe her all the more.

"The knife. Tell me."

"Away, away! Far across the island." The words emerge high, ending on a squeak. She tries to twist out of his grip, but he doesn't let go.

Pan made him a villain, the most fearsome pirate that ever was. Not powerful enough to best Pan himself, of course, but terrible enough to destroy everything and anything else.

"A hole. A pool crying out into the sea." Her words tumble, fast and panicked.

"What does that mean? Talk sense." He shakes her hard enough that her teeth click together.

"Hurting." She protests, pulling weakly against him. "Tears running out into the sea."

She wipes at her own cheeks, wet and salt-tracked. He can't tell if she's expecting mercy or trying to explain. A hole? Running tears? Does she mean a stream? A cave with a stream running out into the sea?

Even though she's babbling nonsense, he's certain she isn't lying. He is Neverland's monster and her fear of him is complete. Hate curdles from his anger, sour and thick. The mermaid disgusts him—a creature as powerful as she shouldn't cower before him. She could tear his throat out with a single snap of her jaws and yet she whimpers and shivers in his grip.

And she has nothing useful left to tell him anymore.

Hunger rises in him, called by her fear. All his forgetting, all his dying, all his loss—it's a void roaring to be filled. The gleaming point of his hook reflects in the wideness of the mermaid's eyes. He's barely aware of raising it before he brings it slashing down, burying the point in the mermaid's eye.

Hook opens his hand. The mermaid sinks, one dead eye fixed on him, the other a hole trailing a ribbon of blood. He watches until she vanishes from sight, then rocks back onto his heels. A cavern with a stream running out to the sea on the other side of the island. Has he seen such a thing before? Did he go looking and fail to find it, or did he give up without even trying?

A magic blade sounds like something out of a children's tale, impossible and ridiculous. But this is a world made by a child, or something that looks like a child at least, so why shouldn't there be such a blade? Why shouldn't a knife be a door, and why shouldn't he use it to step through?

The mermaid is no longer visible, the water still. He wonders if, like him, she will return and remember dying. He hopes she will. Why should he suffer alone?

He wipes the blood from his hook onto his coat and stands. He won't allow himself to forget this time. He won't turn back. And if the knife turns out to be only a useless, chattered tale, he will return here and slaughter every last mermaid, one by one.

BETWEEN TWO WORLDS

LONDON – 1939

Wendy Darling isn't a child anymore. The fact shouldn't surprise him—children grow up in this world, after all. But in his mind, she is frozen as he last saw her, a young girl trailing after Pan. She doesn't belong to this world; she belongs to Neverland.

James watches Wendy Darling, the woman, pelt away from him. Not running from him this time, but running toward a child of her own. Should he find it strange that even with strands of gray in her hair and lines at the corners of her mouth and eyes, he knew her instantly and she knew him?

No. If some part of her still belongs to Neverland, so does a part of him.

Stay. Stay here with me.

Against the day's cold, Samuel's hands are suddenly on his, flesh and blood and wood and flesh again. Dizziness sweeps him, and James leans his weight onto his cane until it passes. Samuel's voice, his ghost, has never come to him outside of their flat before. His worlds, all of them, bleed together, disorienting him.

Stay.

James blinks. The world resolves back into the gray London street, the damp, clumpy snow falling from the sky. Did it ever snow in Neverland? He shakes his head to chase the thought away. A melting trickle of icy water slips beneath his collar, a finger traced down his spine.

He wishes for Samuel's warmth again, regrets the loss of his ghost. He shouldn't have banished him. He needs him here, now. The tug of Neverland is stronger than ever. Wendy Darling reappearing here in this world—it must be connected. Did she feel the door open too? Did she feel the beast slip through?

Last night, he might have dismissed the beast and the door as an illusion, but now he's certain.

And if the door is real, why shouldn't he return? If he's meant to stay in London, he needs Samuel to ground him, to give him some rationale for why he shouldn't run off seeking his ghost, the remains of him in Neverland. Because if the door can open one way, if the beast could step through, then couldn't James himself cross back as well? And find Samuel waiting on the other side.

The thought freezes the breath in his lungs more effectively than the winter air.

The temptation pulls at him, stronger than the desire for smoke or drink. Samuel had always been his anchor, reeling James back when he drifted too far, when he let smoke carry him to the point of unraveling in a desperate attempt to quell his pain. He'd promised Samuel, again and again, that he'd be careful. And again and again, he'd broken that promise. Here, now, everything still hurts, and he no longer has Samuel, his compass, to find his way home.

"Why should I stay when you're gone?" He snaps the words aloud into the cold, puffs of breath hanging like ghosts in the air. A young couple passing close to him startles. The man casts James a wary glance, pulling the woman at his side closer and steering her away.

He ignores them. *Mad Hook. Bad Hook.* Let them think him a crazy old man. What does he care? His leg aches, not just with the cold. He feels the buried fragments of a blade shattered long ago, lodged beneath his skin. Shrapnel. They shift, magnetized pieces tugging him back to where he promised never to go.

Gripping the head of his cane, he walks deliberately against the ache with no destination in mind. He can't remember why he even left the flat—he does so rarely these days. Something pulled at him, demanded he be here at this precise moment to meet a ghost from his past made real.

He can no longer see Wendy Darling on the street ahead. But he's certain now that they've found each other once, he'll see her again. It strikes him—presumably she's been in London this entire time, right under his nose, but they'd never encountered each other. Not until today. There must be a purpose to it. Did Pan ever give Wendy Darling the secret of his hunting beast? Could she have called it here, or better yet, could she call it off if it attacks again?

A faint memory tugs at him—the pale oval of a face surrounded by coppery curls, mouth startled-wide, peering over the rail of a ship—his ship—as he sank into the beast's jaws.

She stood at Pan's side and watched him die. She did nothing to stop it.

James stops suddenly, heedless of the people behind him. The old sensation is there—a sixth sense, reawakened. The swirling snow erasing the street might as well be the surface of the ocean. If he concentrates, he can feel the beast moving, tracking him through London. Tick, tick, tick. Claws clicking over the deck of his ship, claws clicking over the frozen streets.

He glances back and he can almost see it—there, a blunted snout vanishing between two men bundled in their coats, hurrying with their heads down against the wind. The wind. It's too purposeful the way it moves. The clustering snowflakes suggest scales. Teeth. The bite in the air isn't just the cold.

He needs to get away. He needs to hide.

The frozen breath feels jagged in his lungs, but he moves as quickly as his leg will allow. The point of his cane stabs at the slush, his shoulder knocking aside the bodies around him. Someone shouts after him, but he doesn't slow, panic driving him forward. A sharp turn and he barrels through the nearest doorway, finding the warmth and light of a pub on the other side.

Samuel's warning rings in the back of his head again, but James pushes it away. He very much needs a drink right now. And besides, the bitter thought strikes him, hasn't the damage already been done?

He imagines Samuel's disappointed expression. Disappointed, but not surprised. They'd both known James's weaknesses. Samuel had understood, hadn't he? And at the very least, he'd forgiven James, and so, perhaps, his ghost can forgive him now again.

James knocks snow from the worn leather of his boots. As he moves toward the bar, there's a hush like the sea, blood ringing like waves in his head. He hasn't touched the pipe today—or has he? But even without the smoke in his lungs, he feels time coming unmoored. It takes him two tries to climb into a seat at the end of the bar. He is split down the middle. His bones are hollow, salt crystals eroded by the sea.

There was something… Something he was afraid of, wasn't there? A reason he ran to hide here. But when he tries to hold on to it, it slips away from him.

"Brandy." The word slurs in his mouth, but the man behind the bar doesn't seem to notice, or doesn't seem to care as James puts a crumpled note down between them.

When the glass arrives, James can barely see it. It moves, like a bird darting away from his hand. His fingers miss entirely. On the second attempt, he gets the glass to his mouth, and drinks quickly before the entire thing vanishes. Some of the liquid spills, dribbling down his chin, but the rest burns all the way down.

Hook closes his eyes. *No. Not Hook. James.* But even in his thoughts, the name is suddenly ill-fitting, like his coat that pulls too tight across his shoulders, the boots that constrict his feet. The room sways around him like the deck of a ship. He leans his head against the wall beside him.

Samuel, I'm sorry.

Then the wall isn't there, or perhaps he isn't there, and he's falling.

THE NORTH ATLANTIC OCEAN
AND NEVERLAND – BEFORE

Waves roll over the deck, wind battering the ship and pushing it away from the coast. They're so close he can almost smell home, but he fears they'll never make it. He imagines the hull split, spilling its treasures of sugar, molasses, fruit, and wood from the West Indies into the inky deep.

He'd promised Anna their fortune when he left. A dowry for her, if she wanted it, a good life safe from the workhouse. She'd kissed his cheek at the dock and bid him come home safe with worry in her eyes. He'd promised he would. If his bones end with their cargo on the ocean floor, how long until someone brings her word? At least with no body to bury, she'll be spared the cost of his funeral.

The thought is bitter between his teeth, clenched against the wind. Salt-spray drenches him, the water so impatient to drown him it can't resist leaping onto the deck.

Another swell strikes them broadsides. The frantic and useless shouts of the crew are lost in the wind, as the ship lifts, caught and carried to the crest, tilted at an angle that sends him sliding and scrabbling for purchase. The ship finds the pinnacle and hangs above the trough between waves that will surely shatter them. Somewhere in the chaos, someone shrieks a prayer, then time halts.

James blinks. Fetched up against the rail he stares straight down into an abyss that is improbably deep. A stray memory, a story Anna told him when they were children about Charybdis, the monstrous whirlpool set to destroy Odysseus's ship. The thing in the water beneath the ship now is exactly how James pictured that monstrous whirlpool so long ago.

A mouth. Fanged. Ringed in teeth receding into an endless throat of waves. Hunger, given form, and inexorably dragging them down.

He shouts, an incoherent and wordless thing, and the sound echoes back to him in a sudden stillness, as if the storm vanished.

He cannot turn his head to see the rest of the ship, the rest of the crew. There is only this—him clinging to the rail and the mouth in the waves.

It must be a hallucination, an illusion created by the foam. But then how to explain the stars shining in the depths of the mouth, as if a sky existed below the bottom of the world? How to explain the sense of something pulling him downward, not just gravity, but a sense of want? It makes no sense. It—

Crack. The terrible sound of the rail giving way, or a lightning strike splitting the ship in two, or both. Time rushes forward all at once, and James spins, no longer holding on to anything at all. Breath leaves his lungs as the water slams into him. His head rings, and stars burst behind his eyes.

He should be shattered. He should be drowning, but somehow the world is blue and green and black all around him. Salt that might be the ocean or his own blood fills his mouth. Waves close above his head, but somehow, the stars remain, screaming past, as he drowns-and-does-not-drown. He tumbles through the air. He is falling, and it is a very, very long way down.

He wakes to pain with the vague knowledge he shouldn't be waking at all. He is dead, surely. Drowned, or mercifully broken by the waves before his air had a chance to run out. He shouldn't feel anything, yet there is a persistent sensation, like a stick, sharp at one end, repeatedly driven into his side.

"Lay off!" Or those are the words he means to say.

What comes out is a more garbled sound, turning to a wracking cough.

He rolls onto his side just in time not to choke, spitting seawater and bile onto the sand. Grit meets his palms as he braces himself to keep from falling face first into his own sick. He is hollowed out, feverish, and a trembling shakes him from head to toe.

"Have you been kilt, then? Was it the Injuns or the mermaids?" The voice is high and piping, a child's voice, the words nonsensical.

He doesn't have the strength to stand, flopping instead onto his back like a landed fish. The light is very bright. He closes his eyes, trying to drift away from everything, but the jabbing resumes.

"You're not doing it right. You're a pirate. That means we fight. Yaah!" On the last word, the sharpened point of the stick drives into his side again, hard enough to draw blood.

James's eyes fly open on a strangled shout and he sits up. At the motion, his stomach heaves again, but there's nothing to bring up. Grit behind his eyes, his head thudding and spinning, and the relentless sunlight knifing at him. Not dead, but it's all enough to make him wish he were.

"Leave me alone." The words come out slurred, his tongue swollen with thirst.

He squints, trying to focus, trying to make sense of his surroundings. The storm, the shipwreck. They were a week out from home. Could he have washed ashore? But the sky over London was never this blue, and there's nowhere that he knows of in all of England with sand so soft and white.

"You're awfully boring." Scorn marks the boy's voice.

The collection of shadows and angles crouched before him resolves into a child. The boy rocks on his heels, feet bare, his knees sticking up sharply to either side of him, arms dangling loose between his legs. Dirt streaks his skin, deliberately patterned on his cheeks to accentuate their sharpness. His hair, spiked wildly, burns like a copper pot over a flame.

The boy's chest is bare as well. He's scarcely clothed at all except for whatever wraps his waist. James can't quite make it out. It shifts—now leaves, now the hide of an animal. Briefly, it seems the boy's legs *are* an animal's, the joints turned the wrong way, feet replaced by cloven hooves.

Perhaps he is dead after all. This is Hell, and the boy is a demon sent to torment him. Anna told him stories from the Bible as well as Greek mythology. He'd never taken either for truth, but now he wonders. The child might be a satyr, a faun, a minion of the Devil. The wild tufts of his hair do almost look like curling horns.

A glance past the boy reveals no sign of parents, no sign of any other living beings at all.

"You're not a very good pirate." The boy sounds impatient and irritated now.

Anger begins to override the thirst, the hunger, the pain. Who is this child, left on his own to torment a half-drowned man? Why are there no adults to watch over him? No one to fetch help?

"I'm not a pirate." The words are clearer this time. "I'm—"

And he stops. There is a void where there should be…*something*. Information about himself. The name of the ship he came from, the shipping company, the name of his captain. But all he finds is ragged absence, like a plucked tooth. He can tongue the edges, but there is nothing to be gleaned.

"Course you're a pirate. You're not an Injun and you're not a mermaid. What else would you be?" There's such certainty to the boy's voice that for a moment, James almost believes him.

Yes. Of course he's a pirate. What else would he be?

He squints at the child. There's a canniness to his expression, a brightness to his eyes. The way his mouth lifts makes his face look even sharper. It's sly, and despite the bright sun drawing sweat from James's skin beneath his clothes, the boy casts no shadow at all.

"In fact…" The boy leans forward, and there's the suggestion of hunger in his expression; it's unnatural, like the moon rising in the dark wells surrounded by irises that are suddenly no color James can name. "I think you must be their captain."

The way he says it, punctuated by a sharp-toothed grin, sounds like a judge pronouncing a sentence on a doomed man. The boy hasn't moved, but he seems closer, the space folded between them. There's a green scent to the child, an animal scent—James can think of no better way to describe it. Musk and wild and earth, as if the child sprouted from a seed the way a tree would grow.

James glances to the side, wondering if his legs would hold him if he tried to stand, wondering if he could run. A border of trees stands in dark contrast to the brightness of the shore. When he twists around to look behind him, there, just beyond the point of land where the island—and he is certain somehow that it is an island—curves away from view, is a ship. Black-sailed, its belly massive, guns bristling from its ports, its rails and masthead elaborately carved.

He's never seen the like, and yet… And yet, he knows the ship. He knows how its deck will roll beneath his feet, the precise snap of its sails, the way each board and rope will sing in a storm. He belongs to the ship, and it belongs to him.

He looks back to the boy, pulse jagged now. Something has changed. Something is very wrong. The boy's smile is a sickle-cut in his face, the smell of him even stronger now.

James pushes his heels into the sand, trying to back away, trying to stand. But there isn't enough strength in him, and there's something compelling about the child as well. The boy sways in his crouch, a hypnotic motion, and James can no longer look away.

"Yes," the boy says, and the single word twists, a musical tone going on and on like a flute, rising and falling.

It dulls the edge of his fear, dulls everything.

"You're the pirate captain, and that's your ship."

"What—" He swallows, his throat making a dry clicking sound, then tries again. "What about the crew?"

Because how could the ship be there, anchored off the point of the shore if no one sailed it there? The ship must have a crew. And one of them could save him. He can almost see them. Feel them moving around him on the deck, jumping to his command. He has been there before. Or will be there? Has always been?

There's a shifting sensation, like the sand running out beneath him, pulling him down. Only nothing moves. It's something far more subtle and fundamental shifting. Time. Place. Truth.

His heart beats, a painful drum, but he can't express his fear in any meaningful way. He can only stare at the boy with his bright eyes and terrible smile.

"Oh, there were pirates before, but I didn't like them. Your pirates will be much better." Airy, confident, tone shifting even as the boy shifts, as everything shifts, a new truth wrapping itself around him.

The ship changes. James changes. Bones twist beneath his skin, snapping and taking on new forms. His shoulders broaden, his feet lengthen. Even his hair feels thicker, heavier on his scalp, and a new beard roughs his cheeks where a moment before he's certain he was clean-shaven.

In his mind, there's a scrambling, a desperation to hold on to something, but there's nothing to hold. Where was he before now? How did he come to be here? What is his name?

"You'll need a sword. All pirates must have swords. And…"

The boy pauses, putting his head to one side, tapping at his lips as he ponders. Then his smile widens, and he claps his hands, bouncing in his crouch as though he's about to leap into the sky and fly.

"And a hook! You must have a hook for a hand. That will be your name, Captain Hook, and we shall fight all the time and you will be beastly and terrible, but I will always win."

"A hook?" He looks at his hands, considering the long fingers, the palms.

His hands are not a thing he's ever thought much about before. No more than he thinks of his eyelashes, his knees. They are all simply a part of him. But what does the boy mean that he will have a hook for a hand?

"How will—?"

The boy waves his own hand, dismissing the words. Dismissing them so utterly that they curl and dry in his throat, and he finds himself unable to speak again, as though his lips are sewn shut.

"Pirates have hooks for hands and patches over their eyes and wood for their legs and gold for their teeth. Everyone knows that." The boy runs on, his words blurring in his excitement. "And you'll live at the front of the ship and have the finest room and there will be seven crow's nests and a hundred cannons."

Wait, he wants to tell the boy. *That isn't right. That isn't how ships work.*

But the boy would ignore him even if he could speak. The child jumps up so for a moment it seems as though he does hang in the air, impossibly. His feet hover just above the ground, certainly not touching it. James wants to tell him that isn't how boys work either, but his lips remain fixed closed.

The sand beneath the boy is pristine, unmarred by darkness, despite the sun shining directly on him. If he missed the shadow somehow before, he is certain now. His own shadow pools around him; the trees cast shadows and everything else is exactly as it should be, save for the boy.

The boy's feet touch the sand again, and he bends forward at the waist.

"Are you ready?" he asks.

For what, he thinks, but he cannot speak. The boy nods, as if his silence were consent, and he leans back, stretching so far it seems his spine must snap, throwing his head back.

The sound that emerges is nothing he can describe. Nothing that should come from a human mouth, much less the mouth of a child. It rises and falls, trilling like a bird, tolling like a lonely bell, sounding and sounding like wind through a hollow reed. It is an awful noise, in the truest sense of the word. It sounds like an ancient language, spoken by angels and demons before the beginning of the world. He cannot understand it, but at the same time, he knows what it's for—something is being summoned.

He feels the answer rising from the deep, coalescing from the dark, as if all the shadow the boy lacks exists outside of him, scattered about the island, bits of it drawing together to take form. Water sloughs off the back of the creature crawling from the waves. It is mere inches from him, but even so he cannot make sense of it. It is as ancient as the sound that called it, a monster from the beginning of time. A crocodile, but *more* than that. Jaws vast, plated with thick, overlapping scales, eyes burning with all the malice in the world.

The dizzying notion strikes him that the beast and the boy are the same. An invisible tether stretches between them, a monster, but one on a leash and controlled by the boy's hand. There's a third length to the rope as well, with a barbed tip buried in his own flesh, as though the boy has joined all of them so even if he tried to run the beast would still find him, no matter where he might go.

The creature springs forward in an impossibly fast motion, its lashing tail propelling it across the sand, its mouth dropping open. He throws out a hand as if to ward it off and too late he remembers the boy's words. The creature's jaws snap. A neat thing, severing bone. His hand, which he never thought of until now, is simply gone. Unmade, as if it never existed, a smooth and bloodless stump in its place.

The boy leaps into the air again, letting out a triumphant cock's crow, like a rooster calling up the dawn. As the boy touches down again, the world settles into place around them both. A new truth, a new reality.

He is Hook, pirate captain. He is in Neverland. It has always been his home. And the boy, Pan, will be his enemy until the end of time.

LONDON – 1939

James's mouth tastes hot, sticky, and dry. There's a hand on his shoulder, shaking him.

"Up you go. You can't sleep here, old duffer."

He can't have passed out, not after only one drink…but no. He was somewhere else. Someone else. He was in Neverland, with Pan. He feels it still, that other place like a hook buried in his skin, trying to bring him home.

Hook.

And the beast, the beast was here, searching for him. His pulse speeds, but he can't feel the monster. But does that mean he's safe, or simply that they're closed off to each other? He can't find it, and perhaps it can't find him either.

His head pounds. He lifts a hand to it instinctively before he remembers, flinching away before the point catches him. But his fingers are only wood, gleaming with silver. The hand Samuel carved for him. The hand he's worn for years. Only looking at it, it seems strange. It doesn't seem to belong to him. He isn't…

James tries to stand. The floor pitches under him, and the barkeep catches him with a grunt. The man pushes him away again, his expression one of disgust, and the flashing impulse to violence rises. He should clap the man in irons, run him through with his sword.

But he doesn't have a sword. And the man looking at him with pity and distaste doesn't see a captain, or even a war veteran, which might account for the wooden hand. He sees only an old drunk.

"I'm fine." James's tongue is thick, making his words into a lie. He sways, but keeps his feet beneath him with the help of his cane. "Just go."

James does, staggering out into the snow. His head still rings, the world still unsteady, the here and now refusing to stay solid. He scans the street, but there's no sign of anything scaled with terrible jaws trying to take shape. Cold London air slaps his cheeks and slips chapped and icy hands beneath his coat. He tugs the front of it shut, clutching it tight. He just makes it to the alleyway beside the pub before he doubles over, bringing up a thin stream of bile onto the crusted snow. James braces himself against the wall, breathing deep despite the smell, only somewhat blunted by the cold.

The brick resolves, the dirty snow underfoot gaining solidity. The world ceases swinging back and forth and trying to drop out beneath him. James pushes himself upright.

It was an alley very much like this one where he and Samuel first arrived in London, still clinging to each other after the terrible storm. The memory digs at him, sharp as a blade. Time has become unstuck, moments from his life— his lives—catching him unawares, tumbling all on top of each other. Anna bidding him farewell with tears in her eyes. The ship, his ship, carrying him over Neverland's waves. The storm, bringing him here.

He has lived too many lives, all of them filled with loss, weighing him down.

James wipes his mouth. He's about to push himself away from the wall when something catches his eye farther back in the alleyway. It's half-hidden in the shadow of a stack of crates piled against the wall. It might be anything—a sack of refuse, an old soldier sleeping off the drink with nowhere else to go.

Ice grips his spine, and it has nothing to do with the weather.

Leaning on his cane, James approaches. The still form was a man once, but now he is so emptied of anything like life that it might never have been alive at all. James doesn't bother to check for a pulse. Erased, like a hand sheered from an arm with razor teeth as though it never existed at all.

Faint markings, like soot left on the chimney wall after a fire, stain the brick behind the body. It's as though something has leeched out of the man. A shadow, imprinted where he leaned back for a moment, pressing away from the thing he feared before he fell.

Scales and jaws. A living nightmare.

Your dreams are a dangerous thing. Samuel's words again, breathed against his ear, but Samuel is not here, and James resists the urge to turn toward them. He was in Neverland, his dreams shining like a beacon, calling the beast. But Pan was the only one who could ever call the beast, the only one who could control it. Does that mean Pan is here as well? The thought chills James to his core, nearly undoes him.

He remembers drowning.

No. If Pan were here, he would feel it. That he is certain of, even if the tie between himself and the beast is severed. All those years, every time they fought, it was always only one long battle. The moments in-between were barely a respite. He could always feel Pan, like a splinter beneath his skin.

If he can't feel Pan, and his connection to the beast is gone, could that possibly mean that after all these long, terrible years Pan is finally gone too? A spark like hope flares in him, and at the same time, a sick feeling of disappointment. He should have been the one to do the deed, to drive his blade through the child's heart. And if Pan is dead, or gone, then what of Neverland? Because the island was always part of the child too, shaped by his whim. James cracked open the door, but what sort of place now lies on the other side? If the scaled beast is any indication, it is a broken one.

59

He looks down at the dead man again, slumped against the wall. The beast may have the scent of Neverland, but it isn't enough. It drew close to James once again, and missed. Without Pan, the creature is alone, maybe even afraid, snapping wildly and hoping to get lucky. Hoping to catch him.

James's breath steams the air. If he'd woken and left the pub a moment sooner. If the barkeep had tossed him into the cold, the beast might have found its mark.

James steps back, gripping the head of his cane against the stiffness and ache in his leg and forces himself to straighten his spine. How long will his luck hold? He is still here, the last survivor of Pan, except perhaps one—Wendy Darling.

He takes a breath, steadying himself. The thread connecting him to her—he can still feel that at least. Whether or not she has anything to do with the beast, she might prove useful. Old enemies once. Now, perhaps, it is time, for them to be allies at least, if not friends.

ECHOES

J ane sits at the small kitchen table in her flat, arms wrapped around herself. It is the last place she wants to be. She can't stop seeing Peg's emptied body, even though the men from Scotland Yard brought the coroner's wagon and took it away hours ago.

Not it. *Her. Peg.*

After her mother collected Jane from the station—arriving impossibly, as though summoned by Jane merely wishing her there in an unguarded moment of need—after Jane answered the endless barrage of questions, never once raising her voice to shout, "I don't know," as much as she wanted to, there was nowhere else to go but back to the flat. Dusk had smudged the sky when she'd entered the station, but by the time she emerged, her mother gripping Jane's arm as if she might vanish, it had been full dark. They'd missed the last train to Newark-on-Trent.

"Never mind. There'll be another train tomorrow morning. I'll make us supper while you rest." Her mother had guided Jane to a chair, and set about doing just that.

Even though she had longed for her mother's presence, for someone else to take care of her, now the constant out-of-the-corner-of-her-eye motion of her mother moving about the flat grates on Jane's nerves. She wants her mother gone, and at the same time, she can't bear the thought of being alone.

She can't quite fathom how her mother is even here. Jane never got the chance to call her; she simply arrived as if sensing Jane's need. Which means she must have been in London, rather than at home, though she'd never breathed a word of it to Jane.

All through Jane's childhood, her mother had kept the secret of the time she spent in Neverland, when a boy without a shadow came to her window and stole her and Jane's uncles away to a magical land. And yet years ago, that same boy had returned and mistaken Jane for her mother, stealing her away. Unlike her mother, Jane hadn't been given a choice, and in Neverland, Peter had stolen her name, given her drugged tea to keep her complacent, tried to turn her into something she is not.

If her mother had been honest with her from the first, maybe Jane might have protected herself. If her mother had trusted her with the information, rather than assuming what would be best for her—or even worse, simply doing what was best for herself— then Jane might have been prepared, known how to fight back. She wouldn't have lost so much of herself. Now, all Jane can see in her mother's unexplained presence here is more secrets, more lies.

Jane clenches her jaw, listening to her mother in the flat's small kitchen. After her mother had followed Jane to Neverland and brought her home, she'd promised no more secrets. She'd promised Jane she could ask anything, and she would always have the truth. But here it seems her mother is falling back on old habits. Or she never shed them after all.

The thought is a bitter taste in Jane's mouth. The journey they shared should have brought them closer. After all, how many people have gone to another world entirely and come back again? Only Jane, her mother, and her two uncles, as far as Jane knows.

But where her mother clung to Neverland back then as her shield against the world, Jane has done everything she can over the past eight years to distance herself from that place. She promised herself she would never forget, and she hasn't, but the life that interests her is ahead of her, not behind. There is so much more she wants to be than simply the girl that Peter stole. She will be a doctor someday, she will help people, she will do good in the world.

Jane thinks again of the open window in Peg's room, the gap not wide enough for any human to slip through, but what about something inhuman? Could Peter have returned somehow, come looking for Jane and instead found Peg and done something terrible to her? The thought is like a grit of sand, stuck between her clothing and her skin, rubbing her raw. Her mother told her once how all those years she'd held on to the truth of Neverland, she'd always been able to feel it, like a distant whisper of starlight, the sure knowledge of something magical waiting for her on the other side of the sky.

Is it possible her mother felt some hint of Neverland again, and that's what drew her to London? If she had, would she admit to it? Jane knows her version of Neverland is fundamentally different from her mother's, but even after everything, after seeing the truth of it, Jane suspects her mother still misses Neverland somehow.

There are times, dark moments, when Jane can't help thinking it was Neverland itself her mother journeyed for all those years ago, that going back to that place where she'd claimed to have spent the best time of her childhood was more important to her than rescuing Jane. And even now, Jane wonders—for her mother, will one world, this world, the one Jane occupies, ever be enough?

"It's almost ready." Even though she's been listening to her mother move about since they returned, her voice coming from the kitchen still startles Jane.

"What is it?" Something of Jane's thoughts must echo in her expression as her mother comes out of the kitchen, wiping her hands on a dishtowel, her look one of concern.

Jane shakes her head; she doesn't have the energy to even try to explain. Her mother's hand lands awkwardly on Jane's shoulder, a gesture of comfort, but a skittish one.

"What happened to your friend, to Margaret wasn't—"

She twists around in her chair to look at her mother's face, waiting to see what she'll say. It wasn't Jane's fault? It wasn't anything to do with Neverland? Jane wonders which lie her mother will choose, then wonders why she's so certain her mother is lying. Is she being unfair? Her mother is here, and the flat feels too large without Peg, too empty, haunted. Jane should be grateful. But whatever she was about to say, her mother changes direction.

"I only meant that if you want to talk about it, I'm here."

Her mother retreats to the kitchen, almost meek, which is not a word Jane would have thought to apply to her mother before, and guilt prickles in the place of fear. She reminds herself again that her mother is only here to help. The sound of her mother moving about the kitchen resumes, but it's not enough to override the strange quality to the air. There's too much darkness gathered in the corners, a sense of someone standing just out of her line of sight.

Peg is still here. She almost blurts the words aloud, clamping down on them at the last minute.

It's an irrational, childish thought. Jane doesn't believe in ghosts, she can't. She's seen flayed corpses in her anatomy labs, studied detailed medical illustrations of organs and bones. She knows life doesn't continue after death, not in the way most people mean at least. The human body is a machine, capable of breaking down as sure as a loom or a printing press or a car's engine. After a person dies, their body breaks down, it feeds other creatures, flies and worms. The energy of their life might carry on in the insects that eat from them, but nothing of what they were continues except the memories other people carry.

So she must carry Peg's memory, and not do her the dishonor of anything as silly as letting herself think for even a moment that some part of her might literally remain to haunt their flat. The image of the scant opening in Peg's window returns to Jane's mind, as sure as any haunting, more insistent each time she tries to banish it. She doesn't believe in ghosts, but before Neverland, she hadn't believed a person could fly either. As a woman of science, if she's seen evidence of something impossible with her own eyes, shouldn't she leave room to believe that something impossible might occur again? That Peg might…?

Her breath catches; the thought hurts too much. It isn't fair that her time in Neverland should even give her this sliver of hope. She's sick of believing in impossible things. She wants the world to be rational, easily categorized the way it was before Peter stole her away. As a child, she'd collected rocks and butterflies and leaves and labeled them in glass cases and believed that if she tried hard enough the answer to just about any question could be found through study, experimentation, and observation. And now? Her mother's presence only makes it worse, growing the deep ache behind Jane's eyes. With her mother here, she can't forget Neverland or set it aside its promises, as much as she wishes she could.

When they'd returned from the police station, Jane had tried closing Peg's door, as if she could shut out the memory of finding Peg's body. With the door closed, though, she couldn't shake the sense of something lurking just on the other side. But with the door all the way open, she'd felt Peg's empty bed staring at her accusingly. In a way, this is the same. She can't bear having her mother here, and she can't bear the thought of being alone. Neverland is a comfort and a curse, a promise and torture. She can't properly mourn Peg with the terrible hope looming over her that she isn't fully gone.

A sharp memory rises in Jane's mind of her and Peg bundled in their coats, hands tucked into their sleeves against the cold as they'd hurried from class to get back home. Even when Peg transferred programs, they still met up every day—even if one of them finished earlier than the other—so neither of them would have to walk home alone.

"I don't know how you stand it, Jane, I really don't." Peg's nose had been red above her scarf, the sliver of her cheeks still visible was similarly red and wind-chapped. "It's bad enough in my classes, and there are five of us girls altogether. How do you manage being the only one?"

"It's at least partly spite." Jane had allowed herself to grin behind her scarf. "I know some of the professors would rather I was gone, so I just dig in harder to annoy them."

"You're awful." Peg had bumped her shoulder against Jane's nearly sending them both tumbling into the snow.

In that moment, Jane remembered thinking of Peter and his boys, being the only girl among them, and so being told it was her job to cook and tell stories and take care of them all. It had seemed ridiculous to her even as a child. And now, so many of the men at the college are just the same, as though it's never occurred to them that a woman could be a person too, and want things of her own.

It's not only her fellow students, it's the professors too, and sometimes they're even worse. There are those who think themselves well-meaning, as though they're looking out for her, sincerely believing women simply don't have the constitution to be doctors. There are others who outright resent her presence, and she imagines they would refuse to teach her if they could.

Instead, they resort to subtler methods to drive her away. They ask her if she's in the wrong lecture hall. They loudly declare their expectations that she will faint at the sight of blood and ask if she would like to be excused. When they aren't questioning her knowledge and trying to make her doubt herself, they're refusing to call on her, hoping she'll quit. It's exhausting.

One professor had even outright told her that all she was doing was taking the space from a man and denying him the chance to study. He'd confidently told her it was only a matter of time before she got married and had children. A medical education would be wasted on her.

Jane had been so furious she'd nearly slapped him. And if she had, she would have been labeled hysterical, difficult, her actions proof that women's tempers were too hot (even as they were assumed to be too retiring and weak) to cope with the stresses of the medical profession. She'd spent more hours than she cares to admit fantasizing about ways to get her revenge—from idiotic things like filling his desk with frogs from one of the biology laboratories, to pushing him down the stairs and watching him tumble end over end with his academic gown flying over his head.

She'd done none of those things, of course. She'd simply continued showing up to his classes every day, sitting in the front row whenever possible, smiling at him for all she's worth, and working twice as hard as any of the boys. Through it all though, there had been Peg—to commiserate with her, to encourage her. Jane cannot count the number of times they'd saved each other.

Late nights, sitting up together with a pot of tea, complaining about their classes, quizzing each other before exams, proofreading each other's papers. For all her voracious reading, Peg had been atrocious when it came to spelling. She always claimed it was because her mind moved too fast for her hand and her letters got all jumbled up. Jane had teased her mercilessly about it.

An ache presses against the back of Jane's eyes. Not the threat of tears, but the vast weight of the hole left by Peg's absence. Whatever will Jane do without her? The thought makes her feel selfish. She should be thinking of Peg's family, not herself. Peg's other friends. Simon. The thought strikes her, another blade-like twist of guilt— does he know yet? Will she have to be the one to tell him?

A faint smile touches Jane's lips, bittersweet; when Simon had first shown interest in Peg, Peg had been furious.

"I didn't come to school to catch a husband!" She'd stamped around their flat, throwing her hands in the air and letting them flutter about like birds. It was all Jane could do to keep from laughing.

As annoyed as Peg acted, Jane had seen the way she'd blushed at the mere mention of Simon's name, the way a smile inevitably crept onto her lips even as she vehemently denied that any of his interest might be reciprocated.

"It's not like I'm suggesting you drop everything and marry him," Jane had told her, bringing a fresh blush to Peg's cheeks. "All I'm saying is that he's nice and he clearly likes you, so why not give him a chance? After all, you can't study all the time."

How could someone as full of life as Peg possibly be gone?

And now it's as though shadows are continually seeping through the gap between the door to Peg's room and the frame. Jane feels them winding around her ankles, a physical thing she wants to jump up and kick away.

"I'm sorry. It isn't much." Her mother sets a plate down in front of her, and Jane startles again, looking up.

Mistaking her expression, her mother offers Jane a pained smile—sympathetic but uncertain—though she stops short of touching Jane's shoulder or any gesture of comfort. She takes the seat across from Jane, awkward smile still in place.

"Your father does most of the cooking when he's home, and I've never stopped being rubbish at it."

"I'm not hungry." Jane stops short of pushing the plate away. Other words crowd her tongue and she keeps them trapped behind her teeth. *We have to go back to Neverland, you have to show me how.*

There's a door somewhere, and she can feel Peg standing on the other side of it. Something from Neverland slipped into Peg's room and stole the essence of her away, and if Jane could just…

She feels her mother's concern, her expectant watching. What can Jane say? She feels as though she's two people, being torn apart by conflicting truths held inside her skin. It hurts, physically, and she blinks rapidly against tears stinging behind her eyes.

"Jane?" Her mother's voice sounds muffled and Jane shakes her head as if to dislodge water from her ears.

Even with her mother still and sitting in front of her, Jane continues to see the shadow-presence at the corner of her eye—Peg, moving around the room. Two worlds overlapping, one containing Jane and her mother, one containing Peg, her dark hair in its sleek bob curling in to frame her round cheeks, a mystery novel in hand, pausing every now and then to read Jane a particularly delicious passage aloud.

"I can't." The words emerge in a gasp.

Jane stands so quickly her chair tips over backward, crashing to the floor. Her mother is on her feet immediately as well.

"Jane? What is it?"

"What happened to Peg, it's something to do with Neverland, isn't it?" She hadn't meant to say it aloud, but the words are on her tongue, bitter and demanding to be spit out.

Her mother stops, arms halfway raised as if she'd been about the fold Jane into a hug. Her eyes widen enough that Jane sees the flicker of guilt there before her mother can school her expression.

"Oh, I don't—"

Before her mother can get any further, Jane cuts her off, a wild surge of anger rising to sweep away her grief.

"Why were you in the city today? How did you know to come find me before I could even call you?" Jane clenches her hands by her sides, her body trembling with adrenaline, exhaustion, unprocessed emotion.

Her mother's cheeks pale, her mouth snapping shut. It's as good as a confession, Jane's earlier suspicion confirmed. After all, what else would draw her mother here, like a preternatural summons? And what else but something belonging to another world could empty Peg out so completely?

"Jane..." Her mother reaches for her, and Jane pulls away.

"I'd like to sleep now. It's been a very long day." She's too tired to hold back the sharpness in her words and finds she doesn't want to hold it back anyway.

The pain needs to go somewhere, and she can't lash out at Neverland, but her mother is right here—the next best thing. Her mother's expression falls and Jane isn't quick enough to look away. The vindication she wants to feel isn't there, nor the relief. She only feels worse, spreading the pain around instead of lessening it. What's wrong with her? But she lifts her chin, unable to make herself take the words back either.

"I set clean linens on the sofa," Jane says.

"Thank you." The wound is in her mother's voice too; it makes her sound small, fragile, on the edge of crumbling.

Jane wavers. The apology is there. She's on the point of offering to help with the linens, or even offering her mother her own bed, saying she'll sleep on the sofa herself. But her mother's next words drive all thoughts of charity from her mind, ice water drenching her spine.

"Don't worry if I'm not here when you wake in the morning. I'll be back in time to catch our train, but there's some business I need to take care of first." There's a clipped coldness to her mother's words, the vulnerability of a moment ago replaced with fresh armor, meeting Jane's stubbornness with her own.

71

Business. If Jane had any doubts left before, they are gone now. Jane knows, she *knows* that whatever her mother's "business" is, it's to do with Neverland as well.

"Fine," Jane says, her tone mirroring her mother's. "But I won't wait for you if you aren't here on time."

She holds her head up, her spine straight as she steps past her mother, even though all she wants is melt into a boneless puddle on the floor. Her steps don't falter until she finds they've carried her to Peg's door, as if she could just pop her head in and say goodnight before going to bed, and then Jane freezes.

Her breath lodges painfully in her lungs, but she doesn't turn away. The space between the door and the frame shows a slice of the dresser and Peg's narrow bed. She places her fingertips against the wood and peers through the crack.

There's an almost astringent scent to the air, too clean, as though the men from Scotland Yard finished the job started by whoever murdered Peg, scrubbing all traces of her from existence. Jane pushes the door open the rest of the way.

She has the sudden overwhelming urge to find one of Peg's books, its pages dog-eared. She wants to hear Peg in her head, assigning voices to the characters, snatching Jane's own study books from beneath her nose and forcing her to listen.

Peg's hairbrush and a small bottle of perfume, a birthday gift from Peg's mother, are lined up neatly against the mirror. A pair of stockings drape over the back of the chair, while all the rest of her clothing is tucked carefully in drawers. On top of the dresser sits a copy of *The Murder of Roger Ackroyd*, spine cracked open to hold Peg's page. Everything as it should be, as if at any moment Peg will return and resume her life as though nothing happened.

Despite wishing for it, Jane can't bring herself to even touch the book. Peg must have read it three times at least, but this time, she'll never reach the end. Jane moves to the bed, her knees bumping against it. The covers are tucked crisply beneath the pillow, all evidence of Peg's body smoothed away. There should be something to mark that she was here. Jane runs her hand over the top blanket. Is it her imagination, or is the fabric slightly darker here? Like a water stain, but not that at all.

She peels the top layer back. The mark is more distinct, not on the sheet, but underneath it.

Her hands shake as she strips the bed clean, revealing the mattress and the breath goes out of her. A shadow, ragged at the edges like spilled ink staining the fabric. Even as she looks, it seems to grow darker, more distinct, like watching a photograph developing in a chemical bath. The shape is unmistakable—human.

Jane's hand flies to cover her mouth, catching back the sob too late. Now, finally, when she hasn't cried for Peg all day, tears spill forth.

It's like Peg's shadow was ripped from her body, left behind to soak into her mattress like blood. *This* is all of Peg that remains.

OLD ENEMIES, NEW ALLIES

LONDON – 1939

W endy leaves Jane sleeping, guilt dogging her steps through the pre-dawn gray of London. She barely slept, hearing her daughter moving restlessly in another part of the flat, but unable to make herself go to her, afraid of making things worse. She should have told Jane her suspicions immediately; she should have confessed that yes, she'd been in the city chasing some echo of Neverland. But she'd frozen at the thought of saying it aloud. Her daughter had stood before her, grieving, and Wendy should have been there to comfort her, yet it would have felt like rubbing salt in Jane's wound to admit that she hadn't come to the city to see her, that she hadn't intended to let Jane know she was there at all.

Should it surprise her that Jane is angry with her? She'd promised to always be honest with her, but she'd lied again, to protect herself. Is it any wonder her daughter doesn't trust her? She deserves the frost in Jane's voice, the look in her eyes last night when she told Wendy that she would leave her behind if she was late to the train. She was unfair to Jane as a child, withholding the truth of Neverland from her, and now she's being unfair to her all over again.

Slush slides under her boots. Wendy turns her coat up against the chill, tucking her hands into her sleeves, walking with her head down. An additional layer of guilt lies atop the first, because despite everything, Wendy knows she will not turn back. She tried to explain to Jane once what Neverland meant to her, the hold it had upon her, how she could love it and hate it simultaneously. She could see then that Jane didn't understand, would never understand. Wendy barely understands it herself. At times it feels as though Neverland is a sickness in her, a fever that might lie dormant in her for years and then spring up unexpectedly, burning to consume her whole.

The last time she was there, Wendy had torn Neverland apart to save Jane. She'd thought herself done with it forever. But she feels it now—or some echo of it in Hook—and she can't help running toward it. She can't help wanting it to be the land she flew away to as a child, even knowing that land was always a lie.

Wendy lets that lie pull her through the streets now. It's like following a smell or a sound, instinct, leading her to a narrow brick building, knowing beyond a shadow of a doubt that the captain is inside. She pulls open the entry door. The building is old, evident in a slight warping of the stairs, the worn handrail, the water stains on the walls. The same sense that called her here tells her she will find Hook on the top floor.

There's no lift, and Wendy breathes hard by the time she reaches the landing. There's only one door, but as she raises her hand to knock, sudden nerves jangle up and down her spine. For a moment, all Wendy can see is the pirate, sharp-tipped hook poised at her throat, the poppy scent of him and brandied-hot breath washing over her.

The man she saw on the street yesterday didn't look like he could be a threat to anyone. She'd seen the way his leg trembled, barely able to stand. He'd even refused the name Hook. He isn't a pirate anymore and, Wendy reminds herself, this isn't Neverland. He has nothing to gain by threatening her, by restraining her against her will. Peter won't—can't—come to save her anymore.

The door swings open almost as soon as her knuckles touch it, as though Hook had been waiting just on the other side.

"Miss Darling." He doesn't look surprised to see her, stepping back to let her enter.

The gray stubble covering his cheeks and chin seems to have deepened since yesterday. Even out from under the sleet-colored sky, there's a washed-out quality to him.

"I didn't wake you?" There's a faint crack in her voice, a hesitation she wishes she could make disappear. As foolish as it is, a small part of her can't help being a little bit wary of him. Old habits are hard to shed.

"I don't sleep."

He closes the door behind her, and she takes a moment to look over the flat. It's nestled under the peak of the building's roof, the ceiling sloping sharply on either side. A great, round window dominates the wall to her left, like an eye looking out over London. It's a building, firmly rooted on the ground, and yet somehow, it's also a ship. Once she's thought of it, Wendy can't shake the feeling.

There's a stove and a small table. To the right, a large bed partially hidden by a folding lacquered screen. Despite Hook's claim of not sleeping, the sheets are rumpled. Small end tables bracket the bed on either side, and Wendy starts. Atop the table nearest her sits a skull.

"Tea?" Hook's voice draws her back and she finds her cheeks warming as though she accidentally glimpsed something intimate not meant for her eyes.

"Please." She busies herself unbuttoning her coat so as not to be caught staring.

Hook indicates a chair across from a chaise longue in the center of the room, and Wendy takes a seat. In a moment, he returns holding a pot, moving slowly as holding it leaves him unable to use his cane. Looking behind him, she sees two cups with no saucers, a small pitcher for cream, and bowl for sugar all lined up on the counter, waiting to be carried one by one. Wendy blushes all over again.

"Let me help!" She jumps up, but he shakes his head, dismissing her and she fears now that she's stung his pride.

"I don't have many guests, I'm afraid. I'm not used to entertaining." She watches him carry each item and set it down.

He reclaims his cane last before sitting and tucking it against the chair beside him. She watches him pour, trying not to stare at the silvered-chased wood of his hand, which he uses to lightly steady each cup. She thinks of the men whose injuries in the last war required them to be fitted with wooden limbs like Hook's. Even her brother Michael wears a brace now to help with his leg, but Hook's prosthetic seems different. It seems as much a piece of art as a thing of practicality. The wood, grained red in the light, seems to glow. She can't say why, but something about the hand makes her think of love given form.

77

It's yet another thing that makes him seem softer. It's not just his age, it's not just that he's here and not in Neverland. Something else has changed in him fundamentally. If Wendy didn't know him, she would scarcely believe that the man before her is the same man who held her captive on his pirate ship nearly thirty-seven years ago. In fact, it is only because she knows him, because she's looking for it specifically, perhaps, that she sees the outline of the pirate captain beneath his skin, an echo of the man he was once upon a time.

"What happened to your hook?" The words are out before Wendy can stop them, leaving her mortified. "I'm sorry, I—"

To her surprise, Hook chuckles. It is a strange sound, not humor, but something else. Even so, he takes the question in stride.

"I lost it in a storm." He holds out a teacup, and she takes it, adding two sugars.

There are so many things she wants to ask. *How are you here? How did you find me? Do you know what happened to Neverland?* Because it's there, like an ache, a lost tooth she cannot help probing with her tongue. Even after everything, she misses it. It's more complicated than simple longing. Like the space between herself and Jane, Neverland is a wound that refuses to heal.

"How did you know I would come?" she says instead of any of the other questions burning inside her, the ones she isn't ready to ask yet.

"There's been a murder. Perhaps more than one."

The words are blunt, startling her, and Wendy nearly drops her cup. She sets it down before it spills, staring at the former captain. Hook gestures with his wooden hand, the silver embellishments gleaming in the light. There's a newspaper folded on the table.

Wendy takes it and there, in the bottom corner, a small, blurred photograph she barely recognizes, and the name Margaret Thornton. Jane's friend.

The story barely takes up two inches of space, such a small thing for the largeness of her daughter's grief. She'd only met Jane's flatmate once, and then only briefly, but she seemed like a pleasant girl. All at once it strikes Wendy that there's a mother out there missing a daughter. A family whose little girl won't come home to them for Christmas. How did the newspapers get the story so quickly? She sets the paper down and meets Hook's eyes.

"How did you…" Wendy lets the words trail. The story says nothing about a murder, only an unexplained and unfortunate death.

"That girl isn't the only one," Hook says, and still his tone is far blunter than she would have expected. "There is something here in London that doesn't belong."

Her mouth will not close. All she can do is gape at him. His eyes make her think of a storm, of tossed waves. There's something below the surface of them, a shadow, knowledge. She feels it too, though it's nothing she can name, and by instinct, her gaze flashes to the window. She half expects to see another sky beyond the glass, one belonging above a world other than London.

When she'd journeyed to Neverland to save Jane, she'd crawled through the remains of Hook's pirate ship. There, she'd had the sense of ghosts crowded around her, and she'd sworn she'd briefly caught sight of his eye peering up at her from a shard of broken mirror glass. The same feeling takes Wendy now, as if the room is full with more than just the two of them. She's about to ask him what he knows about Margaret's death, and what it has to do with them, but Hook surprises her by leaning forward, laying the barest touch of his wooden fingers against her wrist. The shadow in his eyes vanishes, replaced by something much worse, something utterly raw, broken, and searching.

"You've seen him, haven't you? You went back."

"I… Yes." The question startles her, and what startles her even more is that it isn't precisely a question. "How did you know?"

"It's…" His gaze moves to the space around her as if there's something only he can see, clinging to her like a shadow. It's an unsettling feeling.

"It's a feeling. I can see Neverland on you." As Hook speaks, for just a moment Wendy sees it too, like dust hanging in the air about the captain, but faint, almost imperceptible. It's barely visible, but it is there, marking him as not entirely belonging to this world.

The sound that escapes Wendy is half sob, half laugh. Hook's words and his first question cracks something wide open inside of her. He asked her about Peter, the common monster between them. His next words catch her off guard all over again. There's a kind of hunger in them. He leans even farther toward her, like a man drowning, his life depending on her answer to his question.

"It is possible, once here, to go there again?" There's some loss Wendy can't quite fathom. It's more than the ache she feels for Neverland. If Hook wants to return to Neverland, it isn't for Neverland's sake alone he wants to go back.

"Yes." Despite herself, Wendy's voice almost breaks on the word—even now, even after everything, and she hates the sound of it.

Hook watches her, expectant, the hunger still in his eyes but tamped somewhat. A faint tremor moves his hand until he curls his fingers against it. She notes that he hasn't touched his tea, and even though the sun is barely up, she wonders if he regrets that it isn't something stronger.

"Eight years ago…" Wendy begins, but lets the words lapse. The weight of memory tugs at her, pulling her shoulders down. It feels so much longer than eight years ago, a lifetime, and all at once she wants to let it all go.

The first time she was in Neverland, Hook was her enemy. But might he understand her now, in a way no one else could? With Jane, it is too fraught. She might never have a chance like this again.

"Eight years ago, Peter returned," Wendy says, straightening in her chair. "He'd forgotten about me. After he rescued me from your ship and brought me home, he simply left and I didn't see him again until I'd married, had a child of my own. No time at all passed for him, but I waited, and when he came back, he didn't even recognize me. He thought Jane, my daughter, was me and he took her instead. He didn't even give her a choice, just grabbed her hand and flew out the window with her."

Wendy lifts her cup, sets it down again. There's a knot in her stomach, and she pushes the cup away from her slightly, leaving the tea to grow cold.

"By then, I'd begun to realize that Neverland wasn't the glorious place I'd believed it was as a child. All of Peter's rules, how at times he treated me like all I was good for was cooking and cleaning up after the boys. But then he would be so sweet again, and we had the best times together. He taught me how to fly. He took me on adventures, and when he looked at me, it was like I was the only person in the world who mattered. I would forgive him, then it would all change again and he'd go back to ordering me about."

She pauses, gathering her thoughts.

"Most of that I didn't realize until later. Then I began to question Neverland. Sometimes I even thought about you." Wendy looks up, catching Hook's eye, and sees the startled expression there. "I thought you were my enemy because you were Peter's enemy, but then I began to wonder whether he had you trapped there, playing a role just like he wanted me to play the role of his mother, or at least his idea of what a mother should be."

The hunger dims in Hook's eyes somewhat, the shine becoming something else for a moment. His head inclines slightly, and Wendy feels sympathy for him all over again. Has he been all alone with Neverland all these years as well, with no one to talk to or understand? After a moment, she gathers herself and goes on.

"When it was good between us, I couldn't even remember being mad at Peter at all. But he wasn't just an innocent child, even if he looked like one. There was a darkness in him, he had secrets. He showed me one of those secrets—his true nature—then he made me forget. I came home with a hole in my memories and I didn't even know what I was missing until the night he stole Jane. But I could feel it, like something dark, crouched in the corner of my mind. I threw myself out of my bedroom window to go after them. I was certain, even with everything I'd forgotten, that I still remembered, deep down, how to fly."

Wendy smiles, but it's a wry thing, twisting her lips. It sounds ridiculous, saying it out loud now, but Hook merely nods again, the faintest of motions for her to go on, as if what she's saying is the most logical thing in the world.

"I found the place in the stars where the sky grew thin because I needed to in order to save Jane."

Hook shifts slightly and Wendy catches something like recognition in his eyes. But he doesn't interrupt her or say anything more and so she continues, needing the whole story out of her now that it's begun.

"When I got back to Neverland, I remembered what it was Peter stole from me. He showed me his true self." Here, Wendy pauses, taking a breath. It's clear in her mind, the thing in the cave at the heart of Neverland. The part of himself that Peter tried to cast away. "His true shadow, it was like a beast, and he'd cut it away from himself."

Again, she sees the flicker of something like recognition in Hook's eyes. Had he known all this about Peter too, or is there something else in her story he recognizes?

"I think even Peter had forgotten what he was. Or he had a way of knowing and not knowing all at once." Wendy shakes her head slightly; it doesn't make sense, but nothing about Neverland ever did. "He was very good at forgetting things."

The words hurt, the truth behind them, even still. Wendy ignores the ache though, and pushes on. The part she's coming to is the worst of it, but she needs to admit it out loud as well, even though she knows doing so won't absolve her of the choice she made and the consequences that followed. Even still, she needs to own the pain.

"After I saved Jane, I wouldn't let Peter forget again. I needed him to know what he was and all the things that he'd done, the way he'd hurt people. I sewed his shadow back onto him and made him remember, and it…"

Wendy's breath catches. Not quite a sob, but the words lodging in her throat, sticking like delicate bones.

"It made death in Neverland real when I sewed Peter's shadow back onto him. I made it so he couldn't play make-believe, that he couldn't do whatever he wanted in a world with no consequences." She raises her head again to meet Hook's eyes, waiting for his reaction.

What she sees reflected back is complicated. Pain, memory, something else as well, something she doesn't quite understand.

"There was a boy, Timothy," Wendy goes on, determined to get through the last of it. "One of Peter's Lost Boys, but he and Jane had become friends. He…died. One of the other boys ran him through with a sword the way they used to run each other through all the time in Peter's mock games of war. Nothing happened to him, he was fine. Except when I sewed Peter's shadow back onto him, everything that he'd hidden away, including death, real death, came rushing back into Neverland and Timothy died for real. He bled to death in my daughter's arms. Jane begged me to save him, but I couldn't. But even if I could…"

Wendy closes her eyes for a moment, feeling Hook continue to watch her, and then opens them again, holds his gaze as she makes her last confession. She will not apologize—and perhaps that is what broke things so badly between herself and Jane. She will not apologize for the choice she made, and she would make it again if she had to—Jane or the world. Every single time, she would choose Jane, even if choosing her daughter also meant wounding her to the core.

"I didn't even really try," Wendy says. "I didn't stop or look back to see if there was anything I could do. I grabbed Jane and I ran with her out of Neverland and I didn't look back, because all I cared about was getting her home. Timothy was her first real friend. Jane was too young, she shouldn't have had to carry the weight of a death like that. She blames me for what happened to him, and I understand. I would do the same thing if I were her."

Wendy folds her hands in her lap, finds herself sitting very straight. Though the chair holds her, she feels precarious, hollow, as she balances on its edge. A slight breeze might tip her over and she'll shatter, but she waits to see what the pirate captain will say.

"He's gone then? Pan?" The brightness is back in Hook's eyes, a gleam that gives Wendy pause.

He's asking her for Peter's death, for proof of his old enemy's demise. After everything she confessed to him, that this is all he wants from her lands as a blow. She feels heat rising to her cheeks, the old defensiveness rising in her as well. How dare he? Peter is only a child, and Hook is a grown man desperate to hear of his death.

The anger twists, turning bitter and coming back to Wendy, and she almost laughs, a humorless thing. She is the one who killed Peter. No, not even killed, something worse. She reunited him with his monstrous self by sewing his true shadow back on and then simply left him in the crumbling ruins of Neverland. She didn't stay to make sure she'd set things right, just as she didn't stay for Timothy. She simply ran.

It strikes Wendy that at the end, she truly had wanted to hurt Peter. She'd wanted him to suffer, and she's certain now, looking back, that when she left him, she left him in pain. Death would have been kinder, if a creature like Peter could even die. How can she sit here judging Hook for wanting the same?

After all, they were enemies long before Wendy arrived in Neverland, and after she left as well, she presumes. Except… She saw Hook torn apart, didn't she? Right before she left Neverland, right before Peter brought her home and forgot about her, a terrible creature rose from the waves and consumed Hook. The thought chills Wendy, and now the expression Hook wore when she spoke of making death real in Neverland makes sense to her.

Before she'd sewn Peter's shadow back on, nothing could ever die in Neverland. But all those constant battles Peter had told her of, when he'd fought Hook. He'd told her that he'd made the captain walk the plank, but she hadn't really listened. Hadn't understood, at least, and then she'd seen it for herself. She'd seen Hook torn apart by a massive beast. Peter's war with Hook wasn't like his play-war with the Lost Boys. Peter had let Hook die for real, and he'd brought him back again and again. He'd let him suffer and feel pain and made him live through it all over and over. Wendy is certain of it; that's exactly the kind of boy Peter was. How many times? The thought is a grim one, one that makes her skin crawl.

"I don't know what happened after I ran," she says, and she hears the thinness of her voice, the weariness. "I didn't stop to look back. Neverland was crumbling and I ran, and since then, I haven't been able to feel it. Not until right before I met you, but even then…"

Wendy swallows, her throat suddenly thick.

"It's like knowing a door is there, but also knowing that I'll never be able to open it. That even if I reached for it, I couldn't touch it. It's not even that it's locked, it's just that it isn't for me anymore. I can't return."

The light in Hook's eyes changes—no longer hunger, but something like grief, like anger, all flicker-bright and passing across his features so quickly she can't be sure of them. His hand—the flesh and blood one—finds the head of his cane and grips it, showing knuckles against his skin. It isn't something that he's missing, that he lost, she thinks, it's someone.

In the next moment, he seems to confirm her thought as his gaze moves to the skull sitting on the bedside table. Wendy's pulse jumps, then jumps again when the captain looks back to her. For just a moment, what she sees in his eyes is clear and unmistakable, even if she doesn't understand it—blame. Hook is dangerous; the light in his eyes is baleful, smoldering. Wendy casts around—should she run, find something to use against his as a weapon? But before she can decide, weariness replaces the anger and all hint of violence and hunger go out of the former captain.

"You did what was needful," Hook says. Eyes as gray as a sullen sea, with too many lifetimes built up behind them, meet hers.

There's a finality, a sense of truth settling around her now that Wendy has spoken it all aloud. More than once, standing at her window in London, and again in the house in Newark-on-Trent, she's wondered what would happen if she jumped. Could she take to the sky again, find her way back through a hole between the stars? But every time, she'd shut the window, pulled the curtains tight, turned away. She's certain now, if any doubt remained before, that what she told Hook is true. The door remains, but it isn't for her. She can't return to Neverland, and even if she could, what would possibly remain for her there?

"How did you come to London?" Wendy shakes herself lightly, shaking off the feeling of despair that wants to crawl over her.

"Ah." Hook's expression turns grim, a twist to his lips that isn't a smile, carrying echoes of his earlier pain. "There are magics in

Neverland older than Pan. Or perhaps they are all part of the same magic, the one you spoke of that he forgot."

A wooden box of matches sits on the table nearest Hook. He picks it up, toying with it, his expression contemplative. Wendy registers the pipe laid beside the box, meant for smoking opium, and finds she's less shocked than perhaps she should be.

"There was a knife," Hook says, but when it seems as if he would say more his attention drifts.

Wendy follows his gaze, drawn like a lodestone again to the skull on the table. Loss thickens the air, almost a palpable thing. The way the bone is carved with elaborate whorls, it's not defilement, but an act of love. The patterns, she realizes, match the whorls of silver traced into Hook's wooden hand.

"Samuel," Hook says.

The name means nothing to her. Was he one of Hook's pirates? When she scours her memory, all Wendy can see is Hook himself, his dark, heavy curls, his sneer. The man before her looks so much smaller, folded in upon himself. She recognizes the look upon his face though. Longing.

Wendy's heart goes out to the old pirate captain. Silence lapses between them. Her gaze falls on the folded newspaper again and all at once, she startles. The sky remains leaden in color, but she's already been here too long.

"You said more than one person…was killed. This girl." Wendy touches the newspaper, looking to Hook. "She was my daughter's friend. Is… Is Jane in danger?"

The words rasp against Wendy's throat. She's done it again, left her daughter vulnerable, open. She thinks of a window opening long ago, a silhouette edged in moonlight, and cock's crow. A flicker, if not of guilt, then of regret, crosses Hook's face.

"I am sorry for your daughter's loss. And yes, it is possible she is in danger. I believe something came here from Neverland." The way he answers, Wendy is certain there's more he's not saying.

"How do we stop it?"

"I wish I knew, Miss Darling."

"Wendy." The response comes automatically even as she looks to the door. She would feel it, if Jane were in distress, wouldn't she? Just as she felt it yesterday. "Miss Darling is so formal, and besides it isn't really my name anymore."

"Then you must call me James." She turns back in time to catch the slight quirk to one side of his mouth, almost amusement.

The absurdity strikes her, them introducing themselves like this, when Wendy feels as though she has always known this man. Like hearing a familiar accent when you're far away from home, recognizing a fellow countryman.

"Would you like to come home with me for Christmas?" The words are out before Wendy can stop them, and she presses her lips into a thin line after they're gone.

No, she doesn't regret the invitation. He knows more than he's saying. And if there's something here from Neverland, then if they are all in the same place, they might draw it out. Whatever it is, Wendy would rather face it head on than leave it to skulk in the shadows. And if it is something that does indeed prove itself to be a danger, she will not hesitate to push Hook into its path to save Jane and herself.

"Miss Darling. Wendy." Hook—she cannot quite think of him as James yet—pushes himself to standing and sketches a small bow so she cannot help but see him resplendent in velvet, red coat flaring around him. "I would be honored."

Guilt needles her. Oh, she might tell herself she's being kind. That Hook has no one, and he should not be alone, but her motives are far more mercenary, far crueler. She makes herself smile—a flashing of teeth. And as she does, it occurs to her that even if he guessed her motive, Hook would understand. They are both survivors. They will both do what must be done. After all, perhaps the only reason he accepted her invitation is that he is thinking the exact same thing. Wendy and her daughter might be used as sacrifices to save his own skin.

"Our train leaves—"

"I need only a moment." Hook interrupts her, moving toward the bed to draw a battered travel bag out from underneath it.

She takes it from him gently, holding it open for him to fill, not missing the faint tremor in his leg as if even the empty bag is too much to hold. His expression mixes wounded pride and gratitude.

Hook moves to a wardrobe—taller than she is—standing against the wall. As he pulls it open, Wendy's breath snags. There, buried deep among dark blues and blacks and grays is a flash of poppy— red as bright as blood. The bag slips from her grasp. She takes a step then stops, embarrassed. Seeing her, Hook's mouth quirks upward again, deepening the creases in his skin with amusement.

"You still have it." Wendy can't quite keep the awe from her voice. "I always wondered what it felt like. It always looked so…regal."

She feels ridiculous saying the words aloud, a child again, but the amusement in Hook's eyes softens into something else.

"I was wearing it when I crossed through. It's a little worse off, but…" He lifts the coat, looking at it as if with new eyes, as if

Wendy's interest has suddenly caused him to see the coat for what it is—magic. A piece of Neverland, redder than red, the most beautiful garment she has ever seen. And it doesn't look the worse for wear to her at all; in fact it looks brand new.

He holds it out with a kind of reverence, shaking dust from its folds. Even in the washed-out gray light coming through the window, it's brighter than anything else in the room. He carries it to her, and before she can object, he sets it upon her shoulders.

There's a mirror in the wardrobe door. Wendy stares at her reflection. The coat fits her almost perfectly. Hook isn't as tall as he once was, but she, it seems, is. Or, like everything else in Neverland, the coat's magic fits itself to the wearer. The hem hits just above her ankles, and when she turns a bit to admire it, it flares just the way she remembers.

"It's…" Her throat tightens.

"Keep it," Hook says. "It doesn't fit me anymore."

She wants to object, but with all her heart, she wants to accept the gift. She raises a hand, rubbing the wide lapel between her thumb and finger. It is everything she imagined. Soft, rich, almost a living thing. Even after all these years, the buttons still gleam, and their color is the sun over Neverland.

"Thank you." Tears threaten her eyes and Wendy blinks, turning away. "We should go. My daughter is waiting, and we'll miss our train."

Climbing the stairs to Jane's flat, Wendy feels the same nervousness she felt outside Hook's door, but redoubled, and of a different quality. Hook breathes heavily behind her, even after only one flight of stairs. The toll of years shows in his gait, and she can tell his leg pains him, but he doesn't ask her to slow down. It strikes her, suddenly, that she is older now than he was the first time they met. The thought is at once funny and sad.

Jane gave her a key. Wendy opens the door, pushing aside what doubt she can.

"Jane?" She hates the way her daughter's name sounds uncertain when she says it aloud.

"Mama." Jane's voice comes from farther within the flat, and something in the tone, in the way she says *mama*, not mother, makes Wendy's skin prickle. She drops Hook's bag inside the door and hurries toward Jane's room, stopping when she catches sight of her daughter standing in the room where Margaret died.

Jane turns, mouth open to speak, but then her mouth snaps shut and darkness crackles in her eyes. Wendy sees the moment her daughter takes in the coat, blood red. All at once, Wendy feels foolish, a child playing dress up. Jane's gaze narrows further, shifting to Hook standing behind her mother.

"This is Cap— Mr.—" Wendy falters.

"James." Hook supplies the name smoothly, but it does nothing to lessen Wendy's guilt. She swallows hard, trying to make her voice even.

"What happened?"

Wordless, Jane steps aside. Wendy sees Margaret's bed stripped of its sheets, the mattress tipped up on its side and leaned against the wall. There, on the bare fabric, is the perfect imprint of a human form. A shadow, black as ink, as though cut from Margaret's body and left behind.

THE BLACK BLADE

NEVERLAND – 22 YEARS AGO

Across the water, his ship glows, anchored just where he left it when he jumped at Pan's behest. The sky is a near-solid black overhead, the water reflecting it, his ship the only brightness he can currently see. Is it always night here? He can't remember the last time it was day. This night at least is quiet enough for drunken laughter and music—one of his men at the accordion—to reach him on the shore. His men. His ship. And not one of them came looking for him when he drowned.

A small rowboat waits at the water's edge. Because of course Hook must return to his pirates so Pan's war might continue. He grits his teeth, pushes the boat from the shore, and rows. The oars are perfectly manageable with his hook and his hand, though he can't quite work out the mechanics even as he's rowing. Only that the logic of Neverland dictates that nothing will prevent the cycle starting all over again.

There's a soft thump as the boat fetches up against the ship's hull. No pause in the song or the raucous laughter inside. A rope ladder hangs over the ship's side; Hook climbs. He takes vicious pleasure in scarring the wood, digging his hook in—now clean of the mermaid's blood—as he hauls himself aboard.

His sword bumps at his hip. Didn't he lose it? But like the boat waiting for him on the shore, it scarcely matters. Pan's enemy must have his weapons. There's a sheathed knife at his belt, another in his boot. He's fairly bristling with arms, none of which will help him against the child.

His bootheels beat a counterpoint rhythm to the music rising from below as he crosses the deck. Lanterns illuminate a lone figure at the prow. Hook pauses, a sense of familiarity tugging at him. Why isn't the man below with the others?

Recognition startles him; the man is the one he saw just before Pan made him jump. Hook still can't recall his name, and the fact that he can't bothers him. It shouldn't. His crew clearly doesn't care for him, why should he care for them? They're only fodder in Pan's war, obstacles thrown in the boys' way to slow them down before they reach their prize—Hook himself.

"Captain." The man steps forward, but Hook ignores him, and the man doesn't call after him a second time.

In the mess, liquid sloshes from tankards swung around in careless hands as men gesture in time with the song and swap tall tales. They're all gathered here as if for a celebration. As if they've completely forgotten him, or they're relieved that he's gone.

The faintest of sounds, a light tap of his hook against the wood of the doorframe, but the effect is the same as though he'd fired a gun into the room. The music cuts off with an abrupt wheezing breath from the accordion. All eyes turn to him. Hook rests his hand on the pommel of his sword and steps into the room.

He's gratified when at least some of the gathered faces blanch, but it should be all of them. One pirate at least gives him a sullen look. Harrigan—the name emerges from the fog of Hook's memory. And the next man over is Killdeer; he raises his chin in a slight gesture of defiance as others look away.

"Is this, or is this not, still my ship?" Hook keeps his tone even, hand light on the pommel of his sword.

Shoulders tense then relax, uncertain, glances exchanged around the room. He keeps his attention on Killdeer and Harrigan. Harrigan breaks his gaze, but Killdeer continues to glare, resentment hardening the line of his mouth.

"Has a mutiny occurred?" Calm, level, not raising his voice—and that at last, seems to unnerve Killdeer.

"We knew you'd return, Captain, you always do." Harrigan is the one to answer, words muttered quick and low. He touches Killdeer's sleeve, but the other shakes him off.

"Ah. You knew I'd return, and therefore none of you thought to look for me."

Feet shuffle, men intent on their plates, their cups, gazes anywhere but on their captain. In the corner, Maitland, the boatswain, snuffles loudly, deep in his drink, or perhaps at least a little ashamed.

"Well, that is a relief. As it is a relief to know that I am still captain. And as that is the case, I assume my word on this ship remains law, and that I am the one to say when the beer is opened, when rations are awarded, and when the watch is ignored." He swings his gaze back to Killdeer, who clenches his jaw.

"There was no danger, Captain. Pan only comes for us when you're on board." Killdeer doesn't bother to hide his resentment.

A desperate look flashes in Harrigan's eyes; his mouth opens, but he snaps it closed again. He, at least, seems clever enough to know the thin ice his friend skates upon, but Killdeer seems determined not to be pulled back from the edge.

Does he think he could do better leading these men? Does he think he could kill Pan, even? How would he bear up in the beast's jaws?

"I see." Hook moves closer, close enough to force Killdeer to tilt his head back to maintain eye contact.

"Well, as you have deemed it safe to let our guard down, and there's no need to prepare for an attack, then the men should have plenty of time for cleaning."

Hook allows a smile onto his lips. At the same time, unease creeps around the edges of his awareness. His gaze remains fixed on Killdeer, but in his peripheral vision he sees the boards where Killdeer sits, stained darker than the rest of the floor. Something terrible happened here. Something terrible will happen here again.

Confusion flickers in Killdeer's eyes. Around him, men shift, uncertain whether to relax or whether an order has been handed down.

It is the exact effect he wants, throwing the men off guard. It's a show, in the moment his flair for the dramatic almost equal to Pan's. His crew must learn their places, and it seems they are too stupid to grasp it otherwise.

"You may start." Hook draws the words out, strings the air with tension, showing teeth as he does. "By cleaning up the blood."

He punctuates the sentence with his hook, driven into Killdeer's throat. Crimson sprays in an arc, spattering Harrigan's clothing and skin. Men scramble back, all in confusion, the bench crashing over, but he isn't done.

His hook still buried in Killdeer's throat, Hook lifts the man, gurgling, kicking, and draws the knife at his belt. He plunges it into Killdeer's gut. Death waits just long enough that Killdeer's eyes are able to widen, all the dark of them reflecting Hook—the face of a monster, every bit as terrible as Pan's hunting beast. Every bit as terrible as Pan. He watches the light go out of them, swallowing his reflection. It is immensely satisfying.

Blood wets Killdeer's lips, coats his front. His body hangs limp at last, and Hook lets him fall. The sound is so much spoiled meat hitting the boards, a staining spreading atop the already darkened wood.

He is sick and he is thrilled and if he doesn't leave the ship again now, he will have no crew left to command.

He strides back onto the deck, almost colliding with the man who called after him earlier. The man's eyes widen, staggering back, and now it's a different kind of monster Hook sees reflected in widened eyes.

Crimson soaks the front of his shirt, matching it to the red of his coat. The coat itself, though, almost drinks the blood, leaving no stains. It flares as he turns, but this time when he leaves the man behind, staring after him, it feels like fleeing.

Hook rows away from the ship once more, arms trembling, and not only from the effort of fighting against the waves. The water is choppy where it was calm moments before, tossing the boat, and sweat slicks his brow. He feels feverish, wrong. In the moment, slaughtering Killdeer felt good, right. And now? The way the man on deck looked at him…

Is that who and what he wants to be? Pan's monster, for all time? As leashed as his hunting beast, as unable to change? He needs to get off this bloody island.

He reaches the shore, sloshing onto the sand and dragging the boat with him. The mermaids' sing-song voices echo in his head. *Sad, bad, mad Captain Hook.* He could use a little madness right now. Leaving the boat on the shore, he heads toward the center of the island.

The scent reaches him before the flowers come into view, thick enough to taste, like honey coating his tongue. He finds himself almost salivating, hunger gnawing beneath his skin. When was the last time…? But it doesn't matter. He will sate himself now.

The bushes are half again as tall him, crowding the path with their glossy leaves. The sky has shifted again—twilight hangs over them, as it always seems to at this particular spot on the island. Fireflies blink against the dark, rogue stars dipping into the massive blossoms as if they were bees, and making the petals glow.

He plucks several blossoms, stripping the petals to be crushed underfoot. It is the sap he's after, oozing from the broken stems like blood. Thick enough that when Hook gathers a mass of it, he can stretch the substance, pulling it into long strands with the point of his hook before rolling it again with his flesh and blood fingertips, repeating the process over and over again.

As he works the sap, it darkens—gold to amber. He keeps a pipe on him at all times, carved from bone. When the flower-tar is ready, he crouches in the bushes' shadow. The sap goes into the pipe, and he holds a light under it. As he lifts the pipe to his lips, there's a rustling along the path in the direction he came from, and Hook whirls around.

A face disappears as the leaves shiver back into place, but he can't see it clearly. Pan's feral boys spying on him? Hand on his sword, he listens for the telltale crack of a branch underfoot. There's nothing. If they attack, he'll give them a fight, but he won't give them the satisfaction of chasing them through the trees.

He lifts his pipe again, and draws deep, holding the smoke. The sweetness eats at him, leaving holes in his lungs like moth-eaten sailcloth. When he releases a long stream, it spirals up against the gray-purple sky.

Pale stars prick the twilight, holes punched through the dark. If he could just dig the tip of his hook into one of those pinholes of light, he might tear the sky wide and make his escape. More streams of smoke wind upward. The pipe dangles loose in his hands. Still crouched, his muscles cramp first, and then he doesn't feel them at all.

He sways slightly without rising. The stars move with him. Not quite a circle, but a looping motion, until he realizes they must be fireflies. Or… A memory, half-formed, of lying sick in bed, in a dirty city far away from here, full of rain. Anna, his sister, brought cold cloths for his head. In his fever, he mistook her for their mother, but by then, it was only the two of them.

The same sickness that laid him low had already taken their mother, a fever and endless coughing that hollowed her out, spotted her sheets with blood. A factory accident had taken their father years before, hand caught and the machinery pulling him in, unable to be stopped until it was too late. Anna had peered down at Hook— only that wasn't his name then, was as it?—in exhaustion and terror, afraid of losing him as well. She pushed sweat-soaked hair back from his brow, brought broth for him to drink, and told him stories.

Greek mythology, Bible tales, and faerie stories too. Wee people made of light with wings like insects. Tricksters who might be convinced to help if you left out cream or sweet cakes for them. Have the faeries come to help him now? One darts close and he can almost see the wings beating at its back, its pointed face.

There are faeries here, aren't there? Or there were once. He remembers the dust on their skin. A quick enough hand could catch a faerie and shake some of that dust free. The taste of it had been even headier than the flowers, wild and sweet, peeling him from himself. A sick dread fills him. In a fit of something like rage and something like hedonistic abandon, a determination to plunge himself into oblivion, he'd… The memory surfaces, aching and black. The faeries. He caught and killed every last one, even Pan's favorite. He'd ground their bones to dust, inhaled it and licked it from the point of his hook until every last speck of it was gone.

His stomach lurches. Hook tries to stand, but his legs have gone numb. He falls, catching himself awkwardly on his hands and one knee.

Hands. Two hands. Both flesh and blood.

Is it simply a side-effect of the flower, or something else?

He lifts them to stare. The light twines between his fingers. He wiggles one hand experimentally, then the other. They feel real. Impossible. He whoops with joy before noticing the lights spiraling away from him.

"Wait!" Hook shouts to the dark.

An eddy, like leaves caught on the wind, and the lights dance farther away. His boots slip on fallen petals, crushed to a pulp, leaving the path slick. He half runs. Branches whip at his face, and he barely remembers to raise his arms to shield himself.

Then all at once, he breaks through the trees, coming to a staggering halt on a beach. The lights scatter, falling like foam and sinking through the waves, rising up to become more stars. The sand is flat and white as bone. The sea too, a mirror throwing back the stars and moon. He's almost certain he's never seen this part of the island before.

The only place the water moves is where a stream emerges from the mouth of a cave. Hook sways, unsteady on his feet. The cave the mermaids spoke of. Or, he is flower-drunk, passed out on the forest floor? It wouldn't be the first time. He squints at the cave-mouth, a blur of darkness.

"Captain!" The shout startles him as a hand catches his arm.

He whirls, hook raised to strike. A hook—not a hand—and he feels a flash of regret. All of this occurs in a split second, and yet time also seems to stretch and slow, like flower-tar, so he watches it and lives it all at once, inside and outside the moment simultaneously. Powerless to change or stop it.

He recognizes the pale, delicate man who called after him on the ship. His arm is already in motion. Too late, he tries to stay his blow. The man jerks his head to the side, but the point of the hook skates across his cheek, drawing blood.

Hook falls back, breathing hard. The man touches his cheek, bringing his fingers away red stained. The line of red once opened on the man's flesh unlocks a memory—a similar wound, but on Hook's leg instead and the other man stitching it closed. He can picture the man's expression clearly, pinched in distaste—not for the wound itself, but the violence that caused it. The ship's surgeon. Of course, how could he have forgotten?

Hook still can't remember the man's name. It's almost there and his inability to reach it irritates him, loading a question onto his tongue instead of an apology.

"Were you following me?" The words stretch and warp.

He regrets them, and that annoys him even further. The surgeon winces, touching his cheek again. His bloodstained fingers gleam in the moonlight. Hook has the sudden urge to touch the man to be certain he's real, and not another smoke-born illusion like his briefly restored hand.

"I was…concerned." A blush rises to the surgeon's cheeks.

It catches Hook by surprise. When has any member of his crew ever shown him a moment of concern? He thinks back to the deck of the ship, the man trying to get his attention as he stalked to the mess. And before, when Pan made him jump, a look that was almost sorrow. Hook's chest constricts. He sees again the surgeon deftly stitching the wound in his leg closed, the look of distaste shifting to something else and then the surgeon quickly looking away as he noticed Hook watching him.

The memory unsettles him and he isn't sure why. Hook is suddenly sharply aware of his stained shirtfront. He wishes it were clean. He's embarrassed next to the surgeon's neatness, but why should he be? When has he ever cared about such things before?

"You were—?" He can't quite piece the words or sentiment together. "You're—" He tries again, struggling to summon the surgeon's name.

"Samuel, sir." The surgeon looks down, lashes lowered over his eyes, but not quick enough to hide the flash of disappointment—hurt even.

How many times has the surgeon told him his name before? How many times has he forgotten? Hook has the sudden intense and unsettling desire to place his hook beneath the man's chin, to make him raise his head and look at him again. It's not like the other memories he's lost; something feels deliberate in this forgetting. Why would he try on purpose to forget this man?

Samuel. The name resonates, though he hasn't yet spoken it out loud. The shape of it is familiar on his tongue, a sensation that discomfits him.

The man is a member of his crew, a little kinder than the rest, but nothing more. What does kindness matter here? Hook shakes himself. The air around his head buzzes, a dark ringing in his ears, muffling his words.

"I have to go into the cave."

"Let me come with you." Samuel's eyes are bright, and Hook finds himself almost reaching to touch the surgeon's unwounded cheek before hastily letting his hand fall.

It's only the flower, muddling his head. He came here for a purpose. He has work to do. He doesn't move. One person on this whole damn island cared enough to come searching for him. Another memory seeps into Hook's mind—standing at the prow of his ship, sails bellied full with the wind and running for the horizon. This time, this time at last, he was certain he would break free. Then all at once, the horizon had vanished before him, the island looming there instead, and disappointment had crashed over him like a wave.

He'd allowed himself to hope. But hope and kindness cut deeper than a blade in Neverland.

An inkling of why he'd want to forget Samuel sits uncomfortably at the back of his mind, but he's afraid to look at it too closely.

"It's too dangerous," Hook says. This time, he isn't certain whether the image that rises to his mind is a wish or a memory— the sea calm, the two of them standing at the ship's rail, sharing a drink, a smoke. The image is surprisingly painful.

"Wait for me." He doesn't mean to say it aloud, but the words hang there and Hook doesn't take them back.

He finds he means them, surprised, and Samuel looks surprised as well. Something flickers through the surgeon's gaze—hope, a fragile creature easily startled away. Hook sees the moment the surgeon tries to tamp it down, clearly understanding the nature of this place as well as Hook himself. For some reason, seeing it makes him want to smile, and he fights to keep his expression neutral.

He slips free of his coat, bundling it and pushing it into Samuel's arms. Like a promise, like an anchor to hold Samuel there. The blood on Samuel's cheek has already beaded, on its way to forming a scab. There are other scratches as well. Did Samuel chase him through the woods? Was it his surgeon's face he saw briefly among the bushes, watching him? Watching over him?

Before he can make an utter fool of himself, Hook turns sharply on his heel and strides toward the cave. Samuel's gaze follows him, Hook feels it, like a hand placed on his shoulder, but he forces himself not to look back.

A glow emanates from within the cave. Hook crosses the threshold. The ground is uneven, much like the cave he woke in last time he drowned, only there are no shelves of rock or pools occupied by mermaids. There's only one pool, the source of the glow. It's visible from where he stands, but he can't gauge the distance somehow, the very shape and nature of the cave feel malleable somehow.

The sense that he's not alone cat-paws its way up his spine. It's a feeling of there-and-not-thereness. He takes a step and stumbles, the place he meant to set his foot suddenly treacherous and uneven. He catches himself on one knee and hisses in a breath sharp through his teeth. He's on the edge of the pool; a few inches more and he would have fallen in.

He eases forward for a better look.

The pool is shallow as a bowl. At least he thinks so. Is the flower still messing with his head, or is it the cavern itself? The blue-green light illuminating the water comes from everywhere and nowhere distorting his depth perception. The blade the mermaids spoke of is right there—black, lying at the pool's center, so close he would barely need to wet his arm to the wrist to touch it.

His vision judders, slips sideways. He's looking at two layers of reality stuck on top of each other. The pool isn't a shallow bowl at all but a depthless well that goes on forever, a hole in the world, and a dead woman floats within. He startles back at the realization, nearly losing his balance again, and almost immediately leans forward again, fascinated and repelled.

He struggles to hold both realities in his mind. The shallow bowl. The endless pool. The mermaid's tail forks, once down the middle, or countless times, mirroring the branching realities floating within the pool. Her skin is gray, veined like stone. The lower half of her body is black as ink, undulating as though part of her were spilled into the water. Her eyes are simultaneously open

105

and closed. Hook thinks of the mermaid he killed, one eye gazing sightlessly at him, the other gone.

This mermaid stares right at him with a gaze the color of the fireflies. And at the same time, where her eyes should be, there are only pits of blackness, like a fish-eaten skull. Two conflicting and equally true realities overlapping once again.

He's no longer certain that she's dead after all.

Her hands—tipped in pointed black nails—fold over the blade's hilt, clasping it to her breast. The thought of touching it is a horror. Taking the blade from her would be madness.

Sad, bad, mad captain. Can't beat Pretty Peter. Not at all.

Did he make it this far before? Is this where he lost his nerve, turned away to drown himself in drink and smoke, forcing himself to forget? Hook reaches. This time, he forces himself not to stop. He tries to hold the vision of the shallow pool in his mind, the blade right there, ignoring the dead woman. The blade is within reach, and all he has to do is—

Cold sears his hand even before it touches the water. Plunging it through is infinitely worse, shearing flesh from bone. The dead woman has hold of him. The water has ahold of him, thick as the sap from the flower, like hardening amber. His feet scramble and find no purchase, his arm wrenched in its socket as he tries to pull away.

The dead woman's gaze snaps toward him, seeing him. Once again, he has the sense that her eyes are whole, burning with strange light, and empty sockets, both at the same time. Her gaze—there and not—is worse than the water, not merely flaying skin from bone, but cracking his bones wide to suck the marrow from within.

Her eyes were always open. They never close. They cannot close. Unable to sleep, unable to dream, ancient and seeing everything.

The mouth, filled with needle teeth and blackness, opens as well. The scream is nothing human. He hears it underwater and above, a ringing echo that pierces like an awl. The dead thing surges from the water, clinging to the blade.

Hook falls back, expects to find the creature dripping over him, needle teeth poised inches from his face and black limbs wrapped with crushing strength around his own. But she isn't holding him down and impossibly, he's still holding the blade. In fact, it's burned to his flesh, terribly heavy and weighing nothing at all. He couldn't let go if he tried. Not even when the needle teeth suddenly are there, sinking into his forearm, lamprey-like, turning his blood black and sending it racing through his veins.

He lashes out with his hook, trying to fight free, kicking. None of his blows land. There's a pounding behind him, a muffled shouting, and he remembers Samuel left behind on the shore.

Hook yanks backward one last time, using all of his strength, all of his will. The blade rips free, metal cold as a dead star still burning his hand. And his flesh rips where the needle teeth have hold, pain like he's felt countless times beneath the waves as he's torn apart.

"Captain!" Samuel's voice rises in panic from outside the cave.

A wall of darkness stands between them, a violent wind trying to push him back. Hook grips the blade, crawls forward.

And then he is on his knees on the beach as if the cave were a mouth, spitting him out. His clothes are soaked, clinging to him. His hair, sopping, falls into his face. He tries to push it back, and nearly falls. Samuel catches him.

He's holding the blade. Hook stares down at his hand, expecting to see the flesh black and burned. He expects to see a chunk torn from his arm. Both are whole.

"How long?" Hook croaks the word, glancing over his shoulder. There is something wrong with his eyes. He can no longer see the mouth of the cave, the stream running into the sea. "How long was I gone?"

"I don't know." Samuel breathes hard, voice shaking. "Where did you go? I tried to follow, but there was a wall, a hole, I couldn't find my way through."

Hook tries to stand again, and his legs refuse. He half collapses, Samuel the only thing holding him upright. Leather. The surgeon smells of leather and tobacco. Cigarettes rolled with great care and smoked on the deck on calm and quiet nights while watching the moon.

"I'm quite all right…thank you." He stumbles over Samuel's name. Not because he has forgotten it, but because the shape of it frightens him, fitted too intimately to his tongue.

Hook blinks saltwater from his eyes. Moves his hand to rub his face, and realizes he's still holding the blade.

Moonlight falls on them—Hook, Samuel, and the knife between them. Of the three, only the blade resists the light. Old, pitted, black. Metal or stone, neither or both, Hook cannot tell.

"What is it?" Samuel asks.

Something in his expression makes Hook think of a horse about to shy away from a sting. There is something about the blade in his hand, a blurring buzzing hum. A song not quite heard, a whisper not quite spoken.

"A way out," Hook says.

He turns his hand slightly as if the moon might illuminate the blade at a different angle. All it reveals is the wound on his forearm, not the gash he expected, but a faint half-circle, the clear mark of teeth in his flesh where he could swear his skin was whole a moment before.

"You're hurt." Samuel helps Hook to his feet, and once he's steady, touches his arm with deft, examining fingers.

Hook starts, the impulse to jerk away tightening his fist around the blade, bringing a wave of pain.

"Hold still. Let me look." Samuel's tone brooks no argument.

Hook stills, watching the doctor as the doctor studies him, touch light, fingers skating around the wound in a way that makes Hook shiver.

"This should be cleaned," Samuel says.

"It's nothing. It will heal." Hook withdraws his arm.

"At least take your coat back. You're soaked, and you must be frozen." Samuel lifts the red garment from where he must have folded it neatly on the sand, shaking it out and holding it for his captain.

Hook turns the blade, flat against his skin so he can hold it while he slips his arms through the sleeves of his coat. Samuel's hands linger a moment, as if they would brush sand from Hook's shoulders, though the fabric of his coat is pristine. When Samuel steps back, Hook slides his hand into his pocket, and only there is he finally able to unclench his fingers, let the blade go. He lets out a breath as he does.

His hand aches and he flexes it, but doesn't remove it from his pocket yet. The urge to remain near the knife is irresistible.

"What happened?" Samuel angles his head to indicate the cave, and again the motion makes Hook think of a horse, tossing against its bridle. He almost reaches to soothe the surgeon, an absurd thought, and he takes a step back instead.

"I want no word of this spoken to the crew," Hook says, not an answer, and Samuel looks at him as though he's lost his mind.

Perhaps he has. Mad, bad, sad captain.

Samuel continues to watch him, and Hook cannot quite make himself meet the surgeon's eye. Something has changed. He is different. For the first time in a long time, he has hope, and that frightens him. Maybe it was that, not fear of the dead woman in the cave, that made him turn back before.

"What am I not to tell the crew? You've still explained nothing." Samuel hurries to keep pace with him, and only then does Hook realize he's begun walking.

"Freedom," Hook says, only half in answer to Samuel's question, half to himself. "Freedom."

"I don't understand."

"Neither do I." A grin stretches Hook's lips, and he imagines it is more terrifying in the moment than a snarl.

Samuel lags for a moment, stops, and Hook stops as well and looks back at him. Have he and the surgeon spoken before, shared conversation to pass the time? What does Samuel know about him, and what has he forgotten about Samuel? Does he remember fragments of a life left behind the way Hook sometimes remembers Anna? Does he have a family? A wife, perhaps, even children?

The last thought turns sour in him and Hook scowls. He pushes it away, closing the distance between himself and Samuel until he can clap the surgeon on the shoulder.

"Can you trust me?" It isn't the way he meant to phrase the question at all.

Samuel looks at him oddly. He gets the sense that the surgeon is about to say one thing, sees him gather breath to do so, then change his mind.

"I will trust you, sir." There's a hesitation, a tremor to Samuel's voice, but at the same time, Hook feels the shoulder beneath his hand slacken, tension letting go. "I trust you."

Again, he has the sense of words held back. He can almost hear them; they leave him uneasy, almost afraid. Hook realizes he's taken his hand from his pocket, no longer keeping it next to the blade.

"Thank you." He lets his hand linger for a moment on Samuel's shoulder, then lets it fall.

As he resumes walking, a breeze kicks up and swirls around him. The surgeon's words, the ones Hook is almost certain he heard even though they weren't spoken aloud, brush against his skin as if carried by that breeze. The answer to his question—can you trust me?—but the way he'd meant to ask it. *Do you trust me?*

Always, Captain, always.

THE HUNTING BEAST

She isn't what he expected, the woman Wendy Darling has become. Though what he expected precisely, he cannot say. Someone timid, perhaps, more compliant. He sees her at Pan's heels, only a child, eyes wide in wonder and adoration. He keeps trying to reconcile the woman sitting across from him in the swaying train car with the girl he knew, however briefly.

They were both different back then, and he wonders how she sees him. In the time that's passed, Wendy Darling has grown harder, while he has only diminished, a shadow of his former self. Kinder, Samuel might say. The thought rings bitter in James's mind. Weaker, he cannot help thinking.

One thing James can guess about Wendy Darling is that she does not trust him fully. For that, she has his admiration. She's grown wiser since her time as Pan's shadow. Perhaps it would be to his benefit to refrain from trusting her too easily as well.

After all, she bested Pan where he never could. She made death possible in Neverland. And in doing so, she may have severed the last link to that place allowing Samuel to hold on.

Perhaps he should loathe Wendy Darling.

He glances at her, his enemy's friend. Even as the thought occurs to him, he knows laying the blame at her feet is too easy. Samuel's fate is his fault alone. He brought Samuel to London. He asked for Samuel's trust when he plied the black blade, and again and again after that while he dulled himself with drink and smoke, while he continued to thieve and murder. He made promises, and in the end, he broke every single one.

It strikes James that the woman in the train car with him now is fundamentally different from the woman in his flat earlier. There, she was open, raw, and he felt for a time that he had the upper hand. Now, she is all brusque business, her face creased in lines of concern for her daughter who sleeps on the seat beside her, head resting against the window, breath misting the glass.

An hour and a half to Newark-on-Trent. And then Wendy Darling will welcome him into her home. She had brothers, didn't she? Also trailing on Pan's heels, though never as loyally as her. Will they be there too? He cannot help but picture them as children still, despite the grown woman before his eyes.

Wendy's sleeping daughter he cannot read at all. There's a similarity between the two, a rawness to the girl as well, another open wound, but under it, an anger simmering deep at her core. And no wonder. James saw the shadow on the bed stripped of its sheets—the bed that belonged to the murdered girl. Too perfect to be a stain, and Wendy's daughter had said it emerged over time, faint at first, but fading-in darker. An emergent haunting, much like the stain on the alley wall outside the pub where he'd found the dead man.

Twice now, the hunting beast has snapped its jaws and missed. Wendy told him how Pan took her daughter to Neverland as well. James sees the faint glow hanging about the girl, the same he sees around Wendy herself, but even more sharply defined. Even if the beast's senses are not as attuned to him as they once were, it must be following the residue of Neverland—the one that hangs about all three of them. The beast snapped once, and caught this girl's friend instead of her; it snapped again and caught the man in the alley instead of James. Will they all be as lucky a third time? A question best kept to himself for now, James thinks.

He rubs absently at his wrist, the flesh and bone below the carved wood suddenly aching with cold.

Across from him, Wendy removes an embroidery hoop from her bag. He watches as she makes stitches only to pick them out again, seeming oblivious to his observation. It looks like a ritual meant to calm, the way Samuel on occasion would absently carve figures from wood. As if his hands needed always to be occupied if they weren't actively engaged in healing.

James turns to the window, watching the landscape slide by. The rolling motion of the train reminds him of the best times at sea, nothing but open water and waves, as though they could sail forever, and never find an end. If it had only been that, perhaps he would have stayed, but Neverland was meant as a paradise for one boy, holding everyone else in it a prisoner to his whims.

A newspaper sits folded, untouched beside Wendy as she continues restlessly making and unmaking her stitches.

"May I?" He gestures, and she startles slightly before nodding, then turning her attention back to her work.

He unfolds the pages, smoothing them with his wooden hand. It's a moment before the text comes into focus. Has the type the setters use grown smaller, or is it that his eyes have grown older? He grimaces, considering abandoning the endeavor of reading and trying to sleep like the girl who currently appears dead to the world. Just as he's about to fold the paper, a small square near the bottom catches his attention, mention of an unknown man found dead in an alleyway.

Wendy raises her head and James lowers the paper, meeting her gaze.

"Something troubling?" Her voice is low, so as not to wake her sleeping daughter.

He turns the paper so she can see, tapping the story in question. "The other death you mentioned?" It isn't quite a question.

"Mmm." A noise of agreement.

How much should he reveal? He wants very much to reach for his pipe, to breathe in sweet smoke and let it relax his troubled mind. How long before his hand starts to shake, before he starts to sweat and need breaks him down? He doubts either Wendy or the train's conductor would approve, and he leaves it where it is, tucked into the inner pocket of his coat. For now.

"It seems," he says, thinking of the rough brick supporting him, the way his head swam as he nearly lost himself, "that the beast missed its mark twice. Perhaps it is not the hunter it once was."

"Beast?" A shadow flickers through Wendy Darling's eyes, and James curses himself silently.

He hadn't meant to say so much. He puts a smile on his lips that he hopes is enough to assuage her doubts.

"What else do you call one who has committed a double murder?"

Wendy glances at Jane, a frown shaping her lips before they press into a thin line.

"Nothing merely human did that." Her voice is sharp, her gaze, when she flicks it to him briefly before returning it to her daughter, accusing.

James weighs his words, grateful for Wendy's distraction. She lifts her hand, as though she would brush the hair away from Jane's face, then lets it fall to her lap. Trouble creases the space between her brows. A mother's ache, her concern for her child. The aura of Neverland clings to the girl, rising above her skin, like a certain scent, changing the way she carries herself, leaving a guardedness in her eyes. And if he can tell as much about her at a glance, then surely the monster can as well.

"Beast, then," James says. Perhaps it is better to lay his cards on the table after all. Some, at least, if not every one of them.

"You know what it is?" Again, it is not fully a question.

"Perhaps. What to do with that knowledge, however." James lets the words hang.

Silence fills the space between them once more, stretching long enough that when Wendy speaks again, it startles him.

"If it's come looking for you, why now?" she asks.

The astuteness of the question catches him off guard. Her suspicions align with his—that he is the beast's target, and the two deaths thus far mere collateral damage. Wendy turns the embroidery hoop in her hands, another nervous habit. James tries to guess precisely what she's asking him. Surely she knows as well as he that time works differently in Neverland.

So then, she's asking what has changed, asking him to admit that he reached where he shouldn't have, that he opened the very door she spoke of, one that ought to have stayed closed. That what Samuel told him again and again over the years was true, and he should have believed it all along. His weakness had turned James into a bridge and allowed something terrible to come through.

A memory takes him, sharp where it ought to be dull, the wound long-scabbed by now. The weight of Samuel in his arms. His skin like paper, burned and crumbled to ash. James holding tight, teeth grit, trying to keep Samuel with him by force of will alone, the last two left. But it hadn't been enough.

James had spoken one word, not the words he should have said. If he hadn't allowed himself to be ruled by fear, even after all the years between them, might they have been an anchor? But the word he'd spoken—the wrong one—was, "Don't."

Don't leave me. Don't let go. Selfish to the last. No wonder Samuel had left him alone. James had begged him not to go, yet given him no reason to stay.

Samuel's mouth opened, but whatever he would have said in return never reached James's ears. He'd held Samuel one instant, and in the next, he was gone.

James turns the sound that wants to escape him into a cough, using it as an excuse to reach for the flask, tucked next to the pipe in his coat. Wendy can't begrudge him this at least. The liquid stings going down. He wipes his lips with the back of his hand, and as an afterthought, he tilts the flask in her direction. Wendy shakes her head, but at least the set of her lips is more amused than disapproving. He tucks the flask away.

Perhaps they are both to blame in their own way. A thread snapped. Neverland changed. And yet something remained. A link. The cold iron embedded in his flesh. His ghosts. Always a part of him existed there and a part of him here. It was only a matter of time before he allowed something to cross over. Something left behind in Neverland, hungering and biding its time until his guard was sufficiently down.

NEVERLAND – 22 YEARS AGO

The ship creaks, a gentle sighing of wind making the timber and the ropes sing their own particular song. There's a storm coming. Hook feels it in his bones; he feels it in his missing hand. He feels Pan and the hunting beast like a coiled darkness beneath the skin of the world, waiting to strike. But for this moment at least, all is calm.

Eerily so. The water is flat, the line of the full moon reflected all the way from the hull to the distant horizon. It looks almost solid, a path he could walk over the sea and into another land. If only it were so easy.

He draws the black blade from inside his coat. Despite resting close to his body all through his and Samuel's journey back to the ship, and however many hours it's been since, the metal is cold. Hook still isn't even certain it is metal. At times it looks more like pitted stone. Now, in the moonlight, it gleams like black glass.

A humming note creeps up to the nape of his neck from the base of his spine. It sets his nerves on edge, yet it isn't entirely an unpleasant feeling, and that in itself is unsettling. It feels like power—raw, wild, and dangerous.

"You still mean to use it?" Samuel's voice is soft behind him, but Hook startles nonetheless, almost sending the knife tumbling overboard.

As they'd rowed back to the ship, Hook had explained what he intended to do; he'd largely made it up as he went along, speaking the words aloud to test them. Samuel had listened, doubt in his eyes, but he hadn't interrupted. Now Hook wonders—did the blade whisper the suggestions to him through its strange music, telling him how it wants to be used, or has the flower finally rotted his brain, a thousand, thousand deaths over who knows how many years finally eroding the last of his sanity?

Samuel holds a tin cup in either hand, both steaming. His smile is almost shy as he holds out what might be a peace offering, or perhaps a gesture meant to soften Hook before trying to talk him out of his plan. The wariness as Samuel moves closer, as if the surgeon still isn't certain whether his captain is a dangerous creature, irks him. Hooks slips the blade back into his coat, reaching for the cup and smoothing his expression into something he hopes looks human.

He wants the surgeon's company. At the same time, he's annoyed at himself that he does. Since when did the fearsome captain of Neverland's pirates need anyone's company other than his own? And of all people, why this man, soft and kind-hearted, unsuited for violence or even life at sea.

He lifts the cup with a faint nod, a gesture of thanks without saying the words. He sips, and studies Samuel through the steam rising from the drink. A faint, dark aura surrounds him. He'd seen it first in the rowboat, but now he can be certain it isn't merely his imagination of an after-effect of being in the cave. As he'd explained to Samuel, the black knife is meant to do what any blade is meant to do—cut. He will use it to cut the pirates from Neverland, severing their ties to this place and freeing them from Pan. And he will use it to cut their way between worlds and leave Neverland far behind.

It sounds mad, even in the privacy of his own thoughts. Yet the aura around Samuel is clearer now. It writhes like a living creature, like a kraken from the deep.

Hook sets his cup on the rail, draws a flask from his pocket, and tips a measure into his drink. His hand trembles slightly. If Samuel notes it, he makes no comment. Knowing he must do a thing and actually committing the deed are two different things. As Samuel pointed out in the rowboat, Hook doesn't truly know what the knife will do. He doesn't know what it means to cut the lines binding them to Neverland. He might just as easily be committing wholesale murder.

He tips the flask toward Samuel, who shakes his head.

"I've seen to Killdeer." Samuel's tone is grim, audible disapproval as he leans against the rail. Hook thinks again of Samuel's deft fingers, stitching him closed and the expression on his face then. He pushes the thought away. "His wounds are healing, if slowly. Harrigan is with him."

Hook catches himself on the cusp of offering an apology—not for Killdeer, but for Samuel. Irritated, he tamps it down. He did what was needful to maintain order on his ship, he has no reason to apologize. Yet he finds a kind of excuse tumbling from his lips anyway. He wants Samuel to understand.

"Doesn't it unnerve you? That men die here and return only to die again? That I can tear out a man's throat and then…"

He gestures, letting the words hang against the night's stillness.

Samuel glances at him from the corner of his eye, the prim look of disappointment. How can Hook convey that Pan, that this place, is the unnatural thing and not his act of murder? That what he plans to do next is not yet more violence, but that it will set them free. If no other man among the crew does, Samuel at least deserves better than this place.

Hook sips from the tin mug, frowning in the dark. Tea, with an odd, floral taste, strangely medicinal, but not in an unpleasant way. He tries a different tack.

"I remember drowning, the air crushed from my lungs, freezing in the depths in the coils of a beast's tail. I have felt Pan's blade go through my heart." Hook taps his chest. "And yet I live."

He draws the flask from his coat again and drinks directly. He feels Samuel watching him. Has the surgeon ever died? He thinks not. He's been sheltered, Hook thinks, set apart. Protected.

Again, the tugging sensation, the feeling of willful forgetting. The sense that he may have put something aside that is too painful, too dangerous to think on.

"The life we have here, it isn't living." He leans his forearms against the rail, giving his attention to the lanterns hung from the rails reflecting in the water. It strikes him that perhaps they shouldn't be speaking like this, like equals. He is the captain; he doesn't need permission for his actions, nor comfort or forgiveness for taking them. Hook doesn't move.

"Do you remember anything before this place?" he asks.

Hook doesn't miss the way the surgeon startles at the question, an involuntary movement he covers quickly by rolling a cigarette against the rail of the deck. It's clear Samuel needs something to do with his hands more than he truly craves smoke.

"Sometimes I…" Samuel's voice falters.

Hook turns his head. The emotion on Samuel's face is hard to read—is it fear, regret, a sense of loss?

"I remember a bird," Samuel says at last, his voice soft. "It had a broken wing. I don't remember how old I was, I just remember trying to help and it pecking at me in its fear, its beak tearing me up."

He holds his hands out in the moonlight, turning them as if expecting to see blood or scars. But his hands are white and smooth, long-fingered and delicate. Hook glances away, clears his throat.

"There was… I don't remember who he was to me. Maybe a cousin or a brother. He crushed the bird's skull with a rock. Said there was nothing I could do for it and that death was the kindest thing. I was so certain I could help though."

Samuel spreads his hands as though letting something go. Hook catches himself about to lift his own hand as if he would lay it on Samuel's shoulder and comfort him. He shifts slightly, putting an inch more distance between them.

"I cried. I remember that much. It wasn't sorrow so much as I was frustrated. I know I could have helped that bird if I'd only been allowed to try."

"Is that what made you want to become a surgeon?"

Samuel shrugs. "I suppose. I wish I remembered more. Except sometimes, I don't."

A shudder passes through the surgeon's frame, one he doesn't seem aware of. Hook understands. Memory can be a curse. Especially in this place. It's why he's spent so much time forgetting.

Tonight, though, he wants to remember. His memories suddenly seem precious, something he can gift and share.

"Sometimes I remember," Hook says. "Nothing whole. I had a sister. My mother and father died when I was very young, and my sister raised me. I went to sea to make an honest living for Anna and myself. I thought I would return to her within a year, pockets lined with enough to set us both up for life."

"And then?"

"I discovered the world is not designed for young men to make their fortune by honest means if they weren't already born to it." A sour expression twists his mouth. "I sent home what I could, but it was never enough. I can't tell you how many years passed. I think I was on my way home to see Anna, and then a hole like a mouth opened in the water and…" He lets his words trail, gesturing to ship around them.

"This," Hook says, drawing out a compass and holding it in his palm. "This is all I have left. Proof that there is a world beyond this one."

Anna had kissed his cheek and pressed it into his hand. At least he thinks that's what happened, but sometimes he wonders—did he steal it—the spoils of a pirate—and merely tell himself a comforting story about its origin?

Samuel looks up from the compass to meet Hook's eyes; it's a strangely familiar gesture. Green, Hook thinks. The surgeon's eyes are green, like the waters of a lake, or a particular shade of moss deep in the woods. It's too dark to see if he's right, and there's no reason he should know or notice such a thing.

"I remember you." Samuel's voice is a hush, barely audible, almost as though he hopes Hook won't hear him. "More than

123

that other life, I remember you. Even when you forget."

Even when you forget me. Samuel doesn't say it, but Hook hears it anyway. He suddenly understands the flickers of disappointment he's seen in the surgeon's eyes, the times he looked away as though hurt—ashamed of his vulnerability. Guilt threads itself through his veins. How much has he forgotten, how much has he left Samuel alone to bear?

Though the sea is calm, he's unbalanced, unsteady on the deck in a way he's never been even in the worst storm. There's no reproach in Samuel's voice, and that almost makes it worse. What Hook hears instead is hope—that dangerous and bright thing. It's as though Samuel holds something cupped in his palm, a delicate flower, and it's down to Hook to take it and keep it safe, or crush it in his hand.

Would it be kinder to kill the hope now? Or is that the coward's thought that's made him turn tail and run every time they've come to this point before?

"Tell me what you remember." Hook's mouth dries and his voice cracks. He drains his flask, but it does nothing to steady him, and his throat remains parched.

"The first time I saw you—it's the first thing I remember about Neverland. There was a fight, shouting, blades clashing, men screaming. The air smelled like gunpowder and there was blood everywhere. I was certain I would die. I thought perhaps I had already and I'd found my way to Hell."

A faint, wry smile touches Samuel's lips, self-deprecating – the barest hint of hidden sin beneath the surgeon's veneer. A sudden warmth creeps to Hook's cheeks, his pulse turning over. He tries to imagine what Samuel could ever do to feel he deserves a place in Hell, but just as quickly decides it's an unwise course of speculation.

"And then the Devil himself appeared." If anything, Samuel's smile grows, turns into a grin, the light in his eyes taking the sting from the words as he turns to fully face his captain.

"You stepped out of the blood and the smoke, your skin, your clothes, your hair, coated with gore. You held out your hand and helped me up, told me to go below decks where I would be safe, and then went back to fighting."

Hook wracks his brain, trying to recall the moment painted by Samuel's words, wishing he could see it—live it—again. He tries to imagine himself, a blood-soaked and terrible angel, and wonders why that vision of him should make Samuel smile.

"Do you still think me a monster?" He tries to keep his voice light, but it wobbles. It matters very much what Samuel says next.

The surgeon's expression changes, something Hook can't quite read, or is afraid to. It gentles, and his tone is more serious that Hook would like.

"I never did. I was a stranger to you when you saved me. I might have run you through with a blade the moment you offered your hand for all you knew, but you chose to trust and help me even with death all around. I wanted to think you saw something in me that moment that seemed worth saving." Samuel shakes his head, another self-deprecating gesture, then after a moment, he goes on, softly. Beside him, Hook holds his breath.

"There was something in your eyes, behind all the horror and blood. I don't know how to describe it exactly, but that's what I've always seen. Not the Devil, just you."

Hook has to turn away; Samuel is too bright to look at right now. He can't stand the surgeon's eyes, terrified of being seen in the way Samuel describes seeing him. A tremor wants to start beneath his skin, even though he isn't the slightest bit cold. He tries for lightness again, but what comes out is bitter.

"You might be the only one. The rest of the crew thinks me mad at least, if not a monster."

"Will you give them a vote before you use the blade, whether to stay or leave?" There's only curiosity in Samuel's tone, no judgment. And whatever else might have been there a moment before feels as though it's passed—an opportunity missed, or a terrible reprieve—leaving them only captain and surgeon again.

Hook shakes his head.

"I won't give them the chance to mutiny. Killdeer and Harrigan already plot against me. This is my ship, and my word is law." He makes his voice hard, as if tyranny will give him confidence he doesn't feel.

When Hook glances over again, he sees Samuel's lips flatten, and finds himself frowning in turn. He wants to turn the expression into a scowl, or a sneer. Whatever passed between them, feels raw in its wake. Samuel flayed him, left him exposed, and even worse – now that the scrutiny of his gaze is withdrawn, the knowing in it, Hook finds he misses it.

The urge to bark a command, send the surgeon scampering below decks, almost rises to his lips. He opens his mouth, but Samuel straightens, leaning farther out over the rail and pointing.

"Look." Wonder colors Samuel's voice.

Hook's breath stutters, catching, a thing he hadn't thought possible anymore. Luminous shapes, hundreds of them, glide below the surface of the water. Jellyfish, but they look like rogue stars, streaming across an ocean of night, headed for the distant horizon to spill off the edge of the world.

Samuel leans against the rail, everything but his awe forgotten. Close enough their shoulders nearly brush, the surgeon's hand resting a scant inch from the captain's glittering hook as if unaware of its deadly potential. Hook's chest tightens, ribs aching as surely as if he were being crushed to death by the beast all over again. He is already torn, split in two. He wants—needs—to leave this place. He cannot abide it any longer. Nothing good can persist here.

That spark, possibility he saw in Samuel's eyes, will be snuffed here if they stay. He needs to get out. He needs to get them both out if the fragile blossom held out in Samuel's hands is to have any chance to flourish and survive.

"I hope you'll trust me." He says it quietly after a moment, keeping his gaze on the moving stream of stars lighting the water with their milky glow.

Samuel gives no answer, and for a moment, Hook feels a combined stab of relief and disappointment. Then Samuel shifts, and it is almost an imperceptible thing. The center of gravity moves between them. His shoulder touches Hook's and does not draw away. His fingers rest just beside the point of the hook and they are fearless of harm. Samuel doesn't turn his head, and Hook doesn't dare either, but he hears a smile in the surgeon's voice as he gazes at the luminous water. His proximity and his words, even though they aren't an answer, feel like enough.

"It's the most beautiful thing I've ever seen."

* * *

James stands, stretching muscles grown stiff from sitting too long. They must almost be at their destination. The car sways, and he braces himself, almost falling into Wendy. The motion is so like the rolling pitch of a ship's deck that for a moment he loses himself, disoriented.

Is he back in Neverland? A shouted order locks in his throat. No, he hasn't been in Neverland for years. He isn't... A flicker of motion catches his eye, just beyond the door leading to the next car. He steps forward without thinking, his bad leg nearly failing him. He steadies himself, hearing Wendy's concerned voice behind him and ignoring it as he presses his face to the glass.

The scaled tip of a tail, disappearing out of his range of vision. Hook's pulse hammers. No. Not Hook. He is James. He wrenches the door open, leaning into the space where wind rushes between the cars, where tracks flash past underfoot.

"Captain!" Wendy's voice, the concern rising to alarm behind him. She sounds younger, a girl, forgetting to call him James.

He doesn't bother to correct her; he doesn't answer her at all. But she holds his cane out, and he takes it as he peers down the length of the train. There, the tail again, vanishing into the next car. Roiling, like smoke. Vast and scaled. Impossible. The train jerks, nearly pitching him onto the swaying join between the carriages. Only Wendy's hand on his shoulder, hauling him back, saves him.

"James. What is it?" Her voice is sharp with fear, her eyes wide.

"There's about to be another death." He nudges her back toward their seats. If he is right, the farther they are from what is about to occur, the less attention they draw to themselves, the better.

The less he thinks about Neverland, the more he centers himself in the here and now, the safer he will be.

"What's happening?" The girl, Jane, wakes finally, blinking up at them.

Wendy touches her daughter's shoulder, tension clear along the line of her arm. But instead of answering Jane, Wendy looks at him.

"We have to warn someone."

"More likely than not, it is already too late. And do you want to explain how either of us knows what will occur?"

Doubt flickers in her eyes, and he sees that he has her; she knows he's right. And whatever kindness is in her, her sense of self-preservation is stronger still. Good girl. Wendy opens her mouth, but everything lurches again, brakes screaming protest as the train grinds to a halt. They are not yet at the station. Murmured questions rustle up and down the aisles. After a moment, the door between carriages opens, a harried looking conductor—face blanched and pale—darts a gaze around the car.

"Is anyone here a doctor?" His voice is hoarse, barely above a whisper, almost as if he's afraid of the question being heard.

Wendy darts a glance at James, accusing, but before she can speak, Jane is up, trying to move past her mother and toward the conductor. Wendy seizes her daughter's arm.

"What are you doing?"

"I can help." Jane tries to shake off her mother's grasp, and Wendy only tightens her hold.

The two women glare at each other, jaws equally set, eyes equally hard. There is no mistaking the blood between them. Jane pulls her arm free.

"I'm a medical student." She strides toward the conductor, leaving Wendy looking stricken. "Keep asking in the other cars, but in the meantime, I'll do what I can."

The conductor's expression clearly says he wants to dismiss the girl, but Jane doesn't wait. She is used to this battle, James can tell, and wholly weary of it. She strides past the man, not giving him time to stop her. James can't help admiring her, nor can he help the brief, fleeting thought that she would have made a good pirate. Wendy tries to follow her daughter, and now it is James's turn to catch her and hold her back.

"We would be best off keeping out of the way."

She resists him for a moment, then the fight drains from her. Wendy slumps. Conversation, speculation, ripples up and down the train car. The tension—like a storm gathering over them—is palpable. James finds himself gripping the head of his cane, his knuckles aching.

Time stretches, and yet it seems only a heartbeat before Jane returns, looking worn. She shakes her head, dropping heavily into the seat beside her mother, shrugging off her concerned touch.

"There wasn't anything I could do. There's nothing anyone could have done. It's…" She lets the words trail, turning a haunted, hollow expression toward the glass.

All three of them watch as after a time, the coroner's wagon pulls into the road parallel to the tracks. Eventually, a covered body is carried from the train.

"Just like Peg." Jane's voice is bitter, tired, and angry all at once. She flexes her hand in her lap, and James watches the blood flush and retreat from the skin around her knuckles. She longs to blame someone, he can see it in every line of her posture, the desire to shout and demand an explanation.

Wendy cuts her eyes to him, her expression stony. James shrugs, turns deliberately to look again through the glass. Now is not the time or the place.

The coroner's wagon departs, and several moments later, the train begins to roll again. The conductor passes through the cars, offering apologies for the delay. James notes that he does not stop to thank Jane for her help, and sees the girl note it as well.

When they stand, finally, to collect their bags as the train nears Newark-on-Trent station, Wendy touches James's arm again and he sees she will not be put off this time.

"How did you know?" Her voice is low, urgent.

"I saw something…familiar." How to explain the impossible?

Wendy's fingers circle his wrist, the space where flesh meets wood, and squeezes—a warning.

"You will tell me. Later." She lets his arm go.

James sighs. The train draws to a halt, and he follows Wendy and her daughter as they descend to the cold station platform, each wrapped in their own silences, each of their expressions closed and grim.

10

HOME

LONDON – 1939

Home. But it isn't really. It's her parents' house. The rooms don't know her the way they did in the house in London. And now in the car with them is the strange man her mother dragged along with them. He stinks of Neverland. Even though her mother hasn't admitted it, Jane knows. And she's certain, too, that he's connected to the deaths as well—the man on the train and also Peg.

She listened to him and her mother while they thought her asleep. She doesn't have all the pieces, but enough to confirm some of her suspicion, and the knowledge infuriates her. Her mother promised honesty. She promised Jane could ask her anything. If she confronted her mother, would she tell the truth? But why should she even have to confront her? Why should the burden fall to Jane to drag confessions from her mother like a recalcitrant child? Doesn't she trust Jane? Or does she think her incapable of handling anything but sugar-coated half-lies?

This is worse than the things her mother has hidden from her before. The man, James, knew a death would occur moments before the train's brake was thrown and the conductor came through the cars looking for a doctor. A man's life was at stake, and her mother did nothing. How can Jane forgive her for that? It sickens her now that she thought of her mother as fearless and bold earlier, when it's clear she's a coward.

Jane rests her head against the window glass, her body turned as far away from her mother and James as possible. There's a smell about him, like black powder, like flowers—violence and an incongruous sweetness. She doesn't like him at all.

Part of her wants to lean over the seat, demand the driver take her back to the station. She could get on a train back to London. Better to spend the holiday alone. Only she wants to see her father and her uncles. And in London, all that waits is a cold flat, the memory of Peg's shadow burned into her mattress. The man on the train was the same, as if something had hollowed him out completely. The seat behind him hadn't been stained, but Jane had felt it, a darkness waiting to rise.

When the train crew finds the mark tomorrow, will they remember what caused it? Or will they have already forgotten? She'd seen it starting to happen even as she stood uselessly over the body. Those gathered around her let their gazes drift away, or had them pushed away. They couldn't help it, couldn't hold their focus. It's as though whatever—and Jane is certain now it's a what, not a who—is doing the killing has the power to rewrite reality. It is not just causing death, but making it almost as though the person killed never existed at all.

It's a chilling thought and Jane swears again she will not forget. Not Peg, not the man whose name she doesn't even know. She will hold them in her memory along with the catalog of other things known only to her—her and her mother. Peg, the man on the train, Timothy, and Neverland.

Jane catches herself grinding her teeth and forces herself to stop. It's too late, a headache is already beginning to form.

The car slows and pulls into the drive. Jane sits straighter, peering through the window. The snow here has largely melted, leaving hard crusted patches of white on the flattened brown-green grass. Climbing out of the car though, Jane feels a twinge of guilt—with the war, with so many people unable to do the only jobs they've ever known, it seems wrong that her family should be so comfortable.

She should be happy, she knows. She should be grateful, because who knows what Christmas will be like next year. Will she even come home? Even though she's only a student, she could still volunteer, couldn't she? Surely extra pairs of hands are always needed in the field hospitals, especially hands with training. She could gain practical experience and finish her schooling after the war is done. Most importantly, if she did that, she'd be helping people—like her Uncle Michael, like her father.

As they make their way up the path, the front door of the house opens, and her father steps out. Jane forgets her sourness, forgets everything, and runs to him. Even though her father visits her in the city, it isn't the same as being here with him. Jane is suddenly sharply aware of how much she's missed him. His hug is tight, and even though she's practically as tall as he is now, he still lifts her off her feet and she can't help laughing.

His shirt sleeves are rolled up, and he holds a towel in his hands as if he's just come from the kitchen. He smells warm, like cooking, like comfort, and all at once Jane finds her eyes stinging and she has to blink before he sets her down. Her father smells like home, regardless of whether or not this is the house she grew up in.

"My Jane." His expression changes from happiness to sympathy. "Your mother told me about your friend Margaret. I am so very sorry."

The stinging in her eyes only grows worse and she allows herself to fold into her father once more, buying herself time as she gets her emotions under control.

"I'm all right." Jane pulls away, but her voice remains thick.

She doesn't mention the man on the train; let her mother deal with that. As if on cue, her father's attention shifts. The concern doesn't leave his eyes, but there's fondness there, and then startlement as he notices the man from Neverland. How will her mother explain James? Will she lie? Evade? Give her father half-truths?

She watches as her mother keeps pace with James, who leans heavily on his cane. Her father wipes his hands one last time, then drapes the towel over his shoulder.

"I should have known to expect the unexpected." Her father sounds bemused, more than angry, though still wary as well.

"I didn't know myself until a few hours ago." At least her mother has the good grace to sound embarrassed. "This is James. James, this is my husband, Ned."

Her mother says nothing beyond the man's name, but Jane notes the silent look that passes between them, a promise to explain later.

"A pleasure." James shifts the grip from his cane long enough to grasp her father's hand. Jane notes her mother at the ready to catch him if he falls. "I hope my presence does not cause too much inconvenience, but I do thank you for welcoming me to your home."

"Not at all. We have plenty of food, and we're happy to have you."

James inclines his head, a strangely formal motion. Again, though her mother hasn't said it directly, Jane is certain James and the pirate captain, Hook, are one and the same. The why and how of it don't need to make sense—nothing in Neverland ever did after all.

Who else could James be, after all? His false hand is wooden, but the way he holds himself, Jane sees the echoes of command. There's an air about him of a man used to being obeyed. In her mother's long-ago fairy tales—the stories she'd told Jane instead of giving her the truth about Neverland—she'd made Hook into an enchanted prince wearing a blood-red coat. And there is a bearing of royalty about him, a man who believed himself king above others, at least at one point in time.

Why her mother would invite Captain Hook to their home, Jane cannot begin to guess.

"Well, come out of the cold." Her father ushers them toward the door, but Jane falls back, hesitating.

Something tugs at her. The nape of her neck prickles above her scarf, and it's nothing to do with the wind. She glances at the trees bordering the property. Was there a blur of motion between the branches? She takes a step, but her father calls to her from the door. When she looks again, whatever she thought she saw among the trees is gone.

* * *

Jane surveys the room. It's neat, the single bed made up with a white quilt patterned with tiny pink roses. She wonders if her mother sewed it. There's a dresser in heavy mahogany, matched to the headboard and footboard of the bed. The pink lampshade matches the quilt's pink roses, and there are delicate, cream-colored doilies set atop the furniture that match the curtains. It's all so coordinated and fussy Jane wonders whether it was simply picked from a catalog at random. Even though she's trying to maintain her annoyance at her mother, she can't help the way the thought makes her smile.

Jane's eyes settle on the one piece of furniture in the room that doesn't belong. The bookcase from her childhood bedroom. A globe stuck with pins sits atop it, and the shelves are filled with books she read as a child—*Treasure Island*, books of faerie stories, and books about the natural world. Did her mother put it here, or was it her father's idea?

Jane kneels, running her fingers along the spines on the top shelf. On the next shelf down, in front of the books, is a glass case with a butterfly pinned inside. Holly blue, *Celastrina argiolus*— Jane recognizes the label in her own hand. All the butterflies and rocks and leaves she collected as a child, did her parents keep them all? She could hardly take two steps out of doors without stopping to pick something up, to slip it into her pocket. She must have been impossible.

She sets the case down. There's something missing. Instinct makes her cross to the dresser, pull open the narrow drawer on the left-hand side. There's a rattling sound as she does, and reaching inside, Jane already knows what she'll find. An arrowhead—the one she brought back with her from Neverland.

It sparkles ever so slightly, the chips made to sharpen its edges glinting as if reflecting a different light than the one in the room. Her mother must have put it here; her father never would. A promise, once, between them, that there would be no more secrets.

As she crosses to the window to peer out at the lawn, the knapped stone against her skin seems almost to tingle. A soft tap against the door startles her, a sound so quiet it almost seems as though it's trying not to be heard. Jane tucks the arrowhead into her sleeve, an old habit. She expects her mother or her father, but it's her uncle, already half turning as if he would slip away again. A tension she hadn't realized she was holding on to slithers away from her and Jane opens the door wider, beaming.

"Uncle Michael! Come in." He'd arrived shortly after Jane and her mother had, but between getting everyone settled and eating supper, Jane had barely had a chance to speak with him.

There's a stack of journals tucked under his arm now, and Jane's grin widens. He moves to the bed, free hand gripping his cane, gait stiff. The faint outline of his brace is just visible through the fabric of his trousers—something new her uncle's doctor had recommended to help him with the persistent weakness in his leg.

Jane burns with curiosity—professional, of course—but she would never ask her uncle outright and so she bites her lip. Once he's seated, he draws out the journals with a flourish and a pained smile, setting them atop the quilt.

"Hot off the presses, just like I promised."

"You're wonderful!" Jane reaches for the topmost journal, dropping a quick kiss onto her uncle's cheek as she does.

"Won't any of the patrons miss them?" she asks, flipping to scan the list of articles in the table of contents.

"Amazingly, no. As it turns out, no one but my niece is eager to read the latest in medical science over the holidays." He offers her a wry grin, and Jane feels her cheeks warm.

At the same time, a kind of weariness creeps over Jane. Yes, she wants to read the articles and papers her uncle brought for her, but if she were a man, would she feel the need to push herself to do so as fast as possible when she's supposed to be on break? It isn't just that she can't afford to fall behind, she has to stay ahead, as far as she can, running full tilt so there's no chance that anyone will ever trip her up or catch her.

Jane feels the frown twisting her lips, and she sets the journal down, forcing her face into a more neutral expression before her uncle can ask her what's wrong.

"How is the library anyway?" She keeps her voice light, airy.

"Quiet. Peaceful. Not many people. Just the way I like it."

"Isn't a librarian's whole job to help people find books?" She means it be teasing, but Uncle Michael's shoulders tighten almost imperceptibly before he forces himself to relax again.

"Special collections are less in demand, especially at this time of year. Some days, I can go hours on end without seeing anyone. It's perfect, really." Another flickering smile, and Jane can tell he's trying to make a joke of his words too.

The words and his expression spark a mixture of guilt and regret. Jane can see how hard he's trying, for her sake, and she can see that it pains him as well—merely smiling, merely being around other people, even family. No wonder he prefers the silence of the library and books. She tries, as she has many times before, to imagine what her uncle was like as a child, when he and her mother and Uncle John would play at make-believe in the nursery. She can scarcely picture it. This is the only version of her uncle she's ever known—the one who came back broken from the war, not just his body, but his spirit. The one who retreats so far inside himself at times it's almost as though he disappears.

The ghosted look in his eyes is one Jane knows all too well. She'd seen it earlier, when they'd all been gathered in the kitchen and the radio had switched from holiday music to a news broadcast, which inevitably spoke of the current war. A darkness had come into Uncle Michael's expression, and Jane had clearly seen the moment he retreated within himself, shut away from the world until her mother switched the radio off.

Looking at him now, she can almost see the edges of the mask he tries to keep over his face at all times, the one that tells the world everything is fine. Except when it slips, like now, when he's exhausted, and the hurt comes seeping through. He looks down, trying too late to hide the shadow in his eyes, and Jane bites her lip again.

She wants to tell him she understands. How every day at the Royal College she wears a mask too, smiling and smiling until her cheeks hurt, until a headache creeps its way up her jaw and bursts behind her eyes and leaves her next to tears. It's exhausting, and sometimes she just wants to let it go and scream at the world for being unfair, but outwardly, she keeps right on smiling. It's fine. It's fine. It's all fine.

Jane's hand twitches at her side, halfway to reaching for her uncle's shoulder before she remembers the arrowhead tucked in her sleeve and drops it again. According to her mother, not only had both her uncles forgotten about Neverland after they'd returned from their adventures with Peter as children, but they'd vehemently denied it. Michael especially. It was as though after he'd gone to war and come back, the very idea of a magical land where death wasn't real and children never grew up was too cruel to even contemplate, salt rubbed into the wound of everything he'd been through. The men he'd called brothers who died screaming in pain and weeping for families they'd never see again. Boys who would never grow up and never go home. Bad enough to risk making things worse by telling him it's okay to hurt, to be scared about the new war. How much worse would it be if she accidentally reminded him of Neverland?

When her mother had introduced James before dinner, Uncle Michael had startled at first, but an instant later, Jane had seen not even the faintest sign of recognition in his eyes. In fact, as soon as James has been introduced, her uncle's gaze slid away from the former pirate captain. It was as though Uncle Michael couldn't see him, refused to see him. Unless James was actively speaking, or directly in her uncle's line of sight, Uncle Michael seemed to mentally edit him out, eliding an uncomfortable reminder of Neverland.

Still looking down, her uncle rubs absently at his brace. The moment he touches it, Jane sees him startle, as if he'd forgotten it, as if he'd done his best to edit it out of his reality too.

"Is it helping?" Jane can't help the question, and it isn't professional curiosity now; she really wants to know if her uncle is okay, and if he isn't now, whether he might be one day.

He looks up, his hand jerking away from the brace and his expression stunned, as though he'd already started to drift, to withdraw, forgetting Jane was there and he wasn't alone.

"Some. At times." There's an edge to his voice, then after a moment, Uncle Michael offers her a smile meant to be reassuring—the veneer back in place once again.

It hurts Jane to see it. He shakes himself, using his cane to stand, and leaning upon it heavily.

"The doctor says I just need time to get used to it." He taps the brace lightly with one knuckle, and now the smile spreading across his lips is more genuine. "Once you're a doctor, you'll invent something even better, and I'll be out there running marathons I'm sure."

"I guess I'd better get to studying then." Jane spreads her fingers to indicate the journals, returning her uncle's smile.

She's never seen her uncle walk with anything other than a pained limp; the image of him running stings at the back of her eyes and Jane blinks rapidly.

"Don't forget to sleep and eat occasionally too." Uncle Michael indicates the journals, then draws Jane close enough to plant a kiss on her forehead.

As he steps back, Jane almost tells him to do the same, but she bites back the words. He's an adult, and she has no business lecturing him like a child, no matter how dark the circles under his eyes. The door closes with a soft click behind him and Jane turns to the slim volumes spread across the quilt. Just the thought exhausts her. She can afford one night to herself, can't she? She drifts back to the window, drawing the arrowhead from her sleeve again and turning it in her hand, a soothing motion, despite everything it means.

Tired as she is, she can't even think of sleeping. She should have thought to bring a novel with her at least. And the thought is a blow, leaving her winded, bringing Peg to the front of her mind again. She'd almost forgotten. Almost let her slip away, like Uncle Michael editing the pirate captain from his mind.

Peg's family will spend the holiday without her. Here Jane is, surrounded by the people she loves, and part of her resents it. The thought makes her feel small and selfish, makes her hurt all the way through.

Where the arrowhead in her hand was almost a comfort moments before, now the weight of it drags at her, cold and laden with memory. She will not allow herself to forget, but she can understand her uncle's denial of Neverland, why it would hurt so much to recall. It's a bright lie, a world of fun and games painted in a thin veneer over the darkness underneath. The first time Jane experienced death, intimately, had been in Neverland, and now some shadow of it, some echo, it seems, has taken Peg from her as well. It's too much, Jane thinks, for the number of years she's lived. It's too much to carry. No wonder her uncle disappears into himself entirely at times. No wonder he prefers to forget.

Jane rests her head against the cool glass of the window. There are times Jane wishes she could disappear and forget everything she's seen too.

NEVERLAND – 8 YEARS AGO

Jane turns the arrowhead over in her hand. She managed to find it after shooting it at Arthur, one of Peter's Lost Boys, to stop him from attacking her mother. It feels important somehow, holding on to it. It reminds her that she isn't powerless, even though that's exactly how she feels right now.

It isn't cold in the cavern—if anything, it's far warmer than it should be—but Jane still wants to shiver. It's nervous energy, pent-up adrenaline with nowhere to go. She tucks the hem of her nightgown under her bare feet and tries to take comfort in Timothy's weight nestled against her side. Her mother took Peter somewhere deeper into the cavern. She made Jane promise to stay here, to be brave, no matter what might happen. Stay here, protect Timothy, wait for her mother to return.

But it feels as though it's been ages already and she wants to be doing something. She wants to help her mother, not sit here like a useless lump. She tried again to get Timothy to stand, to come with her and go looking for her mother, but he wouldn't budge. He'd insisted again that he'd been kilt when Arthur ran him through with his sword, even though there isn't a scratch on him. Another one of Peter's stupid rules in his games of make-believe war.

"How long do you think it will be until you're alive again?" Jane asks, trying to keep the impatience from her voice.

Could she leave Timothy behind, go looking for her mother alone? No, she promised to protect him, like a big sister would. He's younger than her, smaller than her, she can't leave him here alone in the dark. Timothy shrugs, looking miserable.

"Sometimes it takes forever and sometimes not at all."

Of course, Jane thinks. Peter's rules. Peter gets to decide everything that happens here, and all the rest of them simply have to live with it. She squeezes the arrowhead, lets it bite into her palm, because otherwise she might scream with frustration.

"What do you think they're doing?" Jane tilts her chin to indicate the deeper part of the cave where her mother and Peter disappeared.

She doesn't expect an answer, but the silence and the waiting is all too much. If she can't do anything to help, she at least wants to hear the sound of her voice and Timothy's in the dark to remind her she's not completely alone.

Timothy begins to shake his head again, and Jane clenches her jaw in frustration. She feels mean and petty, she wants to pinch him until he yelps and jumps up just to get away from her. Make him see that Peter's rules don't control him and he doesn't have to sit here playing dead until Peter says he's alive again. But Timothy freezes, his eyes going wide, and before Jane can open her mouth to ask what's wrong, she feels it.

The ground beneath them shivers and rumbles. Dust filters down from the ceiling above, tiny chips of stone bouncing free and clattering down around them. She pulls Timothy closer, sheltering him as best she can.

"It's okay." Jane tucks Timothy's face against her shoulder. Everything shakes again, and a larger chunk of stone slips free, narrowly missing them as it smashes against the ground.

More dust, more debris. Jane coughs, almost crushing Timothy now. They need to get somewhere safer.

"We have to—" Jane's words are drowned in a terrible roar.

It isn't just the sound of the stone breaking, or the ground trembling. It's something else entirely. Something Jane cannot name.

Timothy stiffens against her, lets out a muffled sound. Without meaning to, Jane lets go, clapping her hands over her ears against the terrible noise going on and on inside and outside of her head all at once. It sounds like the world tearing itself apart. And in the next instant, the stone beneath her cracks, dropping her a few inches, jolting her to a sudden stop, and she lets out a startled cry.

"Timothy!" Dust in her eyes. She can't see him. Panic hammers at her and Jane scrambles forward, feeling wildly over the stone until her fingers find his and she almost sobs in relief.

She closes her fingers, pulling herself toward him, expecting him to squeeze back, to call her name, but he's silent. Everything is still shaking. She loses her balance, but then she's at Timothy's side again, trying to blink her vision clear from the grit stinging her eyes. Her breath stops. Her heart stops and Jane blinks and blinks again, unable to make sense of what she's seeing.

Timothy's shirt is soaked in red. A bright, terrible color that doesn't belong. It can't be blood. It can't. And Jane wants to laugh because it's impossible and it must be a horrible joke. But her mouth is dry and her hands fly to the place where Arthur's sword went through Timothy before and left no wound, where there wasn't even a scratch on his skin, and they come away wet and gleaming.

"No. No. Oh no." Her hands slip, trying to stop it.

There's too much red. It's everywhere. She can't put it back inside no matter how much she tries.

"It hurts." Timothy's voice is small and lost in the rumbling, his lips pale, his eyes glassy. "Jane, it hurts, please."

"It's okay, you're all right, you'll be all right." The words blur. Jane knows they're a lie. She throws her whole body over Timothy's, against the dust, against the shaking, clinging to him as if she could stop the blood with the force of her will. He has to be all right. He has to. She promised she would keep him safe.

The ground still shudders, but over and above it, Jane feels Timothy shuddering too. One last gasp of shallow breath and then it stops and that's far, far worse. Jane feels it, and she refuses it. The words tumbling from her, the promises, Timothy can't hear them anymore. But they are the last thing he heard Jane lying. Her telling him everything would be okay.

A sound rises, tearing out of her, becoming a howl to rival the sound filling the cave and bringing it down around them. Jane clings to Timothy as hard as she can, not caring for his blood or the falling stone or even the far-distant sound of her mother shouting her name. Nothing else matters, only the small body in her arms, and Jane swears to herself she will make it right. She will fix it somehow. She will never, ever let Timothy go.

LONDON – 1939

The moon casts halos around itself, the clouds turning its light smeary. The way the edges of the clouds catch the light makes Jane briefly think of a doorway, of being pulled through the sky against her will. The memory of Neverland is so close, she can feel it against her skin. The memory of Timothy so sharp, so present, she almost feels the weight of him pressed against her side. Her breath tangles in her chest, a sob wanting to break free. It's so real, that she halfway expects to find him peering up at her from the lawn, his eyes wide in the moonlight, asking why she left him behind.

But it is Peg she finds staring up at her from amidst the melting patches of snow. Not a glimpse from the corner of her eye, but unmistakably solid, as if the shadows parted a moment and she stepped through. The arrowhead drops to the floor. Jane steps back, knees hitting the bed, folding her to sit heavily as her legs lose their strength.

In the next instant, she bounces back up, rushing to the glass. Her foot catches the arrowhead, sending it spinning. It must have

147

been her imagination, grief and guilt toying with her. She presses her face to the pane.

Peg remains, peering straight up at Jane's window. Only it can't be Peg, because Peg is dead. The longer Jane looks, the more the subtle wrongness of the figure below her sinks in and her skin crawls.

Peg's smile is too wide. There's something almost doughy about her face, unfinished, like bread kneaded and left to rise. Soft, malleable, the color of smoke.

Jane claps a hand over her mouth, a sour taste rising at the back of her throat. Yet she's already flying down the stairs, out the door and onto the lawn, forgetting she's in her night clothes, forgetting her feet are bare. Her soles hit the frosted grass and she barely feels the cold.

It's more than just the flight down the stairs that squeezes the air in her lungs, and the night's cold only makes it worse, leaving her gasping. Jane wheezes, the exhalation writing ghosts of its own against the night. There's no one here. The lawn is empty.

Jane looks up at her window. A square of light falls on her, and she shivers. She has the sensation of standing inside a space recently occupied by a ghost, a lingering presence clinging to her like a spreading frost. But no footprints mark the grass, save her own trailing back toward the front door in long, wet smudges.

"Peg?" She regrets the whisper the minute it passes her lips and her skin crawls.

What if something answers?

Peg cannot be here. She isn't here. Because something carried her away to Neverland.

The thought rises like a traitor and Jane clamps down on it, pushing it violently away. It's only cruel and wishful thinking. She's too late. She can't save Peg, like she couldn't save Timothy.

But the sensation that she isn't alone persists. As she turns to scan the trees, something swoops toward her. Startled, her heel slips on the slick grass, dropping her, and perhaps that is what saves her. A rush of dark wind passes just overhead. Missing her by inches. Close enough to ruffle her hair.

She feels her arm grabbed and Jane lets out a startled cry.

"Let go!" She kicks out, but her foot doesn't connect, and then she recognizes the pirate captain's voice.

"It's returning." He hauls her up, and stunned, Jane lands on her feet.

James breathes hard. He turns, and Jane turns with him in time to see the shadow rush toward them again. Even though on the train and at the station, Jane saw how James needed the cane to take his weight, he slashes the air with it now, lunging and stabbing, the pirate-prince of her mother's stories come to life.

The shadow tears as the cane passes through it, shredded temporarily and coming back together again. Jane can't make sense of it. An animal, a reptile, but massive and made of smoke and moonlight. And there's more. The air around it roils and churns and there are glimpses of shapes that look almost human, faces rising and then sinking again as if instead of water the creature swims through a sea of ghosts.

Her earlier bravado gone, Jane half drags James back toward the house, expecting any moment to feel teeth sink into her heel. The door flies open as Jane reaches for it, and she nearly collides with her mother, her hair loose and spilling about her shoulders, eyes wide.

"Jane, what on earth—?"

"Inside," James urges, and they tumble through the door.

Jane glances back. She can't help it. And she freezes on the doorstep before her mother can push closed the door. Not the shadow she expected to see surging toward them, but something else, something she cannot fathom or make sense of, and so she can only stare.

A hole. In the sky. Definite this time, not just the suggestion of the door. It's as if the winter night were merely dark fabric, and a giant hand seized ahold of it and tore it, leaving a jagged gap behind. A place where the stars simply stop. Where the thin crescent moon sheds no light. But where there is something else, a thing that can't possibly be. A ship. Falling.

The image stutters. Repeats in a loop.

"Come inside." It is James's hand, rather than her mother's, firm on her shoulder, pulling her over the threshold.

Jane turns to look at him, the grim set of his expression telling her she is hallucinating nothing. Or that the ship is a shared hallucination; he sees it too. Inside, Jane moves to the window, pulling back the curtain. The sky is as it should be. No hole. No ghostly pirate ship sailing across the stars. She whirls toward James, nerves firing so that she doesn't care if she is being rude.

"That was your ship, wasn't it? I know you saw it, so there's no use telling me otherwise. You recognized it."

"Yes. My ship." James's voice is soft, meeting her near-yell with something that is almost sorrow, surprising her into silence.

"What are you two talking about? What were you doing outside?" Her mother's voice trembles as she looks between them.

Fear, concern, and something else. Near-panic, as if knowing there was something there she should have seen, but it was invisible to her eyes.

"You didn't see it." It's only half a question.

Her mother stares at her. Recognition, as though for a moment, she sees the ship, but only as a reflection in Jane's eyes. A piece of Neverland, hidden from her.

"I think perhaps we should sit." James gestures toward the parlor. His leg trembles, and he leans heavily on his cane now even though he wielded it as a sword only moments before.

Jane and her mother remain staring at each other, then Jane is the first to follow the pirate captain. Something attacked her; there was a hole in the sky. She saw it, and James saw it, but her mother did not. Should Jane feel a vicious kind of triumph? Or should she pity her mother? Or neither. Should she only feel what she feels now—numb, stunned.

"May I?" James indicates the cut-glass bottles holding amber liquid set on a narrow, wheeled tray next to the window.

Her mother nods, distracted. Jane watches James pour, grimacing, as though each motion hurts him now after his bold attack on the lawn. He hands them each a small glass of brandy, keeping one for himself. Jane doesn't even want it, but she accepts it, sure to meet her mother's eyes again, daring her to say something, determined to remind her that she isn't a child anymore.

Her mother barely seems to notice though, and Jane feels a petty stab of disappointment. The three of them sit, arrayed around the empty fireplace.

"Will one of you please explain what's happening?" There's a sharpness to her mother's tone, but under it, Jane hears lingering fear.

Jane folds her hands around the glass of brandy, balancing her arms on her knees.

"My ship," James repeats, and it makes just as little sense as the first time he said it. "Or an echo of it. It's how…we left Neverland."

His voice breaks on the word *we*. He drains his glass, seemingly barely aware of it in his hand once it's empty.

"What were you doing outside in the first place?"

There's exasperation in her mother's voice, but she rises automatically, takes James's glass to refill it. She is shaken. Jane looks to her, to the disarray of her hair, the fine lines gathered at the corners of her mouth and eyes.

Her mother, so used to being in control of every situation, a hoarder of secrets, used to knowing more about any given situation than those around her. But here she is, utterly lost. Jane almost reaches out, but ends up clenching her hands tighter around her own glass.

"What did you see?" James leans forward as he asks it, eyes bright.

Jane opens her mouth, closes it again. She shakes her head.

"A shadow. I thought…" She shakes her head again. Falls silent. After a moment though, she looks up. "What did you see?"

"An old enemy. A thing that should not be here. I saw it on the train as well."

Jane turns the pieces she has over in her mind. What is a ship without its captain? Her mother had told her how the captain had gotten his name. A beast, she'd said, something like a crocodile, had devoured his hand. Scales and jaws of smoke, turning and hunting and seeking…

"It's looking for you, isn't it? It doesn't care about either of us." Jane looks briefly to her mother, then back to the former pirate captain. "That thing is hunting you, but something is wrong with it. It can't tell us apart. It smells Neverland, but it's confused. It must have come to the flat following my scent, but it found Peg and—"

Her voice breaks. She can't finish. Her mother and James gape at her. Jane realizes she's trembling, not from cold or fear though, but adrenaline. She wants to leap up, to grab James and shake him. He's the key, or his ship is. They both are, tied together, and between them, they've formed a door to Neverland.

"I fear you're right." James kneads at his thigh, a seemingly unconscious gesture, his expression grim.

"And I think that you ought to start at the beginning and explain everything," her mother says, her voice firm and her expression set.

She hands over the glass at last, but doesn't take her eyes from James's face. Jane looks between them. It's a moment before her mother steps back and resumes her seat, her back very straight.

"Tell me about your ship, and how you came to London from Neverland."

"Wendy Darling." James's expression changes, a wry smile, and he lifts his glass as if to toast her mother. "I would not dare refuse you."

A HOLE IN THE STARS

NEVERLAND – 22 YEARS AGO

The storm's fury is such as he's never seen. The sky roars, lashing the deck with rain—Pan throwing a tantrum, sensing his best enemy about to slip from his grasp. The ship tilts, front end caught by a wave, stern still in a trough, and for a moment, Hook thinks they will capsize. Another storm and another sea superimpose themselves over this one. He remembers a mouth in the waves. Falling past impossible stars. What if they tumble into yet another world, endless new worlds all the way down and never returning to where he started?

But the wave only smashes over them, driving the thought from his mind. His feet slide and it is his hook that saves him, point buried in the wood as another wave hard on the heels of the first drives him to his knees. He tears his hook free as more water swirls across the deck and the ship bucks again. Hook climbs to his feet and sets his stance wide, gritting his teeth.

"Your orders, Captain?" Killdeer's voice is nearly lost in the storm, but even so, Hook hears the edge of rebellion in it, barely contained.

Perhaps he intends to make a move under cover of the storm—Hook swept overboard and Killdeer and Harrigan sailing away with his ship. Hook holds Killdeer's gaze, daring him. They are both soaked to the bone, dripping. Killdeer is the first to look away.

"Get the men up on deck. All of them."

"But—"

"Now!" Hook flings the word with violence, lets the wind snatch it.

Killdeer blanches slightly and goes to carry out the orders. Does he remember his captain's blade in his gut? The point of his hook opening his throat?

Hook keeps his boots planted firm while the deck sways wildly. He told no one but Samuel of his plan. Let the men think him mad if they will. Let them think him incompetent even. By the time the day is done, he'll either have saved them all, or doomed them. But at least he will have done something, made a choice, seen it through, rather than hiding in drink and smoke and waiting for Pan to hunt him down again.

As they emerge, his men are smears of blackness against the howling dark. He scans among them for Samuel, but he can barely tell one man from another. Fighting against the tilt of the deck, Hook climbs to the forecastle, nearly losing his footing as he does. The deck is slick with weed churned from the depths and tossed like garlands to tangle the lines and rails.

"Tonight, we leave Neverland!" He shouts to be heard above the wind; if the men make any response, it's lost in the storm.

Lightning cracks directly overhead. The sky turns to white fire, momentarily burning out his vision. A splintering sound, smaller and more intimate, follows. Hook's vision clears just as the mizzenmast—split like a felled tree—smashes to the deck. Pan has raised all of Neverland's might against him, a child shaking a toy ship. Another wave smashes the breath from him. Hook slides, but a hand at his elbow steadies him. Samuel.

"Surely this can't be all of them?" Hook pushes sopping hair from his face, scanning the men in their huddled knots.

The blade weighs heavy in his pocket. Hook slips his hand inside to grip the hilt. Tiny vibrations sing up his arm and through his bones, reassuring him that he is doing the right thing.

"The men are afraid, sir." Despite the storm, Hook has no trouble picking out Samuel's words. His hand remains on Hook's elbow, and although it's impossible in all the waves and rain, Hook imagines he feels its warmth. Comforting.

"They should be." He clenches his jaw. "Where are the rest?"

"Chauncey led a group onto one of the boats and they struck out on their own. Before you even gave the orders to muster on deck." Samuel looks down. "They would rather take their chances with the storm."

"And no doubt Killdeer put a word in Chauncey's ear." His mouth twists in a frown.

Let them run. Let them drown. He looks past Samuel to Harrigan, and beyond him to Killdeer. Where Harrigan's eyes betray doubt and fear, in Killdeer, Hook sees simmering rage.

"You." Hook gestures at the man standing nearest to Killdeer and Harrigan. "You've just been volunteered."

The man glances at Killdeer, and then back to Hook, torn. Killdeer takes a step as if he would intervene, jaw clenched. Hook turns to Harrigan.

"You, bring him here and hold him."

Samuel's fingers brush the soaked velvet of his coat. Hook shrugs him off, no time for mercy, no time for doubt. The black blade sings hunger through his blood and his fingers tighten on the hilt.

Harrigan doesn't move. For a moment, Hook thinks he will spit. A look of triumph shapes Killdeer's lips, smug, but in the next moment, surprising them both, Samuel takes the man Hook called for by his upper arm, gently moving him closer. Hook remembers the man's name as Samuel draws him close enough to see, Bartholomew. A carved tooth from some great creature hangs around the man's neck on a leather cord. He raises it to his lips and kisses it, murmuring words lost to the storm.

"Keep him still." Hook addresses Samuel.

"What do you mean to do? Whatever rumors you've heard, I swear—" Bartholomew trembles, pleading his case, but Hook ignores him.

"Are you sure about this?" Samuel's look asks him to reconsider, but his grip doesn't waver.

There is a line drawn through the ship, and it is clear which side Samuel stands upon, regardless, perhaps, of his better judgment. But Hook cannot allow himself the full luxury of appreciating it.

"No," Hook says.

Samuel grimaces, but he doesn't flinch or pull Bartholomew away. He holds him firm as Hook studies the shadows writhing in the air around the frightened crewman. Blades are meant to cut.

His arm is up, slashing almost before Hook realizes it. Bartholomew shouts, trying to duck away. The shout cuts off and the ship pitches. When Hook draws back, his hand is slick on the blade's hilt, but he can't tell whether its seawater or blood.

"The captain's gone mad!" Killdeer's shout is snatched by the wind, circling around the deck, echoed as the other men take up the call.

He has to act fast, before it's too late. The men blur like ghosts, scrambling for the rails as if they would rather jump. He shoves Bartholomew away. Lunges for the next closest man, dragging him forward. Maitland grabs his arm, pulling him back, surprising Hook. He'd expected Killdeer or Harrigan, but it appears their mutiny has spread. Hook lashes out, bootheel crunching into Maitland's knee so he goes down with a shout of pain.

Hook leaves the other man to fall on Maitland instead, pinning him with his weight. He brings the knife down. No one moves to intervene, not even Killdeer. The blade meets resistance, but not flesh, Hook thinks. It's something deeper, the man's essence, the knife tearing him in two. Under him, the man stills, only his chest moving with shallow breath. At least Hook tells himself it does. He rocks back on his heels and looks up into the stunned faces, around him, his remaining crew now too frightened even to flee.

"Bring the next man." Hook breathes hard, shaking sodden hair from his face. He's fairly certain that what's wetting it now isn't just seawater, it's also blood.

He thinks of the memory Samuel shared of Hook stepping from the smoke and the chaos soaked in blood, the Devil himself. The death that passed over him and gave Samuel his hand, setting him aside. Saving him.

Music that isn't music winds itself beneath Hook's skin, notes played directly against his bones. The blade sings to him. He's almost certain now. He's doing the right thing. He is saving not only Samuel, but himself, and the rest of his crew. He *is* the storm, the mouth in the sea. He is the blade, and he's cutting them free.

The ship rises, another wave lifting it, but this time there is no accompanying fall, as if the sea itself is conspiring to push them into the sky. Or as if the storm and the waves are one now, all the world water. He remembers drowning. Hook's chest constricts, a moment of panic, but he pushes it down. He tilts his head back, the rain washing him, letting the shouts and terror fall away around him to focus on his breath and his pulse.

Through the rain and the clouds he can't see the stars, but he feels them. He lets himself imagine the points of them in the sky, needing only a line to join the spaces between them to become a door, a way out. His ship lurches and rises again, and he wonders if they are even sailing anymore, if perhaps they're flying. The thought is absurd, rough laughter he traps behind his teeth. Mad, bad, sad Captain Hook indeed.

He slashes the blade—wet with rain, wet with blood, wet with seawater—across the lines of the imagined pattern in the sky. Desire can be a door. If Pan's want for the perfect enemy, a fierce pirate captain to be his eternal foil, could pull him here, then surely it can work in reverse. Surely his will is as strong as Pan's, his wanting tenfold. Hook throws all of himself behind his desire, his desperation becoming belief that he will not let waver. This will work; it must work. He will leave Neverland behind.

He cuts the shape of a door in the air one more time, feeling the sky tear, the motion of it shivering up his arm. It is an impossible thing, but so is this place, so is he. He feels something give, and a cry of triumph breaks from him. The storm continues to batter him, but his ship continues to rise.

Hook lowers his gaze to where Bartholomew lies curled in on himself upon the deck. The man shudders, his form blurs, and Hook catches his breath as he sees the man doubled, one self pulling away from the other. Then in a blink, Bartholomew is gone. Gone. Passed through the door. Out of this world and into another one. Hook lets the laughter free now, aware that he sounds mad and not caring. He's done it. He's opened a door and he cut them free.

The air continues to shiver and hum where Bartholomew lay. He's gone, but Hook can almost see him there still as well. An echo. A shape pressed against the skin of the world, screaming.

It's unsettling, but it must be his imagination. The blade did its work, but there's more work left to be done. He needs to hurry.

"Bring the rest!" Hook shouts.

Samuel leads Harrigan forward now. In the surgeon's grip, Harrigan is too stunned to even protest. His eyes are over-large, his mouth slack. As Hook reaches for Harrigan, Killdeer slams into him. They roll together across the swamped deck and fetch up against the rail, Killdeer on top of him, bearing down. The ship tilts, dropping, the blade's magic faltering. Killdeer will ruin everything.

Hook lashes out at him, missing, leaving himself open for Killdeer to land a blow. Hook's ears ring. Even in the storm, Killdeer's face is terribly clear—a snarling dog protecting something precious to him.

"You won't touch him." As he spits the threat, Killdeer raises a fist to smash into Hook's face again, but a fresh wave sweeps the deck, knocking him off balance.

Hook bucks, twisting, and manages to get one arm free. He buries his hook in Killdeer's shoulder, leaving the other man shouting in pain. Hook rolls free, scrambles up.

The air swarms with shadows, swamping his vision. He swings wildly now, not even looking to see where the blade will bite next, letting the knife itself guide him. He's running out of time. With every cut, Neverland fights back. More and more ropes of shadow lash the crew, trying to bind them. Hook slashes, panting, trembling. Rough hands grab at his collar. He hears the surgeon's voice above the fray, calling for him.

Before he can turn to look for Samuel, the ship lurches again. The blade skitters in his hand, sinking into something soft, catching on bone. There's a tearing, one Hook feels shuddering up his arm and there's a scream—Killdeer?—an animal sound. Hook yanks backward. His feet slip on the deck, slick with more than water now. A body barrels into him, and this time he crashes to one knee. Pain explodes from the point of impact and jars upward.

"Captain!" He catches sight of Samuel, trying to reach him, but Killdeer is suddenly between them.

Hook blinks. Looks down. The man under him, no longer screaming, is Harrigan. Not Killdeer. His eyes are open, glassy, rain and seawater washing streams of red away from him. Hook's arm trembles, his whole body trembles, and still the knife keens in his grip, wanting.

For a moment, Hook is outside his body, seeing himself as Killdeer must see him, as Samuel must see him. Drenched in gore and seawater, chest heaving, knife in his hand, eyes burning mad.

Can none of the rest of them feel the door in the sky? Is he mad after all? Has he murdered his crew?

The tension in Killdeer's jaw, the look in his eyes as he'd spat his threat not to touch Harrigan circles through Hook's mind. Something flickers in Killdeer's eyes, dangerous, rage freed from any need to restrain itself. There are no words when Killdeer roars and launches himself forward.

But it isn't Hook he reaches for this time. Instead he catches the surgeon about the waist—thick to Samuel's slightness—and slams him to the deck. A cry lodges in Hook's throat. He tries to stand, but his knee buckles, bringing on a fresh spike of pain. Rain sluices down the collar of his coat, then fingers tangle painfully in his hair, pulling at his scalp as his head is yanked backward.

"You don't deserve this ship, or these men." Killdeer's face is inches from his own. "And I'm going to take them from you. Every single one. Starting with this one."

He gestures behind him to where Samuel lies wheezing on the deck, then Killdeer smashes a fist into Hook's face. The world blooms with stars, not in the sea or the sky, but behind Hook's eyes. Blood nearly chokes him and he spits red onto a deck already slick with it as Killdeer lets go, bootheels pounding as he stalks toward Samuel.

Hook's skull rings with the aftershock of the blow. But somehow, he's still holding the blade and he swings it before Killdeer moves beyond reach. The point catches. He twists and there's a howl. The world stutters, black and red, a smear like blood across his sight. Hook loses sense of what is here, what is now, time slipping and shattering, a seam somewhere ripping and everything coming apart.

When his vision clears, Samuel crawls across the deck toward him, still wheezing. He half collapses into Hook as Hook reaches for him. Samuel's fingers tangle in Hook's shirt and the lapels of his coat, trying to hold himself upright or trying to keep Hook from falling.

A thin line of blood traces from a cut above Samuel's eye, washing to pink in the rain. All at once, Hook finds his body incredibly heavy. He wants nothing more than to sleep. Only Samuel's body, propped against his, holds him up. Shadows swarm around them, flickering in and out of focus. The ship is too empty and too full, occupied by ghosts. Did he set them free? Or is his crew dead by his own hand?

"Samuel?" Hook's voice is raw, his throat bruised. His face aches where Killdeer struck him.

A low note thrums up his spine, making it hard to concentrate. He can't remember. Who—what—he is. What he meant to do. Samuel's expression is haunted, eyes wide and luminous. Stars. There were stars in the water. He remembers that and nothing else.

"I have to…" Hook raises the hand still clutching the blade as though the metal is seared to his skin.

Bedraggled. Blood-smeared. A true monster. He holds the blade between them, point wavering. Samuel's fingers are still tangled in the fabric of his shirt, the only thing holding him up. Samuel's face is very close to his own.

"I have to finish it," Hook says.

"I trust you." Samuel licks his lips, meets Hook's gaze—steady, determined, afraid. "Captain."

He means to say thank you. Instead, he plunges the blade down. Into shadow, he hopes, not flesh. Samuel's eyes widen further, stars blooming in them, his mouth opened. Blood, red as a poppy, spreads petals across his chest. No. Not blood, Hook thinks, something else. Life. Hook catches Samuel's hand, brings it to the hilt of the blade and wraps his fingers around it before wrapping his own overtop.

They're falling. Rising, the storm and waves catching them up, pulling them into the sky. With his hand wrapped atop Samuel's he turns the blade on himself and plunges it down again.

Pain, such as he's never felt, even dying a thousand times before. Numb fingers slip, ready to let go. Hook cants sideways, still holding blade, his weight still behind it. The final cut, the last tether of shadow holding the ship in Neverland and keeping it from rising through the hole cut in the sky. When it strikes the deck, the blade shatters. Fragments of pitted iron, ancient stone, as cold as stars, bury themselves in the meat of Hook's leg as he collapses atop them.

But they're rising. Flying. They're free.

The wood of the ship screams, the knife and the storm both working to rip it apart.

Hook grabs at Samuel, clutching on to him. It's not just the storm howling. It's Pan, the voice of Neverland itself, raging against its loss. Hook shouts right back, a raw and wordless sound amidst the snap of timbers.

Hook wraps both arms around Samuel, as if after everything, he could shelter him from the storm.

"It's over now," he says. "It's done."

Hook buries his face against Samuel's shoulder. Under the blood and the damp, the smell of leather and tobacco still clings to the surgeon. He feels foolish, small, like a child. His breath hitches, everything hurts. He's afraid.

But if he is going to die, truly this time, he will not do it lying down like a dog. He forces himself to a sitting position, biting down on a cry of pain. He manages to get upright, leaning back against the shattered mast. He pulls Samuel into his lap, and tilts his head back, letting the rain run into his eyes and his open mouth.

"It's done."

The world explodes, green and white and blue. The stars yawn in a terrible whirlpool; the sky is a mouth, and those points of silver are teeth. Hook laughs, a terrible, bubbling sound. A hand grips his. He looks down. Samuel's eyes are open, and they find Hook's.

"I trust you, Captain," he says again.

The ship shudders and blurs and splinters around them. The sky is white and the stars are black and everything is inside out. And then the entire world tears itself apart.

A BODY REMEMBERS

Through the window behind Hook's head, Wendy notes the sky just beginning to shade to pearl-gray, the stars fading to opalescence. Dawn light, but no hole in the sky, no ship sailing through. Wendy tugs her robe closer, cold and unsettled in a way that has nothing to with the lack of fire, or even Hook's story. Not exactly.

Hook. The name returns to her, not James, despite everything he did to escape Neverland. Wendy's frown deepens. She glances to her daughter, sitting on the same side of the hearth as her, but with a respectable distance between them. Jane's head droops with exhaustion.

"It's late," Wendy says. "Or early, rather. We should all try to get some rest."

Jane is the first to stand. She says nothing as she leaves the room, and Wendy listens to her climb the stairs. James is slower to rise, stiff, his leg clearly paining him. Wendy can't read his expression.

"Is the room all right? Are you comfortable?" She falls back on playing the good hostess, though she is uneasy in her own home.

Hook's story is almost too incredible, and yet she has seen a boy separated from his shadow. She herself has passed through a hole in the sky.

"Everything is perfect. Thank you." James takes her hand, wooden fingers under hers, flesh and blood ones briefly patting her own, startling her.

When he lets go, she listens to him make his slow way up the stairs. Was it a mistake inviting him here? Since their arrival, Wendy hasn't even had a moment to properly speak to Ned. What does he think of her, inviting this man—this stranger, her old enemy—to their home, unannounced? And what of Michael? Did she even spare a thought for her baby brother, and what seeing Captain Hook again might do to him?

No. She did not. For all she has grown and changed, for everything she'd lived through, Wendy is still sometimes the callous and thoughtless girl who flew through the window with her hand in Peter's and never once thought to look back or hesitate. All through supper she saw the way Michael's eyes slid away from James, as though with every accidental glance he had to force himself to edit the former captain from reality.

Wendy carries the empty brandy glasses to the kitchen before returning to the parlor. It's still early, but she won't sleep again. It's Christmas Eve morning. The thought strikes her; Christmas Eve morning, but the air hanging about the house feels as far from celebration as possible. Tomorrow will be Christmas Day. She and John and Michael used to thrill on Christmas morning as children, waking early, waking their parents, opening presents and exclaiming over each one.

There were always oranges, and spiced nuts, and something

delicious and roasted for dinner. Before Neverland. Life seemed so much simpler back then.

She moves to the hearth, setting a fire for something to do with her hands. Wendy thinks back to the ruin of Hook's ship on the beach. When she'd returned to Neverland looking for her daughter, she'd crawled through the ship searching for something to use against Peter, something to help her rescue Jane. She'd found Hook's sword. How could the sword have been there though? How could the ship even have been there? Hook himself had said he'd sailed it through a hole in the sky.

But hadn't she felt—without knowing what it was she was feeling—the ghosts of Hook's pirates, moving all around her as she explored the ship? She'd seen Hook's eye, looking up at her from the broken mirror glass on the floor. Is it possible that Hook both escaped and remained? That his pirates crossed through a door in the sky, but that some part of them lingered. Trapped. The thought chills her.

Is some part of the captain still trapped there in Neverland? And what of Wendy herself?

Once invited, always welcome. Once invited, never free.

Wendy shudders, even as flames lick around the wood piled on the grate. She isn't welcome anymore. She saw to that by stitching Peter's shadow, his real shadow, back in place. Jane and Hook both saw the tear in the sky; but she couldn't even see the door, let alone tell whether it was closed, or whether it might open for her once again.

She sinks back into the chair by the fire, but it doesn't make her feel any warmer. She wants to stop time here. She wants to run out into the cold winter morning and keep running. Wendy

Darling, fleeing from the world once again.

It's not just Ned, she's barely spoken to Jane either. She is the parent, the one who is supposed to keep Jane safe, heal all her wounds, and make all the bad things go away.

"Windy." Michael's voice, soft in the doorway, startles her and Wendy raises her head.

"I didn't think anyone else would be awake this early." Michael takes a step into the room, his posture uncertain, leaning on his cane.

Wendy gestures at the chair across from her, and after a moment, Michael sits, stretching his leg out, and rubbing it.

"Mothers never really sleep deeply when their children are home." She smiles, trying to turn it into a joke.

Michael nods, his expression troubled and distant. His ghosts are there in his eyes, as close to the surface as Wendy has seen them in a while. Is it Hook, or news of the war, or both? She has the sudden urge to ask him if he had a bad dream, the way she would in the nursery when they were children, making room for him and John both on her bed, pulling the covers up snug around all three of them and telling a story. Even before Neverland, they'd had their own private world, inhabited only by them.

"It feels like there's something coming," Michael says, a crease marring his brow, lines at the corner of his mouth. "Like a storm. You know when you can feel it in the air?"

When he looks back at her, Wendy catches her breath. She can almost see it—an understanding of everything he chose to put aside, mixed in with everything he's lost.

"I know the feeling." Wendy almost asks him about Hook. In

her mind's eye, she kneels in front of her brother, taking both of his hands. *Tell me what you remember. I know it's still there inside you. Tell me what to do.*

Wendy grips the arms of her chair. If Michael notices the faint tremor, he must put it down to the cold, despite the fire burning between them.

"Sometimes I feel as if I'm not done with the war. Or it isn't done with me. I don't know a better way to explain it." His eyes ask *her* to explain it—loss, confusion, asking her to explain why people can't stop hurting each other.

It breaks Wendy's heart. She has no answers for him, nothing to offer. She rises, not taking his hands as she imagined, but perching on the arm of his chair. She thinks of them as children, when they both would have been slight enough to fit in the seat together. She leans sideways, puts her arm around him. Perhaps that is what she's missing, a thing impossible to have—the ability to take hurt away, to explain away the monsters and protect everyone she loves. The more she tries, though, the harder, it seems, she fails.

Michael resists for a minute, instinct stiffening his muscles. Then he sinks into her so that she can lean her cheek against the top of his head. Tears prick at her eyes, but she forbids them from falling. She can't protect him, no matter how badly she wants to. She can't protect Jane. She can't do anything at all, other than putting the people she loves the most in danger.

LONDON – 1916

Wendy follows nervously behind her brothers, her hands constantly rising as if to reach out for them, then falling back to her sides. Michael's arm is slung about John's shoulders. He left the hospital with a cane, but he's still getting used to it, and John takes nearly all of his weight. Their steps are slow, the tilted angles of their shoulders and bodies all wrong, as if a hard wind were blowing at them both from opposite sides. She wants to help, and she has no idea how.

"Careful, now. This is the tricky bit," John says as they reach the steps.

Just three steps up to their front door, but it seems an impossible mountain. If they could fly, Wendy thinks, and shoves the thought down as soon as it occurs, biting the inside of her cheek.

John's breathing is rough. One step. Two. A catch of breath from Michael, a sound of pain. Wendy's heart lurches through the space between them like the useless fluttering of her hands. Her brother, her baby brother. A grown man. Old enough to put on a uniform and go to war and come home again broken, but a child in her eyes still, and there's nothing she can do to help him.

She keeps her hands ready, stretched to catch them both if they fall, even though she knows their combined weight would knock her down. She holds them that way until John has the door unlocked and they are both inside.

Wendy spent the morning making up the small room at the back of the house that used to be their father's study. Until Michael's leg is further healed, it seemed sensible to install him on the ground floor. Wendy did her best to make it as cozy as possible—she'd even put in a vase with fresh flowers to make the room cheery and bright—but she can't help but fret. There wasn't space to put a bed, but their father's old chair is there, and an ottoman so Michael can stretch out his leg. Michael has said he prefers to sleep sitting up now anyway, when he sleeps. It helps with the pain in his head, the ringing in his ears, which the doctors have assured them will fade.

She watches her brothers, standing awkwardly in the doorway as John installs Michael in the chair. It's high-backed, the wings of it rising up above Michael's head as he slumps down, making him look even smaller—a child's abandoned doll.

"I'll make tea." John's tone is brusque with strain.

Wendy is about to object, to say she'll do it, but he's already brushing past her, back into the hall. It strikes her that John is afraid to be alone with Michael, afraid of his drawn expression and the way the color seems washed from his eyes.

After a moment, she approaches, folding herself into the space beside Michael's chair and looking up at her brother. Michael's face is turned slightly away. The angle of his neck makes his collarbones look sharper, just visible beneath his shirt. Wendy rests her hands on the chair's arm, just short of touching him. The veins on the back of his hands stand out. There's a pallor to him, a translucence, fading right before her eyes. It's as though she can see all the hollow spaces inside him right through his skin.

"Can I get you anything? A cushion? A blanket?" Her voice sounds too loud in the room's stillness.

Michael starts to shake his head, but it's clear even so slight a motion pains him. He presses his lips together, a thin, bloodless line, and the fingers of his right hand, the one farthest away from her, dig into the chair's arm for a moment.

"I'm fine." His voice is scarcely a whisper, pale as he is.

Wendy doesn't know what to do with her hands, doesn't know what to do with herself. Should she try to hold his hand, comfort him? Beyond the door, the sounds of John making tea in the kitchen are just audible. Wendy licks her lips, which have suddenly gone dry, keeping her voice low.

"Do you remember when we were children?" She swallows around a lump in her throat. Michael doesn't turn his head, doesn't acknowledge her.

Wendy's stomach tightens with nerves, a mixture of excitement and fear. Surely, now, after everything he's been through, Michael must remember. What better way to erase the war for him than to take him back to Neverland, at least through shared memories? Fill up all those hollow spaces with wonder so there's no room for hurt.

Her blood sings, the weight of words built up inside of her. She shifts her hands, resting them on top of her brother's arm and leaning forward slightly. She cannot let John hear, but she cannot keep the excitement from her voice either even as she struggles to find the best words, to not startle Michael or frighten him away.

"Do you remember when we went…away? To a place that wasn't in London. Not anywhere in England even?"

Michael finally lifts his head to look at her. There's a sharpness to his cheekbones that for a moment gives Wendy the impression that she's seeing his skull straight through his skin. Michael's lips part. There's a hurt look in his eyes, a weariness, as though he'll ask her to stop, as both he and John have so many times before.

Wendy, please, not this foolishness again. These stories, we're too old for that sort of thing now.

But if she could just make him see, make him understand how good this could be for him. A tremor passes through Michael's body, a shaking beyond his ability to control, as though something deep inside of him is trying to shed by force the memory of what was done to him.

"What if we could go back there? What if I could take you there, and all of this," she waves her hand, indicating his leg, his head, "could just stop?"

Her voice rises, despite her efforts to keep it low. The longer she speaks, the more certain she is that it will work. This, finally, is what will allow her to call Peter back to them. He will see how much Michael is hurting and come rescue them.

"Wendy—" Michael's voice catches.

His eyes swim. In them, behind them, it's as though there are spaces opened up inside of him that didn't exist before. Nightmares crouch there. Ghosts. But she can patch those spaces with stars and make-believe and games of chase and all the beauty of Neverland. She can make him better in a way no doctors, no medicine ever can.

"Don't you see? It's the only way. And I'm sure—"

Michael's gaze shifts, past her, and Wendy looks over her shoulder to see John standing in the door, holding a tray laden with tea. His gaze goes between them, taking in the scene and understanding it in an instant. A frown pulls at the corner of his mouth, eyes an admonishment, and a new weight sloping his shoulder.

"I was only—" She jumps up, ready to make her case.

John sets down the tea tray with a sigh and takes her shoulders. Even as he speaks, he moves her gently, turning her toward the door.

"Perhaps it would be best if you gave Michael time to rest." Not *we* but you, Wendy specifically, closing her out of the space she'd believed to be occupied by all three of them—the Darling children against the world.

Absurdly, she thinks of Peter's games of war, from which she'd

174

been excluded. And even though John's poor vision had kept him from the war Michael fought, here Wendy is pushed to the other side of the sudden wall between them, a world for men and a world for her. But anyone with eyes can see that Michael is hurting, and all she wants to do is make him better, like she did back in Neverland.

"If you would just—" she starts again, trying to step around John, but his hand on her shoulder is firm.

He moves her backward, not pushing, but with an inexorable pressure, a force that will not be moved. Wendy finds herself standing on the other side of the study door, John blocking the threshold. She wants to stamp her foot, to shout, to make them see reason. Why won't they listen to her, why must they so stubbornly refuse to see the truth of things?

"Please," Wendy says, and then, "Michael."

She shifts her gaze, past John, trying to catch her youngest brother's eye. He turns his face away, like a child hiding from a monster he doesn't want to see, almost burying it in the angle formed between the wing and the back of the chair.

"Enough." John's voice is firm, and Wendy's eyes snap back to him, startled to see he's fighting back tears.

Wendy's mouth drops open, but there's nothing else she can say. Beyond John's shoulder, Michael's body hitches. He is utterly silent, but every line of him speaks to heartbreak, a little boy, lost and alone. John removes his hand, and at that, Wendy takes a step back. John closes the door, a final sound, closing himself and Michael away with Michael's grief, and leaving Wendy stranded in the hallway, alone.

A CITY OF RAIN

LONDON – 1917

Water sluices over him, no longer the battering waves of a storm. It takes him a moment to realize the water is rain pouring off the edge of a building. Hook blinks the stinging downpour from his eyes. He remembers drowning. Panic grips him, a fist squeezed about his lungs. But no. He isn't drowning, not anymore, perhaps never again.

He's on his back, looking up at a narrow slice of gray sky. There's a body flung over his, clinging as a man clings to a spar of wood in a wreck. He tries to push himself upright, and fails. There's something missing. The smooth stub of his wrist protrudes from the cuff of his sleeve. His hook is gone.

Bitter laughter rises to his lips, and he chokes it down. The sound turns to a cough, and he uses the other hand to push himself upright. The man lying across him stirs and sits up as well. Samuel. His pulse trips over a beat with unexpected relief.

They came through the storm together, but through to where? He'd been trying to get home, a place he barely recalls; is this the same place he left? All he can see is gray—the gray fall of rain, gray stone, and the gray sky above. Empty boxes and crates and worse crowd the narrow alleyway, thickening the air with stench.

"Captain?" There's a tremor to Samuel's voice; he shivers, whether from cold or shock, Hook can't tell.

Samuel rubs a hand over his face, does it again, a compulsive motion. It's as though he's trying to clear the world around them from his eyes, scrub it away. Samuel holds his hands out, studies them, turns them over.

"It doesn't hurt. It should hurt?" He sounds lost. "Did it work? Where are we?"

"I don't know." An answer to both questions. He feels different, less somehow, and unmoored. A ship without an anchor. He wanted to escape, to be free of that boy and his petty tyranny. But did he ever stop to think what that meant?

His…sister. Yes. He'll find Anna. She'll give them a place to stay, and… But where would he even begin to look? How long has he been gone? She might be married now, or living somewhere else entirely. When he didn't return as he promised, where would she go? And would she even recognize him now?

Samuel stands, and Hook tries to follow him. But once again, he tries to push himself up with his absent hook, and almost falls. Samuel catches him, steadies him, and helps him upright.

"Your hand, Captain." Samuel's eyes widen slightly, and the words *your hand* jolt through him as though the hook were an inevitable part of him.

Isn't it though? He brings his eyes to focus on the smooth stump of his wrist. The phantom pain of jaws closing, severing nerve, severing bone, rewriting him; his throat tightens in response. His pulse speeds, an autonomic thing, leaving him wanting to scramble

177

to hold on to something he lost a long time ago—his self, one he barely even remembers.

But when he reaches after that self, the one he was before, all that comes to mind is stepping onto his ship for the first time, feeling it settle around him like a new suit of clothes, perfectly fit. His feet had carried him to the captain's quarters without hesitation, and it had felt like coming home. There, waiting for him in the center of the pillow on the richly brocaded bed, had been the hook, like a holy relic.

He'd lifted it, seen the marks of wear on the leather cuff, and a stain on the hook itself that made him think of blood. Holding it had left him dizzy with the sensation of being pulled out of himself, something else trying to move in beneath his skin. He'd been afraid, but only briefly. In the next instant, the hook had been pristine again, and he'd slipped it onto the end of his wrist where—as far as he could recall—a hand had never been.

The leather cuff had hugged the end of his arm, molding itself to him. He'd felt the echo of violence clinging to it, the sense that it belonged to another life, another man, and at the same time, the man that it belonged to had also been him. A full circle, the past, the present, his future all collapsed to the single sharp point gleaming at the end of his arm. His ship. His home.

He'd felt his lips stretch, his teeth bared, his steps already carrying him back to the deck to shout orders, knowing his crew would be there waiting for him. Power. A ruthless lust for adventure, for blood, all of it singing through his veins. In that moment, he'd never wanted to be anything else, shedding whatever he'd once been—only a pirate, only Captain Hook.

And now? Samuel watches him as he contemplates the smooth skin, the faint outline of bone underneath. He touches the spot. He's been given a chance to reinvent himself, none of Pan's magic forcing itself on him this time. He has a choice now in who he wants to be.

"It seems I left it behind," he says.

Samuel still has ahold of his arm, and he doesn't shake him off. It's a strange comfort, a tiny scrap of warmth amidst the unfamiliar. Samuel's touch is solid and real through the fabric of his sodden coat. This, he thinks, not the point of a hook that slaughtered so many, this could be his anchor, his self, his home.

"What do we do now? Where to do we go?" Samuel's voice teeters on the edge of breaking.

The way Samuel looks to him, seeking leadership, is suddenly unnerving. He's as lost as the surgeon, not captain of anything anymore. What is he without his hook? Without his ship, or his sword.

"Captain?"

"Don't call me that." The words emerge more sharply than he intends.

Samuel shrinks back, his hand sliding from the wet velvet, and immediately Hook regrets the loss. Hook. The name grates in his mind, worse even than Captain.

"I…" Samuel falters, looking afraid.

All at once, he wishes he could take back every harsh command, every shouted word. He wants Samuel to see him with fresh eyes and none of the weight of their past between them. He doesn't want Samuel to be afraid of him. He has no way of knowing if any of the rest of the crew survived; they may be the only two left in the world—this world, at least.

"James," he says, breathing out, and a burden lifts as he does. "Call me James."

"James." Samuel says the name as though he's tasting some exotic fruit, sweet on his tongue, a precious gift given to him by his former captain.

A shudder, involuntary, passes up James's spine. The name settles on him, like his velvet coat, but an even better fit than the blood-red garment. It feels familiar. Maybe it was his name before, but it doesn't matter. It's his name now—a new name for a new life.

"We should get somewhere dry," he says, unable to look at Samuel anymore.

"Where are we, Ca—James?" Samuel follows him to the mouth of the alleyway.

The rain softens everything. Nothing looks familiar, and yet he remembers the dock, smells the sea, hears a gull cry. He remembers bidding Anna goodbye and promising to return. The world briefly doubles itself. He's here and in Neverland. He's leaving and arriving and leaving all over again, falling through the world. He catches himself on the wall, and Samuel is there again, steadying him.

"London." Speaking it aloud sharpens the edges of the city behind the curtain of rain.

Everything looked different then. Horses. The streets running with shit, both animal and human. This isn't the city he left, not anymore.

"We're in London, Samuel," he says, and he holds the last words in reserve, not daring to speak them aloud. *We're home.*

* * *

180

Another tremor wracks him, despite the covers pulled to his chin, despite the fact that he's sweating, clothes sticking to his skin.

"Here, drink this." Samuel perches on the edge of the bed.

Even the slight weight of the surgeon near him is too much to bear. James's bones ache with the fever working its way through him, leaving him bruised and hollow all the way through.

He fights the urge to slap the bowl from Samuel's hands. He doesn't want doctoring right now. He wants...

James fights a breath, lets it out. Samuel's gaze is steady, concern mixed with a kind of disappointment, judgment without as many words saying that this is precisely what James deserves. The expression drains his anger, leaving misery and self-pity in its place. And the realization that Samuel is still here; he hasn't given up on him despite his raving, despite his sickness. Samuel is still by his side.

"What is it?" James sniffs as he reaches for the bowl, and it nearly spills. Samuel catches it.

"Here, let me help." He holds the bowl where James can reach it and hands him a spoon.

Rage creeps back in. He isn't a child. But then, Samuel has allowed him the dignity of holding the spoon himself, and his hand *is* shaking. He sits up, tamping the anger back down, tamping down the humiliation as well.

Samuel watches for a moment, silent. A frown works its way onto his lips. Not a break in his infinite patience, but something else.

"I may be able to...obtain something to lessen your symptoms," he says after a moment, reluctance in his tone.

"What's wrong with me anyway?" The spoon scrapes against the bowl, an unintentional motion of his hand.

"You're in withdrawal." Samuel's lips crimp again, but James imagines he sees a small flash of sympathy there as well, and a warmth above and beyond the fever touches him. "Your body has grown use to certain...substances which you no longer have access to, and it's in revolt."

Just the words conjure the heavy scent of Neverland's flowers, the smell alone thick enough to bite. Lack makes him dizzy. Samuel sets the bowl aside, but despite the broth, the hollow feeling persists.

"I might be able to find something comparable here, to ease the transition. Only..." Worry flickers in Samuel's eyes, and James understands without his surgeon having to speak it aloud.

The deep pockets of his coat had been enough to save his compass and a small pouch of coins when they fell through the world. The coins—despite their strange markings—had at least been enough to rent them this room. How will they pay their way going forward? What does he know, save sailing and violence? And right now, he's in no condition for either.

"I'll find work," Samuel says, speaking to both of their thoughts, continuing before James can object. "The world is at war, and doctors are always needed in war."

There's a heaviness in Samuel's expression, sorrow. Yes, James remembers. War. He'd dragged them from one world of violence to another, but instead of boys with carved swords here there are whole countries at war, exploding canisters of gas and dropping bombs. Another tremor passes through him, and it isn't entirely to do with his need for the flowers' drug this time.

Samuel's expression is contemplative for a moment before he stands, gathering the bowl. "You should rest. I'll make inquiries."

Samuel moves toward the door, and James has the sudden overwhelming desire to call him back. He almost reaches after him, instinct lifting the arm that no longer ends in a hook before letting it fall atop the covers again. He remembers the hook skittering across Samuel's cheek, unintentionally drawing a line of blood. Whether he wants it or not, whether he intends it or not, he is a creature made only for violence. The thought is bitter, and now all he wants is for Samuel to get away from him. He doesn't deserve the kindness, hates Samuel for it. He hates himself, a pitiable, low creature.

"Captain?" At the door, Samuel pauses, concern in his voice.

"I told you not to call me that." James clenches his jaw against another tremor.

The memory of Anna pressing the compass into his hands, then pressing a kiss to his cheek, rises dizzyingly clear.

So you can always find your way home.

"My coat." He gestures, voice thick. "The pocket."

Samuel obediently fishes within, drawing out the compass. It glints in the light—electric, still a wonder after years, a lifetime, of flickering candlelight. Confusion remains in the surgeon's eyes. When Samuel tries to hand the compass to him, James presses it back into the surgeon's hand.

"Sell it. It may not be worth much, but it's bound to bring something. Enough to let us survive another day at least." He offers a weak smile.

Samuel opens his mouth to object, but James drops his gaze, shame welling in him. "Please."

The word, soft as it is, is strange on his tongue. It tugs at something deep inside of him. He is no longer Samuel's captain. He wants... He wants equality between them. He wants Samuel to help him, stay with him, not because duty demands, but because he chooses to do so. The realization settles heavy in his chest, but James cannot say any of it out loud.

His gaze flicks up again to find Samuel watching him, his expression unreadable. A faint scar marks his cheek, marring the symmetry of his face, yet adding to it somehow, making it more pleasing. It isn't a face like any other, it is uniquely Samuel's, marked by his hand. Guilt twitches in him at the same time as a strange, possessive thought—*mine*.

"I'm sorry." James touches his own cheek reflexively, then looks away again. "For everything."

"Thank you…James." There's the touch of wonder in Samuel's voice again, as if his former captain has become something unknowable and utterly strange. Perhaps he has.

The heat again, nothing to do with the fever, colors James's cheeks. All at once he regrets the electric light for fear it will show too much.

"Rest," Samuel says, his voice gentle. "I'll return soon."

James doesn't look up until he hears the door close, then he dares to lift his head again. The all-over bruised feeling of his body is slightly less for a moment, the terrible pressure of the future easing off him, if only for now. This isn't his London anymore, it isn't home, but perhaps it could be again, in time.

CHRISTMAS DAY

LONDON – 1939

The snow that began to fall in earnest at midday hasn't let up. James watches it through the window, thick flakes driven sideways by the wind until almost everything beyond the glass is erased in a flurry of white. It's a proper storm, unlike anything James can remember seeing in London before, and part of him can't help thinking that it isn't entirely of this world.

He takes another sip from his glass. Wind catches the edge of the house as it whips around it, howling, and for a moment, the flakes rearrange themselves. He sees teeth. A snout. A mouth open to shriek its displeasure with the voice of the wind.

He'd brought his pipe with him, of course, and found a quiet moment to draw in a few lungfuls of smoke from his dwindling supply, guilt dogging him as he did, but he's certain this is no illusion. A premonition, then? The beast is still out there, still hunting them, hunting him, and with all three of them who have been touched by Neverland together now, surely it can't miss. And perhaps that is better. No more hiding, cowering, hoping the creature will miss its mark and his luck will hold.

He will face it as befits a captain encountering his foe of old.

"We're, uh." A hand touches his shoulder, and James starts. "We're just about to sit down to supper, if you're ready."

Ned, Wendy's husband. He withdraws his hand quickly, rocking back a step. He looks uneasy, and James makes an effort to smooth his features, to look unthreatening. Sometimes, whether he wants to be or not, he is still the pirate captain, Hook rising to the surface to bury James. The way Ned looks at him, wary, makes James think the man must have tried to get his attention several times before now, only touching his arm as a last resort.

"Apologies, I was lost in thought." He is a stranger here, an intruder in their home, but he does not want this man to be afraid of him. He does not want any of them to be afraid of him. "And thank you. I'll be in in a moment."

James leans heavily on his cane, making a show of it, moving slowly. In truth, he needs a moment to collect himself, to make certain the veneer is in place. He's been slipping more and more recently, the opium helping and harming in equal measure as memories pull at him and try to unanchor him from time. He cannot afford to get lost, not here, not now.

A sharp nod from Wendy's husband and he withdraws, his movements still skittish and uncertain. James glances back one last time to the window, searching for teeth, searching for jaws in the storm. There's nothing, but the feeling of waiting, of a confrontation ticking ever-closer through the storm.

* * *

James braces his arm in his lap, trying again to tighten the straps of the wooden hand Samuel carved for him. He no longer shakes thanks to the opium and laudanum Samuel secured for him, but neither saves him for being purely clumsy. Even though they don't carry the strength of Neverland's flowers, at least the drugs take the edge from his yearning, keep the fever and cramping at bay. They quiet the nightmares, and give him some measure of peace.

As he tries to line up the strap with the buckle, the hand slips again and he nearly growls in frustration. He's sick at himself, his helplessness. He needs to be able to do this on his own without Samuel helping him.

Samuel has assured him over and over again that he'll grow accustomed with practice, but at the moment, James feels useless. He's grateful, and the hand is beautiful, expertly carved, decorated with whorls of silver, and yet in some way he can't explain, it unsettles him.

It isn't the mechanics of the hand itself, it's what it might mean. It is the memory of Samuel's face as he returned late from his work and presented James with a wooden box. When he'd opened it, James had seen at once that the hand wasn't merely functional, but a work of art. There's a warmth to the wood, not merely blond or red, but a bit of both, the natural grain of it somehow suggesting grace and motion.

He hadn't asked where Samuel obtained the wood, or the silver, but some part of him couldn't shake the feeling that somehow it had been carried over from Neverland. Something about the hand spoke of magic, and when he touched it, the wood had been warm, as if it held on to the light of another sun.

Had he carried the wood with him for this sole purpose? Or had he planned to make the hand for James even before, in Neverland?

There had been such hope in Samuel's eyes as he offered up the box, a light that caught James utterly off guard. Waiting for James's judgment, fearing disappointment. James had felt anything but. But when he'd looked up from the open box in his lap, utterly at a loss for words in the face of the surgeon's kindness, James had been stunned all over again to see sorrow.

Samuel had softened his voice and delivered news James had expected, but still hadn't prepared himself for fully. Samuel had found Anna, buried in a small churchyard, over fifty years ago. He'd been even more right than he'd known when it had occurred to him that the London he'd returned to wasn't the London he'd once called home. Years had passed, decades, the century had turned. While he'd been gone, Anna had grown, married, had children and grandchildren, and died after living a full life without him.

Holding the box with the hand in his lap, he'd tried to picture her grave. Would the stone be worn, or well cared for? She would have been buried next to her husband, he assumed, under a different name. Did her children and grandchildren visit? Did they lay flowers? Samuel had offered to take him there, but James had shaken his head.

"I'm a different person now," he'd told the surgeon. "Her brother never really came home."

Samuel hadn't seemed surprised, and James had wondered then if the hand was meant almost as a distraction, to soften the blow.

"I can help you try it on, if you'd like." Samuel had indicated, offering a saddened smile.

Words born of pride, making him want to snap a refusal, curled and died on James's tongue. He'd allowed Samuel to help, watching the surgeon's face rather than his hands as he secured the straps to hold the hand in place, utterly unable to look away. Samuel's touch was light and sure. And he'd found himself blushing when Samuel looked up, hating himself for it.

"How does it feel?" Samuel had asked.

James had barely registered the hand at all, stupidly spell-caught and feeling foolish for being unable to turn his attention away from the man kneeling before him with hope in his eyes. But the answer he'd given had been honest either way.

"Perfect."

The door bangs open. Startled, James nearly drops the hand, catching it just before it hits the floor. Samuel stands in the doorway, rain-drenched, pale and shaken.

"What is it?" James rises too quickly, and his leg reprimands him with a sharp pain that makes him catch his breath.

Normally, Samuel would key to the pain immediately. That he doesn't tells James, as much as his haunted expression, that something is truly wrong.

As quickly as his leg allows, he moves past Samuel to close the door. One-handed, and using the stump of his other wrist for support, he takes Samuel's coat from him, and hangs it near the door. Water pools at Samuel's feet. His hair hangs into his eyes, soaked as well, though he scarcely seems to notice. James retrieves a towel, hands it to him silently, then sets about, as best he can, making tea.

189

"On the way home, past the docks…" Samuel's voice shakes, the words trail.

James turns. Samuel's eyes are glassy, not seeing their flat, but something else entirely. His expression is hunted, as though something terrible might have followed him home. With one hand, James pours hot water from the kettle. He carries cups and the pot one at a time to the table in the center of the room, then gently guides Samuel to a chair.

In the months since they've been here, Samuel's work has brought them enough to move from the small, rented room they occupied when they first arrived to the entire third floor of a building looking out over the city through a window shaped like an eye. There's a small stove where they can prepare meals, and a bathroom one floor down that would be shared with other tenants if the floors beneath them were not currently empty. A building no one else wants in a neighborhood where others would prefer not to live.

There is only one bed, which James gave over to Samuel, ignoring every one of his protests. The place is Samuel's rightly, paid for with his coin. When James sleeps, which is rare enough anyway, it is on the chaise near the window.

His existence is by Samuel's grace alone, and as much as he wishes he could repay him, at the moment, James feels useless.

Samuel rubs his arms against a chill, as if finally noticing he's soaking wet. James puts a teacup in his hand and takes the chair opposite him.

"The docks," he repeats, prompting.

There is only one reason why Samuel would be at the docks, because there's no logical route that would carry him past the water

190

on his way home. Somewhere in the pocket of his sodden coat, still dripping on the floor, is a waxen envelope filled with opium. Guilt needles James. Whatever happened to Samuel that has him so shaken, it is only because he was there on James's account.

There are no obvious signs of bruising or violence. His pulse rises and falls again—fear and relief two sides of a single heartbeat.

"I saw…" Samuel hesitates, his eyes are once again those of a man looking to his captain for guidance, leadership, assurance that the storm will not sink them.

"Maitland," Samuel says finally, and James can only stare at him.

The name means nothing, and then it does, and memory rushes back to him, like a wave, rocking the deck beneath his feet. Maitland. The boatswain. How could he have forgotten? The blade in his hand and the storm raging, the deck slick, cutting and cutting at shadows.

"Are you certain? Did you speak to him?"

"I…" Samuel's hand jitters, tea spilling over the edge of the cup.

It shakes badly enough that James leans forward, taking it and setting it aside.

"At first it was as though he couldn't see me. He was unloading crates. I stood right in his path and still he looked right through me."

Without the cup in his hand, Samuel is steadier, but he still looks as though he might leap up and bolt, a rabbit wary of a hawk about to stoop.

"I thought he would walk right into me. It wasn't the crate he was carrying either. He could see over it. But…" Samuel shakes his head. "There was a…thinness to him, like when people tell stories about ghosts."

James stands, goes to the shelf beneath the window and returns with a bottle. He pours a measure of brandy into Samuel's cup. Samuel grimaces as he swallows. But he looks grateful when he sets the cup down, and something in James warms.

"I said his name, and it's only when I spoke that Maitland saw me. He startled, like he was afraid. And…" Samuel rubs a hand over his face, as if to rub away the memory.

"He dropped the crate. It broke open and oranges went rolling everywhere." A hysterical edge rises in Samuel's voice, and James tightens his grip on the bottle in his hand.

"He collapsed. The other men went right on working, like once Maitland saw me, we were invisible to everyone else." James thinks of his ship, the storm, the blurred sensation of seeing his men and not at the same time. Ghosts, split between this world and Neverland. Samuel continues. "I tried to lift him. He tried to speak, but I couldn't understand him. Then he…he fell apart in my hands."

"Fell apart?" James knows his tone should be kinder, gentler, but he can't make sense of Samuel's words.

"Like wet newspaper, coming apart in the rain. He…dissolved. I can't think of a better way to describe it."

Samuel picks up his cup, drains it, and unasked, James refills it with brandy alone this time.

"He was a solid, flesh and blood man one moment, and then he wasn't anything at all. Like he was rooted in this world until I saw him, and then he remembered he'd once been something else.

I think... I think he remembered Neverland, and it killed him."

The cup rattles in Samuel's hand. James takes it again and sets it aside. The motion puts him closer to Samuel than he intended to be.

"What if the same thing happens to us?" Samuel asks, dark pupils at the center of his eyes wide and drinking the light.

"It won't." James says it with as much confidence as he can, but his voice betrays him by catching.

He wants the words to be true, and more than that he wants Samuel to believe them. He wants to keep Samuel safe, and even more than that, James wants him to feel that safety. Because he's no longer certain what he would do without him.

It isn't just Samuel's coin, paying for the roof over their heads. If it came to it, James would find a way to survive. He is stubborn, above all else. But from the moment they fell through the world and into London, neither of them had even once considered going separate ways. They hadn't even asked the question.

Guilt flickers through him. It strikes him—he'd forgotten about his other pirates. Until Samuel mentioned Maitland, he hadn't once considered their fate once he'd opened the door in the sky and severed the shadows tying them to Neverland. At least, he thought he'd severed the ties, but he hadn't been sure—not then, just as he isn't sure now. He should have looked for them, they're his crew and he should be responsible for them. But once he knew Samuel had crossed with him safely, nothing else really seemed to matter.

"Why aren't you more bothered by this?" It isn't quite an accusation, but it's edging on one, as if Samuel knows exactly what he's thinking.

James flinches, trying to hide the motion with another sip

from his cup. Samuel is afraid; James understands. Anger is always easier than fear, always safer. If Samuel needs to lash out to protect himself, James won't fault him, but he won't apologize either.

"We're safe. That's all that matters." He doesn't mean it to sound flippant, cruel, but it does.

He sees it the moment Samuel's eyes shift—moss green shading to slate gray, like clouds coming down over the sun. Samuel's hand closes into a fist against the table to stop it from shaking.

"You don't know that. Just like you didn't know what would happen when you came here. You blundered ahead and you didn't ask and…" Samuel's voice trembles too.

He looks stricken, not just by his own fear, but by his daring in talking back to his captain, in challenging his rule, even though that's not what they are to each other anymore.

"Samuel—" James reaches, unsure exactly what he means to do, perhaps lay a comforting hand on the other man's arm, but Samuel jerks back, sending his teacup spinning to shatter on the floor.

"No. I can't." Samuel stands rapidly, chair legs scraping the floor. He leaves it unsaid what he can't do, burying his fingers in his hair and tugging as if he could pull free the sight of Maitland crumbling before him.

James tries to logic it out. Samuel is a scientist after all—if he can appeal to his rational mind he might soothe his worries. James has never once felt on the verge of crumbling. He is real and solid, yet he hasn't forgotten Neverland, comfortably astride two worlds, and if he ever feels too much the tug of one or the other, he has Samuel to remind him that it's within his power to choose who he wants to be.

Perhaps it's that. He and Samuel have each other. The rest of the crew, he presumes, were scattered, left to their own devices. It was easier for them to become lost, or there was already less of them to begin with. He never asked—he never thought to, never cared to—whether any of them remembered a life beyond his ship and the sea. Maybe whatever of them remained when he cut them free from Neverland was too fragile to be sustained for long.

None of this is comforting though. Samuel lowers his hand, half turned away. The hunch of his shoulders speaks misery even more than his voice, which is soft, still looking away from James while he speaks.

"Sometimes I feel…hollow, like part of me is missing. Don't you ever feel it? Like there's something I'm forgetting, a name on the tip of my tongue, or…" He lets the words trail.

James stands, using the chair for support. His hand lingers in the space between them with no firm decision as to where it will land. Why is this so hard? Compassion. Caring. He's no stranger to pain, but he's always been the one feeling it or causing it. This—healing—is Samuel's territory, and he's utterly lost.

"It's like part of me still exists there. Whatever…Peter did to us changed us, and I can't help feeling that one day it will call me back as though we never left at all."

"You're not like Maitland. You're not like the others."

"Why?" Samuel faces him now, the motion all at once pleading and accusing. He needs something from James, a tug James feels like a thread tied deep within his core. "Why am I different? What keeps me safe?"

Me. The word is there like a thunderclap, but he doesn't say it aloud even as it changes the air pressure in James's chest, flipping the world upside down. Defeated, Samuel drops back into his chair, shoulders slumped. But he's still looking at James, asking for assurance that nothing bad will ever happen to him.

An ache stretches all the way through him, a hollow, but not like the one Samuel described. It's a specific hunger, and if he let himself, it would be easy enough to fill. Because he knows exactly what it is that's missing, what he wants. And it isn't some undefinable piece of him left behind in Neverland. It's right here.

He forgot Maitland. He forgot the other pirates. Because nothing besides Samuel had been worth remembering.

James moves a step closer so his shadow falls over Samuel. Close enough that his leg almost touches Samuel's where they splay almost boneless. For one terrible moment, James sees it—a thinness—and he imagines Samuel vanishing the way he described Maitland crumbling. He will not let that happen.

His breath tangles in his throat, heart beating a rhythm that's almost painful. Everything hangs on the cusp, waiting to tip over into the moment that has been there ever since they crossed, hunting him, haunting him, as sure as Pan's stalking beast, but a thousand times kinder and more terrible.

He places the stump of his wrist alongside Samuel's cheek, against his scar. Samuel doesn't pull away. His face is already tipped up toward James with naked wanting, asking for comfort. James's touch nudges Samuel's chin up further. James holds him there a moment, holds his breath a moment, to see if Samuel will startle back like a spooked horse.

His eyes are only green now, the clouds receded. James hears the faint catch in Samuel's breath—the shift from one kind of need to another.

There's barely any space to close now when James finally leans down to put his lips against Samuel's. He tastes brandy and tea, heat and fear and hunger. He threads the fingers of his hand through Samuel's hair, still rain damp. He pulls Samuel to stand with him. For once, his leg doesn't ache, and he's able to move almost with ease.

The floor sways beneath them, the deck of a ship. Crashing them into each other and tipping them back toward the bed. Samuel's bed. Only it isn't. Because it has always been their bed, and like everything else, it isn't even a question between them.

James works at the top button of Samuel's shirt one-handed, frustrated when it won't yield. In his impatience, he tears it. The button makes a soft sound hitting the floor and rolling away, and a small wave of shame takes him—that he should be so undone by this man who never belonged among his pirates—too kind, too good.

"Let me." The gentle curve of Samuel's smile, the look in his eyes, takes the shame away immediately. It is what James has wanted since they first arrived here, for things to be equal between them. And now they finally are.

Samuel undresses them both. It is a slower, more methodical thing than James would ever have accomplished. For the first time since arriving in London, he wishes for his hook; he is used to navigating the world with it, and with it he wouldn't feel so helpless. He could simply slash the buttons from both of their clothing in a single motion.

But there is virtue in Samuel's method as well. The delay, the anticipation. James shivers. Samuel's smile deepens. Not a surgeon and his captain anymore. No part of James is in command of even himself now, let alone anyone else. His legs tremble, weak, and he decides to simply abandon himself to it. It is only a matter of a single, light push to the center of his chest—that and Samuel's eyes, green and steady on his own—toppling him backward onto the bed. Their bed.

A ship, tossed at sea, and this, a haven in the midst of the storm. An anchor for each other, giving weight to the promise he tried to make moments ago. James will hold on as hard as he can. He will not let Samuel go. They will keep each other safe from disappearing. This, here, the hunger sweeping through him— greater and sweeter than his hunger for any drug—is real. James lets that hunger consume him. He lets himself consume, so that every space in him is filled, and there is no room for any world but this one.

Neverland cannot touch them. Not ever again.

LONDON – 1939

Snow taps against the glass, thick and fast. James feels it at his back, the storm growing worse. Even though he's a stranger in her home, Wendy has given him the place at the head of the table, perhaps so she can keep an eye on him. Wendy and Ned sit opposite each other next to him, Michael beside his sister, Jane beside her father.

The table fairly groans with food, candles lit in the spaces between the plates and cups for wine. The strains of music swirl, just on the edge of his hearing. Not Christmas music, as would suit the occasion, but an old drinking song, something his men would sing. He's certain no one can hear it but him. There are flickers, shadows, moving around the edge of the table like ghosts. He tries not to look for Samuel among them. When the wind circles the house, even though the exterior is brick, James hears the creak of boards on a ship.

He is here and he is not here and something terrible is coming. He lifts his glass. It doesn't feel right to offer a toast, but at least he might thank his hosts. He opens his mouth and just then the wind comes like a battering ram, striking the window behind him. The glass shatters. Darkness screams through the room, extinguishing the candles. James throws himself forward, old memories of cannonballs splintering wood making him instinctively seek cover. Chairs crash over, but Jane is the first to rise.

"It's here." The wind snatches her words, tearing them away.

James raises his head. Another gust eddies snow into the room, which unerringly finds the back of his neck. But the ice tripping the length of his spine is nothing to do with the weather. The beast is there. Do the others see it? Open jaws, and a long, scaled tail.

"He's the one you want. He's here." Jane makes a grab at his shoulder, as if to push him into the beast's path.

The creature turns, lashing, snapping. At last, James thinks. And he sees what took the beast so long. Its eyes are moonlight and smoke, blinded by cataracts. Not Pan's creature anymore, but some broken fragment of it. But who holds the leash?

He pushes Jane away, and his hand goes to his hip as he tries to get his feet under him, but of course his sword is longer there. His cane leans against the wall and he stretches, managing to snag the tip of it and pull it close enough that he can lever himself up. And just as soon as he does, pain doubles him over, like a hot poker driven into his thigh, the shards of an ancient knife, shattered and buried there at once burning and freezing.

As he bends with the pain, the beast sails over his head. Jane shouts a warning, but too late. Michael, the last still seated at the table, is right in the beast's path. Jane lurches toward her uncle, but misses. James looks up in time to see the shadow-beast strike Michael Darling full force in the center of the chest. Rather than emptying him though, it sinks into him. The chair topples over backward, Michael with it, both crashing to the ground.

Wendy yells, scrabbling over broken plates to reach her brother. A steady wave of pain throbs up James's leg.

"Michael. Can you hear me?" Wendy shakes her brother.

As she bends over him, James sees not the man, but a boy with a mop of blond hair and wide blue eyes clutching his sister's hand, another boy with moonstruck owl eyes behind over-large glasses on her other side, all three crowded together against the mast of his ship.

"It's in him." Jane's voice shakes, anger just as much as fear. "It didn't kill him. Is it because he's been to Neverland too, even if he doesn't remember?"

She asks the question out loud to no one in particular. Is that what the beast meant to do to him, James wonders, burrow inside him? Did it mistake Michael Darling for him?

"Perhaps we should—" Ned begins, but whatever he is about to suggest is cut off by Jane whirling away from her uncle and toward James, her teeth practically bared and a wildness in her eyes.

"It should have been you."

He steps back, startled by her fierceness.

"You brought that thing here. You…" She lets the words trail, and for a moment, James thinks she might strike him.

"Jane." Wendy reaches for her daughter's arm, a gentling motion. "What—"

Jane spins toward her mother now, her eyes bright, her anger leaving her shaking.

"It should have been him. It came hunting him, but it found Uncle Michael instead, after it killed Peg, after…" Jane takes a shuddering breath. "It found the hollow and hurting place inside Uncle Michael, and now it's a part of him."

Wendy raises a hand to cover her mouth. Above her splayed fingers, her eyes are terribly bright—guilt and loss. For a moment, James can almost see the thoughts flickering behind her eyes— the creature took her brother, but it never once turned to her.

Michael stands, an unnatural, jerky motion. It's like his body is made of wood, someone else pulling the strings. In the next moment, as Michael moves, James thinks no, more like a suit moved by the body inside of it. Michael's cane lies on the ground, knocked over when his chair fell. He takes a step without it, the brace evident beneath his clothing perhaps the only thing keeping him from falling, the pain utterly ignored, because it is nothing to the thing inside of him.

"Michael?" Wendy reaches for her brother, who looks straight past her, straight at James.

At Hook.

There, like an arrow, shot straight to the heart of him. Recognition, and the old name falling back upon him. His pulse thuds. Michael's lips open, and it's a moment before sound emerges, and when it does, it's as broken and unsteady as his motion.

"Captain."

The voice coming from Michael Darling's lips is not Michael Darling's at all. It is an amalgam of voices. Harrigan. Killdeer. His lost pirates.

"We waited." The voices fracture, stutter, rise and fall, laced with an animal growl.

Michael's eyes, glassy in their focus, are muddy brown, and James is almost certain that Michael Darling's eyes, until a moment ago, were blue. Because they aren't Michael Darling's eyes, he thinks. They are Killdeer's, and Harrigan's. Maybe Maitland and Bartholomew as well. All the pirates he freed, or tried to free.

"We waited, Captain. For you. Hook. And you didn't come. You forgot about us, but we didn't forget. You. We remembered. The beast remembered."

James stares at Wendy's brother, at the thing—the things—inside him. Pan's beast, his pirates, some terrible amalgamation of all of them at once. Fragments of his pirates left behind in Neverland, the trapped shades of them making some terrible deal with Pan's hunting beast to find him. How, he wonders, has it been for them? How long have they suffered, blaming him for their demise? Brown eyes glare at Hook. Brown, tinted with a sick yellow-gold. The creature, the creatures, wearing Michael Darling like a second skin fix Hook in their gaze, and the look they turn on him is one of pure and utter hatred.

"We waited." A smile, nothing human, with too many teeth, stretches Michael Darling's lips. James grips the head of his cane. "Until you got careless. Hook. Until you opened. The door. And let us in."

THE HOLLOW BOY

LONDON – 1939

Jane steps back, anger and adrenaline draining to leave her shuddering as if with the cold. The tiny movement takes her much farther away, leaving her watching the scene unfolding as if she has no part of it at all. Her mother takes her place in turning to shout at Captain Hook. When Uncle Michael lunges suddenly, his wrong-colored eyes fixed in loathing upon the former pirate captain, his voice and movements broken, her father and mother are both there to catch him.

"Don't hurt him," Jane says, but her voice is small and lost in the chaos.

It's still her uncle, only there's something else wearing his skin. A scaled beast, the thing that killed Peg. But not just that, because it speaks with the voice of a man—multiple men.

Jane's thoughts snag on that, a weird mixture of sickness and hope. The beast was in her mother's stories, the enemy of the pirate-prince who she now knows to be Captain Hook. It killed him in at least one of her mother's tales, but here he stands in her parents' home, whole where her uncle is now broken. The rules for death are different in Neverland. Did the beast kill the men whose voices it uses to speak now? Or are they part of the beast somehow? One thing Jane is certain of is that she's looking at the beast that killed Peg. And she saw Peg on the lawn last night before the beast appeared—does that mean some part of Peg is inside the beast too?

The thought leaves Jane dizzy, her chest constricting.

There's broken glass everywhere, the wind and snow still howling in through the missing panes. Uncle Michael twists, leaning his weight forward. He looks straight past Jane. He doesn't seem to see her father either, though their bodies are braced against each other, her father trying to hold him in place. Uncle Michael shouldn't be stronger than her parents together, but it's clear they're struggling to hold him, even with his bad leg.

"We should tie him to a chair," Jane says, louder now, and all eyes turn to look at her. She feels like a stranger, an intruder, as the room falls silent. "So he doesn't hurt himself."

Or anyone else, is the part she leaves unsaid.

"I'll find something to cover the window." She needs to be doing something, and her decisive motion is enough to shake everyone else into action.

Jane returns with a sheet, a hammer, and a handful of nails. Her mother and father move Michael across the hall into the parlor. Jane rights one of the chairs, shards of glass slithering and crunching as she climbs onto the seat to reach the top of the window. The knot in her stomach remains at the thought of Peg somehow trapped by the beast, and her uncle, a prisoner in his own body. At least she hopes something of her uncle remains.

The chair wobbles. A hand at her elbow steadies her. Looking down, she sees Hook. She wants to be angry all over again, but she's just weary. She sets to work pinning the corner of the sheet in place with a nail, stretching it to the opposite side, then climbing down to repeat the same on the bottom as he watches her.

It feels good to be doing something, anything. Jane finds her hands remarkably steady. If she can just keep busy, find something useful to do, everything will be fine. The front of her dress is damp with snow by the time she's done, and she's cold. She takes a moment to survey the ruins of Christmas supper, the crackers by each place, the meal her father worked so hard on now grown cold. She bends to pick up a fork knocked to the ground, and Hook speaks softly.

"Don't you think we'd better join them?"

Jane doesn't look at him, but takes her time setting the fork back in place, straightening as if they might all sit down again at any moment despite the broken glass and the sheet pulling and snapping taut behind her. She wants to tell him to mind his own business, that he doesn't understand a thing about her family. This is all his fault.

But there's nothing left to do here, so she steps past him, and Hook follows her. Jane listens to the point of his cane tap the floor, focusing on her breath, on keeping her pulse steady. A fire crackles in the hearth, a cheerful counterpoint to the scene—her mother standing directly in front of her uncle, her father off to the side, looking uncertain.

"Michael?" Her mother touches her uncle's shoulder gingerly.

The sound that comes from her uncle's lips is a stuttering growl, caught somewhere between animal and human. He whips his head around, snapping his teeth, and her mother stumbles back. Uncle Michael keeps his teeth bared, almost a grin, too wide and too wild, as if the thing inside him changed the very structure of his bones.

His attention shifts to her as Jane steps forward, his eyes narrowing, the shine of them unnatural. It makes her think of something bright glinting underwater, a coin dropped into a dirty puddle.

"Jane, don't." Her mother reaches for her, alarm in her voice, but Jane ignores her.

Uncle Michael watches her approach. Or rather, the thing inside him watches. Jane searches his face for some evidence of her uncle trapped behind the shadow inhabiting him.

"He's still in here." The grin on Uncle Michael's face turns nasty, his narrowed gaze plucking the thoughts from Jane's mind.

"My uncle isn't the one you want." Jane's voice is steadier than she would have imagined. "Why don't you leave?"

All three of the adults watch her, waiting instead of any one of them taking charge. Tightness knots her belly. Another growling sound emerges as Uncle Michael's gaze slips past her, to Hook, and Jane understands it for frustration.

"You missed, and now you're stuck."

Baleful golden eyes turn to glare at her, then slide back to Hook again.

"He must suffer." The effect of the overlapping voices coming from her uncle's mouth is truly unsettling.

Part of her wants to strike the creature, even wearing her uncle's face. She imagines slapping him so hard his head snaps backward, blood threading from his nose. The impulse to violence shocks her, and she keeps her hands clenched firmly by her sides. Shadows move beneath her uncle's skin.

"Jane! Don't let them—" Her uncle's voice, a gasp like a man breaking to the surface of a wave, and then the words cut off, his head rocks backward as if she had struck him after all, a motion of such violence that Jane expects the crunch of bone.

Her uncle's body twitches, still bound to the chair. It's as if he's fighting for control. When his head comes up again, Uncle Michael's nose is bleeding, a thin line of crimson tracing its way to his upper lip, just as she imagined.

Did she strike him? Jane looks down at her hands, breathing hard. No. But the thing—the things—inside him have the power to hurt him.

"Michael!" Her mother moves forward.

Jane stops her mother, a hand on her arm before she gets too close. The curve of her uncle's smile, which is not her uncle's smile, tells Jane he would snap again, sink his teeth into her mother's hand.

"We have to take him to Neverland." Jane drops the words into the airless room. "That's where they belong. That's where he belongs too."

She gestures to Hook. Her voice surprises her with its calmness, its evenness, and at the same time, her pulse stutters. The rules of death are different in Neverland—hadn't she thought as much earlier? Perhaps there is a chance she can save Peg after all.

"Jane, you can't—" Her mother starts to protest, but Jane rounds on her, her fear, her nerves, all of it spilling out as anger.

"Why? Because Neverland belongs to you?" There are so many other things she could say, but Jane chooses words she knows will cut.

Her mother's eyes widen, face paling as though struck. Jane feels as if she's breathing very hard, as if she's run a long way. She was never given a choice to leave or stay. Peter stole her away. She lost Timothy. And now she's lost Peg as well. She needs someone to blame and she chooses her mother, because who else is there?

"Jane, that's unfair." Her father's voice is soft, wounded.

He's right; Jane knows as much, but if she doesn't hold on to her anger, she's afraid she'll collapse under the weight of grief.

"Neverland is unfair." She meets his eyes and the hurt in them almost undoes her. He's standing on the outside, only wanting to help her, help her mother, keep them all safe, but there's nothing he can do.

"I didn't—" Her mother's eyes shine, but Jane waves her words away, lifting her chin against the stinging in her own eyes.

"The captain and I were able to see the tear in the sky." Jane does not say pointedly that her mother could not; she does not look at her mother either. "That means the door is open to us, and we can go through it."

She's being cruel, but for so long it's felt as though her life hasn't belonged to her, and now she is finally reclaiming it. Peter stole her, yes, and her mother stole her back without giving her a chance to say goodbye to Timothy, to try to set things right. This is her chance to reckon with Neverland, maybe to help Peg, and to set one thing right at least to make up for all the things that have gone wrong.

She turns to face Hook. His expression is hard to read, but Jane keeps looking at him as she finishes what she has to say, because if she looks at her mother, her resolve might shatter.

"We will take my uncle to Neverland. We will undo whatever's been done to him. You will fix this, and you will not let anything harm him." Jane lays the last like a charge, partly to see what the pirate captain will do, but more so because she means it.

This is Hook's fault. The shadow followed him here, hunting him, killing people in trying to get to him. Jane means to hold him accountable.

"Yes," Hook says. There's a slant to his shoulders, weariness in his voice, but to his credit, he does not look away.

"Then it's settled." Only then does Jane turn to face her mother. She waits for the challenge. She waits for words that will break out into a fight. From the corner of her eye, she sees her father, distress clear in his expression. Part of her feels as though she's acting like a petulant child, throwing a tantrum. But doesn't she deserve to be a little childish? She had to grow up too fast, watching Timothy die, carrying the weight of his death. Her mother—an actual grown up—should have protected them both, but instead, she'd left Jane to take care of Timothy alone and she'd gone off to take her revenge on Peter. Had she ever stopped to think what it would do? No, she'd plunged ahead, childish in her own way, so certain she was right. And she'd refused to apologize for her actions, convinced still that she'd done the right thing. So how can Jane possibly think of forgiving her?

Jane expects her mother to draw up, to demand to go with them, to forbid Jane from going. Instead, her mother lowers her head. The look in her eyes the moment before she does—raw pain, loss, a grief Jane can't fully understand—nearly breaks her. Jane knows what Neverland was for her, but for her mother, it was entirely different. And there is the heart of it, the thing Jane knows deep down and doesn't want to acknowledge, because anger is safer, it's easier, armor to pull around herself to keep from getting hurt. Her mother will not apologize for what she did all those years ago, because she did it to save Jane. She made an impossible choice, let Timothy die, and tore Neverland down, all to bring Jane back home.

The thought leaves Jane breathless, chest aching with regret, but she swallows down whatever words she might say, and waits for her mother to speak.

"I understand," her mother says quietly.

She does not tell Jane to be careful. She does not tell her to come home safe. Is it defeat, or is she finally giving Jane her full trust, recognizing her fate lies in her own hands—to go or stay, to fight or flee, her choice, and her choice alone?

"Thank you." Jane says it so quietly that only her mother may hear, so quietly, she isn't entirely certain she's said it aloud at all.

The words are painful, spoken around the sudden lump in her throat, and for a moment, she wants to take back all her anger and blame. Instead, she reaches out, and squeezes her mother's hand. Their eyes meet and then, just as quickly, Jane lets go and turns to face Hook.

"We must be ready to leave as soon as the rip in the sky returns."

LOST GIRL

LONDON – 1939

Wendy pauses with a hand on the doorknob, key in her other hand. After a moment, she drops the key in her pocket without using it, and turns away. Whatever else he may be in this moment, he's still her baby brother, and she can't lock him in like a prisoner. Michael didn't fight them when they moved the chair to the small back room on the ground floor, meant to be quarters for a maid when the house was built. It makes her think, too, of the room at the back of her childhood home, her father's former study where Michael had first taken his convalescence after the war. But that was a self-imposed exile. How many times had he locked the door against her, preferring to be alone than suffer the only comfort she had to offer? Neverland.

That he seems utterly uninterested in breaking free unsettles Wendy. It is as though Jane's intention to take him to Neverland is exactly what he wanted all along. But to what end?

The key weighs heavy in her pocket as Wendy returns to the parlor. She's tired, but she has no desire to sleep, restless, feeling uncomfortable everywhere in her own home.

James stands before the fire, stirring logs with the iron poker with his cane leaning up against his leg. It is as though the mere idea of returning to Neverland has brought some of his old strength back, another thought that leaves Wendy uneasy. He wears his overcoat, ready, as Jane said, to leave at a moment's notice. The duffle bag Wendy helped carry to the station sits ready nearby. Though the coat is dark wool, not blood-red velvet, his stance is that of a pirate, a captain.

The fire poker might as well be a sword, his back straighter. It even seems he has grown taller somehow.

"I invite you to my house on Christmas, and now you're about to take my daughter and my brother away." She cannot quite summon malice into her voice, only weariness, and James turns with a faint smile on his lips.

"I should say rather it is your daughter who plans to take me away." He sets the iron poker back in its place, and he is just a man once more, no longer a captain or a pirate.

He studies her, and Wendy doesn't flinch beneath his gaze.

"She resembles you, and I imagine she is very much like you were at her age."

"I was far worse." Wendy allows herself a small laugh, mirthless. After a moment, she moves closer to the fire.

"Your brother," James says. "He remembers nothing of Neverland?"

It isn't precisely a question.

"Michael... When we came back from Neverland as children, I think he found a way to split himself in two. In order to keep living every day, he locked a part of himself a way, and simply never looked at it again. It's the same with the war. He closed off another part of himself, sent the part of him I used to know somewhere deep inside where he couldn't be hurt and all the killing and violence couldn't touch him."

Wendy feels James studying her.

"Everything he went through in the war, it's like Jane said earlier, that left…spaces inside of him. All that fracturing he did of himself, that's how the creature, creatures, got inside."

A shudder passes through her, despite the warmth from the fire.

"Your daughter is right. It was here for me," James says, his tone flat. "And you would have rather it had simply gone about its business, torn me apart, and left your family alone."

"Yes." Wendy finally raises her eyes to meet his, no apology in her tone. His expression tells her James expected none; his words were not even a question.

He knew the things that spoke with her brother's mouth, the pirates he left behind. The story he told about his ship and the knife, the magic he wielded without understanding—whatever he did must have trapped some part of them there, tied to Hook, but unable to follow.

"I am sorry to have brought this upon you." He inclines his head slightly. "And I will do whatever I can to set it right."

"Keep her safe, if you can," Wendy says, and despite holding her back as straight as she can, holding herself together with all her will, her voice trembles. "Keep them both safe, whatever it costs."

She spent so much of her life waiting—for Peter's return, for proof that she could hold up to show her brothers that she did in fact know her own mind. Not delusional, not a liar. The girl left alone, left behind, and now she must become that again. Wendy hates it. She hates that she cannot go with Jane to keep her safe. She hates that she cannot protect her little brother, and must trust both their lives to a man who was once her enemy.

If James has an answer for her, Wendy never gets to hear it, because at that moment, Jane races down the stairs.

"It's back! The rip in the sky is back."

Like James, she's dressed in her coat. Underneath, she wears a pair of trousers Wendy sewed herself, with deep pockets, and one of Ned's old shirts. Jane carries a satchel slung over her shoulder. Ever-practical—her daughter wouldn't return to Neverland unprepared. Jane's cheeks are flushed. She looks like an excited child and a confident and mature young woman all at once. Looking at her, Wendy aches.

"What is it?" Ned comes to the top of the stairs.

"It's time," Wendy says. "You and James had better fetch Michael."

Doubt flickers in Ned's eyes, and Wendy's heart goes out to him. He's had eight years to grow used to the idea of Neverland, and yet he hasn't seen it with his own eyes. He can't possibly understand what their daughter intends to do. Part of him may think both Jane and Wendy mad, even now, and Wendy doesn't blame him. If their positions were reversed, what would she think?

Even with the doubt though, Ned comes down the stairs, going to fetch Michael. As he passes her, Wendy sees hope that she will change her mind, put her foot down, or give him the relief of telling him it's all an absurd joke. She does none of those things, and when they're alone in the hall, James following after her husband, Wendy turns and takes her daughter's hand.

Without a word, she leads Jane outside. Jane already wears boots, but Wendy is only in her slippers, uncaring how the cold soaks through them as she moves to stand on the lawn. The snow has stopped, but clouds still scud across the sky, playing hide and seek with the moon.

"Show me where?" Wendy asks.

Her breath frosts the night. Jane turns her head to look at her as Wendy continues to scan the dark. She can see nothing—save for the way the moonlight catches on the ragged edge of the clouds, casting halos as the wind tugs them past.

"There." Jane points, and Wendy follows, sighting along her daughter's arm, but there's still nothing.

It hurts in a way she can't fully explain, even to herself. She knows what Neverland is, and still, there's an ache in her that goes all the way through her and leaves her feeling cold. She remembers the night Peter took Jane, and how she couldn't get warm afterward. It's like that now, only worse, a deeper chill, settling into her bones for good.

After a moment, Jane lets her arm fall, and Wendy turns to her. She busies herself buttoning her daughter's coat, not allowing her hands to be still, not meeting her daughter's eyes. Jane stands for it, and Wendy feels a kind of awe coming off her, as if Jane expected a fight, and cannot quite understand her mother's silence.

"You'll want this." Wendy draws a length of Christmas ribbon — a pale silvery green — from one of her pockets. She slipped it in there absently earlier, and now it seems as though she carried it around for precisely this purpose. "To tie your hair out of your eyes so it doesn't get in the way."

Jane takes the ribbon, her eyes shining, holding it and staring at her mother. Then a little catch of breath, and Jane turns to look back up at the sky again.

"I hadn't thought how we would even reach it," Jane says.

Wendy glances back to see James and Ned leading Michael between them. Michael's hands are still bound. The eerie smile remains on her brother's lips, the unnatural light in his eyes. Wendy turns her attention back to her daughter. As if by instinct, James and Ned stop a few paces away, giving them space.

Wendy turns her daughter gently, looking her square in the eye. She allows herself to smile, even though it is a fraught thing, even though the greater part of her wants to cry.

"You'll fly, of course," Wendy says.

Jane's eyes widen. Her mouth opens, but before she can speak, Wendy shakes her head slightly, going on before she can no longer get the words out around the growing thickness in her throat.

"You remember how. Fill up every space in yourself with the knowledge that you can do this, because you've done it before. Leave no space for doubt, then aim for the second star to the right and keep on straight until morning."

The words taste like ash, a sob caught in Wendy's chest and threatening to break her open. Jane closes her mouth. Wendy feels a tear, tracking hot on her cheek, and she lets it fall, not bothering to wipe it away. She steps back, her voice hoarse, but still hers to command.

"You can do this, Jane. You will." She believes it with all of her heart, seals up all the spaces for doubt in her own body, so there is only room for her sure knowledge about Jane.

Her daughter will succeed. It doesn't matter that Wendy

herself is being left behind; in this moment, there is only Jane and the journey she must undertake and nothing else.

Wendy steps back. Once. Twice. The space between herself and her daughter grows exponentially as she does. Ned is at her side then, and his arm goes around her shoulders. The solid warmth of him grounds her, keeps her from falling apart.

James takes Michael by the elbow. He moves to stand beside Jane, and Michael doesn't resist him. After a moment, James lays his wooden hand on Jane's shoulder. Wendy remembers how it felt the first time she stepped out of her window holding Peter's hand. She remembers how she leaped from her window again eight years ago, returning to Neverland to save Jane. How full her heart was, how heavy, and she lets it be that again—bursting with pride in her daughter, banishing fear, willing Jane to fly.

And she does.

Jane puts her hand over James's and grips it. She sets her chin, and Wendy imagines her fixing her sight to that guiding star that Wendy can no longer see.

Then Jane's feet are no longer on the ground. They lift, James and Michael alongside her, the stars framing all three of them. Ned makes a sound of wonder. For her part, the sound that breaks from Wendy is not quite a sob and not quite a laugh.

"Our daughter is actually flying." Ned shakes his head, as if he can scarcely believe it, even seeing with his own eyes.

"Yes," Wendy says, watching until her own eyes ache, until she can no longer see Jane or Michael or James against the field of stars. "She absolutely is."

THE BURNING SKY

NEVERLAND – NOW

Being pulled through the sky is like being pulled through his own skin. Turned inside out, stretched, and drawn along the length of his spine. James is traveling to Neverland. He is Neverland. And an incessant screaming slices its way through his very being.

He remembers drowning.

His body wants to thrash, but someone has ahold of him in an iron grip, and he remembers Wendy Darling's daughter, Jane. He remembers the purpose of their trip, and peels them apart from now, disentangling the two until he can breathe again.

They do not land so much as crash. The air goes from his lungs, and for a moment, all he can do is lie on his back, wheezing, while starbursts of gray explode behind his eyes. Through the ringing in his head, he hears the faint rush of the tide. The salt-smell is the sea he knows, so different from London.

There's a shout nearby and James manages to raise his head to see the boy—Michael, though not truly a boy anymore—try to run. His hands remain bound, but he uses his elbows to lever himself to his feet, staggering a few steps along the beach until his bad leg betrays him, and he goes down with a grunt. Whatever lives inside him is still at least partially bound to Michael Darling's flesh, and in the end, that is what might save him.

Jane catches up with her uncle, breathless. She gets a hand on his shoulder, to help him or to keep him down, James can't tell. It occurs to him that it's dark, a strange kind of dark. In his memory, the sky over Neverland was always an aching blue or a velvety black, speckled with stars and gilded with moonlight. This is something else, a low, sick, burning color, the girl and her uncle indistinct against it.

A brilliant flash lights the sky, freezing everything in a stuttering series of tableaus—Jane trying to keep hold of Michael, Michael throwing his weight back to knock her off balance, Michael kicking out with his good leg, barely missing catching Jane directly in the jaw.

James forces himself up, his cane sliding in the sand and fighting him. He expects his own leg to buckle, but the twinging ache isn't there. Instead, there's a low kind of hum, a resonance trapped inside his skin, like music played using his bones as instruments. And layered overtop of it is the new, bruising hurt of his fall from the sky, but that is easy enough to ignore as he strides toward where uncle and niece tussle on the sand.

Strides. Yes, he thinks, because Captain Hook does not have a bad leg. Only James does, and here, he is… Here. Two jagged halves that do not quite make a whole crushed together. He is. He is…

"Stop!" His voice echoes command.

He grabs Michael by the collar, hauling him bodily away from the girl with strength he didn't have a moment ago. He tosses Michael to the sand, where the boy blinks eyes gone momentarily pale again in utter confusion. James shifts his grip, holding the cane like a sword, though still at his side. A threat implied.

Jane's eyes widen. James sees it clearly when the sky cracks with light again, and for a moment, the object in his hand actually is a sword, blade crimson-slick. He isn't certain which of the two pathetic wretches before him he means to run through first.

He is…

He steps back, shifting his grip until the object in his hand is only a cane again. The light goes on flickering, and he tilts his head up to look at the sky.

It is bloody—there is no other word for it. Black clouds pile against the dark, their edges jagged each time the lightning strikes. Only it isn't lightning. It is…seams, cracks, pulsing, like the space behind the sky is on fire. Michael Darling glares at him, or rather, something else glares at him through Michael Darling's eyes. Jane, for her part, looks stricken.

"You, up." James points his cane at Michael, just short of striking him.

Michael growls, low in his throat, but he climbs to his feet. The wet sand has soaked damp patches into his clothing. He sways, but does not fall.

"There's rope there." James speaks to Jane without taking his eyes off Michael. "Secure him so he can't run off again."

Jane fetches the rope lying coiled on the sand, but once she has it in her hands, she makes no further move.

"What is it?" Impatience creeps into his voice.

"I know this place." Jane scans the shore. "This is where I landed the first time I came to Neverland. The ship... But it's different."

James follows her gaze to the dark, broken bulk farther down the shore. How could he possibly have missed it? His ship. *His* ship.

He steps past Jane, ignoring her when she calls after him. He keeps walking until he stands before the curving hull. The prow now points toward the wrong-colored sky. Half a ship. A broken thing. It shouldn't be here at all. He sailed it through the stars. He tore it apart. The fragments of the broken blade in his leg hum.

James—or is he Hook now, he's not certain anymore—rests the tips of his fingers—wood chased in silver—against the hull. The light catches in the decorative whorls, like ribbons of blood dripping from his hand. An echo of voices, shouting against the storm. Rushing all around him, scrambling to secure the lines as the sea and the wind conspire to tear them apart. He strains to hear Samuel's voice, to feel him amidst the thronging ghosts trapped in the wood. He aches, and it's a terrible thought. He doesn't want Samuel here, not like this, and yet... Just to see him again. Just for a moment.

The same wanting that opened the door between worlds in the first place.

The hand resting against the hull isn't wood at all; it's a bright curve of metal, the tip wickedly sharp. The deck sways and creaks underfoot. A coat of red, the color of blood and poppies swirls around him. He is—

"Captain!" Not one of his men calling him, but Jane, her voice sharp with alarm.

James lets his hand fall. Not a hook. Wood and silver gleaming dully in the light. He turns to look at Jane. She's looped the rope clumsily around her uncle's waist, dragging him behind her.

"That's a terrible knot." James indicates the poor job she's done. It would be no work at all for Michael to undo it.

"Well, I'm not a sailor," Jane snaps, and James can't help the smile as her concern gives way to annoyance.

"Luckily, I am." He instructs her how to tie the rope properly. Michael watches with sullen eyes, but makes no further attempt to escape.

"What happened when you were here before?" he asks.

Jane is a quick study, her second knot far more secure than her first. He tests it with a quick pull.

"This is where Peter brought me. He gave me a tea that made me forget myself." Jane frowns. "Something made of flowers, I think."

Flowers. A sick, dizzy longing hits him, a need like claws buried in his skin, like a voice screaming in his ear. No matter the quality of the opium Samuel obtained for him in London, it could never compare. He wants it, suddenly and deeply, like the need for air, the only thing that can save him from drowning. A tremor passes through him and James clenches his jaw. Jane continues, her tone thoughtful.

"My mother told me the beach was the first place Peter brought her as well. Only the ship wasn't wrecked then." She points to the slick, dark water. "Perhaps it's part of the door. A hole between this world and home."

"Indeed." His ship, and perhaps the tether holding part of him here.

It tugs at him even now, like the tide lapping in the dark. The ship wants him to tread its boards again, even broken. It wants him to be the pirate captain he is not, and the longer James spends standing here, the more he has the sensation of standing exactly in a door such as Jane described. It is not a comfortable feeling.

He turns, striding back down the beach. His bag lies just beyond the reach of the waves and a pang goes through him as he crouches to open it. Jane huffs as she trots up beside him.

"You brought luggage?" Her face scrunches, just now noticing the bag, seemingly unsure whether to scold him or to laugh.

There's only one thing inside James truly needs, and he lifts it reverently, cradling it in the crook of his arm. The blood-light splitting the sky catches on the silver whorls chased through Samuel's skull as it did the whorls in his hand. Was it wrong to bring him here, all for his own selfish reasons? But he was never the strong one; it was always Samuel. James cannot image doing this without Samuel at his side.

Holding the skull steadies him. He's only aware of the smile on his lips when he raises his head to find Jane staring at him, expression shading to disgust.

"What is that, some sort of war trophy?"

"No." James curls his body protectively, smile turning to a scowl.

"Ah, the surgeon." Michael's lips produce Killdeer's voice, dripping with scorn.

His smile is not human, but a reptilian thing. The sick-gold light back in his eyes, brighter than before.

"I remember. Your little pet. Your toy. Or was it the other way around?"

The words are slick, voices braided together, sliding like oil. He feels them along the bones of his spine. The voice sounds most like Chauncey's now. Mutinous, treacherous soul. The coward, who fled. A growl answers it, from the other side of Michael's mouth, like the voices arguing among themselves. James wants to spit in disgust to hear what he and Samuel had together reduced in such a way.

Hook doesn't even realize the sword is in his hand again, his arm raised to slash down until Jane steps between him and her uncle, her eyes shocked-wide, but not backing down, willing to take the blow.

"Don't hurt him!" She holds her hands out as if to catch the sweep of his arm. Over her shoulder, Michael grins.

"Jane, sweet Jane, thank you. You would never let anything happen to your old uncle, would you?" The voice is cloying, like honey if it could rot.

Jane's face becomes a storm cloud, and she whirls, her body shaking with adrenaline as she points a finger at her uncle's face.

"Not another word from you, or I'll let him strike you next time. Better yet, I'll strike you myself."

James can see she means it, and he feels a strange surge of pride toward this girl he barely knows.

"We should go," James says softly.

"Where?" Jane turns to face him.

"I'm not certain, exactly. But I'm sure it will come to me."

Jane opens her mouth as if she will object, but James can see she doesn't have any better suggestions. Instead, she merely shrugs, moving to follow him, pulling on the rope binding her uncle more roughly than necessary so he stumbles behind her as he falls into line.

* * *

Smoke leaks from James's mouth as he leans back in the chaise. The light through the window makes a pattern on the ceiling in the shape of an eye, the city looking down at him. He imagines looking back through that eye, seeing every part of London at once—the tops of all the buildings, the glittering line of the Thames. As if he's flying.

The door opens and closes again, and James drifts, listening to Samuel putting packages away. It's comforting, like the hush of the sea on the rare days when the waves were calm and Pan had no plans for starting a war. Days when his time was his own, and they could simply sail.

The sound of a wracking cough shakes him from the illusion and James sets his pipe aside, rising. The opium, no matter the quality, loosens its hold easily enough. In fact, if he doesn't concentrate on remaining in a half-dreaming state, the world comes rushing in all at once. Just as he was once cursed with eternal life in Neverland, he now seems cursed with eternal wakefulness, eternal awareness of everything around him.

As such, it isn't merely the sound of Samuel's painful cough – he feels it as well, an ache in his chest, but Samuel waves him away when James reaches for him.

"It's nothing."

"You're a terrible liar." James nudges Samuel toward a chair. "And you work yourself too hard."

He feels Samuel watching him as he takes over putting away the rest of the packages. Despite James's urging, Samuel remains standing, one hand braced against the back of a chair, as if the slightest movement might unleash another coughing fit. He's convinced Samuel to take laudanum occasionally, but even that he uses sparingly enough.

"You could stop," James says, keeping his tone as even as he can, as if nothing rested on Samuel's answer.

A fist squeezes James's chest. He doesn't turn around, but he feels Samuel tense. They've had some version of this conversation dozens of times before. And James can't seem to help saying the wrong thing at every turn, protesting that he could take care of them both, that Samuel doesn't need to work himself to the bone, spread himself thin to the point of vanishing. He's braced for a fight, so it startles him when there's a chuckle from behind him instead.

"What?" James turns.

"I know that look."

"What look?" It emerges defensive. James holds a box of tea against his chest like a shield. This is new; he doesn't know what to expect.

"Your guilty and feeling sorry for yourself look. You can't wait to beat yourself up for the fact that I work so hard and have a good wallow in your misery."

Samuel shakes his head, but the faint smile on his lips takes some of the sting from the words. Some, but not all. James opens his mouth and closes it again, feeling pinned.

"Has it ever occurred to you that I like my job? That I do it because I want to and not because I have to, and that I would work this hard regardless of you? My entire world doesn't revolve around you." Samuel steps forward, takes the tea from James's hand to place on the shelf.

As he steps away, he lets his hand casually brush James's shoulder then drift to the small of his back—a brief spot of comfort and warmth. It doesn't entirely take the hurt away, nor does it distract James from the suppressed cough that crackles in Samuel's chest. Samuel's knuckles are white where he grips the back of the chair, leaning almost all his weight onto the piece of furniture.

"I can help people." Samuel cuts James off before his protest can rise this time. His cheeks are drawn, but there's an almost manic shine to his eyes. "The people other doctors won't help."

There's an openness to Samuel, a rawness as well, as if every moment in this city causes him pain. Not his pain, the pain of those around him. In Neverland, the hurts he encountered, however horrific, were at least self-contained and all dealt to pirates who participated willingly in the violence. Here, though, a whole city sprawls around him full of addicts, fallen women, the poor, the indigent, those who would otherwise slip through the cracks without him, and Samuel's heart bleeds for every single one.

James wonders though, after his paying clients, how many who cannot afford to pay him anything does he see? A complicated feeling twists through him, a stab of misplaced jealously, a kind of pride, and topping it all, fear.

"You can't save the whole world." James mutters it, compensation for the fact that he hadn't meant to say it aloud at all.

Samuel's heart is in the right place—of course, it always was—but if he burns himself out trying to save all of London's destitute? What then? The irrational itch of jealousy returns, the wild desire to scour London's streets of its vermin and keep Samuel for his own.

"No, but I can try." Another fit of coughing chases the words.

Each wracking sound is a blade driven through James's skin. His shoulders rise, a bony and useless defense. No storm has broken between them this time. Some perverse part of him wants to go on needling Samuel until it does. He's comfortable with the fight, with tempers flaring on both sides to burn themselves out later in heat and forgiveness. This weariness, this reason, though, he cannot grasp. It twists itself around and slips through his hands.

Despite Samuel's gentle remonstration that his world doesn't revolve around James, that his pain and his choices are his own, there's a deeper truth at work. When James tore them apart to bring them here, something essential was left behind. He's always known Samuel to be the stronger of the two of them, but much less stubborn, much more forgiving of the realities of the world. James—Hook, when need be—will rage against London and Neverland both as long as he can. He's too proud, too full of anger to let something as petty as death take him. But Samuel is different.

How much longer will Samuel be able to hold on? And the worse question still—how much longer will he *want* to?

"You should rest," James says.

There's a different kind of storm coming, not a fight, but a slow and creeping thing as terrible as Pan's hunting beast. He's felt it for months now, a thing hovering in the corner of his vision that he's tried to ignore, as if by avoiding looking at it head-on he can deny it exists at all. But the knowledge is there, sure and unsettled in his bones. What's wrong with Samuel is not merely exhaustion and overwork, and it's not merely physical.

James doesn't sleep, but when he smokes, sometimes he dreams. In those dreams, he sees Samuel standing in the corner even as

Samuel lies fast asleep beside him—like a precursor of his ghost, haunting him. His lips move, shaping words without sound: *Let me go.*

He's selfish, keeping Samuel here. He knows as much, and knows as well that he doesn't intend to change. If he could forbid Samuel from leaving, if he could chain him to this life, he would. Because yes, he is selfish, and he hasn't entirely forgotten how to be cruel.

"And what would we do for money while I rest?" Samuel asks.

"If you'd just let—" James clenches his jaw, edging back to anger, to territory he understands.

"No." Samuel's voice matches James's sharpness, but the weariness remains underneath.

He knows James, well enough to know he's being pushed toward a fight, and he's tired of it all.

"I know how you'd get us money." A shadow passes across Samuel's face, expression grim, deepening the bruised quality of his skin.

The way the light strikes him, it's almost as though James can see right through him. He half expects Samuel to mouth *let me go,* but he merely stands there, gaze challenging until James is the one to look away.

James clenches his flesh and blood hand, braces it in a fist against the counter. How can he make Samuel see that what he is could be good for them too, that no one else matters? As long as they've spent here, as much as James has rooted himself in this life they've made, it's only a matter of thought to call Hook to the surface of his skin. Samuel has plied his own trade of kindness and healing to keep them alive for this long. If Samuel would only

229

let him, James could do the opposite, unleash his own particular talents for cruelty and violence.

After all, he's done it before. He hadn't even thought twice the first time he slipped a hand into another man's pocket and relieved him of the notes he found there. It had come to him as easy as breath, and he'd found himself doing it again and again until it had become reflex anytime he'd left the flat. Other habits returned just as easily—cheating at cards, extorting money based on secrets let slip by inebriated men.

He'd justified it by telling himself that no one was truly getting hurt. But in truth, James hadn't really cared. He reveled in it. What did the people of London and their tiny lives matter to him? If they were stupid enough to spill their secrets, to allow themselves to be bilked at cards, or were careless with their wallets and purses, how could he be blamed?

If only he could find a way to make Samuel see as much. But Samuel is stubborn in his own way, stubborn about all the wrong things, refusing to see this is the only thing James is good at, the only thing he will ever be good at.

The look Samuel gives him now—disappointment—only furthers James's fear that Samuel is not only tired of this conversation, but the larger fundamental difference between them. James cannot change who he is at the core.

And deep down, James fears that is the crux of it, the paradox of their situation. He is not worthy of Samuel's kindness, and it can only be a matter of time before Samuel realizes it. Yet if James buries Hook too deep, lets himself become the kind of person worthy of Samuel, then he will not be able to survive the moment when Samuel inevitably decides to let go.

Better to hold on to the monstrousness. Better to embrace it. And he has. In the time they've been in London, he's done worse than thieve and cheat at cards.

There'd been a night when he and Samuel had been returning from a pub. Still, thick, the air dewed and distorting the lights around them. The streets had been strangely empty, as though no one existed save for the two of them.

Until a man had stumbled drunkenly from the pub doorway after them. James had marked him when they'd been inside, casting glances, expression sour—as if James's and Samuel's very existence offended him, as if he felt their happiness was undeserved and wanted to take it away. Samuel hadn't seemed to notice, and so James had schooled himself rather than walking over and striking the man. For Samuel's sake.

"Oy!" The shout had echoed, the man himself apparently not content to let it lie—a single word like a slap, and James had stopped.

Samuel had glanced back then, seen the man, and tried to urge James on. And James had tried. He truly had, letting the man's slurs roll off him. He hadn't acted until the man had grabbed Samuel's shoulder, yanking him backward, sick of being ignored.

The decision hadn't even been a conscious one. Like taking a breath after holding it for so long, a red haze had descended over him. Cane in hand, hefted and smashed into the man's face, breaking his nose instantly. The bright shock of blood had only urged him on. He'd hit the man again and again, even as the man pleaded, as Samuel tried to drag James off him. And the entire time, his stance had been steady, and his leg hadn't ached once.

Hook, utterly eclipsing James.

He'd come back to himself crouched over the man, smeared with blood, riffling through the man's pockets, and had found Samuel looking at him in horror. Samuel's face had been paler than the fog around them, almost a ghost, staring at James as though he'd never seen him before, as if he'd forgotten who and what he could be.

The moment James straightened, using his cane again as it was intended, Samuel had startled away from him. In that moment, Hook remained too close to the surface, released and now refusing to be tamped back down. Instead of remorse or guilt, anger had snapped in him and James hadn't been quick enough to keep it at bay, lips twisting into their old sneer.

"Would you prefer I'd let him kill you? You should thank me."

Samuel had taken one step back, the sound of his heel overloud on the stone, his breathing harsh and shallow. James himself might have been hurt, however unlikely, but no fear for him had showed in Samuel's eyes, only fear *of* him.

"You don't know that." Samuel shook his head, green eyes catching too much light in their wideness.

Sickness roiled in James's gut, cold against the anger. Deep down, he'd wondered if Samuel was right. What if defense was only an excuse? Hadn't it felt good—hadn't *he* felt good, killing, breaking his promise? More like himself, more alive and more useful than he'd been since Neverland.

"What do you expect when you ally yourself with the Devil?" In the face of Samuel's horror, he'd tried for a grin, but the expression slipped off his face and twisted into something nasty. "Do you expect a mad dog to cease biting merely because you put it on a leash?"

He'd shaken bloodied hair out of his face, expression hard where he met Samuel's gaze. It would have been easy to apologize, to back down, but none of that had been in him. He'd wanted to push, to see where and if the bond between them would break. He'd been spiteful enough, and deep down, self-loathing enough, that some sick part of him had wanted to drive Samuel away.

Samuel's expression had crumbled, hurt, and James had leaned into the hurt, putting pressure on a bruise. He'd thought that Samuel understood. That he knew James for what he was, saw him, and chose him anyway. Had he merely been waiting, hoping, for him to change? Did Samuel see James as that same broken-winged bird he'd spoken of a lifetime ago, cutting his hands to ribbons with its beak when he'd only been trying to help?

"Do you remember what you told me about the first time you saw me? You didn't seem bothered by my bloody-mindedness then. A terrible angel to protect you, a weapon to keep you safe so you wouldn't have to dirty your own hands?"

He'd bared his teeth, a half-feral grin, not caring whether his words were true or if he even believed that Samuel felt that way. He'd only wanted to wound, dealing in another kind of violence after the death of the man lying crumpled at his feet. He'd felt more like Hook than ever.

"If I'm a monster, then let me be a useful one."

"You're not…" Samuel had shaken his head, the hurt in his expression deepening, seeming almost on the verge of tears.

"Why then? Why stay?" James's own voice had turned rougher than he would have liked, smaller.

"I always saw more." The words caught, ragged, like sailcloth tearing to shreds in Samuel's throat; Hook—*James*—barely heard it.

"You're not a dog," Samuel had said. "And you're not a monster. Behind the Devil, I saw that you could be whatever you chose—if you chose. Not just what Pan made of you." Samuel's tears slipped free at last. "That's why I stay. Because I care. And because I do love you. But you do have to choose."

Samuel turned his head, ready to leave.

"Wait." James had caught Samuel's arm, then frozen, staring at Samuel's sleeve and the smear of crimson he'd left behind, a bright accusation.

"I'll try." The words were harder than James would have thought, but he meant them.

He'd always meant them. Like he'd always meant to keep Samuel safe, apart from the worst of everything, including himself. He'd meant to protect him; he'd meant to be better, to deserve him.

"Let me try?" James had managed to meet Samuel's eyes, just barely, to see the conflict on Samuel's face.

Fear had curdled in James's belly, and words had caught in his throat. There was a bridge, one he wasn't yet willing to cross. And so he'd turned away from the hope, the shadow of expectation Samuel couldn't quite keep from his expression.

Because I care. And because I love you.

Why couldn't he say the same in return? Instead, he'd deflected, hoping at least to make Samuel smile, to forget his disappointment and save his decision of whether to stay or go for another day.

"You forgot the other reason you stay."

"What's that?" A small amount of wariness had showed in Samuel's eyes.

"I'm devastatingly handsome." James had flashed a grin, made it as brash as he could. At the same time, he'd held his breath, hope a fragile thing ready to shatter in his chest.

"Well, there is that, yes." The corner of Samuel's mouth had lifted, and relief, a tide, had washed over James, set to drown him.

But how long would it last? Behind all his words and underneath the anger, there'd been fear. Of Samuel leaving, of losing himself. Because he had tried to change. He'd become something more, but in that moment, he couldn't find it anymore—Hook rising to claim him as though he'd never left Neverland. And he'd wanted it. He'd wanted to kill and soak in blood and never be anything other than a bloody pirate.

As always, Samuel had been the one to cross the bridge, to heal the rift between them, or at least bandage it for a time. He'd been the one to reach through the space between them and pull James back from the edge. He'd placed a hand alongside James's cheek, the look in his moss-green eyes unraveling the bloody pirate captain to find the man underneath.

"Are you with me?" Samuel had asked, and when James hadn't had an answer for him, hadn't even understood the question, Samuel leaned his forehead against James's own.

"Are you with me, here, or are you determined to lead a life antithetical to everything I stand for as a doctor sworn to save lives?"

James had swallowed, throat gone thick. Despite the dark, the fog, there was nowhere to hide from Samuel's gaze. It occurred to him that the alarm should have been raised by now. He'd just murdered a man, but time seemed to have stopped, holding them here in this moment—a far worse reckoning than any that could come from the law.

"Because if you're with me, then you should be with me. Here. In London. In this life. Not always half in that other world. Stay here." He'd pressed a hand to James's shirt, despite the blood there, breath warm on James's cheek, and James sharply aware of his heartbeat against the palm of Samuel's hand. "Stay here with me, where you belong."

"What about you?" James had closed his eyes, unable to bear Samuel looking at him any longer. "Are you with me? Because if you're only with me because you're hoping I'll change, then you may be disappointed, and that isn't fair to either one of us."

They'd stayed like that for a very long time, holding on to each other as they had once upon a time in a storm.

He can't remember now if Samuel had answered him. James remembers that he tried though, to be what Samuel saw in him. He *is* trying.

"Promise me you won't turn pirate again." Samuel's voice is soft, bringing James fully back to the here and now. "My sickness will pass, you'll see. There's no need for you to do anything…rash."

Samuel's lips are pale around his smile, a brave front. Does he know his words are a lie? Does he truly think the sickness will pass, that he'll get better, or does he merely want to keep James in check? There isn't as much bitterness in the thought as James would have expected. In this moment, he would happily be leashed as long as it meant Samuel would stay by his side.

"I promise." The words come easily, perhaps too much so. The same promise he's made countless times before, intending to keep it every single time.

James crosses the room and lays his hand against Samuel's cheek. Stubble rasps against his palm as Samuel leans into the touch. Here, in this moment, James truly does mean it. He wants to be the man Samuel believes he can be, no matter the consequences, no matter how vulnerable it leaves him.

"I'm tired." Samuel closes his eyes.

"Sleep," James says. "I'll wake you for supper."

Samuel doesn't move, and for a moment, it seems as though he'll fall asleep leaning against James's hand. There's a blurring at Samuel's edges, and again, James sees him as a ghost. *Let me go.*

If Samuel knew how afraid James is, would he fight harder? But surely he must know, mustn't he? Even though James hasn't said it aloud. He must know, after all this time, what James is, and that he *has* tried, and will keep trying for Samuel's sake. Surely that must be enough.

James swallows around the ache in his throat, around words like something barbed that he is unable to spit out.

He watches Samuel move toward the bed. Samuel turns, curling on his side beneath the covers, his breathing soft and regular. It doesn't change when James sits lightly on the edge of the bed beside him.

"You're stronger than you think." The covers rise and fall gently over the topography of Samuel's body—a jagged landscape, too much bone and not enough flesh holding him together.

James's breath catches. He wants to argue. Tell Samuel that he—not James—is the strong one and always has been. He remembered, all those years while James forgot, he carried the burden for both of them, and what use has James ever been? Could he order Samuel, as captain to surgeon, to stay? It would

237

be cruel; it would be selfish. But he can see himself doing it, and Samuel obeying.

Samuel's breathing deepens. James is about to rise, but after a moment, Samuel's voice comes again, slurred and half-wrapped in dreams.

"You've always been kind to me. Why can't you be kind to the rest of the world?" James has no answer for him. "Why can't you be kind to yourself?"

The second question is so much worse, hollowing him out. Samuel doesn't seem to expect an answer; the lines of his body go slack beneath the covers. Even if James did have an answer for him, Samuel wouldn't hear it.

Why can't he be kind to world? Why can't he be kind to himself? Because once upon a time, Pan broke him, rewrote him, and made him into the villain in his private tale. Because as that villain, James died a thousand times and was born again, and he remembers every one of those deaths—teeth in his skin and the air crushed from his lungs. He remembers what it is to be run through with a sword wielded by a child, and he remembers what it is to drown.

He cannot be kind to himself, because he does not deserve kindness.

A part of him fears that the scarcely-more-than-a-boy who left his sister on the docks with a kiss and a promise he never intended to keep was only ever a veneer over the cruel thing he became when the beast severed his hand. He was always made for violence, for blood, for a blade, and Pan only set that nature free, stripped the skin to show his red and terrible self to the world. Samuel is the best part of him, the only good part. What will James do when he's gone?

James raises his hand as if to touch Samuel's shoulder, wood and silver gleaming softly in the light. A word sits heavy on his tongue. He lets his hand fall.

Samuel already does so much. He already fights so hard to stay, and James knows that it isn't on his own account that he does so. He stays for James's sake—loyalty, selflessness, a desire to take care of him. If it weren't for James, he would have let go long ago, crumbling like so much wet paper in the rain.

It's only a matter of moments before the gentle sound of Samuel's snore drifts through the room. Despite his promise, he does not wake Samuel for supper. He lets him sleep, looking him over occasionally and waiting for the troubled creases on his brow to straighten themselves out. They never do.

NEVERLAND – NOW

They move along the beach. The sky doesn't change. It remains red and bloody, the tide sluggish and relentless as it washes over the sand, though it never seems to rise or withdraw.

Jane does a quick hopping double step to close the space between them. She's let the rope out to its fullest extent, and Michael seems content to trail behind them, even dragging his feet on occasion to further slow them. The maddening smile never leaves his lips, taunting without saying a word.

James tries to avoid looking at the boy, but he notes how Jane continually glances over her shoulder as if unable to stop herself. Her movements are skittish, haunted, caught between equal parts fear of and for her uncle.

"Why do you carry that, if it's not a trophy?" she asks, her eyes flicking to the skull then quickly away again. "What did Uncle—

What did he mean when he called it the surgeon?"

James sighs, lifting the skull to the level of his eye without breaking his stride. He still carries his cane, but he needs it less and less here.

"His name is—was Samuel. He's someone I loved very much. Someone I love. But I never told him as much and it is my life's greatest regret." The sky's eerie light rests in Samuel's eye sockets and makes the silver chasing in the bone gleam.

Now, when it is far too late, the word comes easily—*love*. It leaves a bitter taste on James's tongue.

A frown tugs at Jane's lips. James resettles the skull in the crook of his arm as she chews his words over. She carries regret as well, plain to see. Not a beau, he thinks, perhaps her mother? It's impossible to miss the tension between them, so that may well be regret weighing on Jane now. Or perhaps there's something more.

"You were here when Neverland broke," he says, as much to distract himself as her. "What happened?"

"I…didn't see, but my mother told me what she did. She sewed Peter's shadow back onto him and made him whole. But it broke everything else. I guess it made it so he couldn't lie anymore about this place, or what he was, and it made death here real. And my friend, he—"

Her voice breaks, and Jane lets the words lie. Timothy. The boy Wendy mentioned. Perhaps that is the regret the girl carries. James can almost see it, a weight upon her, a shadow wrapped around her and dragged behind her with every step.

A shudder passes through her, and James feels unease himself. All the times he died in Neverland and returned. If he dies here now, it will be for good.

"And this was…?"

"Eight years ago." Jane does not look at him as she answers.

Eight years. Samuel had started to fade long before that. In the back of his mind James had been holding on to hope that Wendy Darling was to blame, that he could lay Samuel's death at her feet, rather than his own. But no. It is all down to him.

If he hadn't listened to the mermaids. If he hadn't consumed the flower. If he hadn't sought the blade.

The flower. He stops suddenly, making a sharp turn so the water is at his back, facing in toward the center of the island. The blade.

"I'm going about this all wrong."

"What are you talking about?" Jane hurries to catch up as James strides forward again.

A grimace tugs at his mouth. No, he is going about things exactly right, because this is always where he was going, was it not? The heady, sticky-sweet scent of flowers swirls around him, a memory, but tangible and real, a thread tugging him farther inland.

"There's something here I need."

James quickens his pace even further. Jane lets herself fall back a few steps. Behind her, he feels Michael's grin. And inside James, the hollow gnawing at his core grows and grows into a hungering roar.

LOST BOYS

NEVERLAND – NOW

Everything is the same and everything is different. As they walk, Jane tries to pick out familiar landmarks. But she was here such a relatively short time, with Peter always pushing her or dragging her about, and it's been eight years since then besides. The murky light makes it even harder to discern whether anything they've passed might be familiar. She can barely see her hand in front of her face in the red-tinted light, and the pirate captain—she can't think of him any other way—is setting an increasingly ridiculous pace.

"Would you slow down?" Jane calls after him, but either Hook doesn't hear, or chooses to ignore her.

When she first met him, he was an old man, and needed a cane to walk. Here, he's something else entirely.

"I said wait, will y—" Jane's words cut off as a root catches her foot.

She loses her grip on the rope, and a moment of panic takes her, then a hand at her elbow, steadying her.

"Why are you following him? Coming here was your idea. Who decided he should be in charge?" The voice at her ear carries just enough kindness and concern that for a moment she can convince herself it is her Uncle Michael and not something—several somethings—wearing his skin.

But the sly smile and the weird light in his eyes, picking up the red of the sky now even though they are under the trees, betray him immediately. She jerks her arm away.

"Do you even trust him?" Michael asks.

"I don't trust either of you." Jane frowns, annoyed at the question, and more annoyed at herself because it didn't occur to her until Michael asked that she *doesn't* have to follow Hook.

He doesn't have any more idea of what he's doing than she does. He said as much himself. For all she knows, he'll decide suddenly he wants to kill her and add another skull to his collection. She could be searching the island to see if some remnant of Peg really was carried here by the beast. She could be looking for a while to cure her uncle. She bends down to snatch up the trailing end of rope. Michael's smile only widens.

"I won't try to run."

It's unsettling, seeing the smile on her uncle's lips, any smile at all. She allows a little slack into the rope, but doesn't let go. Michael holds up his hands, a shrug.

"You see? I'm still here."

"What do you want?"

"To kill him." Michael tilts his head toward Hook, his voice eerily cheerful. Like the smile, it doesn't belong to him, all wrong, like an ill-fitting suit hanging from his shoulders.

"Why haven't you, then?" If she can understand the thing inside her uncle, maybe she can find a way to get rid of it without hurting anyone.

"I want him to suffer." Michael lowers his hands, peering around as though they were merely tourists on holiday, intrigued by the local flora.

Jane realizes she's lost sight of Hook. A spike of fear goes through her, resentment close on its heels. She doesn't want to care what happens to him. She doesn't want to follow him. All she wants is to find a way to fix what's wrong with her uncle and get them both back home. And she has no idea how to do that.

She pushes aside a heavy branch, ducking under its trailing leaves. A clearing opens up before her, and her pulse trips. There's no mistaking it, even fallen half to ruin without Peter's magic sustaining it. A tangle of rotting platforms and walkways winding through the trees; a wall of timber surrounding a cleared patch of ground. It's Peter's camp, where the Lost Boys slept, where she ate soup made from stones, and told Timothy a story when he couldn't sleep.

Jane lets the rope slide from her hand. It makes a soft sound as it drops. Scattered stones and smudges of ash mark a long-ago extinguished fire. Jane counts the remaining platforms, trying to guess which one she sat on with Timothy, all those years ago.

She can almost conjure the sound of his crying, soft and muffled, trying not to let any of the other boys hear. She pictures his eyes, wide in the moonlight. His gentleness. His trust in her when she promised to keep him safe. His body, lifeless on the cavern floor.

She turns back toward her uncle whose hands are in his pockets now as he studies the trees. She peers at him more closely. She saw Peg's ghost on the lawn, didn't she, right before the beast attacked. She could still be in there somewhere, carried along with the pirates, and if so, could Jane set her free? Hope makes

Jane catch her breath. What would Peg think of this place? Would she find it beautiful, even ruined?

As if feeling her studying him, her Uncle Michael turns slowly, hands still in his pockets, uncanny smile spreading on his lips. He cocks his head to one side.

"Are you looking for her, your little friend? What was her name? Meg?"

Jane takes a lurching step forward, fingers curling. Her uncle makes a *tsk*ing sound, brown-gold eyes stopping her motion and pinning her in place. The expression in them is the most terrible thing she's ever seen—heartless and cold. Beyond anger, beyond a desire for revenge. Cruel, simply for the sake of cruelty, with it meaning nothing.

"I'm so sorry, little Jane." His voice is anything but. "But we ate her all up. You see, we were so hungry when we arrived, and she was delicious. We are of this place, and she is not. The only thing she was good for is fuel."

Jane flies at her uncle, no longer caring that he is her uncle, wanting only to get at the thing burrowed under his skin. She wants to tear through muscle and bone to rip the creature out by the root. She can't bear its words—the idea that Peg was only fuel, that it might burn her uncle up as well—a convenient vessel to allow it to carry out its purpose.

Her hands are outstretched, but Michael neatly sidesteps her and Jane overbalances, crashing to her knees. Her body heaves, a sob shuddering through her. It isn't fair. Peg had so much life left in her to live and she's gone. And stupidly, childishly, Jane had held on to the hope of saving her, because Neverland had primed her to believe the impossible—that a person could die and come back, that they could be dealt a sword wound and not bleed. But that isn't how things work in the real world. And it isn't even how things work in Neverland anymore.

Jane tilts her head back, letting out a raw-throated sound of frustration and sorrow. The sound empties her, but brings no relief, only leaving a space inside her that is at once too empty and too full.

Slowly, her eyes focus and the white shape looming above her that she's been looking at without seeing suddenly clarifies. A skull, set atop a sharpened stick, driven into the ground. Jane lets out a startled yell and scrambles backward, colliding with her Uncle Michael behind her.

Amusement plays across his features. He holds up a hand, still bound, to help her up and Jane stares at it in disgust. Anger and fear roil together with nowhere to go. She wants to slap his hand away, but just then, figures—a dozen, more, she can't tell—rush out of the dark between the trees. Jane scrambles to her feet and finds herself pressed against her uncle's side.

Jane tries to face every direction at once, assessing the new threat. Restless motion boils through the clearing, making it impossible to tell how many surround them. The thunder of footsteps is everywhere—a sound like bare feet, but also like hooves. The figures shift and blur. It isn't just the motion, it's something else. Even as Jane tries to fix one of the figures in her sight, it blinks between forms.

Recognition strikes Jane breathless. These are Peter's Lost Boys, the ones who played hide and seek through the woods with her and killed a boar to give her a welcome feast. Except they're not boys anymore, they're men, or they're something else altogether.

Not ghosts—they're as real as they ever were, except broken, like the sky, like Neverland itself. It's as though they're experiencing every possible moment in their lives at once, every iteration of their being, constantly pulled and stretched so thin she can almost see through them, yet held together by whatever twisted power still remains in this place.

Jane fixes on a tall, lanky boy with the skin of an animal draped over his shoulders. Even as she looks at the boy, she sees a man with tangled hair and a matted beard. She sees a child, streaked in blood and crying. And she sees a body that is neither animal nor human. She sees all the ways that Peter changed the boys around her over time, bending them out of true, hurting them, breaking them and putting them back together to suit his whims.

When her breath catches again, it's on something like pity. This boy. She knows him. Before she can speak, though, the boy's face twists in rage. In the next instant, he's upon her, knocking her down.

There's a stone in his raised fist, and Jane manages to jerk her head to the side just as he brings it smashing down. He lifts it again, lips peeled back from his teeth. There's barely any breath left in her body where he holds her down, but Jane wheezes out a name.

"Arthur?"

It's enough to make the boy pause. It's enough for Jane to wiggle free, to scramble backward. His gaunt face is dirt-streaked, but she knows those eyes, they haven't changed. Hard and mean.

Another of the men—the boys—reaches for her. He shifts between forms too fast for her to guess who it might be, if it's someone she used to know. Jane crawls on hands and knees, avoiding his grasp, but getting tangled in the strap of her satchel instead. She bangs her chin and fresh tears sting her eyes, pain now, not fear. She rolls away, desperately avoiding a heavy object hurled in her direction. The rock Arthur used to try to bash her face in. At least he doesn't have it in his grip anymore.

"Do something! Won't you help me?" Jane shouts to her uncle who stands watching in amusement.

"Uncle Michael! I know you're in there. Please!"

Before she can get beyond his reach, Arthur is on her again. He flips her, getting a hand around her throat and squeezing until starbursts of gray pop before her eyes. His hands are small, blood-slick, a mere child. Is this the way Arthur looked before he came to Neverland? He's slight enough for a moment that Jane is able to get a knee up, to shove him back. Her vision clears momentarily, but then he is the Arthur she knew again, the tallest of the Lost Boys, wiry and strong enough to hold her down.

"It's me, Jane." Her voice is strangled.

No flicker of recognition in Arthur's eyes.

Jane gropes at the satchel, the edges of her vision threatening dark again. What does one bring to a magical, impossible land? She'd thought to supply herself with practical things, items she was certain would be useful anywhere. A roll of bandages. Small scissors to cut them. A bottle of iodine. A hooked needle and thread for stitching wounds.

Her arm tingles like its falling asleep. Her fingers are clumsy, refusing to obey her. Spots dance before her eyes. Faces blur above her as the other boys loom close. From what seems like a great distance, she hears cheering. They're hunting the boar. They're bringing it down. Soon enough they will roast her and dine on her meat.

Jane's fingers close. She grasps the handle of her scissors and yanks them free. With whatever strength she has left, she swings her arm and buries the small points of the blades in Arthur's face.

He howls, reeling back from her, blood welling from between his fingers as he claws at his cheek where the scissor handles protrude. He's bearded and stinking, caked in dirt. He's a boy, scarcely half her height. He's the boy she remembers, bleeding and furious.

Jane scrambles up just as Arthur yanks the scissors free, tossing them away. He lets the blood flow, and she thinks of the cave, ages ago, how she punched him in the nose and made him bleed then too. How he ran Timothy through with his sword. How Timothy died.

Jane's vision washes red. She rushes at Arthur—the boy, the man—ready to tear him apart the way she'd been ready to tear her uncle apart minutes ago. She's meant to be a doctor. She's meant to save people. And right now, she doesn't care about any of that. It's what Neverland does to her. Makes her want to hurt and hunt and destroy and forget everything else. The other boys fall back; without Arthur's direction, they're lost.

"Run! Run, you scurvy rats, or feel the wrath of my blade!" The voice booms through the clearing, and Jane skids to a halt.

One of the boys—a boy in truth now, one she almost recognizes – lets out a whimper. It is a pure sound of fear, a child confronted with a nightmare vision, the monster from under the bed, the shadow lurking in the dark. Jane looks where he's looking, and her own breath catches.

Hook—sword brandished, eyes the red of a demon's, hair the black of a raven's wing, and coat flaring about him. His hand is not the wooden one she knows him to wear, but a hook, wickedly sharp and wickedly bright. The boys scatter, feet pounding the earth, vanishing among the trees.

Jane's heart goes with them, the instinct to run, to flee the demon almost overpowering until the captain takes another step forward, resolving only into an aged man, holding a cane, breathing hard. Except he isn't only one thing. Two versions of Hook stand before her overlapping, both equally true.

"You're the only one they ever feared." She remembers her mother's stories—an enemy fierce enough to terrify the boys, but one Peter could always defeat.

"Captain Hook?" The voice trembles, and Jane turns.

Her uncle's eyes are wide and stricken, a grown man still in shape, but his expression a little boy's. This is how he must have looked in Neverland, Jane thinks, when he and her mother were children, a lifetime ago.

She takes a step toward her uncle, reaching out for him. And it *is* her uncle, if only for a moment, if only for now, Jane is certain of it. He's terrified, just as the Lost Boys were, fleeing their enemy of old.

Hook was her uncle's enemy once upon a time too. He kidnapped Jane's mother and her uncles, held them captive on his pirate ship as bait for Peter to rescue. Only her uncle doesn't remember any of it. Or didn't, until now.

Confusion floods Michael's eyes. His lip trembles. The ghosts are gone, stepped aside to let him see the world around him—an act of pure cruelty. Michael's features twist, like he's trying to escape himself.

"Jane?" The look in his eyes pleads with her to make everything make sense—as if he were the child, and she the adult.

"It's okay." Jane steps forward, taking her uncle's arm.

"Don't," Hook says just as Michael's body goes rigid and boneless all at once, his head slumping forward.

His breath rasps, a sound that turns into a wet, bloody-sounding chuckle. When he raises his head again, the sick-gold light is in his eyes, the blade of a grin across his mouth.

"Soft-hearted child." Michael brings his bound hands up, catching Jane on the chin just where she struck it against the ground.

Her head snaps back, ringing with the blow, and she tastes blood. She staggers, then she spits on the ground, wiping red from her mouth with the back of her hand. The fractured multitude inside her uncle chuckles again, but Michael is still visible, a ghost trapped inside his own skin. He's still terribly afraid.

"Come along." Hook takes her arm, drawing her back. Jane resists a moment. Even bleeding, she wants to go to her uncle, help him.

Hook's grip is insistent though, and Jane allows herself to be led. It's a moment before she realizes she's left Michael's rope behind. When she turns back, her uncle is behind her, holding the rope out to her with a mocking bow.

HOW SWEET THE BLOOM

NEVERLAND – NOW

Hunger gnaws at him that has nothing do with his stomach. Hunger, need, weakness, desire. It hollows him out, even as it speeds his pace. James almost feels he could run, despite the dark and his age and a leg that hasn't fully been under his control for years.

Except here, it is. Here, he is the immortal pirate captain Hook. He is ruthless and angry, and even death can't defeat him. And it hurts. All the living. Pan's blade running him through a thousand times. Teeth gnashing and tearing him apart beneath the waves. Drowning. He feels it all, and he continues existing in the face of it, and only one thing can make it stop.

"Don't look at me that way." James speaks through gritted teeth to the skull cradled in his arms, empty sockets turned up toward him in judgment and sorrow. "You don't know what it's like. You can't know. So just shut up."

You've always been kind to me, James. Why can't you be kind to the rest of the world? Why can't you be kind to yourself?

He's aware of Jane crashing through the brush behind him, her uncle in tow, but their presence barely registers. He doesn't care if he loses them. Nor does he care if they overhear him talking to Samuel, or what they think of him if they do.

It isn't like the countless times he's spoken to Samuel's memory before, resting his fingertips against the bone, or caressing the silver chased through the skull. The way he hears Samuel's voice here feels real, not just a memory. Concern, admonishment, a voice with breath behind it telling him he's too reliant on his drugs. For all the circumstances, the conversation feels almost natural.

"Who's the one who introduced me to opium anyway?" he snaps, even knowing it's unfair and unkind.

"Only to help you." The reply, fading, like the wind carrying it away. "And it isn't opium you're chasing now, is it?"

There's a quality to the words, like wind blowing through a reed. Samuel had given him opium to dull his pain. To dull his reliance on a flower not found in London, hoping eventually that James might cut back to laudanum, and from there cease using opiates all together, but he'd never gotten past that first step. One of the many ways he'd failed Samuel over the years. He'd always had an excuse – life simply weighed too heavily on him, his existence too abrasive.

The circumstances are different now though, and Samuel has no right to judge. He needs the flower to find the blade, what remains of it that isn't buried in his thigh. He's certain it must still exist, and that it must be the key to undoing what was done. In the heart of the storm, he couldn't have severed all the ties fully, the tendrils of shadow binding him to Neverland. He left a door open, and now he needs to see the door not only closed, but destroyed entirely.

* * *

Promise me. Promise me, won't you?

Samuel's words trail him, pressed upon James with the fever-heat of skin, Samuel grasping his hand before he'd left the flat and gone out into the night.

Promise.

Had he? James can't remember. Opium still winds through his blood, keeping the answer to the question at bay. He doesn't want to break a promise to Samuel. But he can't ignore the shine that had been in Samuel's eyes either, his sunken cheeks. Samuel can't work, he can barely get out of bed. What else is there? How else will they live? And he is determined that Samuel *will* live.

James turns, his step not quite aimless, only appearing so while carrying him steadily away from the density of lights, into the more shadowed and seedier streets where fewer eyes watch, where those that are watching watch only for their own skins with little care for others. He feels the reassuring weight in his pocket, the blade carried there.

The soft lap of water, the weedy scent of it. Even though the docks are a few streets over, James smells it, hears it—the sea calling to his blood. Without seeing it, he can picture the way the light breaks on the water, the oily shine of it as tiny waves kiss the pier. He turns again, following the sound of someone singing off-key, the sound warbling through the streets and calling to him.

The establishments here cater primarily to those who work the docks, going straight from their shifts—ripe with sweat and sometimes the scent of whatever cargo they've been hauling –

straight to a worn stool and a pint, two, more. The grinding weariness of their lives, as much as the drink, makes them careless. Makes them easy prey. He's practically doing these men a favor, like the man who comes into view now, the source of the off-key song. One hand is braced against the wall, the other ostensibly aiming as he pisses against the bricks.

James doesn't bother letting the man finish. No dignity in life, no self-respect, and none in death either. For a moment, he doesn't need the cane as he slides the blade in clean. The man grunts, a sound of surprise, then slumps forward into the filth and the damp. James lowers him almost gently and goes to work swiftly.

He empties the man's pockets, taking the ring from his finger. A cheap band, thin. It won't get him much, but it's something. Could he have simply stolen from the man without taking his life? James pushes the thought away. Crouched at the back of his mind, Hook smiles. James whistles a snatch of the man's tune, picking up the thread of his song and carrying it with him as he wends his way back home.

He opens the door on the terrible sound of Samuel coughing, a bloody, wrenching sound that immediately steals James's own ability to breathe. The last dulling effects of the opium peel away to reveal a world too sharp and too bright. He left Samuel sleeping peacefully, looking better, he'd thought, than he had in days. His pulse thumps, panic replacing the last shreds of his drug-induced dream.

All the lights are out in the flat, leaving only the faintest glow of city light seeping in from outside. Samuel's entire body shudders on the bed, wracked with pain. The edges of him flicker, and James's heart drops straight through his chest to his soles.

"Samuel." It's scarcely a whisper, but Samuel's eyes fly open.

"Captain." Not James, as if all the time between now and Neverland never happened.

Samuel's eyes are open, but not focused. James stops dead in the act of reaching for Samuel, breath rasping in his lungs. There's blood on his hands. He can't possibly touch Samuel in this condition. He stares at them, one flesh, one wood. They're clean.

Or are they? He did just kill a man, did he not? Or did he hallucinate leaving the flat? Relive the memory of what might have been, or experience a premonition of something that might still occur? Time doesn't always behave around him. He isn't always certain of when he is, or where.

"It's me," James says, but the words come out rough, and he isn't certain Samuel hears him. Nor is he entirely sure what he means by them. Is he himself, or more accurately, which self is he?

But Samuel's expression softens into a smile, or at least an attempt at one. His body relaxes somewhat, but even that is an effort, and the shadow of pain doesn't lift from him. James grasps his hand, the feel of blood tacky on his skin still clinging to him, even though it's only in his mind. At least he hopes so.

"I'm here," he says. "I've got you."

He wants it to be true, but the edges of Samuel still flicker. James thinks of all his lost pirates. He didn't witness their deaths, but Samuel did. He made it his mission to track down every last one of them. And those he didn't find found him, like they were called to him, a beacon of compassion to witness them and see them for what they truly were in their last moments before they crumbled away.

Their ghosts crowd Samuel's eyes. The weight of all that death, dragging him down. James tightens his grip until he imagines Samuel will cry out, but he never does.

"You can't have him." The words are almost a growl. James clenches his jaw. Speaking to Neverland. Speaking to Pan. Speaking to the past he swore to leave behind.

He'll fight any force, any demon, to keep Samuel by his side. But there is nothing. Nothing but weight and time and a life stretched too thin.

"James." A whisper so soft James can pretend he doesn't hear it. His name, but there are other words hidden within the shape of it: *Let me go.*

Words laced with pain. His stubbornness isn't James's; it is compassion that's kept him here, caring. It is James himself, and that is no longer enough.

The breath shatters in James's lungs, broken edges digging in so he expects his next intake of breath to drown him in blood. This is the end he's felt coming for them for too long. He isn't ready. He'll never be ready. Samuel needs to hold on.

"I—" And even now, the words lodge in his throat.

He cannot let them go, cannot crack the last shell of the fierce and bloody pirate captain who would never be so weak as to admit to his heart aloud. An anchor, but not a chain. A guiding line for Samuel to follow back to his side.

"I—" Silence, as loud as any shipwrecking storm, howling through the room.

James's fingers close. Within the terrible strength of his grip, James finds himself holding only ash, only sand. Samuel's hand is there in his, and then it isn't, the rest of him following even as

James throws himself onto the bed, gathers Samuel's crumbling form into his arms, and clings to him as hard as he can.

"Don't. Don't go." He says the words over and over again, until they mean nothing.

Samuel's eyes are twin candle flames in the dark, then they are nothing at all. James holds only a skull, and that fact that it remains feels like both a gift and a painful mockery. Why should this linger when everything else is gone?

Rage breaks in him like a wave, rising up from the ocean of loss that is the greater part of him now. He wants to hurl the skull against the wall, smash it to pieces, curse the skies and death itself and above all, Pan, for even now taking everything from him.

But he does none of those things. James brings the skull to his lips, which tastes of salt now, and, weeping, rests one last kiss on his lover's brow.

NEVERLAND – NOW

The scent hits James before the flowers come into view, and he rushes forward, panting, open-mouthed as if to drink the air. There's a thickness to it, like syrup, already blunting the edge of his pain, and at the same time, making his hunger even worse. Even in the dull light, the petals glow, like embers, like the blossoms are aflame. He imagines he could almost breathe in the smoke of them without doing anything at all.

"What are you doing?" Jane's voice is sharp and she catches his arm, yanking him backward. "Don't you know what those are?"

Her eyes are wide in the dark, a hint of fear, but stubborn anger as well.

"Of course I do." James pulls his arm away roughly. "Do you?"

"If you know, then why would you…" Jane lets the question trail, disgust clouding her expression. For a moment, it looks like she will abandon him to his vice, but then she catches his arm again and tightens her grip. "They're what Peter used to make the tea he gave me when I first arrived in Neverland. They make you forget yourself."

Revulsion is clear in Jane's features, and for a brief moment, James feels that revulsion himself. The fierce pirate captain a coward, running from himself, hiding inside the numbing effects of the bloom.

"Forgetting myself is precisely what I need." He steps past her, shaking her off and seizing one of the blooms, snapping it from its stem.

His pipe—he left it in his bag on the beach. He'll have to make do. Thick sap oozes from the broken end of the flower and he touches it to his tongue, then sucks at it greedily. The effect is immediate, lightning to his spine, an old friend, coming home. Jane makes a sound of frustration beside him, but James can't help but smile. A slow, syrupy thing in its own right.

"Are you sure?" He holds out the blossom to her, hearing the slur in his words. She smacks it from his hand. He barely feels the blow.

"Disgusting," she says. And then she says, "What would he think of you?"

James stares at her. The words come from Jane, but they're not hers. Her voice, but not, because how could she know?

She's barely looking at him, glancing around as if she expects a fresh attack any moment. James can't stop staring at her. A second mouth has opened across her cheek, just above the line of her jaw.

It speaks in a hissing whisper, even as her lips remain closed.

"What would he think of you? No better than an animal. All hunger. Like a pig rutting in filth. You would break his heart."

James's own heart thuds against his ribs, painful, running too fast. His first instinct is to take more of the sap, to chase the vision away. But he isn't holding the flower anymore. He looks down, noticing the other blooms now, scattered and trampled as if underfoot. Not merely shaken by the wind. Harvested, he thinks. Tasted. By whom? The boys who attacked them at the camp?

And why should it surprise him that Pan would drug the boys in his thrall, as Jane claimed he drugged her, keeping them loyal to him? In Pan's absence, why wouldn't they turn to the drug again to dull the horror of their existence? Feral things, trapped here, abandoned by their leader. He'd seen the skull at the camp. How long had it been before the boys turned on each other, slaughtered one of their own?

The thought brings him a kind of grim satisfaction. After the number of times he tried and failed to even wound them, here they are, doing the work for him. At the same time, some deep-buried sense of pity swells in him. They are in-between things, trapped as he was in a life they never asked for, not boys in truth any longer, but not men either.

He plucks another flower, devours more of the sap. He extends the blossom to the bound man this time, ignoring Jane. Michael. Yes. He remembers a child bound with rope a very long time ago. He tied the rope himself. Lashed the child to the mast, and waited for Pan to come. James chuckles to himself.

"Don't you dare!" Jane's tone is furious, stepping between James and her uncle.

"But he's in pain," James says. "Anyone can see that."

Michael Darling is hurting. His ghosts—not ones from Neverland, his own, the ones he carried here with him—are clear in his eyes. Men dying. James sees them, reflected in Michael's eyes. The scars of a war.

"Can't you?" James points, clumsily.

His heart goes out to the boy. He was never a soldier, but he understands endless battle, endless death. He understands what it is to be the only one left, the one who survives.

Jane turns to look at her uncle, her expression pained, caught between the two of them. There's a kind of aura about her, a shimmering gold, and he has the urge to run his hands through it. It's hurt. It's armor. She's like Samuel in so many ways, caring so much about everyone around her that it vibrates from her on a frequency he couldn't see until now. Should he warn her of all the ways the world will try to break her, wear her thin if she lets it until she crumbles to ash?

"Jane?" It's Michael Darling's voice, and James turns his head.

Michael, once again surfacing from the shadows. This might be the truest James has seen him—Michael Darling himself, and not anything else.

"Promise me you won't go to war." Michael moves swiftly, surprising James, catching Jane off guard.

"What are you—?" Jane tries to step back, but Michael grabs his niece by the upper arm. His expression is that of a man who fears being pulled under by a vast tide, speaking quickly while he can.

"Promise!" He shakes Jane, and tears start in the girl's eyes. "I see you there in the tents, in the blood and the screaming, and I can't..." His voice breaks, his hands fist around the lapels of her

261

coat, dragging Jane closer until it looks as though he'll swallow her whole.

His eyes are bright too—bright with ghosts and tears.

"I—" Jane catches a breath, but there are no words.

James watches them from a distance, removed by the flower, fascinated. These children of Neverland. These broken things.

"James?" The voice breaks through everything, his name, clear and heartbreaking.

Samuel stands at the edge of the trees, almost swallowed between them. He's dressed not as James last saw him, but as he was in Neverland—the surgeon's clothing he wore on the ship. He looks young and lost. Smoke and silver, like an opium dream given flesh.

James takes a step, reaching, and now his leg does fail him, folding and crashing him to the ground. Samuel's skull flies from his grasp and rolls across the forest floor to rest at the ghost's feet. James wheezes for breath. He tries to claw his way toward the skull, toward Samuel. He's vaguely aware of a crashing noise behind him, like someone plunging through the brush, and he ignores it. It isn't important now. What's important is—

"Samuel." The name rasps as James struggles for another breath.

His fingertips reach, but the skull is so far away, the toes of Samuel's boots are so far away.

Samuel isn't looking at him, but at his own skull. There's a dispassionate curiosity to his gaze, and it surprises James how much the expression hurts him. He wants to tell Samuel to look away. What will it do to him, seeing his own death? Does he know James is at fault?

"Don't," he wheezes, but Samuel ignores him. He bends at the waist, but instead of picking up the skull, his fingers pass right through it.

"What did you do to me?" Samuel's head snaps up, his gaze fixing James, fixing Hook, burning silver rage.

"I didn't... I'm sorry." James pushes himself up, crawling toward Samuel.

His fingers brush Samuel's knee, reach for the hem of his coat. His touch passes straight through the ghost of his lover, leaving him grasping at nothing.

"Please," he gasps. There's salt on his lips. There's something he needs to say, before it's too late. A spell to hold Samuel with him, an anchor to keep him from drifting away again.

"I—" But before he can get any further, Samuel throws his head back and howls, a chilling, inhuman sound.

The silver mist of him dissipates and James is left alone in the clearing among the sick-sweet scent of bruised petals. He collapses, misery dragging him down. Samuel is gone. And dully, he is aware that Jane is also gone. Even Michael is gone, along with the ghosts filling him. James is as alone as he's ever been—his only companion, Samuel's skull.

CHASING GHOSTS

Jane watches Hook converse with empty air, speaking to it, and listening as though it responds. She wants to strike him across the face, snap him out of it. She can't have the pirate captain and her uncle both unraveling on her. It's too much.

Michael spoke to her. He begged her not to go to war. It wasn't the shadows inside of him. It was Uncle Michael, and he knew somehow, even though she's told no one in her family that she's even considering enlisting as a nurse. What's the sense in waiting for soldiers to come home broken, like her uncle, if she can be on the front lines? There, maybe she can do some good before it's too late.

Her uncle had sounded so afraid. It's as if the ghosts in his eyes told him her intentions. The way he'd said it, it was as though he really could see her, her future, among men crying out in pain. She's used to her Uncle Michael seeing ghosts, but nothing like this. And now Hook maybe be talking to ghosts of his own, and she isn't sure she can bear anymore.

But, of course, there is more.

"Jane?" The small voice from behind her pierces straight to her heart.

Jane knows what she will see before she turns. It's impossible, and yet there is no other way things can go. She came here looking for Peg, hoping to save her, and she'd failed. Now, here is another failure, staring her in the face.

Jane turns to face Timothy and says his name—a choked version of his name that's half sob, half broken laughter.

She watched him die. She held him in her arms as he bled out and his body went still and cold.

He peers at her with moon-wide eyes, unchanged, and she runs to him even knowing he can't possibly be here. It's an illusion – Neverland, or whatever remains of it, playing with her head. And none of that matters. She runs to him, and Timothy's eyes widen further.

"You promised you'd keep me safe and you let me die. You let them hurt me." Tears start and he whirls on his heel, sprinting away from her.

Jane is much taller than him now, her legs so much longer. It should be nothing to catch him, and yet he weaves between the trees, always just ahead of her, a flash of silver vanishing in the dark.

"Wait! I'm sorry!" Jane pants, her coat flapping, hot and weighing her down.

She wiggles free of its sleeves, shedding it behind her like skin as she runs, but keeping the strap of her satchel clutched tight. It occurs to her that she's left Hook and her uncle behind and she decides she doesn't care. She has to catch Timothy.

She scrambles over a fallen tree, over tumbled stone, climbing. Sweat sticks her clothing to her skin. She stretches, wedging her fingers into whatever gaps she can find, reaching after handholds. She doesn't give herself time to think, and because she doesn't, climbing is the most natural thing in the world. It's eight years ago, and she's playing follow the leader with Peter and the boys, and she will not be left behind.

Jane's foot slips, and she bangs her shin painfully, hissing in a sharp breath. Blood seeps through the fabric of her trousers even though the cloth itself didn't tear. She forces herself to keep climbing. She can't see Timothy anymore, but he must be just above her.

Their positions reversed from the night they climbed to the cavern where he died, the first time she promised him everything would be okay, and he almost fell. And her mother saved them.

The satchel slung across her body bangs against her hip as Jane hauls herself up until she can plant her knee on a plateau, then push herself to standing. Her legs and arms tremble with the effort. There's nowhere farther to go. She's at the top of a spill of stone that looks as though it was shattered by a giant fist.

Her hair hangs in her face, and Jane takes a moment to untie and retie the ribbon her mother gave her. As she does it, there's a sudden pang. She remembers her mother braiding her hair when they finally found each other in Neverland—a moment that was absent and tender both. Her mother should be here. Jane blinks rapidly, and tucks the strands of hair the ribbon refuses to hold behind her ear.

No. She doesn't need her mother, or anyone. She can do this on her own.

The red and flickering sky feels closer without trees in the way, as if being higher up means that all she would need to do to touch it would be to stretch herself a little taller. She knows that isn't the way the sky works. Except maybe in Neverland it does.

A jagged crack, like black lightning, races across the bloody red. Jane catches sight of stars, briefly, and they make her think of home. She strains to catch a glimpse of Hook's pirate ship, ghostly and tumbling through the skies. There's nothing. Nothing except the sketched suggestion of something that looks almost human. Human, but vast and stretched across the bowl enclosing the world. Like a boy, but with horns and hooves.

She must be imagining it. Her mother stitched Peter's shadow back onto him. She made him into a monster. And then? The thought is too terrible to contemplate, and she tears her gaze away from the sky.

Except she can still feel it. It makes her want to drop to her knees and cover her head. She wants to crawl under the rocks so the terrible thing in the sky can't see her. Because there's a sense of attention, the sense of a waiting pause as if something impossible and ancient is sweeping its gaze over the exposed plateau where she stands.

Jane does drop then, digging at the rock, burrowing in a senseless panic so that it's a moment before it fully registers that there is somewhere to go. There's a gap, just wide enough, even though the satchel drags at her as she tries to worm her way through. A new fear seizes her, squeezing her chest tight. She'll be caught between the rocks, or they'll shift and crush her. She scrabbles at the strap, fighting the tightness that tells her to gasp in shallow breaths because there isn't enough air.

She forces her breathing to remain even, forces herself to relax. Struggling will only make things worse. Fear is her enemy and if she gives into it, then she will get herself wedged, or in flailing and clawing to escape, she will be the one to shift the stone and cause the collapse. Deep, even inhales, followed by exhales. There is enough space, enough space even to work the strap of the satchel over her head and push it ahead of her.

The way widens, and Jane is even able to get to her hands and knees rather than slithering on her belly. Then all at once, her hand comes down on nothing, and Jane plunges forward, her heart dropping, her body dropping, air whistling in a throat that has suddenly closed to a pinhole, refusing her even the relief of a scream.

Her shoulder bangs painfully against the stone, arresting her fall. Pain blooms, erasing everything with white heat, and it's a moment before she can convince herself she isn't falling. Her head hangs downward into a space that she can't make sense of at first. And then she can, because she knows this place. Where else would Timothy's ghost run to except the place he died?

Jane shifts her weight, and her shoulder screams in response, a grinding of bone against bone. There's nothing else for it but to scream back—not pain or fear, but sheer frustration. She will not let Neverland break her.

Using her good arm, Jane levers herself up. Agony spikes through her, making her eyes water, and she squeezes them closed, breathing and breathing until she can be sure she won't be sick or pass out. Slowly, she shifts her body, trying as much as possible not to jostle her arm, until she's seated on the edge of the hole that breaks through into the cavern below.

In the gloom, she can't quite gauge the drop. She hauls her satchel around, hoping the canvas itself is enough to shelter the contents. Jane lets the bag fall, holding her breath to listen. Not that long until she hears it thud to the ground. It can't be that far.

Or at least so she tells herself. Because what choice does she have? She can't crawl back the way she came, not with her shoulder the way it is. She has to go farther in.

Jane takes a deep breath, an irrational thing, as though she's about to dive into the ocean. She pushes herself off from the lip of stone, and for a moment, she's certain she's thrown herself to her death. Then she remembers to tuck and to shelter her arm if she can, and manages somehow to hit the ground with knees bent rather than legs rigid, staggering to the side and catching herself in a crouch instead of collapsing in a heap.

Only it's her bad arm she catches herself with and Jane lets out another scream, voicing all her agony and frustration in a cry that leaves her throat raw. Darkness threatens the edges of her vision, but she forbids herself from passing out. Somehow, she's able to stand without falling, taking a deep, shuddering breath as she does.

Another wave of sickness sweeps over her as Jane bends to retrieve her satchel, hanging it from her good arm. As gently as she can, she probes her wounded shoulder. More water stings her eyes, and Jane catches a breath, freeing tears.

Not broken, she thinks, only dislocated. At least she has a concrete diagnosis, and problem to solve. She must think rationally, think of herself as just another patient, and take things one step at a time.

There's a trick she saw one of the younger doctors at the college perform once, one of Simon's friends. He'd laughingly called it a miracle cure. She and Peg had gone with him and Simon and two other doctors in training to the pub for a drink. The young doctor, Ethan, had only just completed training at the college himself, and now worked as a teaching assistant part time, while also working at one of the local hospitals.

It had been an icy night, and as they'd been leaving the pub, one of the other men—Paul—had slipped, landing badly and dislocating his shoulder. Peg and Jane had immediately insisted he needed to go to the hospital. Ethan had promised, however, that he could fix it himself, and it would take less than a minute. He'd seen a man do it at a traveling show, and it was the easiest thing in the world.

Jane had been horrified, certain Ethan would only make things worse. She'd argued, accusing him of being drunk and a show-off. What had finally reassured her, at least a little, was Ethan's own admission that he'd initially been convinced that the traveling showman had been a phony too. But he'd watched carefully as the man performed his miracle, and then he'd lingered until the exhibitions closed, and he'd plied the miracle worker with drinks until he'd explained his wondrous cure.

Jane had only relented though when she'd made Ethan promise that he would explain every step to her in turn. To her surprise, he'd agreed. He had treated her just as he would a male colleague, expecting her to keep up and understand immediately, not assuming she would be squeamish or flinch away.

The trick, he'd explained, was getting the injured person to relax, holding the arm straight by the patient's side with the elbow bent, and applying very gentle and steady outward pressure while massaging the muscles around the joint until they relaxed. The shoulder would then slip back into place on its own, with not even a hint of pain.

She'd held on to her doubt, but watched Ethan like a hawk. As much as a tiny part of her had wanted him to be wrong, yet another braggart overstating his skill to emphasize how much more qualified he was to be a doctor than her, she couldn't argue with the results. Or his method either. His calm explanation of the process, his steady, jocular tone, had put Paul at ease. There'd been something almost hypnotic to the rhythm of his voice— something else he'd learned from the miracle worker at the fair— convincing Paul's body to do the work for him. She'd seen the joint slip back into place just as Ethan promised and Paul hadn't so much as felt a thing.

Here, in a cavern, in an impossible world, Jane doesn't have the luxury of alcohol, or Ethan's steady assurance. She'll have to do it on her own. If only she had taken Hook's flower.

A rough chuckle escapes her, enough to send another jolt of pain through her, sobering her. The longer she waits, the worse it will be. She lowers herself gingerly to the ground. There's a stone she can use to brace her arm, elbow at a ninety-degree angle. She won't be able to apply pressure and massage her muscles all at once. She'll have to rely on the weight of her body, leaning away from her arm, and hoping it will be enough.

She forces herself to take a deep breath. Another. *Think happy thoughts.* Her mother's voice in her head, saying the words a lifetime ago. Jane fights down another rough laugh, one that threatens to turn into a sob. Happy thoughts have nothing to do with flying; even young as she was then, Jane had guessed that truth. But she understands now what her mother was trying to do—chase away doubt, not allow room for fear. She has to do the same thing now.

"It's just like flying," Jane says aloud, and her voice echoes weirdly in the cavern.

Another deep breath, and she eases her good arm across her body, focusing on steady breaths, a steady pulse, as she massages the muscles in turn. She leans. She expects a spike of pain and almost tenses against it, but there's a feeling that she can't quite explain—the joint popping back into place—and she can scarcely believe it, her breath catching, and then let out again in a whooping victory cry.

She moves her arm. It doesn't scream in pain. She tests her range of motion, and it's all there, as it should be. She laughs, wiping at her eyes, tears of relief now. She can barely believe it worked, but it did, and she scrambles to stand. At the motion, the fabric of her trousers pulls against the wound on her leg, and Jane laughs all over again. She'd forgotten all about her scraped shin.

Digging in her satchel, Jane retrieves the iodine, and the bandages. She doesn't have her scissors anymore, the ones she buried in Arthur's cheek. Rolling her trouser leg carefully away from the scrape, she swabs it with iodine and wraps a length of bandage around it, tearing it awkwardly, and tying it off. She lowers her trouser leg. There's nothing to be done about the bloodstained cloth, but at least she can be fairly certain now that infection won't set in.

It's hard not to feel a little invincible. If only her mother could see her now. How proud she'd be.

The thought is swift and unexpected, and it nearly takes Jane's breath away all over again. Jane lifts her head, forcing her scraped chin not to wobble. But the ache of the thought remains, like a bruise. If Jane doesn't look at it too closely, doesn't prod at it, then she can pretend it isn't there. She must focus on what she came here for in the first place—Timothy.

Her eyes have adjusted to the low light in the cave. It should be utterly pitch black, but there's a faint, hazy grayness, like the sky before dawn. Jane doesn't question it, the source of the light. It needn't make sense. In fact, she would be surprised if it did. This is Neverland, after all.

The thought leaves her giddy, a kind of wild humor that might overwhelm her completely if she allows it. She moves carefully, wary of the uneven stone. She slides her feet rather than lifting them, remembering the melted-wax unevenness of the ground, the columns of stalagmites and stalactites. There's just enough luminescence—whatever the source—to make out the crystals winking in the walls.

That much hasn't changed. Despite the shattered interior, this part of the cavern at least is the same. The only thing missing is the burning glow, the heat like a furnace roaring somewhere deep within the cave. As Jane moves onward, she sees more evidence of the damage done. Great tables of rock forced up at jagged angles, as if pushed from underneath by a buried giant waking from its sleep. Cracked columns like felled trees.

She remembers the cavern shaking, tearing itself apart as she begged her mother to go back for Timothy.

She swallows around a painful lump in her throat. The light, whatever it is, seems to be growing brighter. She moves toward it, then stops, her pulse wanting to stop with it, every part of her going cold.

The light brightening the cave, gleaming off the crystals and shattered stone, comes from Timothy. His ghost, standing solemnly with his head bowed, his hands folded in front of him, like a sorrowful guardian. He stands over his own bones.

A sob breaks from Jane. She rushes forward, kneeling, drawing pain from her scraped shin and ignoring it. She lifts her arms, but she isn't sure whether to reach for Timothy's ghost or his bones or neither. He raises his head, eyes meeting hers, and his expression stops her completely. His eyes are dark wells, drawing in the light, holding in a pain far too big for his tiny frame.

"I died twice," Timothy says, barely a whisper. His voice is terrible in the dark and Jane wants to stop her ears, but forces herself to listen. "It hurt, Jane. It hurt so, so much."

"I know." Jane draws a ragged breath, tears thickening the words so she barely gets them out.

This is a moment she'll never get with Peg. As much as it hurts, she has to be here for Timothy, for both of them, and for herself as well. The ache of looking at him is as fresh as the moment Timothy slumped against her, the moment his wound became real, crimson blooming across the shirt whose tails he used to chew on, the same shirt his ghost wears now. She remembers how he didn't even cry; how death came for him too quickly for that. Only a faint whimper, a truncated sound as he clutched her, and begged her to make it go away, to make him better.

There'd been nothing she could do. Jane remembers her hands slick with blood, trying to staunch the flow. But the blood had kept on going, Timothy's life bleeding out before her eyes.

There is nothing she can do now either. Timothy is dead, and he has been for years. Or for moments. Time means nothing here, and the pain is fresh for both of them. There is nothing Jane can do to take it away. She can't go back. The only way through is to go deeper.

274

"I know," she says again. "And I am so, so sorry. I'm sorry I left, and I'm sorry I couldn't stop it, but I'm here now, and I'm not leaving you."

She reaches for him to fold him in her arms, remembering the way he would burrow into her side for comfort when he was afraid as she told him a story.

But her arms go right through him, and she ends up holding nothing.

The motion tilts her forward so she almost falls upon his bones. She cradles them instead, lifting them gently, and holds them against her body, sobbing.

Timothy weighs nothing. There is nothing left to him at all. Everything bright and beautiful about him is gone, but Jane doesn't let go.

"Once upon a time—" Her voice breaks. She squeezes her eyes closed, tears scalding her cheeks.

She can't do this. She can't. She has to. She will.

"Once upon a time, there was a boy who was very far away from home, and a girl who was far away from home too. At first, they were both afraid, but they found each other, and became fast friends. They took care of each other, and went on many adventures, and neither of them had to be alone or afraid anymore."

She wants it to be true so badly. She wants it with every ounce of her being. She feels Timothy's ghost watching her, feels the deep, wounded wells of his eyes. She feels it when the glow fades, and when she finally forces herself to look again, he's gone. Jane doesn't know if it's forgiveness, but she hopes, at least, it is peace.

She looks back to the bones cradled in her arms. She can't leave Timothy alone in the dark again. But she can't carry his whole skeleton out with her either, as small as it may be.

The answer comes to her, known the moment the problem occurred to her, and she shoves it away with violence. The thought sickens her, and at the same time, she knows there is no other way. Jane lowers Timothy's skeleton. She arranges it as carefully as she can, curled on his side, as though sleeping. She feels the fragility, how easily the bones would come apart. She hates the knowledge, that this thing will be easy to do when it should be impossible.

It's worse than bracing herself for relocating her shoulder. It's worse than anything she's ever done, except watching Timothy die in the first place. She takes his skull between her hands. It's so small. She forces herself to look into Timothy's eyes, even though he doesn't have eyes anymore. She forces herself not to flinch or look away, and she twists his skull free.

Jane's breath goes out in a rush. She'll never get it back again. She'll suffocate here.

Then her body turns traitor, breathing in again. She is still alive. Peg may not be, Timothy may not be, but she is, and she has to keep going.

Jane nestles the skull in her satchel, like tucking Timothy in. She'd imagined once, what it would be like to be his big sister. Well, she has to be big and safe and caring one more time. She has to protect him. She lays her hand over the shape of the skull in her satchel and rises.

"Hold on, Timothy," she whispers. "I'm taking you home."

NEITHER PIRATE, NOR GENTLEMAN

The girl is gone. Her uncle too. And Samuel as well. Unless they were never here to begin with, and he hallucinated them all. Perhaps he only dreamed leaving Neverland, and now he's awake, back where he began. Samuel's skull looks up at him, baleful, reproaching. James's limbs are heavy, but his head is light, disconnected, his tongue and throat sticky with flower sap.

He can't sit in this clearing forever, going over in his mind what he doesn't have. The boys—the men?—the feral creatures left in Pan's wake might return at any moment. How long will their memory of fearing him keep him safe?

James pushes himself up. He's unsteady, his body suddenly remembering its aches. He is not the pirate captain any longer; he is not the man he became in London, the veneer pulled over his past. He is nothing, in-between. But at least he still has his cane. And Samuel. He tucks the skull into the crook of his arm. Should he search for the girl? She's probably better off without him.

Either his eyes have adjusted to the gloom, or the sap has sharpened his senses. One path leading from the clearing seems brighter than the rest. The tip of his cane sinks into the leaf-litter, nearly unbalancing him, but he carries on. It's as though he's wading through blood-warm water, each of his legs attached by long, pulled strands of tarry opium. His progress is slow, but at least he's moving again.

He has it in his mind that he should return to the cave where he first found the blade. If the old bitch-siren is still alive—as undying as he once was—he'll demand answers. If not, perhaps he'll drown himself in her pool. Or perhaps he could call Pan's beast to him, whatever remains of it have been crammed inside Michael Darling's skin, and allow it to devour him whole. The thought makes him chuckle, a sound without mirth.

It's too quiet, too still. Neverland should ring with voices—bird-voices, boy-voices, Pan's, which was always both, even those stupid chattering monkeys. All James hears now are muffled booms of distant thunder. Like cannon fire, he thinks. Two vast ships sailing across the red sky, locked in eternal battle.

The tree line ends, and the beach begins. White sand, soft and powdery, though it looks almost pink under the glow from the sky. This is the far side of the island from where they landed, if his geography is right, but in this place, it's impossible to tell. There's an oily motion to the tide, a slickness, like ink crawling up the shore and retreating again—an unsettling motion.

Carefully, James removes his boots, sets them aside before stepping barefoot onto the sand. He glances at the sky, and immediately regrets it. There's a sound like shattering glass, like bells ringing, and an animal roaring in pain. It's like nothing he can name, and the sky tears wide, a mouth, a maw. Stars glitter like broken teeth, and smoke pours forth, and for a moment, the roiling shape of it is the beast that devoured him a thousand times.

James falls to the sand, covering his head with his arms. Jaws open. He feels it rather than sees it, the beast twisting in midair to fall upon him, engulfing him. He can't scream. Darkness, like a physical thing, and he breathes it into his lungs. Consuming him from the inside out. He's choking. Drowning. Scales wrap him, a powerful tail crushing, rolling and rolling in the depths. His ribs creak, on the point of shattering. His chest won't expand, he cannot get enough air.

Then all at once, the beast is gone.

James blinks. He is alone on the shore, cowering like a child. No, not quite alone. Someone watches him from a few paces away.

He picks himself up slowly, a new kind of dread pooling in him. Samuel, but not as James saw him in the clearing with the flowers. Samuel as he was just before the end—gray, ragged, worn, and fading. A wave of shame fills him. James scrambles to retrieve Samuel's skull, brushes the sand from it, and stands as straight as he can. The sadness in Samuel's gaze tells him he is a pitiable thing. Worn as he is, Samuel is still young. He never wanted Samuel to see him grown this old, not unless they were growing old together.

James's breath catches, and he cannot get it to restart. The whole world seems to hang still and waiting as Samuel approaches. He leaves no footsteps on the sand. He isn't really here, and yet James feels seen, flayed, stripped bare. He doesn't even realize he's trembling until Samuel reaches out a hand, and James finds himself taking it automatically. The hand he reaches out in turn shakes, but it is his hand, flesh and blood, not wood—a phantom hand to touch his phantom lover.

"Come along, I'll show you the way." Samuel's voice is a sigh.

He turns as if to lead James toward the far end of the shore, the curve of rock, and the memory of a line traced in the sand where water once ran from a cave mouth and into the sea. James finds himself leaning back, digging his bare heels into the ground until Samuel looks back at him with a questioning expression in his sorrowful eyes.

"Last time we were here." James swallows, begins again. "Last time we were here, you tried to stop me."

"I could never talk you out of anything. When your mind was set, there was never any changing it." A faint smile, but touched with sadness. Samuel shakes his head slightly.

Promise. Samuel's hand slipping from his, hot and hollow and frail. *Be kind.*

James licks his lips, dry suddenly as the shore underfoot. He wants to protest that Samuel's words aren't fair. He stopped killing for him, stopped thieving. He stopped being a pirate. Changed everything. Became a kept man. Became less.

But no. He never did anything of those things. He never changed, though he pretended to.

And there it is. The thought, stark in his mind, matched to the pain in Samuel's eyes. James hears it, understands it without Samuel ever saying it aloud: *Is that truly what you think? That changing would have made you less, rather than us together becoming more?*

James's mouth opens. Closes again. He wants to deny it, but the words lodge in his throat. His damned, stupid pride. The words he never allowed himself to say. And still he cannot say them aloud.

Samuel tugs gently at his fingers, and this time, James allows himself to be led. He is too stunned to do otherwise.

"You're determined to do this thing." Samuel's voice drifts back to him, blown on a lonely wind, even though the air is eerily still. "I won't let you go alone."

What is it that he's even trying to do? James is no longer sure. Set something wrong right? But how? He plunged in the first time not knowing what he was doing, wielding a blade, a magic he didn't understand. He was like an animal in a trap, gnawing off its own leg to be free, not caring for the consequences. It had cost him his crew. It cost the lives of innocent people in London who simply happened to be in the wrong place at the wrong time.

Perhaps the way to end this all is to end himself. Hasn't that been the problem all along? Killdeer and Harrigan stalking him, killing to get to him. If he simply removes himself from the equation, they won't have a purpose, and they won't have the satisfaction of winning.

James stops. They're at the mouth of the cave. A faint glow hangs around Samuel, a luminescence matched to that of the pool he remembers from so long ago. Samuel looks back at him again, something almost reassuring in his smile, but touched with regret as well. James tightens his grip on the skull, ducks, though it is unnecessary, and follows Samuel inside.

The stone underfoot is uneven. He almost slips, but Samuel is there to steady him. The only light comes from Samuel's skin. The pool wasn't that deep into the cave. James remembers that. So whatever light it emitted then is gone. Even as the thought occurs to him, his next step nearly takes him over the edge, and he reels back, losing his balance and landing hard on his tailbone.

Samuel drifts beside him. When the shock of pain subsides, James can just make out the pool, faintly illuminated by Samuel's glow. Or rather, he can make out the place where the stone of the cave floor stops, and something else begins. He has a faint sense of it as liquid. But at the same time, it is simply a lack of light, a negative space, a hole in the fabric of *here* that is something else. Or perhaps nothing at all.

He crawls forward, squinting, but it doesn't help. The light fails, resisted by the black. He has a sense that he's leaning over water, but he can't see it clearly. A chill emanates. Not quite a breeze. Cool damp. He has the sudden image of a rotten arm reaching up to seize him by the throat and drag him down. He sees a rage-filled face, sharp angles of cheekbones and razor teeth tucked behind thin lips. The mermaid, the oracle, whatever she was. The black of the pool is the black of her eyes and he imagines her still sleeping there, dead and not, and he rocks back onto his haunches, wrapping his arms around his bent knees as he crouches at the edge of where he feels the pool to be.

"What do I do?" He isn't really asking Samuel, but he looks up anyway.

He feels very small. He wants Samuel to give him advice, remove the weight of decision from his shoulders, but Samuel merely shakes his head.

"I can't tell you that."

James wants to shout at him, ask what good he is then when Samuel's expression breaks, shifting from disappointment to sympathy. As his expression shifts, so does he, moving to James's side, crouching beside him, and placing a hand on his shoulder.

It doesn't sink through James's skin, and for a moment, he can allow himself to believe that Samuel is really here. He can allow himself to feel warmth from the touch, everything in him leaning toward it and drawing comfort and strength and reassurance from it.

"I'm only here to make sure that whatever you do, you don't have to do it alone." The smile Samuel offers this time touches his eyes, it cracks James open so his pulse stutters and his breath snags.

"I think I know." He doesn't really, but he didn't know what he was doing last time either.

It's about belief. A leap of faith. He isn't sure what he believes in when it comes to the larger question of his life, but in this moment, he believes the blade—or whatever remains of it—waits for him in the black pool, and he will have to reach in to get it. Because if Samuel can be dead and still here by his side, if his ship can be broken on the shore when he sailed it through the sky to freedom, if he can be James and Hook both, then this is also true. The blade is broken, its fragments buried in his leg, but it is in the pool waiting for him too. That's the logic of Neverland.

The dead mermaid oracle also waits beneath the surface, as does the nightmare beast from his worst dreams, beady black eyes just below the level of the water, glaring hate. All of these things are true, but he's not going to let it stop him.

Using his other hand, James curls the articulated fingers of his wooden hand into a shape like a hook to catch the hilt of the blade. Then without giving himself any more time to doubt, James throws himself forward all in one motion and plunges his arm into the black.

It's like having the limb severed at his shoulder. The arm sheared clear off, too quick and clean to feel the pain. Then the pain comes a moment later. A burning cold, the sense of reaching through and back to his own past, when he did this the first time. The sense of being here and another part of him being somewhere else.

His arm is no longer his to command. He can't move the muscles; the whole thing might as well be carved of wood, not just the hand. He has to trust. He has to trust that somehow his fingers caught something before he wrenches himself back and falls gasping onto the cave floor.

He can't lift his arm. He can't do anything for a moment but breathe against the burning cold. His eyes water. He struggles to lift his head, turn it toward the dead weight of his arm. He can barely see in the dark, but far away from him is his hand and there is the blade.

Paler than the black blade had been all those years ago. Gray, and he still can't tell if it's metal or stone. Pitted. There are pieces missing, and his thigh aches, like calling to like.

"Did I...?" The words are a wheeze, not enough breath to complete the question.

Samuel crouches beside him, brushes a hand across James's brow. He feels the touch, whether it's truly there or not. James is about to speak when something terrible happens to Samuel's face. It crumples, like smoke collapsing inward to fill a sudden displacement of air. Something dark and terrible swings through the place where Samuel leaned over him a moment ago, and James barely has time to register what's happening.

Michael Darling stands over him with a stone in his hand, and he brings it crashing down on James's skull.

THE BLACK BLADE RETURNED

NEVERLAND – NOW

James wakes tied to a mast, and filled with the sense that his life has come around in a circle, returning him to a place where he never meant to be. At any moment, he'll hear Pan's taunting voice, a circle of boys will jeer and dance around him, and he'll be forced to walk the plank again. He'll drown.

He waits, his arms aching from being forced behind him, his head aching where it was struck with a rock. Bruised, battered again, but still not dead. And no Pan. There is only the weird flickering sky overhead, and a canted deck below him.

James laughs. A dry and hollow sound that turns into a cough that makes his chest ache. His ship. Michael Darling has brought him back to his ship and lashed him to the mast, their roles reversed from what they were many long years ago.

He remembers the rock that struck him, the way it passed through Samuel's face on the way to him. He turns his head slowly, a motion that makes the world swim, sends pain spiking behind his left eye and makes him want to vomit. He closes his eyes, waits for the sickness to pass. When he opens them again, the dizziness remains, but less now.

He'd allowed himself to hope that Samuel's ghost would be there, looking over him, but he's alone. No. Not alone. Not quite. Ropes creak, and a breeze carrying salt and the scent of the waves stirs across his face. The deck bows beneath the weight of feet that aren't quite there, and James hears a distant shout. Voices, calling back and forth to one another under the snap of sails.

Even though the ship is grounded, shattered, the deck tilted, he feels it roll. His crew. They are here too, all around him. They are almost visible, a thickening in the air, places where the world blurs.

"Will you give them orders, Captain? Will you command your crew again?" Wisps of smoke-ghosts part and re-form around Michael as he climbs the tilted deck toward James.

His step is sure—the limp plaguing the real Michael Darling buried deep—his smile a sickle in the dark, and his eyes the eerie gold of old coins. The golden eyes of Pan's hunting beast. The beast's teeth are in Michael Darling's smile as well, an unsettling thing.

"Will you order them to die again? Slaughter them a second time?" Michael stops, head tilted slightly as if considering James, as if genuinely curious as to what he will say.

When James doesn't answer, Michael sighs, shaking his head as if disappointed. James can no longer quite pick out the separate voices of his pirates—Killdeer, Harrigan, Chauncey. They blend into one.

"We waited here for you for so long, Captain. Ages, lifetimes, and it was no time at all. But all of it was spent hating, until we finally found a creature that hated you as much as we did. We never could control it quite the way Pan could, but luckily it wanted you badly enough that all we had to do was point it toward the door. Pity it was only a stupid creature and couldn't get it right even on the fourth try." Michael looks down at his body, the body he wears, and shrugs slightly.

"It'll have to do."

James remains silent. There's no point in answering or protesting his innocence either; he had cared about his own escape, and he'd cared about Samuel's. It hadn't mattered to him if the rest of his crew lived or died. He'd forgotten about them the moment he crossed into London.

"Do you remember when you tied me to this mast?" Michael's voice, the voice coming out of his mouth, is casual, conversational.

He resumes his pacing, circling around James. The voice sounds like Michael's now, but James is certain the words are Killdeer's, or Harrigan's. "I was only a child then."

"You're not Michael Darling." James can't turn his head far enough to follow Michael's movements all the way around him, but he feels pressure at his wrists where the ropes cut into them.

He listens to the footsteps stop behind him. Silence for a moment, save for the phantom breath of wind and the fluttering of sails.

"No. But his body is mine now. Ours. And I don't intend to return it. It is a pleasure to have flesh again." As he says it, the rope binding James loosens and he falls forward.

He tries to put his arms out to stop himself, but only one obeys. The arm he plunged into the pool to retrieve the blade hangs useless at his side, dead weight. The other one prickles, pins and needles as blood returns where the ropes restricted the flow. Too late. His face smashes into the deck and James groans.

"*Tsk, tsk*. The great Captain Hook. How low you've fallen." More pacing steps, and Michael comes to a stop before him, the toes of his boots inches from James's face.

It hurts, but James uses his one good arm to push himself up, enough that he can raise his head at least and spit blood.

"You missed." Michael crouches so his face is almost level with James.

"Kill me and get it over with, if that's what you intend to do." James tilts his chin toward the blade, held loosely in Michael's hand.

Michael turns his head, tracking James's gaze as if only now recognizing the blade in his hand. It's all for show, theater for James's benefit, and he has no choice but to play along. If their positions were reversed—as they were once before—he would do the same.

"Soon, but not yet." Michael holds the blade up.

The weird light shows the gaps in its substance. The blade, like the boys in Pan's camp, flickers—there and then not, whole and broken. Existing in more than one state, more than one time.

"There's more to be done yet." Michael lowers the blade, and offers another unnerving smile.

James feels a pull, like the air around the blade is humming. Michael holds out his other hand, and James stares at it. When he doesn't move, Michael reaches, impatiently hauling him to his feet.

"Don't you remember all the pompous speeches you made on this deck? Swearing this time you'd finally best Pan?" There's a mocking edge to the words. "Now it's our turn to speak."

Michael keeps his grip on James, even though he's on his feet now. James's other arm, the one Michael isn't holding, continues to hang uselessly at his side.

"I'm going to bring them back. All the pirates you slaughtered. But first, I need something from you."

Michael moves closer, stepping James backward. James ends up with his back against the mast again, pinned, though the pressure from Michael Darling's hand is slight. There's a compulsive power to him, and that, more than any physical touch, keeps James still. It's the hunting beast's eyes in Michael's face, a little bit of Pan's hypnotic power, still caught in this world.

And then, there's something else, something behind the gold in Michael's eyes. Not the pale, washed-out blue, but a deep brown-green, a dark hazel. Harrigan's eyes, and they're sorrowing. For just a moment, Michael's expression is fathomless loss, not his own. Did Harrigan actually care for the lost pirates? Does he actually mourn them? Or perhaps one pirate in particular. Killdeer. A sudden image of Harrigan's face, stricken and full of rage as the terrible pirate captain—not James, Hook, though aren't they one and the same really—casually buried the sharp point of his hook in Killdeer's throat.

Perhaps it's only his imagination, or a faulty memory, but for a moment, James can believe it. Harrigan is the one trying to set things right, and James, Hook, is still the villain of the tale after all. He opens his mouth, but never gets to speak. Michael's hand shoots downward, plunging into James's thigh.

James screams. Michael's fingers pass impossibly through his skin, digging into the meat of him. The shattered pieces of the black blade shift, drawn by Michael's touch, and when Michael yanks his hand back, they come free.

Michael steps back, and James collapses to his knees, breath emerging in a whine. There's no blood. He can see his leg, whole, even though his vision swims with the aftermath of pain, but he feels the wound nonetheless, open and raw. A piece of him, pieces of him that never belonged there in the first place, torn free, leaving him...less.

He pants, his body shuddering, but manages to raise his head. Michael leans down, until his face is inches away from James's own. He raises his hands, bringing them together, the ghost blade and the fragments of the original. A sound like a thunderclap, a displacement of air, and when Michael draws his hands apart again, the black blade is once more whole.

James cannot rise, he cannot fight back, but there is this small dignity at least. He hasn't fallen face down again. Yet. He will die on the deck of his ship, if not on his feet. He will die, at least, with the ability to raise his head and look at the sky.

Michael traces the blade through the air, a rough circle. At first, there is nothing, and a taunt rises to James's lips, a sneer curling them. Whatever the shadows inside Michael intended to do, they have failed. They know nothing more about wielding the blade than he did all those years ago.

But Michael makes a second pass with the blade, a third, and a thin silver line appears in the air, shivering, like the knife tip has etched it upon the dark. A door. A gap. A wind blows through, rain-wet, a storm from a lifetime ago, and the ghosts follow on its heels.

James can only stare as the shadows of his former crew solidify before him. Not human, not flesh and blood and bone, certainly. Shapes that have weight, that carry anger, directed toward him. He counts them, faces twisted in rage, names coming back to him where he never cared to remember them before—Bartholomew, Hawkins, and Dart. The ones who were lost, the ones he cut, but who never made it through to London. Chauncey, who left under the cover of the storm, with a boat full of mutineers. Maitland, who made the crossing with them, who Samuel watched die. They're all here.

"Some of these men left before I even used the knife!" James shouts over a rising wind. "They turned traitor. I had nothing to do with their fates. Their deaths aren't on my hands."

Michael glances at him, the repository of yet more shadows, ones James can see shifting behind his eyes.

"You tethered us all to the ship when you used the blade. You trapped us here."

"How could I have known?" James grits his teeth. It hurts, but he forces himself to stand at last, breathing hard, hoping his wounded leg will hold his weight.

Pieces of him shift, grinding like bone against bone. Bits of him have come loose, unmoored. If he isn't careful, he will crumble to dust. Like Maitland. Like Samuel. He lifts his head, pushed by the wind, swaying with his own unsteadiness, but still standing. He takes a step toward Michael, who ignores him; it's like wading through sand.

The deck underfoot is slick, wet, a storm raging only where the ship sits, even grounded on the shore. James feels himself sliding, shoved by the wind, wave-rocked. He loses count of the shadows gathering in the dark. Is this all of them, his whole crew, the ones who sailed through the gap with him to London, the ones who crumbled in their half-lives, unable to survive without the fragments of themselves they'd left behind?

He scans the faces, sick fear pooling in his belly. He forces himself to meet their eyes, or at least try as their faces shift and blur, fading in and out of each other. Mouths open and he catches fragments of words like a cold-blowing wind. These pirates, these half-lives, yes he had a hand in their undoing, but in truth, they were undone before he even met them. They are what Pan made of them. And so is he. Still Hook, even after all this time. Still their captain.

Michael speaks again, taunting, and James has no trouble hearing him above the howling wind.

"Are you looking for your surgeon? He's here too."

Michael takes ahold of one of the shadows, pulling the figure roughly forward. James's heart lurches and falls. He wouldn't know the shadow from the others. There's barely any substance to it, no features that are recognizable. It is a thin and wasted thing, frightened, not of Michael Darling and the creatures inside him, but of James. Of Hook.

It doesn't matter that the shadow doesn't bear Samuel's face. The ache inside him tells James that this is him, the part of him the black blade cut away and left behind. Frightened. Trapped. Alone.

James almost expects to see himself among the shadow pirates, but no, he always carried Hook with him, able to pull him on like a coat, to summon the captain from beneath his skin. When he cut them free from Neverland, he did the poorest job on himself – always caught between two worlds, like a bridge, like a door. His dreams, the ones Samuel warned him about, always drawing Neverland's eye. That bridge, that road between worlds, must have only made things worse for the remnants of the pirates left behind – taunting them, pulling them toward their captain, but leaving them unable to follow. Until he'd finally opened the door.

The heart goes out of James. He wants to look away from Samuel's ghost, but he can't. Entranced, he steps forward, his hand raised. His fingers, the flesh and blood ones, graze the shadow's cheek, as if brushing away a tear.

"I'm sorry," James whispers.

Tremors wrack the shadow in Michael's grip. It flinches from James's touch, and Michael leers.

"This is what you made of him," Michael says. "What you made of all of us."

James feels the other shadows gather close, hungry, hollow, and wanting.

He thinks of the bodies left behind in London, drained and emptied from the inside, husks with nothing left inside. That's what they mean to do to him. Erase him like the hunting beast once erased his hand. The pirates and the beast will empty him out and pour themselves inside his skin. They will take whatever is left of his life and live it using his body, but everything that ever made him James, or even Hook, will be gone.

"Do it, then," he murmurs.

He looks away, no longer able to bear the un-gaze of the shadow that Harrigan-Michael-Killdeer claims to be Samuel. He wants to deny that it could even be possible, that Samuel could come to this, but the doubt won't leave him. How many times has he thought himself over the years that his actions killed Samuel by slow degrees, ruined him even as he tried to save him? Now here is the evidence before his eyes.

The fear in the cowering figure undoes him. This is what he deserves. As captain, he should have gone down with his ship.

He never should have escaped, he should have stayed, bound, as these shadows were, rather than running like a coward. He expects Michael's blade at his throat at any moment, but instead, there's a voice at his ear.

"That isn't me."

Samuel.

James whips his head around. The silvery ghost, the one who stood with him in the cave—the one, if he is being honest with himself, who may only be a figment of his mind—offers a pained smile. It is the same smile Samuel wore at the end, the smile of a man aching to go, but trying so hard to hold on. For James's sake, not his own.

"Whatever I left behind doesn't matter," Samuel says. "The best part of me, always, went with you."

Whether Samuel's ghost is really here with him, or whether it's only his own mind, trying to offer him mercy, it is enough. Enough to wake his love, his rage, his bloody-minded stubbornness. Hook, the immortal pirate captain, is not ready to die just yet. He thought it himself just moments ago—he is still what Pan made him. He is still these men's captain, and this is still his ship.

James throws himself forward, through the thickening mist of ghosts, crashing into Michael Darling and catching him off guard. He lets his weight bear both of them down, and they hit the deck together. The blade goes skittering out of Michael's hand. James ignores it, going for Michael's eyes with his good hand, going for his throat, anything he can reach.

They grapple. Michael twists and bucks beneath him, throwing him off. James is amazed at the strength in the body that seemed so frail when they first met. He's amazed at his own strength. But Michael Darling isn't himself, after all. He is the stitched together fragments of who knows how many lost pirates, fueled by their terrible and unreasoning rage. He is the hunting beast, leashed to his lost pirates' purpose. But James, too, is stitched together of all the things he's been in his many lifetimes—legion fighting legion.

They roll together, sliding down the slanted deck. James's wooden fingers trail uselessly, scraping the boards. If only he had his hook. He could bury it into the wood. Or smash it into Michael's face.

Michael hits him, a quick blow in the same place he struck earlier with the stone. Stars burst behind James's eyes. His head rings and for a moment he can't breathe, can't move. The weight lifts from him. He struggles to rise, then Michael is on him again, and he has the blade in his hand once again. James just manages to raise an arm in defense so the blade slashes a line of fire across his forearm, soaking his sleeve with blood.

Numbness tingles in the blade's wake. Deep cold. Is this how he will go? Death by a thousand tiny cuts? How long before he succumbs? His vision fades in and out, consciousness wanting to leave him. He slumps to the deck, breathing hard. Michael advances on him.

Is it blood running in his eyes, or rain? He can barely see. He's drowning. Failing. Falling. Somewhere, far away, over the howling storm, someone calls to him.

"Captain!" Not another ghost. The girl. Jane.

James pushes himself halfway to sitting, holding his side. Crimson leaks between his fingers. Jane climbs the deck toward them. She's holding a sword. She doesn't look like she knows how to use it, but it doesn't seem to matter. As her uncle turns toward her with a snarl, she brings the hilt down with all her strength, smashing it into his shoulder.

It's enough to throw Michael off balance. Enough to make him drop the black blade, fingers spasming and going numb. Enough that Jane can duck past him and grab James by the arm, trying to haul him up and away.

James just manages to grab the restored black blade as Jane pulls him upright. He almost drags her down, dead weight, bleeding, his limbs barely under his control.

"Come on." She grits her teeth, tugging at him again.

The satchel at her side bulges. It's an odd thing to notice in this moment as Michael regains his feet, advancing on both of them. But James feels the pull toward it, the sharp awareness of what the girl carries there.

"Samuel." He reaches, forgetting he's holding the blade, and the point nearly tears the bag's canvas before Jane tugs it away, glaring at him. Abashed, he slips the black blade into his coat pocket where it hums against the phantom ache in his thigh, the place where its fragments were buried only moments ago.

"I found it. Him." Her eyes are wide, wild, as she glances back toward her uncle. "Let's go."

She tries to pull him up again. Michael's progress is slower now. His limp returned, or a new one discovered. Maybe James actually managed to wound him. He pushes Jane away. She stumbles back a step, but doesn't leave. Brave, stupid girl. Once again, she reminds him of Samuel, not caring for her own safety as she tries to help everyone else.

296

"I promise I won't hurt him." James follows her gaze toward Michael; the fear in Jane's eyes isn't entirely of her uncle, it's for him as well. "I promise."

He's broken a lifetime of promises, more than one lifetime, but this last promise he intends to keep. It takes all his strength, but he forces himself to stand. One side of his body lists, but he's upright, gripping the blade. He meets Jane's eyes as the thing inside her uncle limps toward them.

"But you have to promise something in return," he says. James grins. It is a pirate's grin. "Bury me with him."

He points toward the satchel at Jane's side. Her eyes widen further, but she nods. His lips stretch, a feral and terrible grin, not belonging to him, but belonging to a pirate captain.

"Now, get the hell off my ship." Jane gapes at him, and James summons up every last bit of fierceness and command that he can to bellow at her. "Now!"

From the corner of his eye, he sees Jane scramble toward the rail. He turns all his attention to Michael. He squares his stance, as much as he can with his wounded side and trailing arm, facing the shadow army of pirates behind and inside Michael Darling.

It's time for him to be a captain one last time. It's time for him to go down with his ship.

THE LAST PIRATE IN NEVERLAND

NEVERLAND – NOW

Deep marks cross the sand as though something heavy was recently dragged across it. Jane's stomach sinks, the unshakable feeling that something terrible has happened, is about to happen, is happening right now. She shouldn't have left her uncle behind. She shouldn't have run off chasing Timothy's ghost. And she wouldn't take her actions back for the world.

She touches the satchel at her side, taking comfort from the outline of bone beneath canvas as she follows the marks along the beach. She's bruised, scraped, exhausted from finding her way back out of the cave. She wandered for what felt like hours in the dark, but it might have been no time at all, until she finally found another way out. Then, not knowing where else to go, she returned to the beach. The place she first woke in Neverland.

She pauses to take a breath, to take in the sweep of the landscape before her. She's almost grown used to the red-black light flickering across the sky so it's a moment before Jane realizes something is different. Wrong.

She draws to a halt. The marks in the sand lead back to the ruined pirate ship, her time in Neverland come full circle again. And all around the ship, the air is strange. Dark. Thickening. It's like looking at a storm, but not one that's happening now. One that did happen. One that will happen. She's seeing it and not seeing it, like looking at the Lost Boys flickering between states of being, past and present, and it makes her head hurt.

Jane has a terrible sense of being too late. She has to get to the ship, and it's the last place she wants to be.

Electricity dances across her skin, raising the tiny hairs on her arms. Merely walking forward is like pushing against a gale force wind, her steps sliding backward, grit blowing into her face. She raises an arm to shield her eyes, tightening her grip with her other hand on the satchel.

All at once, the wind stops. The ship blinks from existence. The ship falls from the sky.

Jane chokes on a startled shout, scrambling backward. It's impossible, but the ship plummets, smashing onto the sand, wood and debris flying everywhere. She trips over her heels, lands hard on her backside. She stares. The ship falls again. She feels the impact, thudding, shaking the ground. The ship falls and falls and falls again, an endless loop. Pushing down fear, Jane climbs to her feet, and against all reason, she runs toward the ship instead of away.

Overhead, a storm rages. Overhead, the sky is clear, crystal blue. And it is burnt red-black. It's like she's seeing three overlapping pieces of time, or more. She catches sight of someone else on the ship. She expects Hook, or her uncle, but it's a woman, and Jane's pulse trips so she almost misses a step and falls.

She knows, even without getting a clear look that the woman is her mother. Her mother is here. It doesn't even occur to her until she's at the ship, falling breathless against its side, hauling herself through the broken hole, that the woman who crawled into the ship just ahead of Jane is her mother as she looked eight years ago. The day she rescued Jane from Neverland.

She almost laughs, a wild, uncontrollable thing. Time is broken here, more than ever. Why shouldn't she see an echo of her mother along with all of Neverland's other ghosts?

Her mother moves deeper into the wreck of the pirate ship and Jane scrambles to follow. Loose strands of hair escape the braid trailing down her mother's back. She wears wide trousers, her shawl tied around her waist. The shadow of her mother ducks and vanishes through a doorway, and for a moment, Jane can't breathe.

Her mother isn't here, but she was. Jane remembers the story, how her mother raided the pirate ship and found Hook's old sword before setting out to face Peter. Before finding Jane. A fragment of that time has slipped into the now, and seeing it is like being struck a blow, surprising her with how much it hurts. Jane pulls herself forward, climbing, sliding—a game of follow the leader. She almost shouts, but she knows her mother wouldn't hear her.

And then her mother is there again, striding straight toward her, climbing back out of the ship. She doesn't see Jane. She doesn't exist in the same place and time, and she passes right through Jane. Jane clutches at herself, as if she could catch the trailing wisps of her mother. But when she turns, her mother is already gone. She's been gone for eight years. The slanted corridor of the ship is empty.

Jane's heart pounds. She's alone, but she sees again the determination etched on her mother's face as she strode from the ship with Hook's sword at her side. The fierceness, the anger. And all at once, Jane sees her mother at a remove—a woman hurting, afraid, and taking all that hurt and fear and turning it outward. A woman prepared to fight for her daughter, for herself, and do whatever it takes to bring them both home.

Jane presses a hand to her chest again, to the ache there. It's like a bruise, and she pushes against it, hard. She wants to feel that pain. And she wants to push it through and out of herself and have it gone.

Perhaps she's been too full of her own anger to even try to see things from her mother's point of view. Yes, her mother had a choice in coming to Neverland—a choice Jane herself had never had. But Jane does have a choice in what she does going forward. Deep down, she knows what happened to Timothy wasn't her mother's fault. It was easier to blame her, to blame herself even, than simply accepting that life is big and unfair and no matter what either of them did back then, nothing would change. Jane had promised herself once not to forget Neverland, but not to live in the past either. Perhaps it's time to live up to that promise, to find a way back to her mother, and move on.

She's always known her mother is not simply one thing, but a bundle, a contradiction, like any other person. The thought strikes her like lightning—her mother is human. At the same time the absurdity of the thought hits her. Of course her mother is human. She is flawed. And she is a being separate from Jane, but linked to her inexorably. Not just her mother, but her own person as well, and that is precisely what makes them capable of hurting each other. The love between them, binding them together, clashing against the simple fact of living in two separate skins, each trying to discover who they are.

Jane braces herself against the ship's wall, dizzy with the realization. When she gets home, she will try. She swears, she will try to see her mother on her own terms, and hope that her mother can see her on hers. They will find a way back to each other, and maybe their relationship will never be perfect, but it won't be for lack of trying. Jane won't let them simply drift apart, closed off from each other, each lost in their own separate worlds.

She pushes away from the wall. Moves down the tilted corridor, and steps through the doorway and into the room her mother exited. It's as her mother described it—the remains of broken furniture, and shattered mirror glass. And then it's even emptier still, and the scant light seeping through the yellowed window glass is a baleful red again. And then the sky is blue, and the room is whole, and Jane feels waves swell beneath the deck, lifting it.

The room, the ship, flickers between states so fast they blur together. In one of the realities, perhaps more than one, there's a sword beneath the bed. Neverland is a place of impossibilities, even, or especially, when broken. And if she believes hard enough, it means the sword will be there for Jane to find.

She presses herself flat to the floor, stretches her arm out as long as she can. Her fingers grope. There is nothing, nothing, then all at once, a hilt beneath her hand, and Jane grips it tight, yanks it free before it can vanish again. She straightens, holding the sword in wonder. She sweeps it through the air once, imagining her mother doing the same, and giddy laughter takes over her.

Jane turns, ready to leave the ship when something catches her eye. Half buried in the torn remains of linens covering the bed, something metallic glitters. She moves the torn covers aside to reveal the hook nestled there.

As she reaches for it, the room tilts. She throws out a hand to steady herself and the hook's sharp tip catches her skin, tearing a line of red down her arm. Jane sucks in a breath, snatching her arm back and automatically covering the wound. It isn't deep, but sticky blood seeps between her fingers. She wipes her hand on her trousers, digging one-handed in her satchel, careful not to touch Timothy's skull, until she finds the rolls of bandages again.

It's a clumsy job, but she manages to wrap her arm before turning her attention back to the hook. She should leave it alone. The air buzzes around it, an almost magnetic pull drawing her, leaving her reaching for it again without meaning to. Gingerly, she lifts the weapon by its leather cuff.

Because that's what it is—not just an appendage to replace the hand of a wounded man, not here. That's not how Neverland works. It's a thing made for violence, and even now, Jane imagines the metal rust-stained with blood. Like the ship, it flickers—clean and bright, and then gory in the next instant, and she almost flings it away from herself, but she finds she can't let it go.

The ship tilts again, nearly knocking her off her feet, shaking her from her reverie. Wind batters it, and the timbers groan. What happens if the ship falls from the sky again while she's on board? Or has that already happened? She has no time to lose.

She retrieves the sword, holding it tightly in one hand, holding the hook in the other—pinched between two fingers by the leather cuff and held as far away from her body as possible. The ship sways as Jane returns the way she came, struggling to keep her balance with her hands full.

Her foot strikes something, and it rattles across the deck. Shock travels through her as she looks down and sees a skull. She almost drops the sword to reach for her satchel, but it's much too big to be Timothy's skull. She recognizes the silver chasing; it's the skull Hook carried here with him, the one he claimed belonged to someone he loved. He wouldn't be parted from it willingly, so if the skull is here, then Hook must be here somewhere as well. And possibly not of his own accord.

Setting the sword aside, she lifts the skull gingerly, holding it a moment before tucking it into her bag alongside Timothy's. The canvas bulges as she resecures the strap and regains the sword and the hook. She takes a deep breath, and climbs up onto the deck.

Jane emerges into chaos. A storm rages, wind whipping and stealing her breath, leaving her lungs empty and burning. She gasps, squinting through rain that isn't there. The deck is crowded with shapes. Most of them aren't solid. There's a sense of absence, like the absence she felt in Peg's room, and for a moment Jane is rooted. Her boots have fused with the deck, and she can't move.

The brief thought flashes through her again that she will find Peg here, and just as quickly she tamps it down. Peg is gone. And Jane would not wish her, any part of her, here in this chaos even if it meant the chance to say that she's sorry and say goodbye.

After a moment, her mind assembles the jagged, broken pieces to make sense of what she's seeing. As much sense as can be made, at least. Her uncle and Captain Hook, fighting, surrounded by a maelstrom of ghosts. The shout is at her lips before she can stop herself.

"Captain!"

Everything pauses and seems to hang still. She sees the world in individual, disconnected moments. Hook lifts his head to look

304

at her. He's wounded. Her uncle looms over him, holding a knife. Her uncle is not her uncle, and something terrible will happen if she doesn't stop it.

Jane doesn't think. She drops the hook and charges forward. Brings the sword down hilt first, striking her uncle in the shoulder as hard as she can. It's just enough to hurt him, to make him drop the blade he's holding. Then she's grabbing at Hook, pulling at him. They need to run.

The air swirls thick around them, not just a storm, or at least not a normal one. The deck swarms with shadows, faces that are almost human rising to the surface and sinking again. Hook pulls free of her grasp, taking her arm in turn and steering her toward the rail. Now it's Jane's turn to shake him free.

"What are you doing? I can't leave my uncle."

Jane looks back to Uncle Michael's crumpled form. He groans, already pushing himself upright, filled with unnatural strength. Even so, she moves toward him before Hook catches her, pulls her back.

"I promise you, no harm will come to him. I will set things right." Hook's eyes are wild in the swarming dark.

Is he still under the influence of the flowers? Does he have any idea what he's saying? Jane feels unsteady, filled with the sense that this moment is taking place in more than one time, bits slipping free, looping over themselves, happening and not happening all at once. If they could stand outside this moment and recount it to each other, would their stories match?

Jane shakes herself, tries to pull free, but Hook's grip is iron. He doesn't look like the old man she first saw standing behind her mother at the door of her flat. Jane sees the outline, the ghost

305

of someone else laid atop his skin—black hair flowing over his shoulders, a red coat, flaring at the hem.

Behind the wildness in his eyes, there is something else—bloody rage, bloody determination. The eyes of a pirate. But maybe in this place that Peter built for endless games of war, that isn't such a terrible thing. Jane stares at the sword in her hand. She used it to hurt her uncle, even if he isn't her uncle right now. At the thought, revulsion fills her. She isn't a pirate, she's a doctor, or she will be one day, and in order to do that, she needs to leave this place behind. She can't do what needs to be done to fix Peter's violent world, but Hook can. She turns the sword in her hand and holds both it and the hook out to him.

"These belong to you."

Hook stares for a moment as if seeing the weapons for the first time, as if he will refuse them. Then he nods, taking the sword and the hook awkwardly in one hand, the arm with his wooden hand hanging uselessly at his side.

When his eyes meet hers again, she doesn't see the pirate—or rather she sees the pirate and the old man both—eyes the color of the sea in a storm, filled with violence and filled with sorrow.

"Promise me you'll bury me with him."

Jane's hand goes to the satchel at her side. The skulls.

"I will."

"Good." The smile Hook, James, gives her is as wicked and sharp as the blade in his hand. "Get the hell off my ship. Now!"

He's an old man, bleeding from more than one wound. And he's a pirate captain, hair black, eyes flashing. He is terrifying, and Jane runs almost without meaning to, scrambling for the ship's rail.

There's a roaring like the wind in a storm and a thousand tormented voices screaming all at once. She wants to look back, to see what's happening, to make sure Uncle Michael is safe. But there's a percussive blast, like a hand set between her shoulder blades, shoving.

An explosion rocks the deck, like a strike of lightning, like the world folding in on itself. Jane flings herself over the rail or she is thrown, the land and the red–black sky trading place, stars showing through that belong to a world other than this one, while the lightning shatters everything over and over again.

She hits the sand, hard, the breath knocked out of her, grit in her eyes and her mouth, coughing, choking. She's on dry land, but she's drowning.

A CAPTAIN GOES DOWN
WITH HIS SHIP

NEVERLAND – NOW

The man, the boy, Michael Darling, climbs the deck toward him. At least they are evenly matched now. One of Michael's arms hangs useless at his side, numb where the girl smashed his shoulder with the sword James now holds. His sword. Hook's sword. The sword of a captain.

He'd never thought to see it again. But then, he'd never thought to return here either. The air shudders and howls around him, the shades of his lost pirates hungering to tear him apart. Michael continues to climb the deck, sick-gold eyes fixed on James. When he smiles, he shows teeth with blood on them.

Even though he doesn't have his cane, even though the deck tilts wildly beneath them, Michael Darling seems to have no problem walking. The pirates inside of him, Harrigan, Killdeer, infuse him completely, insensate to his pain. James takes a step back, another. Not running, but buying himself time.

Survive. It's what he does, against all odds. The immortal pirate captain, unable to die. Turning to violence to save his skin over and over, almost despite himself. Stubborn, and perhaps more than that. Cursed. Breaking his promise to Samuel every time, unable to shed Hook's skin, unable to let go, but fighting on and on, no matter the cost, always hungering for more life no matter how much blood he had to spill.

Now, perhaps, at the end of everything, he can finally put his cursed existence to good use. Become Hook one last time, and then let him go.

Still backing up, Michael still advancing, James scrambles at the straps holding his wooden hand in place. It drops, thudding to the deck, and his heart goes with it. Not just losing a piece of himself, losing the best part of him, the person he tried to become. His gaze sweeps the howling maelstrom, the mass of shadow pirates swirling closer, snapping teeth and grasping with fingers twisted into claws. But they're still insubstantial for now. They cannot hurt him. Only Michael Darling can.

James dodges around the shattered remains of the mast as the ship rocks and he nearly loses his balance. He's running out of time. He searches and finds the faint glow that is Samuel. His light is a candle's, guttering in the wind. The shadows whipping around him seem to tear pieces of him away with each pass, wearing him down. But Samuel doesn't move, he remains fixed where he is, and though his eyes are silver now like his skin, James sees the warmth in them where they meet his own.

"I'm sorry." James's voice breaks, the words catching in his throat and tearing it bloody, leaving everything else to emerge in a whisper, pained and raw. He doesn't even know if Samuel will hear him; he can only trust that somehow, even if he can't, he will still understand.

"I never said the words, and I always should have. But even though I didn't, they were still true."

Samuel's mouth opens as if he would answer, but James can't bear to hear. His eyes sting and blur. He turns away, jamming the leather cap of the hook over the stump of his wrist.

He bellows—a raw, wordless sound.

It's like fire running through his veins, waking up his arm again in the worst possible way. The hook fits itself to him like it always did, claiming him, swallowing him whole. He tilts his face to the sky, teeth bared. A shadow jitters there, like a boy, but not a boy at all. A monster who made him a monster in turn, one who was never human.

"You won't best me," he says, the words for himself more than the boy who once was. "Not this time, Pan."

On the last, he looks down, slashing out and sending Michael Darling tumbling back, catching him off guard. Hook leaps over the fallen mast, sword point at Michael's throat. He could kill him, it would be easy, and for a moment the impulse to lean his weight on the blade and end it now rises in him. But he made a promise, and he's done breaking his promises. At the last, he will finally keep one, and he will make it count.

Even so, he lets the blade's tip kiss the side of Michael Darling's throat, drawing a tiny bead of red. It shines under the red of the sky, and James's pulse thumps in response, something like hunger. Michael growls at him, only it is Harrigan and Killdeer. It is Pan's hunting beast, hate shining through the eyes of the body all of the lost fragments have occupied.

Michael's good arm, the one his niece didn't smash, jerks to the side, a feint as if he would roll away from the blade. But Hook is faster, even if James is not. He brings the curved sword down a hairsbreadth from Michael's face, stopping his motion. The shadow of fear passes through the sick-gold of Michael's eyes, and his throat bobs as he swallows hard.

James lifts his arm, Hook's arm. The point of his newly regained hook glints in the light, and the fear deepens in Michael's eyes. Even Harrigan and Killdeer cowered in terror of him once.

While he has the pirates cowed, Hook draws the black blade from his pocket, trading his sword for it. Michael Darling is completely disarmed now, and the pirates inside of him are frightened. Perhaps not frightened enough, not yet, and perhaps some of the fear may belong to Michael himself, but Hook can use that.

The deck sways, and he widens his stance, riding with it. The storm whipping around them is the same that battered them years ago, when he first wielded the blade. Time collapsed around them, as it always does in Neverland. And now, he must play the villain one last time.

Hook crouches, grinning, his face close to Michael's, the black blade held just above his chest. And underneath his skin, James's heart beats hard, and his pulse constricts against the weight of drowning. He is afraid too. What he's about to do might be mad, it might gain him nothing. The shadows might win in the end. But impossible odds never stopped Hook before.

He considers Michael Darling. Hollow—that's what Jane had said of her uncle. That the war had hollowed him out and left spaces for the shadows to crawl inside.

James lets the tip of the blade rest against Michael's skin, just below one of the buttons on his shirt. Teeth bared, breathing hard, Killdeer and Harrigan watch him through Michael's eyes to see what he will do. He raises the hook again and holds it where they can see, lets the shadow of it fall across Michael Darling's face.

There is a hollow inside of him too. Carved by loss, carved by grief that remains unhealed after fifteen years. He has lived hundreds of lifetimes, barely knowing himself, turning away from the truth, the goodness, in fear, just as many times as he died and was reborn. He wore violence like a second skin, as if it could keep him from pain, and all the while it wore away at him. The hollow space inside of him is so much vaster than Michael Darling's could ever be, vast enough to contain multitudes. And he will welcome them in.

"Has a mutiny occurred?" Hook asks softly.

He brings the hook to rest against Michael Darling's cheek. Inside, Killdeer and Harrigan and whatever fragments of the others they've gathered flinch away.

"You won't win," Killdeer snarls. "You're old, you're frail. You're—" His words cut off as Hook presses the tip of the weapon that is his hand against Michael's skin, not hard enough to break it, but enough to make it known.

"Wrong. I am still captain of this ship. The men aboard, whatever state they are in, are still mine to command. They always have been, and they always will be, even you."

He does not give himself time to doubt. He promised Wendy's daughter he would save Michael Darling, but even so, he plunges the black blade into his chest. The blade does what all blades do, cuts one thing from another, but unlike other blades, this one operates on a level more fundamental than flesh. Michael gasps, mouth wrenched impossibly open, as though he would scream, but instead of sound, only shadows pour forth. His body arches painfully. The darkness whips around him, howling where

Michael, where Killdeer, where Harrigan cannot—a scream of utter, frustrated rage.

Hook stands, an easier motion than it has been in years. Before he can give himself time to doubt, he turns his hook on himself, burying the point in his chest and dragging it downward, opening a way to the hollow within. Pain—but no worse than he's felt a thousand times before in the beast's jaws, at the end of Pan's blade. He follows the hook with the black knife, changing the wound into something else, a gaping, hungering maw. Because in this world, desire can be a door, a knife can be a key, and a man—a captain— can contain multitudes. Hook uses the blade to hold the wound open as his voice rings above the storm.

"I am still your captain, and I command you. You wanted my flesh and bones. Come take them, if you can."

Michael Darling's body shudders, shadows still pouring out of him. Darkness swirls around Hook and he grits his teeth against the pain, against the urge to pass out. Too stubborn to die. He must remain so for just a little while longer.

The first shadow strikes him like a blow, almost knocking him from his feet. But he has ridden out worse storms, and he manages to keep his boots planted on the deck as the darkness burrows into him. His clenches his jaw hard as a second follows, and a third. He cannot breathe. He is drowning in the air, on dry land as shadows choke him and fill up the spaces inside of him. And yet there is more space to fill. He is vast enough to hold them all.

They flow faster now, pulled, called, unable to resist. Like water filling his lungs, they batter into him, but he refuses to fall under the weight even if he staggers. Every part of him is raw, bruised. Every part of him aches and the shadows claw at him from the inside now, tricked, trapped, desperate to get out. But he will hold on to all of them, keeping them bound inside his skin.

Wind and rain lash at him, a storm in truth now as the ship rocks beneath him. Hook faces the darkness down, and as he does, the darkness grins back at him.

His pulse skips, drops a beat, and his nerve almost falters. James, inside Hook, gives way to a moment of panic, sweat prickling his skin, his limbs trembling. Pan's hunting beast roils out of the air, eyes no longer moon-blind, but burning gold and full of hate as they ever were. Hook restored and his immortal enemy restored too.

"There you are." Hook's lips twist, a sneer.

Of course it would be the beast at last. Its massive legs swim in the air, thick armored scales glistening with rain. Its jaws open, not hunger, but a smile. It knows him. It understands him. And he knows it as well.

"Well, come on, then. What are you waiting for?"

Still holding the blade against his wound, Hook doesn't give himself further time to doubt. He lashes out, driving the point of his hook into the beast's eye. The creature thrashes—both solid and smoke—but Hook doesn't relent, dragging the beast toward the wound in his chest.

Whatever the hunting beast expected, it was not this—an embrace, Hook's very own death roll. He wraps his arm around the beast, crushing it tight in a terrible hold. He pulls his other arm free beneath it, holding the black blade. He keeps his grip, forcing the beast so close there is no space between them, so close they might as well be the same. Two beasts, created by Pan, born for violence, locked in an eternal battle to the end.

Jaws close, teeth sinking in, but still Hook doesn't let go.

"A good captain always goes down with his ship, and I was the best of them."

Bearing the beast down with him, Hook lets himself fall. He plunges the blade into the deck, shattering it again, as he did all those years ago. Inside him, the ghosts of all his dead pirates scream. The ship falls and falls and falls again. Plunging into the sand. Plunging up into the sky to break against the teeth of the stars. Everything howls and rips apart. The world goes white then black. Lightning cracks the sky and Hook laughs while James weeps, rooted to his sinking ship by the tip of an impossible blade, and this time, he will not let go.

Now, the blade is no longer a door to step through, but an anchor to keep him secured where he was always meant to be.

25

BURIALS

Jane's eyes stream when she's finally able to blink them open. She is not drowning after all. She's lying on the sand, staring up at the wrong-colored sky. She pushes herself up, despite her body's protests, every part of her feeling bruised. The ship is gone. Her heart lurches and she scrambles up, falls, stands again, and breaks into a run.

"Michael! Uncle Michael."

There's a crater in the sand where the ship shattered, or rose, or sank. Jane still isn't sure what happened. All she knows is that it's gone. But a body lies crumpled where the ship stood and her throat squeezes tight, tears starting in her eyes.

Then a cough. A gasp of breath. Jane rushes forward and falls to her knees at her uncle's side, touching his shoulder. He sits up, blinking at her with eyes that are pale blue and no longer stained sick-gold.

"Jane? Where are we? What's—"

She throws her arms around him, squeezing him tight. There's no missing his thinness, the fragility of his bones, but she can't make herself let go. She's crying and laughing all at once, and it's a long moment before she can make herself pull back, wiping the tears from her cheeks, to look at him.

"You're never going to believe me when I tell you."

The sky is red-black, flickering. If Jane allows her gaze to stray to it for too long, she begins to pick out a shape she doesn't want to see—a massive thing, that might once upon a time have looked like a boy, maybe never quite human, but human in form, and now no longer anything like it at all. She looks down at the holes dug in the sand instead, one long and rectangular, the other square and small. Her arms ache with the effort. There's sand under her nails, in her hair, worked into her skin.

They did the best they could with bits of driftwood and stones as tools. Her uncle helped her dig, in silence. Now, he sits beside her on the sand, legs stretched out, his head tilted back, watching the sky.

"It's him, isn't it?" His voice is very soft, very small. He sounds like a young boy. "It's Peter."

Jane doesn't want to look where he's looking, but his question stops her cold. She forces herself to glance, just for a moment, at the sky. It hurts in a way she can't explain, and she looks down again, looks at her uncle and the awe and terror written on his face under the red-dark sky.

"Yes. I think so. What's left of him."

Her uncle doesn't say anything else then, but keeps watching the sky, the figures, while Jane turns her attention back to the ground. How much does he remember? Something in his voice sounds to her like someone waking from a very long dream. And if that's the case, she wonders what will happen to him when he does.

Part of her expected it to be different, as if once the shadows were driven from him, her uncle would finally come back to himself. A self she's never really known, only seen glimpses of. But he brought his own ghosts to Neverland, and those haven't left. Maybe they never will.

If she goes away to war, will it happen to her too? But her father went to war and returned reasonably whole. She tries to push the thoughts from her mind; there will be time for them later. Perhaps she can still find a way to help people without breaking her uncle's heart.

Jane shifts her gaze to the bones. Along with Michael, in the crater where the ship had been, she'd found a skeleton, one with only one hand. The bones looked old, as if the man they'd belonged to had died a long time ago. She lifts them now, as carefully as she can. They weigh nothing as she shifts them to the makeshift, shallow grave.

She takes the larger, carved skull from her satchel, nestles it into the crook of the skeleton's arm. She lets her fingertips rest against the silver patterns for a moment, feeling she should say something, though she didn't know either man, not really. They were stories, dreams belonging to another world. But for a time, their world crossed her own.

"He loved you very much." It's the only thing she can think to say, seeing in her mind's eye the pirate captain's expression as he'd held the silver-chased skull. "And he's sorry he never told you."

She lets her touch linger a moment before pushing sand into the grave until she can no longer see the bones. Then she turns to the second, smaller grave. Her hand rests on the flap of her satchel. For a moment, she can't make herself reach inside. She doesn't want to let go. Timothy deserves so much better than this, an unmarked and shallow grave under an eternally burning sky.

But she can't bring him back to London either. Whatever else this place was to him, it was also home. Once he was happy here. There were times when the only things were games and stories, no bedtime or rules. And he could fly.

Jane scrubs fiercely at her eyes. The grief inside of her is too big to let go. It sits in her chest, in her throat. Tears stream from her eyes, but instead of bringing relief, the ache just goes on and on. It isn't fair.

She kneels, setting Timothy's skull in the hole as gently as she can.

"Once," she whispers, like the beginning of a fairy tale. But the word breaks, and she can't get any further.

Everything smears and blurs in her vision, she's crying so hard. A hand touches her shoulder, and she looks up. Uncle Michael stands beside her, looking down at her. He doesn't need to know who the bones belong to in order to understand her sorrow. He doesn't have to know where they are, or what happened to know that Jane hurts, all the way through, and to reach out and offer her comfort in her pain.

She covers the hole as quickly as she can, wordlessly saying she's sorry, wordlessly saying goodbye. There's a picture in her mind of Peg and of Timothy and she holds on to them as tightly as she can and then lets them go. When it's done, she rises, and brushes the sand off her trousers. She takes her uncle's hand, smiling at him through the tears.

It's time to go home.

NEW YEAR'S DAY

LONDON – 1940

Wendy raises her head, losing the thread of Ned's words in mid-sentence.

"What's wrong?" Ned touches her hand.

"They're back." Wendy is already on her feet, running toward the door.

She plunges onto the lawn and stops, head tilted to the sky. Frost sparkles on the grass, crunching under her feet. The sun is barely risen, the sky still pale. Ned comes up beside her and takes her hand.

This time, Wendy sees it when the door in the sky opens. It's faint, but visible, and all her breath catches and stops in her throat. Pale stars glimmer behind her daughter like a frame of diamonds set in a blood-red sky. And behind Jane and Michael, Wendy can see clear through to Neverland.

Her heart lurches. It aches. The thread stretched between herself and that other place is suddenly there again, tugging at her core. All she would have to do is follow it. She's stretched, yearning, almost rising on her toes, almost leaving the ground.

And then without moving, she slams her heels back down to the ground as firmly as she can, focusing all her attention on her daughter instead. Jane is home, and that's the only thing that matters.

Jane touches down, Michael beside her, and Wendy rushes forward, but stops short of where her daughter and her brother stand. Did Jane see the moment Wendy's gaze drifted past her and still wanted, despite everything, to run toward Neverland? How can she explain that she is broken, but she wants to heal? How can she explain the fear that finding her way back to Jane in this world will be ever so much harder than it was in Neverland, but that she will never give up, never stop trying?

Wendy opens her arms like a question. Jane steps into them. For a moment, it feels like the years falling away between them. Jane is a little girl again, and nothing is complicated. Then Jane stiffens, almost imperceptibly and steps back. It's too soon, and Wendy fights down the urge to cling to her as Jane steps around her to hug Ned. The way she hugs him is purer, less fraught. It hurts, but Wendy understands. There's still a trust that needs to be healed between them; there's still work that needs to be done.

"Windy." Michael's voice sounds as young as it ever did in the nursery, tugging at her.

Wendy turns to her brother. He's pale, shaken. He looks the way he did the first day she and John brought him home from the hospital. Like part of him is still trapped somewhere else, gone away so far that she will never reach it.

Back then, she begged him to remember Neverland, the only way she could think of to try to find him and bring him home again. He's been there now, been and come back again. Wendy can almost see the light of that other place resting on his skin, a shine, a shadow, and her hand trembles as she raises it to Michael's cheek. It's wet with tears.

He starts at the touch, but doesn't pull away. His eyes focus on her. They are clear blue, empty of shadows, but not of ghosts. He puts his hand atop hers, pressing it to his cheeks, leaning into her touch like he needs to reassure himself that she is in fact real.

"I saw..." His voice breaks. His entire body shudders. "I saw..."

Peter. Neverland. The Lost Boys. All the things the world promised him as a child, all the things the war and return to the real world took away from him. A sob breaks free, and Wendy folds him in her arms, holding her baby brother as he shudders against her.

"Shhh." Her hands stroke his back, holding him to her to show that she is real and not going away.

What else can she say? Telling him that everything will be okay is a lie. Telling him it was all a dream would be equally cruel. There is nothing to say, no way to be sure how much he'll remember, if he'll remember, or if he'll go away inside himself again and forget, because it's less painful, easier. All she can do is hold him in this moment, be here for him, listen as he finds the words to tell her what happened. He's gone so far away, and so far into the real world, into places she can't follow. All she can do is be here for him when and if he finds his own way home.

"Well?" Wendy asks softly, just one word, and she can barely bring herself to say even that, holding her breath, afraid of the response, afraid of silence.

She's been bursting with questions all day, holding them back, and now she and Jane are alone in the kitchen. The air is warm, the lingering smells of cooking still in the air. Since Ned prepared most of the meal, Wendy had insisted on washing up alone. She was surprised when Jane had quietly risen to join her.

Jane's arms sink almost to the elbows in soapy water. She washes and rinses a plate, and hands it silently to Wendy. Perhaps she'd simply had too much company with John and his wife and their young daughter arriving soon after Jane and Michael had made it home. Blue smudges mark the skin under Jane's eyes. She must be exhausted, Wendy realizes. Several days passed here while they were gone, all the time between Christmas and New Year's. Her daughter hasn't slept in that entire time. She's barely had a moment to herself to breathe. She still hasn't had time to process her grief over Margaret. Peg.

"You don't have to," Wendy says quickly. "I can finish up here if you'd like. You should go upstairs and rest. John and Elizabeth will understand."

"No, it's all right." Jane turns from the sink, leans her back against it.

Wendy automatically hands her a towel, and Jane dries her hands and stands there holding it.

"I thought it would be different," Jane says softly.

Wendy forces herself to be patient, hold back her questions. At first, she's afraid Jane won't say more. Her daughter twists the towel between her hands, frowning, not looking at anything in particular.

"It was... I don't know. Not like I remembered, but also like nothing had changed." She looks up at last, meeting Wendy's eyes.

323

"I don't know how to explain it. Everything was…it was broken, not like the last time at all, but it felt frozen somehow."

"Stagnant," Wendy says, and the word surprises her. Jane nods, her eyes bright with not-quite-tears.

The ache is there again, the thread bound around Wendy's heart, and she carefully puts the feeling aside. It strikes Wendy that despite everything, part of her never really did grow up, never learned who to be without Neverland. She has to believe there's still time for that now. That part of her life is done, and she's ready for a new adventure.

"I…found Timothy," Jane says. Her voice is soft, so full of hurt. Wendy steps forward, stops, unsure what to do.

"I buried him." Jane looks down, and now the tears do fall.

Wendy closes the space between them, lifts Jane's chin gently. She smudges the tears away with her thumb, then she puts her arm around Jane's shoulders. After a moment, she draws Jane into her and she presses her cheek against Jane's hair.

There's so much to say, so much to figure out between them. It's all uncharted territory, and Wendy isn't sure how she'll navigate it. But she's determined find a way.

There will be time later, if Jane wants to tell her, what happened to James, what happened to the shadows, but Wendy promises herself she won't push. Neverland isn't hers. Or rather, her Neverland isn't Jane's. She isn't owed her daughter's experiences, like she isn't owed Michael's. If Jane wants to tell her story one day, then Wendy swears she will be there to listen.

Holding Jane against her with one arm, Wendy's free hand strays to her pocket—an old, nervous gesture she's barely aware of making—until her fingers close on the hard shape there and she draws it out. The arrowhead from Jane's room, the one from Neverland. She remembers vaguely going into Jane's room to tidy up, restless and worried for her daughter, unable to sit still. She'd found the arrowhead on the floor. Has she been carrying it this whole time, switching it from pocket to pocket every time she changes clothes without realizing it, just waiting for her daughter to come home?

She almost laughs, but stifles the sound. It's enough though for Jane to draw back slightly and catch sight of what she's holding, a frown shaping her lips.

"I found it in your room. I didn't realize I had it." Wendy feels caught out as she extends the arrowhead to Jane.

She watches her daughter take it gingerly, as if it's a thing that might burn. The stone looks duller in the kitchen light than Wendy remembers. Jane's frown deepens and Wendy feels a fluttering in her chest. Has she ruined it all between them again? Jane turns the knapped stone over in her hand, then closes her fingers on it a moment. The expression on Jane's face is like that of someone listening hard to catch a strain of music drifting in from another room. Wendy finds herself holding her breath until Jane opens her hand and sets the arrowhead on the counter beside her with a gentle click.

"I can't feel it anymore," Jane says.

It's not exactly sorrow in her voice, or loss, but there's a sense of emotion, one too complex to untangle and name. Wendy feels an echo rise within her, the feeling of wanting to simultaneously run toward and away from something as hard as she can. It's a place where a splinter has always been, forced beneath her skin, and when it's suddenly gone, she misses the feel of it there. Jane raises her head and meets Wendy's eyes.

Jane lifts her hand. Her fingers trace the air above the arrowhead without touching down. As she lets her hand fall again, Wendy catches it, pressing her daughter's fingers.

"I know," she says softly. "I understand."

It surprises her when Jane is the one to step back into their embrace, bowing her head against Wendy's shoulder like a child seeking comfort after a bad dream. Wendy can almost feel the ache through her daughter's skin, almost too big to ever heal, but she will try. They will try together.

She feels her daughter shiver against her. Exhaustion, grief catching up with her. Wendy takes as much of Jane's weight as she can, letting Jane lean against her, trying to absorb the burden, make it easier to carry. It's all she can do for now. Be here, in this world, right here and waiting for when her daughter needs her.

EPILOGUE

LONDON – 1951

A crisp autumn wind tugs at Jane's hair and swirls fallen leaves around her feet. A particularly bright leaf, all gold and flame, detaches itself from a branch just as she passes underneath it, and the chubby boy at her hip reaches after it as it drifts past her head. Jane smiles. Despite the breeze, the sun is warm and the sky achingly blue—a perfect day.

She nudges open the shop with her hip and the bell overhead jangles. The space behind the counter is empty, but a moment later, her mother's head appears from behind a dress form in the corner with a look of surprise.

"Jane!" Her mother pulls pins from her mouth, tucking them into a pocket as she comes forward, and Jane can't help laughing at her distracted air.

"You didn't forget about supper, did you?"

"No, of course not. I only lost track of time." Her mother gestures back toward the dress, half pinned, on the form behind her.

"Timmy, aren't you going to say hello to your nana?" Jane turns her hip with her son toward her mother, bouncing him slightly.

Timothy grins, then buries his face against her neck in mock shyness before peeking at her mother and giggling. Jane ruffles his blond curls, causing him to squirm in her arms.

"You can set him down if you like." Her mother gestures around the shop. "There's nothing he can hurt here, and nothing that can hurt him. Everything is tucked away."

Her mother pats her pockets, and Jane gratefully lowers Timothy to the ground. It never ceases to amaze her how the boy seems to grow every time she takes her eye off him for even a second.

"I honestly don't know how you manage it all." Her mother sounds genuinely admiring, and Jane can't help another smile.

"Pure luck. Ethan sees most of his patients in the morning, and I see most of mine in the afternoon, so it all works out. And Simon is awfully good about coming around to help out whenever he can."

When Jane looks up, the pride in her mother's eyes catches her off guard and she has to look away for a moment. The light coming through the shop window throws the shadow of the curling letters painted there onto the floor at Jane's feet—Darlings. She toes the shadow, smiling.

"Have you decided?" Her mother's tone is carefully neutral, trying to keep safe footing in a conversation they've had before.

It's not precisely an argument, but tension laces the air every time the question arises—will she and Ethan stay in London another year, or will they go? This time, instead of a defensive response leaping to her tongue, Jane finds a strange ache as she straightens her shoulders.

"We're staying in London." Her mother's eyes brighten, but Jane hurries on. "But we do still mean to travel, when Timmy's just a bit older. There are so many places in the world where Ethan and

I can do some good. The earthquake in Tibet, the war in Korea. Doctors are always needed, and I want to see the world." Jane feels the restless weight of it all as she says the words.

She thinks of the globe in her childhood bedroom. Thinks of where she's been and all the places she hasn't seen yet. She'd promised her uncle years ago that she wouldn't go to war, and she'd kept her word then, but all over the world is hurting and she longs to do something about it.

"You can do good here too."

"I know. We are. And we will again." Jane offers her mother a smile she hopes she'll understand. "We're not leaving England for good. We'll always come back. I wouldn't let you miss this one growing up entirely." Jane nudges Timothy, who looks up with a wide grin, the sunlight catching his curls and making them shine.

"My daughter, the world traveler and the hero." Her mother steps closer, lifting a lock of Jane's hair absently and smoothing it as she flicks it behind Jane's shoulder. "I always knew you would do great things."

The ache is there again and for a moment, Jane's throat is too thick to answer. She's used to arguments from her mother, contradictory ways, but this is almost too much to bear. She steps around her mother and son both, closer to the dress form, for somewhere to look until she's certain her eyes won't betray her with tears. She promised herself once that she would always look ahead, not back at might-have-beens or what-ifs. She's seen the dangers of living solely in the past, and she's ready for the next adventure, her and Ethan both, helping people, like she always wanted to do.

Jane plucks at the hem of her mother's dress in progress, running the fabric through her fingers.

"Pockets?" she asks over her shoulder, though she already knows the answer.

"Always." Her mother joins her, close but not quite touching. "I thought it would look quite nice on you, actually."

Jane startles, half turning. Lines crinkle at the corners of her mother's eyes. Her hair, gathered in braids wound around her head, is almost all gray now, but strands of copper still peek through. No matter how much time passes, there's something ageless about her mother, as if time draws close and then falls still again, waiting for Wendy Darling's say so to move on.

Jane looks back to the dress, a color like periwinkles and the summer sky. It's not the sort of thing she would normally wear and yet looking at it, she can picture herself at a party, dancing with Ethan, and a smile touches her lips.

"It's lovely." Jane's voice trembles slightly, then she gestures toward the door. "Should we go?"

"Let me get my coat." Her mother disappears into the back and Jane lifts Timothy onto her hip again. His weight is sweet and sleepy against her now, and he rests his head on her shoulder.

More than just stopping time, her mother seems to have turned it back now, the sun catching in the threads of copper in her hair so they blaze and overwhelm the gray. But brighter still is her coat, blood and poppies, flaring at the hem where it falls at the perfect length, fitted to her mother's shoulders, her body, her height, no matter how any of them may change over the years. Rich and brand new, though Jane knows that in truth the coat may be more than a century old.

"You still have it."

Her mother's eyes sparkle with mischief as she loops her arm through Jane's and leads her to the shop door.

"Only for special occasions," she says.

Her mother locks the door behind them before regaining Jane's arm—a pirate, a queen, a wild creature out of a story at her side. Together, they step out into the bright autumn day.

Acknowledgments

Sometimes when you're mired in the process of your novel, it feels like you're laboring alone and no one else could possibly understand the world inside your head. Then you take a breath and look around and see all the amazing people helping you along the way.

First and foremost, thank you to everyone who read *Wendy, Darling* and had nice things to say about it. Your encouragement and enthusiasm bolstered me while writing this book.

Thank you to Sophie Robinson, my very patient editor, who helped me hone and focus the story through many revisions, and even helped find it a title. A huge thank you as well to the entire team at Titan for everything from editorial work, to making the book look gorgeous, to getting it out in the world.

Thank you to my agent, Barry Goldblatt, for believing in my work, and for providing excellent feedback.

A huge thank you to Fran Wilde for her thoughtful reading and amazing advice, and thank you (always) to A.T. Greenblatt, Stephanie Feldman, Fran Wilde (yes, she deserves to be thanked twice), Sarah Pinsker, and Siobhan Carroll, for being wonderful critique partners and wonderful friends. This novel wouldn't exist without all of you. I deeply appreciate you listening to me talk out plot points, complain, and occasionally cackle with glee.

There are several people I need to thank in general for their friendship and support over the years, and for overall being wonderful—Matt and Amy Bush, Therese Marmion, Jane Wightman, Janet Ankcorn, Janis Morrow, the Gibson Family, E. Catherine Tobler, Eugenia Triantafyllou, Scott Andrews, Usman T. Malik, Suzan Palumbo, John Wiswell, and Arley Sorg.

Always, always, always I owe an incredible amount of thanks to my husband and my amazing family (including the four-legged members).

Finally, thank you to J.M. Barrie for creating Captain Hook in the first place so that I could take so many delightful liberties with his character.

A.C. Wise is the bestselling author of *Wendy, Darling* (Titan Books, 2021), two collections published by Lethe Press, *Catfish Lullaby*, a novella published by Broken Eye Books (2019), and *The Ghost Sequences*, a short story collection published by Undertow Books (2021).

Her work has won the Sunburst Award for Excellence in Canadian Literature of the Fantastic, as well as twice being a finalist for the Nebula Award, twice being a finalist for the Sunburst Award, and being a finalist for the Lambda Literary Awards. In addition to her fiction, she contributes semi-regular review columns to *The Book Smugglers* and *Apex Magazine*.

@ac_wise

www.acwise.net

For more fantastic fiction, author events,
exclusive excerpts, competitions, limited editions and more

VISIT OUR WEBSITE
titanbooks.com

LIKE US ON FACEBOOK
facebook.com/titanbooks

FOLLOW US ON TWITTER AND INSTAGRAM
@TitanBooks

EMAIL US
readerfeedback@titanemail.com